ALSO BY THOMAS M. DISCH

NOVELS

The Genocides (1965)

The Puppies of Terra (1966)

Echo Round His Bones (1967)

Black Alice (with John Sladek; 1968)

Camp Concentration (1968)

334 (1972)

Clara Reeve
(as "Leonie Hargrave"; 1975)

On Wings of Song (1979)

Neighboring Lives
(with Charles Naylor; 1981)

The Businessman: A Tale of Terror
(1984)

The M.D.: A Horror Story (1991)

SHORT STORY COLLECTIONS

102 H-Bombs (1967)

Fun with Your New Head (1968)

Getting into Death (1976)

Fundamental Disch (1980)

The Man Who Had No Idea (1982)

POETRY

The Right Way
to Figure Plumbing (1972)

ABCDEFG HIJKLM NPOQRST
UVWXYZ (1981)

Burn This (1982)

Orders of the Retina (1982)

Here I Am, There You Are,
Where Were We (1984)

Yes, Let's: New & Selected Poems (1989)

Dark Verses and Light (1991)

CHILDREN'S BOOKS

The Brave Little Toaster (1986)

The Tale of Dan de Lion (1986)

The Brave Little Toaster
Goes to Mars (1988)

LIBRETTI AND PLAYS

Ben Hur (1989)

The Fall of the House of Usher
(composer, Gregory Sandow; 1979)

Frankenstein
(composer, Gregory Sandow, 1982)

The Cardinal Detoxes (1990)

INTERACTIVE SOFTWARE

Amnesia (1986)

THE PRIEST

THE
PRIEST

A GOTHIC ROMANCE

THOMAS M. DISCH

Alfred A. Knopf

NEW YORK

1995

THIS IS A BORZOI BOOK
PUBLISHED BY ALFRED A. KNOPF, INC.

Copyright © 1994 by Thomas M. Disch

Library of Congress Cataloging-in-Publication Data
Disch, Thomas M.
The priest : a Gothic romance / by Thomas M. Disch. — 1st ed.
p. cm.
ISBN 0-679-41880-6
1. Catholic Church—Minnesota—Minneapolis—Clergy—Fiction.
2. Extortion—Minnesota—Minneapolis—Fiction. 3. Child
molesters—Rehabilitation—Fiction. 4. Minneapolis
(Minn.)—Fiction. 5. Time travel—Fiction. I. Title.
PS3554.I8P75   1995
813'.54—dc20   94-26093
                                           CIP

Manufactured in the United States of America

FIRST AMERICAN EDITION

For Phil Marsh

Hoopster, hipster,
excellent role model

Kill them all. God will look after His own.

—ARNALD-AMALRIC, *Abbot of Cîteaux,*
at the massacre of Béziers, 1209

Kill 'em all! Let God sort 'em out.

—*a popular U.S. T-shirt, 1986*

THE PRIEST

1

The grass was unnaturally green. Jelly-bean green or the green of golf games on television, though come to think of it that was grass too, televised grass but grass nevertheless. Golf was the only game she enjoyed watching because there were no rules to keep track of. You only had to sink the ball in the hole and count the number of times you'd hit it. People could have played golf here except for the headstones. So many names and for the life of her she couldn't remember which one she was looking for. This one was nice, all speckledy gray-pink, ALPHONSE BURDETT, but imagine being married to someone called Alphonse, and in any case Alphonse Burdett had died in 1951 at the age of—? She did the arithmetic from his birthdate, 1878. Seventy-three, when he died in 1951. She could be pretty sure that ruled out Alphonse Burdett.

And look, right here on the next stone, CECILIA BURDETT, BELOVED WIFE, 1904–85. She felt almost as though Cecilia had caught her flirting with Alphonse at one of those awful senior socials with Kool-Aid and Oreos. She could remember things like that, general things, but not particulars, the names and faces of people who assumed she remembered them and when she couldn't then assumed she was an imbecile. But there were *places* she could remember with the clarity of a slide being flashed on a screen. Living rooms with all their furniture, backyards, the enormous produce department of a supermarket somewhere, a room in a basement with just one tiny window near the ceiling and large rhubarb leaves screening the window. She only had to close her eyes and they were there for the summoning.

It was like a detective story, in a way. If this is the bedroom I remember, with this wallpaper with a tangle of pastel blue and pink roses, and this maple chest of drawers, and this crucifix with a frond of dried palm bent double and attached to it with a rubber band, and this rug that's faded to match the greenish tan of the chenille bedspread—then who am I, the person who can remember it all so clearly? Was it *my* bedroom? For that matter, is it still?

She sat down on Cecilia Burdett's headstone with a sigh of gratitude and looked at her poor tired feet and marveled at her shoes. A woman of her age wearing tennis shoes. Though if she'd had to walk about all over this grass in a proper pair of shoes it would not have been easy. The sunshine was nice. She could feel it right through the sleeves of her sweater. A cloudless blue sky, a friendly sun, the lawn yielding with each footstep, what could be nicer.

It occurred to her to wonder, what if *she* were Cecilia Burdett? How could she be sure she wasn't? What if this was heaven? With the beautiful weather and no one around, it was peaceful enough to qualify, and four headstones off was a bouquet of her favorite flowers, daffodils. It might not be the heaven she'd been led to expect, but probably no one really knew what heaven would be like, or God for that matter. Once, perhaps, she'd had clearer ideas on the subject, the way she'd known whom to vote for, once, or how to sight-read a piece of music, but all those clear things had gone blurry. Usually that blurriness didn't bother her. It could even be pleasant. She could settle for a heaven without trumpets and angels and everyone speaking in Latin, a heaven that was just an increasing, agreeable blurriness with everything slowly darkening until the stars began to be visible.

But what presumption. To suppose *she* was in heaven, without so much as a stopover in purgatory, not to mention the worst and likeliest possibility. She might not be able to remember her name but she could remember her sins well enough, and all the confessions that had been lies, because she *knew* she'd go right back to the same sin, like a Weight Watcher returning to sticky buns. Even now, if she went to confession, could she make a sincere act of contrition? Once the temptation was gone, could you claim any credit for resisting it? Assuming it was gone. At least of the birth control that was a safe assumption. But of him? When she reached for a memory of him it was always of some cheap motel room or the backseat of a car. Or a booth in a bar with neon beer signs and his long white fingers playing with a cardboard coaster advertising Hamm's. She could remember the fingers but not the face. She could remember the guilt but not the love that had made the guilt worth bearing.

A black car, a very nice one, long and expensive-looking, glided into view and moved toward her with a sound of crunching gravel. It came to a stop like a boat butting up to a dock, and when the driver got out she could see, even this far away, that he was a priest. It was almost as though her guilt had summoned him here. The priest lifted his right hand, greeting her or blessing her, she couldn't tell which. She waved back and then, lowering her hand, felt the back of her head to be sure her hair was presentable.

When he'd come near enough not to have to raise his voice, he said, "I thought I might find you here."

How to reply? He seemed to know who she was, but she couldn't return the compliment, though there was something vaguely familiar about him. Perhaps he just had that kind of averagely good-looking face, less than a movie star, more than a nobody. Mousy brown hair with the part a little off center like the younger sort of TV personality. Well dressed, of course, but what priest isn't, really, in his uniform of black suit and Roman collar? The shoes, however, struck a false note. They were sneakers disguised to look like proper shoes by being all black. A priest shouldn't be wearing sneakers, even black sneakers.

"Father," she said, "how nice to see you."

He stopped beside Alphonse Burdett's gravestone and gave her a peculiar look, a mix of puzzled and peeved. "Mother," he said softly, "how nice to see *you.*"

She realized at once and with a keen sense of embarrassment that she'd done it again, forgotten everything. But even with him there before her, calling her his mother, she didn't recognize him. Her memory was as useless as a dead lightbulb.

"Are you all right?" he asked.

"Oh yes, I'm fine. It's such lovely weather." Then, when he just stood there with the same perplexed smile, she asked, "And how are you?"

"Worried, actually. They called from the Home right after breakfast when they realized you were missing, but I was away from the rectory all morning. So it wasn't until noon that I finally heard from them, and then there was a parish business meeting I had to be at."

"I'm not *missing,*" she insisted, a little resentfully. "I'm *here.*"

"No one knew that, Mother."

"Well, I knew it."

For no good reason she began to cry. The warmth of the tears on her cheek was an actual comfort. A luxury, like the sunlight and the smooth, mowed lawn. Maybe in heaven you would also cry a lot.

The priest took a small package of Kleenex from the inside breast pocket of his suit, removed a tissue, and offered it to her. It seemed unpriestlike to be giving someone a Kleenex instead of a clean handkerchief. But she accepted it and dabbed at each cheek, blotting up the tears, which, obediently, ceased to flow.

"I don't know why I do that," she declared, forcing a smile.

The odd thing was that she did know that she was prone to such outbursts but that she didn't know a basic fact like her own name. Couldn't remember, even now, this man who'd addressed her as his mother. A priest!

Did she have other children as well? A husband somewhere? She'd no idea. Yet she knew she was a Catholic, as surely as she knew her own sex. She knew she was old, but not how old; poor, but not how poor; educated, but not how well. She could remember being in churches and schoolrooms and even hospitals, but only abstractly. Their names, like her own, had been erased, like names on a blackboard, leaving just a smear of white chalk dust.

"Would you like to go visit Dad's grave?" her son the priest asked her.

She made a joke of her own unknowingness: "Your dad or mine?"

He bowed his head and lowered his eyes and offered not the glimmer of a smile. "My own."

"Sure, why not. Is it far? I mean, can we walk from here? I'd prefer to walk."

"It's not far," he said, and led the way among the markers, following no path but as sure of his direction as if he were walking through the rooms of his own house. They went by the graves of MARTIN SWEIGER and his wife GERALDINE; of SGT. JOHN KOSKINEN, who'd died in 1944 at the age of twenty-two; of EDWARD and PATRICIA MANGAN; and of an entire SHEEHY family who'd all died on the same day in the late seventies. She pointed out to the priest how each of the markers had the same date of death.

"Don't you wonder what happened?" she asked, to which he only nodded. "Probably a car accident," she theorized.

"Probably," he agreed.

She wondered if he knew what actually had happened to the Shee-hys and if he thought that she ought to, too. He must be irked by her forgetfulness. After all, what people said about someone who had gone through some enormous change was that his own mother wouldn't recognize him.

"Well, here we are," he said, taking up a semiprayerful position in front of a wide, white, knee-high marker not far from where the Shee-hys were buried. It was set up like a double bed with the husband's name on the left, PAUL BRYCE, and his dates beneath:

FEB. 9, 1902

*

NOV. 23, 1949

On the left side of the marker the name of MARGARET BRYCE had already been incised in the marble, and a birthdate as well, MAY 14, 1919. Apparently Margaret Bryce was not yet dead.

Apparently, *she* was Margaret Bryce.

"A little premature, isn't it?" she remarked caustically.

The priest raised a questioning eyebrow.

"My name on the stone," she explained. "It seems a little overeager to me."

"Well, Mother, it was your decision. Maybe it was a way of economizing. I wouldn't know. You didn't consult Petey or me at the time."

"How *is* Petey?" she asked, in a tone that dared him to doubt she knew who Petey was. "What's he up to?"

The priest made a little grimacing frown and then a glance that showed that he knew what she was up to. "Petey's fine, I imagine. We're not that closely in touch, you know."

Of course she *didn't* know, and he must know she didn't, and so his vagueness was deliberate. He was being mean.

Well, she could be just as mean.

"Father," she said, "I have to go to confession."

Already he looked embarrassed, and she'd just got started. "Here?" he said.

"We could scarcely have more privacy, could we?"

"But don't you think . . . another priest . . . ?"

"It came to me just now. The memory."

He sighed. "As you please." He made a sign of the cross at her, and she did the same, kneeling down on the grass. "There's no need to kneel," he told her, but she stayed where she was, looking down at the fingernails of her folded hands. They were painted the pink nearest their natural color. "Bless me, Father, for I have sinned. I don't know when my last confession was, but this sin goes back to long before whenever that would have been."

"It's probably something you've confessed before now, Mother. So there's really no need—"

"No, I'm sure I never spoke of it. It would have been too embarrassing. It has to do with him." She nodded curtly toward the white stone with the name of Paul Bryce on it. "You see, he's not your father. Not your real father."

"Mother, really, this is not appropriate behavior."

"Neither was his. That's what I'm trying to explain."

"Mother, get up off the ground."

"From the first we never needed birth control. But you know what I used to do? I used to confess that we did. 'Cause everyone else did. They complained about how it shouldn't be a sin, and they wouldn't have complained unless they were doing it, would they? So I complained, too. So they wouldn't suspect the real situation. So, he was not your father. Your father was someone else. That's my *true* confession. I can't tell you *his* name. I promised I never would. And what good would it do you to know now?"

"Will you get up, Mother?"

"Have you absolved me?"

"You'll have to confess that sin to someone else. I simply don't believe you. I think you made the whole thing up on the spot, out of spite. Forgive me if I've misjudged you."

"It's true that I forget a lot of things. And the fact is, I couldn't tell you your real father's name if you asked. But the man buried under that stone is *not* your father. *Mea maxima culpa.*"

He got his hand under her elbow and lifted her up off her knees. "Well, thank you for that, Mother. And Happy Mother's Day."

"Is it Mother's Day?" she asked, astonished.

"No," he said, pursing his lips. "And it's not April Fools' Day either. Now, let's go home, shall we?"

2

Of the four couples whom Father Cogling was preparing for the sacrament of matrimony, one had telephoned to the rectory an hour beforehand to announce that they'd be unable to come ("Darryl is tied up at work," Darryl's fiancée had explained), and another simply hadn't shown up. So here he was in the little meeting room partitioned off from the parish hall, facing half the number he'd addressed last week, when he'd instructed them on the subject of birth control. It was no surprise to him that Darryl, who was half Jewish, should have chosen to be absent, for Darryl had been more inclined to score debating points than to receive instruction, pleading for the use of prophylaxis in various hypothetical situations and unable to grasp the simple idea that the only morally acceptable form of birth control is self-control, period. Darryl and his fiancée were college graduates.

When Father Cogling had been a seminarian at Étoile du Nord Seminary on Leech Lake in the forties, Archbishop Cushing of Boston had made an address to the CIO in which he'd observed that not a single bishop or archbishop of the American hierarchy was the son of a college graduate. It was a source of regret to Father Cogling that this could no longer be said to be the case. College education was one of those insidious features of modern life that seemed to betoken progress but led, more often than not, to doubt, the decay of authority, and sin. This was so, sad to say, even of those who attended Catholic universities. Even the seminaries, those that had survived, were not proof against the corruptive tendency of a so-called liberal education. Their present condition was a sword in the side of the Virgin Mary.

Father Cogling had a particular veneration for the Holy Mother and recited the rosary in her honor thrice daily. It was Mary who, by her mercy and chaste example, would restore the Church to spiritual health. Revelations had been made by the Virgin through the Blessed Josemaria Escriva de Balaguer, both warnings and promises, which were not generally known and which Father Cogling was not at liberty to share, except with some few other initiated souls. Extraordinary things were to happen—miracles, catastrophes, terrible judgments from which there could be no reprieve without the Virgin's interces-sion. Meanwhile, until those prophecies came to be fulfilled, the rot would go on, the fabric of the Faith would decay, heresy and indecency would flourish, and the Madonna herself would be made an object of ridicule.

Though not in this parish, not here at St. Bernardine's, not while Wilfrid Cogling could help it. He might not be the pastor any longer, those days were past, and perhaps it was just as well. As Father Pat kept pointing out, he was entitled to enjoy the rewards of retirement. And it wasn't as though he were idle. He still said two Masses on Sunday, still heard confessions, still attended as many parish events as Father Pat himself, if not more. The hard part had been surrendering the habit of authority and deferring to judgments he knew to be mistaken or ill-considered. He often wondered if it would have been easier spending these years of semiretirement in another parish than St. Bernardine's, but when he considered the other priests he might have had to deal with, he knew that God had been merciful to him. Father Pat might be lax in some doctrinal matters; he might err on the side of novelty in his approach to the liturgy (altar girls, indeed!); but he was sound in the things that counted. He didn't equivocate about abortion or sins of unchastity or other matters. Father Cogling had no patience with those priests—and they were no longer exceptions to the rule, they had become the rule—who sided with opinion polls against the Holy Fa-ther. Were there opinion polls in hell? Probably! And probably one hundred percent of the damned were of the opinion that they should be in heaven, and the results of the polls were published every morning in hell's own newspaper and broadcast on TV, and there were protest rallies organized by demons, and long processions of the damned wail-ing and singing "We Shall Overcome."

The two couples in attendance had arrived together, five minutes late. The younger girl, whose name was Alison Sanders, explained,

"We waited outside for the others, but then . . ." She smiled an apologetic smile and glanced sideways at her boyfriend.

He finished Alison's sentence for her. "They didn't come. We figure they must've got scared off."

"Sometimes," Father Cogling observed, taking the joke in earnest, "our second thoughts are wiser than our first impulses." He remembered now that this one, with the Clark Gable mustache and the Spanish-sounding surname (which he'd forgotten), was the smart aleck. Not an arguer, like the Jew who hadn't come back, but a scoffer, a smiler, a know-it-all.

"I mean to say," the priest went on, "that you may decide as a result of these talks that marriage is *not* the right path to take at this point in your life. You may decide that it would be wiser to achieve more financial security before you take on the responsibility of raising a family. You may find that you haven't prepared yourself *spiritually* for what will be the most important day in your life. These talks aren't like modern high schools that have to graduate every student who manages to sit through four years of classes whether they've learned anything in those classes or not."

The other couple nodded their heads in unison, assuming an expression of submissive attentiveness. The man's name was Robert Howell, he'd been brought up Catholic, and he was a rookie fireman in the suburb of Eden Prairie. The woman's name was Denise, and she'd had no religious upbringing. "Though," she'd said at the last meeting, "I do believe in a Higher Power." She'd said it in that confiding, sugary tone of voice that implied she was doing God and Father Cogling a favor. Father Cogling didn't like her, but he thought she could eventually be converted and would make a suitable wife for Robert Howell.

"Before we begin," said Father Cogling, folding his hands and lowering his eyes, "let us prepare our hearts with prayer." He waited until the four of them had also assumed an attitude of prayer and then prompted: "Our Father . . ."

Of the lot of them, only Alison Sanders articulated the phrases of the prayer in a crisp and audible manner. She also, to her credit, dressed in a manner both modest and becomingly feminine, in a flowery dress that showed her figure to advantage without being in any way too bold.

The same could not be said of Denise, who had dressed for the occasion in blue jeans, a Twins sweatshirt, and tennis shoes. Her fiancé, with his long hair and the gold chain around his neck and an earring in his left earlobe, was actually the more feminine of the two. Father Cogling had been reproved by his pastor on more than one occasion for making disparaging remarks about the fashions adopted by what Father Pat called "the youth culture." As though young people lived in a separate world with its own norms and customs. As though they were Ubangis or Hottentots! But it was true, as Father Pat had many times pointed out, that there was nothing inherently immoral or indecent in hair that touched one's collar or, for that matter, in an earring. Such things were not declarations of degeneracy, at least not necessarily. So, as reluctant as Father Cogling was to tolerate such fads and foibles, he held his peace. If firemen wanted to look like fairies, so be it. His lips were sealed.

The prayer concluded, Father Cogling smiled a wise, priestly smile and made eye contact with each of the four young people in turn. Then, his eyes still focused on Alison, he said, "We all must be so grateful for our mothers. I know I am. Not only for my earthly mother, who passed to her reward some time ago, God bless her, but even more the mother I share with all of you here, and with"—he dipped his head reverently—"Jesus. Our mother who is the Queen of Heaven—the Virgin Mary."

Out of the corner of his eye he saw Alison's fiancé making a characteristic grimace, italicized by the thin line of his mustache. "That presents you with some difficulty, Mr. . . . ? I'm sorry, my memory isn't what it was."

"No problem," the boy said. "You can just call me Son."

"Son?"

"Yeah. I got to call you Father, right? So you can call me Son. Who needs last names?"

"Well, Son," Father Cogling resumed imperturbably, "you seem to have some difficulty with the idea of the Virgin Mary. Many Protestants do, including some theologians. It is one of what they like to call the scandals of our Faith."

"I'm happy to hear I'm not alone."

Alison whispered, "Greg, please."

Father Cogling raised his hand as though in benediction. "I prefer to think of these matters as mysteries of the Faith. Mysteries in the sense of puzzles that the rational mind, unassisted by Faith, can never solve. The Virgin Birth, for instance, is in some ways a more mysterious, or challenging, concept than Christ's conception in the Virgin's womb."

"Excuse me, Father," Denise interrupted, "but I don't see the distinction."

"The distinction is that Mary *remained* a Virgin *after* the birth of the Christ child. In the Latin phrase, she is *Mater inviolata*."

"No shit," Greg marveled. He had the decency at once to blush.

Father Cogling smiled benignly. "It is amazing, is it not? It defies common sense. It is . . . miraculous!"

"You mean," Denise asked, "that it was like a cesarean section? He wasn't delivered normally?"

"Indeed: He was delivered supernaturally."

"You're saying," Greg put it as bluntly as possible, "her hymen wasn't broken. The baby came out *through* the hymen."

Father Cogling nodded.

"That is weird. That is incredible."

"Hey, come on, lay off it, will ya?" Robert Howell counseled. "Give the guy a chance."

"Ah, but Robert," Father Cogling insisted, "he's quite right. It *is* incredible. Quite literally. Without faith it is something one *could not believe.*"

"And you're saying," Greg insisted, "that for me and Alison to get married in the Church I got to believe that?"

"No," said Father Cogling. "I'm only explaining what most Catholics believe concerning the Virgin Mary. Not even all Catholics. No pope has ever declared Mary's postnatal virginity an infallible truth. I think Pope John Paul *may* do so: That has been my prayer these many years. But there *are* some Catholics who are skeptical in that regard."

"So," Greg said, "it's like Ripley: Believe it or not."

Father Cogling glared at the young man in silent remonstration before answering, "You might say that."

"Thanks. I appreciate your generosity."

"Greg," urged Alison, "please."

Father Cogling waved away Alison's distress with a motion of his hand. "The reason that I called the matter to your attention was to emphasize the importance that the Church places on the matter of chastity."

"Uh-huh," said Greg.

"Not only before marriage," Father Cogling went on, "but

throughout marriage." He paused, inviting an objection. When none was forthcoming, he continued: "Chastity not in the sense that you are to remain virgins after you have been married—that privilege was reserved for Mary and Joseph—but, rather, in the sense that the pursuit of hedonistic or sensual pleasure should never be the object of the conjugal act. Procreation, rather, is the goal of marital love."

This time it was not Greg who intruded on the priest's discourse but Denise, who, from sitting and staring expressionlessly at her clasped hands, suddenly burst out laughing. A single convulsive snort of laughter that she at once did her best to stifle, but then there was a second snort, and then laughter outright. "I'm sorry. I'm reverting to high school or something. Excuse me a minute—" She stood up from her chair. "Is there a lady's room here?"

Father Cogling smiled primly. "Outside and at the other end of the hall."

As soon as Denise had left the room, her fiancé got up and said, "Yeah, excuse me, too."

"So," said Greg brightly, when there was only himself and Alison and the priest left in the room, "you were telling us about the Virgin Mary and the opportunity for chastity in marriage."

"I take it that chastity strikes you as somehow ridiculous," the priest said, abandoning even a pretense of civility. It was clear to him that this young man belonged to the new generation without any sexual compunctions whatever. Father Cogling had encountered others like him in this very room. It distressed the priest to think that such a young man might receive the sacrament of matrimony before the altar of St. Bernardine's. It distressed him, as well, to think that the boy would involve a decent Catholic girl in his perdition. Indeed, it was likely that the process had already begun. Father Cogling knew all too well from his experience in the confessional how rarely these days young women entered into matrimony without having already forfeited their virginity. What had once been the sinful exception was now the damnable rule.

"Surely. Let us discuss chastity in marriage, as the subject interests you. The patron saint of this parish, Saint Bernardine of Siena, actually had some vivid things to say on just that topic. For instance, Saint Bernardine, following the Decree of Gratian, declared that while it is wicked for a man to have intercourse with his own mother, it is much worse to have *unnatural* intercourse with his own wife. That's to say, any form of sex that leads to an ejaculation outside the proper vessel."

"You mean, like a hand job?" Greg marveled.

"If by that you mean masturbation, yes, certainly."

"You're telling me, Father, that if I jerk off, that's worse than if I fuck my mother."

"Greg! Please!"

"Sorry, honey. But I don't know the theological terms for this sort of stuff. And the Father here doesn't seem to mind my language. The important thing is we should understand each other, right, Father?"

Father Cogling nodded. "And to answer your question: Yes, masturbation would be a more heinous offense than incest, so long as that is conducted in a natural manner."

"By natural you mean without using birth control?"

Father Cogling nodded.

"But if I used birth control while I had incest, *that* would be a whole lot worse?"

Father Cogling nodded. He had used the teachings of Saint Bernardine before to similar effect. Bernardine of Siena confounded and scandalized unbelievers. Non-Catholics were unaccustomed to the rigorous exercise of logic in matters of morality. "Well," Greg drawled, "I'd better be sure my mother knows about this."

But Denise had left the room, and with her went the only audience for his obscene humor. Father Cogling lowered his eyes with conspicuous modesty but not before he'd noticed, with satisfaction, that the young man's fiancée looked stricken. Mixed marriages were almost always a mistake. Perhaps this young woman might come to realize that, even at this late date, two weeks short of the day appointed for her wedding. The gift of grace is unpredictable and sometimes even inconvenient. Caterers must be paid even when a wedding is canceled. But it's a small price to pay when one's soul is at stake.

"The reason I bring up the teachings of Saint Bernardine," Father Cogling resumed, after a suitable interval, "despite the fact that his message is so . . . unfashionable, is because I know of no better way to impress on non-Catholics the importance we attach to the matter of birth control. It is not a foible, or a pious fable, or a moral option that might be changed in the course of time, the way Catholics once had to abstain from eating meat on Friday but now are under no such obligation. We are *absolutely* opposed to artificial methods of birth control, and as the husband of a Catholic woman, you must make a solemn and unconditional commitment to observe that prohibition in the conduct of your own married life."

"You got it, Father," Greg said. "As solemn as you like." He stared at the priest with naked hostility.

At that moment there was a providential knock on the door. It was Robert, announcing a phone call for Father Cogling on the pay phone in the main hall. Father Cogling excused himself to Greg and Alison and went to the phone.

"Hello," he said into the receiver.

"Wilfrid, I'm glad you're there." It was Father Pat, the pastor of St. Bernardine's.

"Pat—how is your mother? Did you *find* her?"

"She was out at the cemetery, as we thought she might be. She was in fine spirits, considering."

"And . . . mentally?"

"Alzheimer's is a one-way street, Wilfrid. Her memory always gets worse, there's no improvement to be expected in that area."

"But we can pray."

"And that's about all we can do. In any case, that's not why I called. Why I called is two separate things. First, I wish you would speak to your friend, Mr. Ober. He's got hold of a list of the members of Agnus Dei and has been phoning them systematically in a tone that was described to me as menacing. I realize some people think Gerhardt sounds menacing when he says hello. *I've* spoken to him before, but he doesn't seem to listen to me. He nods his head and says 'Yes, Father,' and then he's right back to the same tricks. Maybe he'll listen to you. I know he's zealous, but isn't it enough for him to be involved in setting up the maternity center? He *must* learn discretion."

"I'll talk to him," Father Cogling promised. "Though I doubt it will do much good. Gerhardt's a little like your mother. As you point out, he nods his head and then goes off and does just what he wants to anyhow. What's the other thing?"

"I'd like you to be on duty for me tonight. Something came up that I have to tend to."

"Tonight is the Rosary Society?" He didn't wait for an answer. It was Wednesday, which was when the Rosary Society met. "Fine, I'll be there."

"You don't need to be at the whole meeting. Just show your face and eat a cookie or two."

"Anything else? I should be getting back to my couples before they start the Reformation all over again."

"They're being difficult?"

"Nothing I can't handle."

"I'm sure of that, Wilfrid. Well, thank you." He hung up.

"You're welcome," Father Cogling replied dryly. "And enjoy your night out."

3

After he'd exited 694, Father Bryce drove to the far corner of the first large parking lot he came to. The lot served a mini-mall that housed a liquor store, a gun shop, a Chinese takeout, a carpet factory outlet, and two bankrupt businesses, one that still featured a sign in its window:

WATERBEDS

50% OFF   LAST DAYS!

It was already dark at seven-thirty, and only the liquor store and the Chinese takeout were still open.

He'd left the rectory in mufti—tan dress slacks, a plaid sport shirt, sneakers—but even so he felt exposed and identifiable. If not as a priest, then as someone belonging to that part of the world where priests and what they stand for are a consideration. He found himself wishing the basic wish of his adolescence: that he could inhabit another body entirely, one that was larger and stronger and hairier, a body in which he could feel authentically masculine. The kind of body he had all through his life lusted to possess—not as a lover would possess his beloved in his embrace, but as a demon possesses, inhabiting another body, taking it over and evicting the prior tenant. Could there be a more hopeless desire? a more misguided paraphilia, or any sillier? And yet how many others there were stuck in the same daydream, flies in honey. It seemed at times the essence of homosexuality. Please, sir, would you be my mirror?

But no, that side of his character was more likely the result of having grown up as a twin, rather than of his being queer. Petey and Paddy, they make our hearts go pitty-patty. Karen Olsen had made up that jingle in the third grade, and it had followed the Bryce twins all the way through sophomore year at Ramsay High, at which point Patrick and Peter had escaped the daily psychic torsion of twindom by taking diverging paths to their disparate futures—Patrick to Étoile du Nord Seminary, Petey to a juvenile correction facility in Anoka. If they couldn't be identical, then they'd be opposites. Still the same symmetry.

Out of the Adidas bag on the seat beside him, Father Bryce took a small jewelry case covered with synthetic velvet, which had contained, some Christmases ago, a silver crucifix and chain. Now it held his mustache and a bottle of gum arabic. Twisting the rearview mirror aside to help, he dabbed the stickum onto his upper lip and deftly positioned the false mustache. Then he waited for the gum arabic to dry. In the mirror the mustache looked full and fierce and not quite his own, a mustache someone else had grown (Petey perhaps?) and he'd adopted, without making allowance for the contours of his upper lip (smiles were dangerous, grins impossible) or the more meager character of his other visible hair. Yet that was often the way with *real* mustaches, he'd been assured by the barber in Chicago from whom he'd bought the thing. And it was only natural that *he* would think it looked bogus, since he knew it was. But strangers who didn't know him wouldn't think to question the authenticity of his mustache. They would only think, what a show-offy mustache, and, with the addition of sunglasses and a baseball cap, the mustache would be all they would notice. He would be invisible behind it.

At least that was the theory, and his hope.

He debated whether he should allow himself a drink. Not now, certainly, with the further drive ahead of him. Alcohol had begun to affect him erratically. Twice he'd escaped DWI citations by virtue of his Roman collar. Tonight of all nights he dare not take that risk.

So, with a sense of steely resolution, he ignored the delectable orange neon of LIQUORS and returned to 694, then followed it east through Fridley and New Brighton until it swung south proper and metamorphosed into 35E. Just before the highway crossed into St. Paul proper, he exited again onto Little Canada Road. And there in another bankrupt-looking mini-mall, as per his directions, was the tattoo parlor—Knightriders Kustom Ink—the only business with its windows still lighted. A single large Harley stood heraldically on the asphalt before the window. The lot was otherwise empty.

He couldn't believe that it had actually come to this, that he was submitting to such an outrageous demand. But what was the alternative? Prison. Even if he ran away to some other state, gave up the priesthood and tried to hide behind an alias and a false mustache, eventually he would be hunted down and brought to trial. They had their hook in him up through his butt and into his gut, and no amount of wriggling could help. It was this or prison or suicide, and he'd had three weeks in which to prove to himself that he didn't have the nerve to kill himself. He'd gone so far as to read *Final Exit*, and he'd had a supply of the requisite pills for the last three years, ever since he'd cleaned out his mother's medicine cabinet after she'd been taken to the Home. So it would not have required much in the way of physical courage. But what it required he lacked.

Did he then, secretly, deep down, still believe in hell? Was that what stopped him? Hell and its associated demonologies had been the first part of his faith to go, first fading into something vague and symbolic, the hell beloved by the more liberal interpreters of Dante, and then simply disappearing into the mists of a more and more mythological afterlife. By the time of his ordination he had reached a tacit understanding with his confessor that *all* beliefs of a pictorial or narrative nature were equally idolatrous, golden calves at whose devotions priests perform rituals for the benefit of those unable to face the dark truths shared by those initiated to secrets of the inner temple: that the tabernacle is empty and God an eternal, inapprehensible Absence. A cloud in a sky that is everywhere cloudy. He was in no hurry to get there.

The time has come, he told himself, it has to be done. But at the last moment before leaving the car he decided that it might be prudent to deposit his billfold and wristwatch in the glove compartment. When he opened the glove compartment he realized it wasn't the dictates of prudence he was responding to but his addiction. For there, where he had no memory of having left it, was a nearly full pint bottle of Jack Daniel's. So much for his good intentions of only twenty minutes ago.

He uncapped the bottle and took one slow, grateful swallow. The bourbon worked its usual magic at once. The impossible suddenly was possible, the undoable on its way to being done. He transferred billfold and wristwatch to the glove compartment, and after the benediction of another, slower, better-savored sip of whiskey, he got out of the car and tucked the bottle in his back pocket.

He checked to see that the car doors were locked and the windows rolled tight. He checked to see that his mustache was in place. He even brushed his Adam's apple with his fingertips to be sure he was not wearing his collar, a gesture that had become semiautomatic in situations when he was off his clerical leash.

The interior of the tattoo parlor, visible through the front window, fairly vibrated with excess of fluorescence, the way some supermarkets do. Its furnishings were as minimal as those of any church basement. Folding chairs along the walls and a single threadbare couch. One end table stacked with magazines. Some free-standing ashtrays. Nothing to distract from the framed samples of the tattooist's work that covered the walls from knee level almost to the ceiling. The effect was like wallpaper—if hell were to have wallpaper.

Then, as though summoned, the tattooist appeared through a door at the back of the shop. He seemed about Father Bryce's own age, with the usual abrasions and scuff marks of middle age—receding hair, a small potbelly, a scruffy beard irregularly tufted with gray. Reading glasses hung pendantlike across his chest from an elastic band. As he approached the front door, he walked with a pronounced limp. No vision of macho glory, certainly, and no visible tattoos, for he was wearing a plaid flannel shirt that covered his arms to his wrists.

The tattooist's eyes met Father Bryce's through the shop window. He paused a moment with a questioning look, and then, as though the question had been answered, he smiled, exposing the decayed stumps of his incisors. He opened the door and thrust out his head. "You the guy called about the custom design?"

Father Bryce nodded.

"Okay! I got your money order, the stencil's done, and we're ready to roll. I'll just switch this sign around"—he flipped over the OPEN sign on the door so that it read CLOSED—"to guarantee ourselves some privacy. Funny, you didn't knock or anything, but I had a feeling you was out here. Come on in."

He could still say no, he thought, even as he stepped across the threshold into the shop's pulsing fluorescent glare. He was under no physical compulsion. His will was still his own.

The tattooist turned the bolt that locked the door, then held out his hand to be shaken. "Wolf."

It took Father Bryce a moment to recognize what the man had said as an introduction. "Wolf," he repeated, taking his hand. "Glad to meet you."

Wolf maintained his grip on Father Bryce's hand, waiting to be offered a name in return.

"I'm Damon," Father Bryce said.

"Damon the Demon," the tattooist said with a smile revealing more of his dental problems. Instead of releasing his hand, Wolf tightened his grip. "You came to the right joint for your ink, bro. Hail fuckin' Satan."

"Right," said Father Bryce weakly. Then, thinking, When in Rome, he made a more complete surrender. "Hail fucking Satan."

"I'll tell you something, Damon," Wolf said, letting go. "I consider it a privilege to be putting this design on you. A fuckin' privilege. Most guys come in here, they look around for maybe an hour at the flash on the walls, and they bullshit with each other and ask prices on designs you know they are never going to go for, the really heavy biker shit, and at last if they don't just walk out the door with 'Maybe next payday,' they get a scroll with the name of their fuckin' girlfriend, or 'Mother,' or what I do the most of for some reason, a panther-and-snake, like these here."

He tapped a finger on a framed panel bolted to the door at the back of the shop. Beneath the clouded plastic was an assortment of crudely drawn panthers, some by themselves, some in contention with large snakes, all in the same heraldic pose, the panther rearing up, a snarling head in profile facing right, forelegs lifted and the right leg flexed, as though the creature were climbing the flesh on which it was tattooed, from which each claw extracted its own distinct drop of blood.

"Don't get me wrong. This is a good basic design. It says something. And we all got to start somewhere. But the kind of work you're talking about, man, that is a once-in-a-lifetime opportunity."

Wolf opened the door blazoned with the rampant panthers. "We'll be in here." He waited for Father Bryce to enter.

He felt like a prisoner being shown, for the first time, to the cell he is to occupy for the rest of his life. It was about the size of his own bedroom at the rectory, some fourteen feet square and windowless. Where his bed would have been was an old-fashioned barber chair of white porcelain and shredded black leather, which was flanked on both sides by a shallow white Formica counter, with shelves above it, that held the implements of the tattooist's trade. An oversize lightbulb in a metal cone was suspended above the chair.

"You can hang your stuff over there," the tattooist said, pointing to a coatrack with a black cowboy hat on it.

Father Bryce nodded and began unbuttoning his shirt, first at the cuffs, then down from the neck. There were no hangers, so he hung the shirt right on the hook. Then he pulled his T-shirt up over his head, taking care not to disturb his mustache, and stood before the tattooist bare to his waist.

"You'll want to take your pants off, too," the tattooist said as he started snugging his right hand into a surgical glove. "We'll start off by laying out the whole design. From crotch to clavicle." He tapped the top of his shoulder. "That's this bone here."

Before he took off his pants, Father Bryce removed the bottle of Jack Daniel's from his back pocket.

"You came prepared, I see," Wolf observed. "Better go easy at first. Some guys got no problem drinking and inking, others puke their guts out. If you're used to the booze on like a daily basis, you probably won't have any problem. Myself, I got to stay away from the stuff. Nobody wants to get tattooed by a drunk, right?"

Father Bryce nodded. He uncapped the bottle, drank from it, and screwed the cap back on. He unbuckled his belt, but then it was as though he were thirteen again, in the locker room of Ramsay High School, having to undress for the first time in his life in front of strangers. He felt a warmth of embarrassment suffuse his face. He unsnapped the snap at the waistband and pulled down the zipper, and then he stood there holding up the pants, blushing and paralyzed by shame.

"Hey, pal, if you got a hard-on, don't sweat it. I'll tell you a trade secret. Most guys got boners while they're getting inked, the ones that ain't creaming in their pants. It don't mean you're a faggot or anything like that. It's just your body's natural response to the needle, know what I mean? It's like when you hang someone, the guy comes. I guess it's sort of like you get one last chance."

"No, it's not that. I just didn't know what . . . The bottle . . ." He handed the bottle to Wolf, who put it on the countertop. He got his pants off and hung them on the hook beneath his shirt. As though Wolf's words had been a snake charmer's tune coaxing a cobra from its basket, Father Bryce found himself getting an erection, along with the related symptoms—a dry mouth, a hollowness in his chest, a tightness about the temples and around to the back of his neck.

"Come over here," said Wolf. "I want to show you the design. You're gonna like this."

He spread open a tattered tabloid newspaper on the counter, the *Weekly World News* for April 7, 1992. The headline announced, in two-inch-high letters:

SATAN

ESCAPES

FROM HELL

A smaller boxed subheadline explained how this was done:

13 Alaskan oil rig workers killed
when the Devil roars out of well

In evidence of this event there was a photograph: In a typical oil field landscape with tanks and drilling rigs, one of the rigs was spouting flames which rose to become a gigantic roiling cloud of smoke, the billows of which formed an unmistakable snarling face, with fanglike teeth and a beaky nose and white, pupilless eyes.

"Here's what you sent me," said the tattooist, "and I've got to say it is a pretty un-fuckin'-believable photograph. Like you said on the phone, if it's a fake it's a real professional job. And here"—he rolled out a scroll of white paper—"is the design I worked out. There's no horns on the face in the photo, but I figured it's Satan so you'd want horns. The horns'll spread out from just above your tits to your shoulder blades, and Satan's chin'll be about three inches above your navel. It's a serious piece of work. I figure the face'll be all blackwork, pretty much like in the photo, but the flames around it can be different colors, mostly red, but some blue and yellow. Basically it'll be like the Technicolor version of the photo, except down below where you've got the guy on the horse with the torch. I made him a Viking type, but that could be changed. I could do an Indian, or a Mongol warrior, or a storm trooper, all depending. So—what do you think?"

"It's really . . . big."

"For sure. I figure it'll take about ten hours, but we can get the basic outline on tonight if you can hang on for two hours or so. You like the horseman okay? His mustache is kind of like yours, did you notice that? Talk about strange coincidences. I mean, till just now I never saw your face."

"I like the whole thing," Father Bryce assured him.

"I should also point out, down here on the left, under the pile of skulls, I signed it—'Knightrider.' That wasn't in your specs, but a piece on this scale, I'd like to sign it."

"That's fine. So, should we get started? You want me in the chair?"

"Yeah, but first, why don't we go over and stand by the sink and I'll zap off your hair there so it doesn't get all over the place. You're a pretty hairy guy."

"Zap off my hair?" Father Bryce repeated with dismay.

"Your body hair, where the tattoo goes. You got to be smooth if I'm going to tattoo you, right?"

"Uh-huh."

"You hadn't thought of that? It's funny, a lot of guys don't. I've had some guys decide to get a tattoo on their biceps when they were thinking of getting it on their forearm, just 'cause they didn't like the idea of shaving off the hair. Anyhow, with a piece like this you'll probably want to *keep* it shaved. At least anytime you're going to be showing it off."

The tattooist took an electric clippers from the countertop and plugged it into an outlet by the sink. "Next," he said. The clippers, when he switched them on, made a buzzing sound that seemed the audio equivalent of the flicker of the fluorescent light.

Father Bryce walked over to the sink and watched in the mirror of a medicine cabinet as his chest hair was shorn away in long downward swathes, falling in clustered curls to the newspaper that had been spread across the linoleum floor.

At each further indignity, he would think, This isn't happening to me. But it was. Now the tattooist was pulling down his underpants to get at his crotch hair and thereby exposing his state of erection. Exposing, which was the truly shameful thing, that he was someone who would in such circumstances be *able* to have an erection.

"Wha'd I tell you?" Wolf remarked, pushing Father Bryce's cock forward, out of the path of the clippers. "Just the idea of getting inked will get a guy stiff, it never fails."

To Wolf's credit, he dealt with the matter clinically, in much the same way as a nurse or orderly at a hospital might have approached the same task.

"Okay," Wolf said, switching off the clippers. "That didn't hurt, did it? But the needle will, I can guarantee you that. So maybe you'll want another drink?"

Father Bryce shook his head.

"Or whenever, just tell me." Wolf spread a large towel over the seat and back of the barber chair and nodded for Father Bryce to sit down. The terry cloth of the towel was damp and a little chilly.

"You don't have to start biting the bullet yet. We still got to transfer the design from stencil to skin. And because of the size of this mother, that means four separate stencils. Anyhow, you may be one of the lucky ones."

"The lucky ones—how's that?"

"Some guys manage to get off on it. Like some guys get off on taking a punch when they're boxing. I wouldn't count on it, it's not that common. Mostly you grin and bear it. The tough part is when the needle gets closest to the bone. Like here." He tapped Father Bryce's collarbone. "But everyone's different. I had a guy come in and get a spread eagle across his chest, no problem. Then he comes back and gets this snake wrapping up over his hip, where's he's got a lot of cushioning, and he blacks out. Which may be the easiest way to handle it. Like they say, what you don't know can't hurt you."

As he talked, Wolf began to apply the stencils, moistening the shaved skin of Father Bryce's chest and stomach with a sponge, then positioning each stencil carefully and pressing it to the damp flesh until the skin bore a transferred image for the tattooist's needle to follow. As if he were in a dentist's chair, Father Bryce kept his eyes closed and tried not to think about what was being done and to ignore the tattooist's chatter. One anecdote followed another, each one a little parable about the satisfaction to be gained through suffering. Father Bryce had given more than a few homilies on the same subject, and he felt a professional respect for Wolf's skill in engineering the right attitude in his customers so that instead of dreading what he was about to do they would welcome it.

"Okay, Damon," Wolf announced as he peeled off the last stencil from Father Bryce's abdomen. "We're ready for serious shit."

He took up the tattooing gun and positioned the tip of the needle over the middle of Father Bryce's chest just below the rib cage. He tapped the on/off switch with his foot and with a high-pitched electric whine the needle bit into flesh.

Father Bryce's first reaction was simply relief to know the extent of the pain he would have to bear and to know that it was bearable. It was not as bad as he'd feared, nothing like the pain of a dentist's drill, which the instrument in Wolf's hand so much resembled. It couldn't be shrugged away or ignored, but it was not such a pain as the Jesuits knew at the hands of the Hurons (or, for that matter, the Cathars at the hands of the Inquisition).

"Tattoos do things to people," Wolf observed, keeping his eye fixed on the slow progress of the needle as it traced a line of ink and blood across Father Bryce's flesh. "They get changed. Not just in the way that's obvious. Like they say, what happens is more than skin-deep."

Father Bryce flinched as the needle hit a nerve that caused the dull pain to flare, momentarily, into something bright and intense. He began to sweat.

"You become a different person," Wolf went on coolly. "I've seen it happen to lots of guys. Chicks, too. Not always. Some guys get tattooed the way they go to work where their dads went to work. Like, it's part of the job description. But you're not that kind, I knew that even before you come in. Not with a design like you were asking for.

"Some designs are like doorways, you know what I mean? They're like there's something inside of you that can't get out until the tattoo is there, and the tattoo *lets* it out. That's how it was for me, man. Five years ago, you know what I was doing? I was a fuckin' CPA. I shit you not. A tax accountant for a big company. So what happened was I went with a buddy of mine who had this bike that's like a toy for weekends, and we drove to this rally in Wisconsin, and there was this tattooist there working out of a Winnebago. We got stewed and then we got tattooed. I got a wolf, the head of a wolf, on my shoulder, where I figured no one would see. But *I* saw it. And I knew the person with the tattoo was not the same person who put on the business suit and commuted to work every day. And gradually Wolf, the person with the tattoo, took charge. The other way of looking at it—my wife's way—was that booze took charge. But really the booze was like a switch, or the stuff Dr. Jekyll drinks in the movie when he wants to become Mr. Hyde. It sort of greased the hinges on the door. But the tattoo was the doorway."

Wolf put down the tattoo gun, took a Kleenex from a box on the counter, and dabbed blood from the zigzagging line of Satan's teeth. "How's it going? Startin' to get into it?"

Father Bryce nodded. He fixed his eyes on the filament of the bulb overhead and tried to will his mind into the same state of whited-out blankness.

The pain began again almost at once, and Wolf went on: "I got a theory. It goes along with why I called this place Knightriders, which is not because of the movie. It's to do with armor. This all comes out of another time I was getting tattooed, when I was dropping acid and I got this idea that the tattoos was like a coat of armor. I was close to having full coverage by then. It wasn't like the tats was some kind of bulletproof protection—there's guys who had that idea, but most of 'em are dead—it was more like the knight is riding the horse, and armor is riding the knight. Like the armor is some kind of alien that takes over what you do. Like the tattoos get to be in charge. They *ride* us. Can you dig that, Damon?

"Damon?"

Father Bryce nodded once, he could dig it, and then, as the vomit he'd been trying to make himself swallow spilled down across his cheek, he fainted dead away.

IV

Silvanus de Roquefort, Bishop of Rodez and Montpellier-le-Vieux, was attired with unusual splendor to celebrate the Feast of Saint Macarius, which falls on the second of January, which was also the anniversary of his consecration. Ergo, all the pomp. But a more practical purpose was served by the layers of vestments in which he was encased—alb, tunicle, chasuble, and pallium, to mention only those that served to keep out the chill—for it was unusually cold in the abbey church of Notre Dame de Gevaudon. In the morning hours the church lay within the shadow of the escarpments of the fortress of Montpellier-le-Vieux, and only the dead who were interred there—many de Roqueforts among them—could have taken comfort in their surroundings. For the larger part of the congregation, who must stand beyond the altar screen in the as-yet-uncompleted nave, beneath a canopy of dripping rushes, there could be little sense of a holiday being celebrated—the third within eight days—but only of a mortification to be endured. As he ascended the pulpit to deliver his homily, the Bishop could not resist feeling a certain satisfaction in the evident misery of those assembled before him, for their presence attested eloquently to the power that had brought them here so much against the grain of their own fleshly will—the conjoint power of the Bishop de Roquefort and of Holy Mother Church.

"My dear children," the Bishop began, speaking not in Latin but in the language of his listeners, "the flesh is evil. In that matter the heretics among you are correct. Whether they go by the name of Cathars, or Albigensians, or Waldensians, heretics know that much. Heresy has a nose, and it can smell corruption. For what is our flesh but meat, and what does meat do after only a little while? It decays, it rots, it becomes a lodging house for maggots. You will all die—the fat merchant and squinch-eyed lime-burner, the gravid mother and the nursing child, priest and prince and prisoner—none will be spared, all will become dead meat, a feast for worms, a noxious thing that must be buried where it can't be seen or smelled.

"And then, when it has been lodged within the earth, when the soil is packed tight about its face as though it were an onion or a radish, why, what then? Why, that is only the beginning of your terrors. For then—and the day will be soon!—the trumpets of Judgment shall sound, and the dead shall be raised, like onions torn up from their bed, and merchant and mason and mother and child shall stand naked before their Judge, with their sins written on their skin as though it were parchment. On the merchant's skin a dog gnaws a bone as a token of his greed and gluttony, and the Judge surrenders the merchant to the demons waiting to run him through with a spit, like a chicken that's to be roasted, and then in the undying fires of hell he will be turned on the spit as he screams in endless pain. On the mason's skin the Judge reads marks of sloth and lechery, and he is given over to the citadel of hell, where through eternity he is crushed by the weight of the stone he must bear up an endless steep incline as jeering demons scourge him with whips. And the mother's skin is a veritable nest of vipers, as lusts that were invisible writhe up from within and spread across her skin, and *she* is given over to the demons, and how they deal with her I may not say, though you may all imagine it quite well. And her child that nursed at her breast? What of that child? That *unbaptized* child? Its skin is black with the stain of original sin, and that child is forfeited to hell as well, as are all who die unbaptized or unshriven. Without the sacraments, outside the Church, there is no salvation! This is what Augustine says: *Noli credere, nec dicere, nec docere, infantes antequam baptizentur morte praeventos posse ad originalium indulgentiam peccatorum, si vis esse catholicus.* Which is to say, Do not believe, or say, or teach that the unbaptized infant can be forgiven original sin—not if you wish to be a Catholic.

"My dear children, this is why heresy must be hunted down and extirpated. This is why there can be no clemency or compromise, for the aim of heresy is nothing less than the destruction of the Church and the triumph of Satan. The heretics would pull us all down to the pit with them, if they could have their way. I have heard some say that the Crusaders were cruel and merciless after the capture of Béziers. That the slaughter of so many of the city's inhabitants—in fact, of all of them—was merciless and un-Christian. But against heresy there can be no mercy, not from God, nor yet by God's deputy here on earth, His Holiness the Pope, in whose name and at whose urging the Crusaders fought. There was opportunity for the citizens to leave Béziers with their Bishop, and that opportunity was refused. And before that they might have surrendered the heretics among themselves, but no, that demand could not be met, for it violated their rights as the *free citizens* of Béziers."

The Bishop paused to savor the irony of that phrase. He knew there were those among his congregation who had claimed a similar autonomy for the "free citizens" of Montpellier-le-Vieux, who felt that heresy was a sin like other sins, a matter for the conscience and the confessional.

"And so, my dear children, those *free citizens* of Béziers stood upon the ramparts of their city, thinking themselves safe from retribution, and taunted the armies assembled below them and hailed down missiles on the cavalry in their armor and the *routiers* in their rags. But it was those ragged mercenaries who breached the gate and threw into confusion those *free citizens*—but let us call them by their true name— those *contumacious heretics!* And slew them, man, woman, and child! And burned their free city of Béziers to the ground. The very cathedral was sundered in two as a judgment for having sheltered heresy.

"O my dear children, accept the fate of that city as a warning to yourselves. Surrender your heretics to the Holy Inquisition. You may speak to your confessors in confidence, or if you lack confidence in your confessor, if you fear he may not be zealous, then you may approach the Holy Office directly. If you have but doubts or misgivings concerning a friend, a neighbor, even a relative, share them with us that the cleansing may begin. If you do *not*, if you shirk the hard task now, you may pay a terrible price later, when your shepherd will not be present to protect you."

The Bishop lifted his crozier, symbol of his pastoral authority. He scanned the faces of the congregation before him and took note of those whose eyes dared meet his own. Among them were those of

Bonamico, the master mason from Lombardy, whom the Bishop knew to be a skeptic and libertine, like so many of his confraternity. Bonamico resented having been impressed into the Bishop's service, along with some thirty other Lombard workmen who had been employed, at much better wages, in repairing the fortifications of Carcassonne. Their employer, the Viscount of Aude, had not been in a position to gainsay the Bishop's request, since he was beholden to him for his appointment as the military governor of the newly pacified region. Bonamico's work had been near completion, in any case. The mason resented his forced service in the construction of Notre Dame de Gevaudon and had twice attempted to flee his obligation, for which the Bishop had been obliged to make an example of him. After these floggings the man's baleful glare was not to be wondered at. The Bishop did not care about dark looks or mumbled curses, so long as Bonamico and his Lombards accomplished the special, covert task assigned to them. Then he might receive the wages of his insolence.

Nearer the pulpit from which the Bishop regarded his flock was a figure toward whom it was more difficult to maintain an attitude of tolerance and forbearance. Though her face was obscured by a veil of black lace, the Bishop was certain that the eyes of Marquesia de Gaillac, could they be seen, would have shone with an enmity and malice more implacable than Bonamico's. One of the woman's daughters had been married to a known Cathar, Jean Cambitor, and the Bishop was quite sure that the faith of Madame de Gaillac was cut from the same heretical cloth. Indeed, he suspected that she was a *perfecta*—the Cathars, among their other abominations, admitted women into the ranks of their apostate clergy.

Just the sight of the woman, standing before him with every outward sign of respect, infuriated the Bishop, who was stirred thereby to take his homily in a direction he had not planned, telling his flock the instructive story of a certain man of Brabant who discovered the unholy practice of certain midwives who, when they deliver a child, dedicate its life to the devil. The man had hidden himself and seen his own daughter act in this manner in the delivery of his own son, and he'd seen his newly delivered son climbing up the chain by which the cooking pots were suspended. In terror at what he'd seen, the man insisted that his child at once be baptized. When the child was being carried to the next village, where there was a church, they had to cross a bridge. The man would not allow his daughter to carry the child over the bridge but, putting a sword to her throat, insisted that the child must cross the bridge by himself. Being compelled, the midwife put down the child and invoked the devil by her art, and suddenly the child was seen on the other side of the bridge.

The Bishop paused at this point in his remarkable tale to allow its fearful import to be digested. There was much to mull over: the perfidy of women, and of midwives in particular; the extraordinary power of Satan and of those, even infants, dedicated to his service; and—this above all!—the obligation of a good Catholic to prefer the Church's well-being above his own or his family's. For the conclusion of the story, as the Bishop now related, was that the man accused both his daughter and his wife before the Inquisition, and the two women, after a period of purgation, were burned at the stake.

Did Madame de Gaillac feel the particular relevance of this tale? Did she shudder within her dark veil? Did she have some premonition that she might share such a fiery fate? Those leagued with the devil sometimes are gifted with second sight, but never in matters touching their own welfare. In these they are blind, or even deceived, for the Father of Lies is impartial in the matter of deception.

The Bishop concluded his homily with a tribute to Saint Macarius, who was a pupil of Saint Anthony and one of the Desert Fathers. The Bishop told how the skull of a pagan had spoken to Macarius, revealing secrets concerning the governance of hell, where the Jews were consigned to a deeper pit than the pagans. But deeper than the Jews, the skull revealed, was the place reserved for unregenerate and heretical Christians, closest to where Satan himself, the Archfiend, was bound to a burning gridiron with red-hot chains. As he screamed, he would reach out and seize the damned and press them, like clusters of grapes, into his insatiable maw. Not all of these details derived from the particular revelation of Saint Macarius. The Bishop collated many sources in painting his picture of the afterlife that awaited the Church's enemies. His aim was not scholarly exactitude but vividness, and when he descended from his pulpit, he felt he had achieved his aim.

In the sacristy, the Bishop dismissed the abbot and the deacons of Notre Dame who had assisted at the Mass and was divested with the aid only of his famulus, Abbé St-Loup, who had acted today as thurifer and as a result still gave off a penetrating odor of frankincense. Abbé St-Loup was a short, plump cleric of fifty-four years notable rather for his skill at beekeeping and viticulture than for his piety. He was also, unfortunately, the Bishop's half brother, one of many such offspring that the Bishop's father, Aimeric III, Count of Roquefort, had sired in his headstrong youth outside the bonds of wedlock. Most of these blots on the good name of the family had found places of service in the de Roquefort household or had been shipped off to the Crusades, either to the Holy Land or to Toulouse, where they'd killed infidels and heretics and, such was God's will, been killed themselves. Of all Aimeric's bastards, only St-Loup survived, thanks to his having been dedicated to the service of the cross rather than that of the sword. For that reason as well, he had become the particular charge of his ten-years-younger, legitimate half brother, Silvanus, who felt toward him a temperate but implacable detestation that St-Loup answered with a fawning deference and sly insinuations of fraternal affection. He was a thorn in the Bishop's side but, as so often in such cases, the Bishop could not be quit of him. He was a wound that would not heal for picking at the scab. The Bishop needed to have his half brother about to torment, and by having him about he secured his own misery as well.

"Your Grace was most eloquent today in his homily," St-Loup declared with a cringe of reverence as he accepted the crozier from the Bishop's hand and began to remove the enamel pins that secured the seamless fabric of the pallium. Then, lest this seem insufficient: "Your Grace is always eloquent."

"Never mind my eloquence. Mind the pins!"

"Indeed, Your Grace! The pins—and the pallium! Such a privilege to be allowed to assist in your disrobing when you wear the pallium. I feel almost as though I were touching the garment of our Savior Himself."

The Bishop was, in fact, somewhat vain concerning the pallium. It was a vestment usually reserved for the use of the Pope and of archbishops. Its wool came from special lambs that had been blessed by His Holiness on the feast day of Saint Agnes, January twenty-first, and then entrusted to the canons of St. John Lateran and raised by nuns of an order particularly devoted to this task until they were ready to be shorn. In all Europe there were only eight episcopal sees whose bishops were privileged to wear the pallium: Autun, Bamberg, Dol, Lucca, Ostia, Pavia, Verona, and the Bishop's own diocese of Rodez and Montpellier-le-Vieux. It was a distinction that the Bishop could not help but suppose prefigured further distinctions to come. But to hear

Abbé St-Loup speak of it in his tone of oily sycophancy was a defilement, as though the garment's white wool had been besmirched with excrement.

"Oh, look at this!" the Abbé marveled, holding up the rarest of the pins for the Bishop's closer admiration. "Is this an amethyst? Or is it a chip from very heaven's dome?"

The man exposed the black stumps of his teeth in a grimace of pious cupidity, and the Bishop, unable to repress his annoyance, swatted at the hand holding the pin as at a fly.

St-Loup yelped as the point of the gold pin penetrated the soft heel of his hand. A gout of blood formed where the skin was pierced, and before the Bishop could back away from him, the gout swelled to the size of a small grape and dropped down across the pallium, where it formed a slantwise red mark like a virgule just below the Bishop's pectoral cross.

"Clod!" the Bishop screamed in dismay, for he knew, at the first sight of the stain on the wool, that it was indelible, that some faint trace of St-Loup's blood would always remain upon the pallium, which itself was irreplaceable and inalienable—almost, in a way, the Bishop's second skin, for whoever received the pallium knew that he was destined to be buried in it. Even to lend it to another cleric, howsoever high his office, was not permitted. And now the Bishop's pallium had been soiled forever by this oafish prelate's mongrel blood.

The Bishop grasped hold of his crozier and struck Abbé St-Loup across the face. The gilded and bejeweled shepherd's crook made a formidable weapon. The Abbé covered his face with his hands and fell to his knees, begging forgiveness. The Bishop struck him again, slamming the bottom end of the staff into the small of his back.

"Mercy, my lord!" the Abbé gasped.

Not by any impulse of mercy but from a sudden, searing pain that spread across his own chest, the Bishop desisted. Now it was his turn to gasp, and to fall to his knees. But of whom could he beg for mercy? What instrument had dealt this terrible pain? He tore at the vestments that wrapped him, layer upon precious layer, trying to discover the source of his suffering and to assuage it. He dropped the crozier, cast off his miter, clawed at the golden chain from which his pectoral cross hung pendant, but he no more had the power to remove the chain than if he'd been a blackamoor trying to tear off his fetters.

The pain was unbearable. It was as though he were being flayed alive. As though the single enameled pin that had pierced the Abbé's flesh were now puncturing his—not once but infinitely many times.

The Abbé, still prostrated on the stony floor, saw the Bishop's paroxysms with such astonishment that he forgot, at first, to be fearful. "My lord?" he ventured timidly.

But the Bishop had become quite oblivious of him. It almost seemed—but this was a terrible thought—that he had been possessed. The Abbé scrambled to his feet and backed toward the heavy oak door of the sacristy.

The Bishop summoned up the strength to command: "Leave me!"

The Abbé left with no more persuasion.

The pain continued, but with some abatement, so that the Bishop was able to remove his pectoral cross and to slip the pallium from his shoulders. But with the folds of the pallium bunched about his knees, he found it impossible to untangle himself from chasuble, tunicle, alb. He collapsed to the floor with his arms spread across his chest, his fingers clutching his shoulders, as though to protect himself from his invisible torturer.

But the torturer continued his work and even became, for an instant, visible—if not to the Bishop's physical senses (for he'd pressed his eyes tight-closed), then to some other organ of apprehension.

The man was a scrawnier St-Loup, the same gray-tufted beard, the same tonsure, but strangely dressed, with a curious device of wires and glass mounted on his nose and ears. He smiled at the Bishop and spoke in a strange language, which the Bishop nevertheless understood: "Good timing, Damon. We're almost done with the outline. I'll show you where we are."

The man put aside the instrument of torture and held up a speculum of incredible rarity and precision. Slanting its silvery face, he showed the Bishop his own naked, bleeding torso—and rising from it, yet intrinsic with it, a face of smoke, the face of hell itself, dim but undeniable.

"What do you say to that, Damon?"

"It's Satan," the Bishop whispered.

"You bet your fuckin' ass it's Satan."

The Bishop turned away his face from the smiling, demonic visage in the speculum, closed his eyes, and found himself once more on the sacristy floor. The vision of hell had vanished and, with it, the worst of the pain.

He knew what had happened. Hell had claimed him for its own. His sins were to be punished, as he'd always feared they would be. Perhaps not at once. Perhaps he might be spared some hours or days. But the yoke had been placed on his shoulders, the collar was about his neck.

5

"Hello," said the answering machine in a voice that could have been anybody's. "You've reached 555-0023. Sorry there's no one home. If you would like to leave a message, wait for the beep."

She waited for the beep, which seemed to take forever, and then she said, "Petey, hello, are you there, this is your mother."

She gave him more than ample time to pick up and then, when he refused to, she continued: "Well, whether you're there or not, I hope you're all right. I had another little episode today, but I'm fine now. There were chicken tenders for dinner, and I always like that, but the cook here doesn't know how to make a cake and I swear she uses Crisco to make the frosting. This was not really my idea, calling up, but if I refuse to call, that goes on my record and I get the third degree from my counselor. 'Why aren't you using your phone privileges, Mrs. Bryce? Are you angry with anyone?' As though I had anything to get angry *about!* Anyhow. Your brother came out to the cemetery and found me there, and I remember there was something I told him about your father, and now I can't remember what. But something you'd want to know, too. He's a priest. Well, of course, you'd know that, wouldn't you? What are you? I know what you *look* like, because the nurse, who's sitting on the other side of the ward at this minute, knitting, pointed you out in the picture on my dresser, the one with just the two of us, and I've got to say, you ought to lose some *weight*. Your brother is much trimmer, and he's your twin. I do remember some things. I mean, about the two of you. But mostly back when you were little. Or even teenagers. I remember, vaguely, that you used to fight. I guess with boys that's inevitable. And you would always get the worst of it. Which is funny when you think that it's your brother who became the priest. Is this machine still recording me? Anyhow, this should satisfy the nurse about my mental equilibrium. For tonight, anyhow. Oh, it just came to me, isn't that always the way. It was about your father—not Paul, your real father. And I've told you already, haven't I? I never told your brother, but I did tell you. Years ago, when we got drunk, after Grandpa McCarthy's funeral. You should have seen the look on your brother's face when I told him today. I didn't say who it was, only that it wasn't Paul. And he didn't say a thing, but I had a feeling that he was pleased. You were, weren't you? I mean, who would *want* Paul Bryce for their father? Not that the alternative is so much better, I guess. In fact, that was what was at the back of my mind just now, when I agreed to have the nurse dial your number. I can remember his face, sort of. Not bad looking, but no Clark Gable either. I remember he wore a cassock sometimes. But then I *also* remember him wearing one of my dresses. It's like watching Geraldo on TV, some of the strange people nowadays. Then, too—only *then* people didn't talk about it on TV. They didn't talk about it at all. Anyhow, I can't for the life of me remember his name. But I think I told you. So you would know and I don't, which certainly is a peculiar situation. *We* could go on Geraldo, as a team. Anyhow. It's nice talking to your machine. I always feel we've got this special bond, your machine and me.

"Bye."

His mother was always so much friendlier and more interesting when she talked to his machine than when she had him on the line that Peter Bryce rarely picked up the phone when she called in the evenings. He'd even taken to recording her different messages on the answering machine on another tape as a kind of keepsake. Possibly he might play it at her memorial service, assuming there was one, and that he'd be attending it, which lately had come to seem a more and more unwarranted assumption.

After she'd hung up, he rewound the tape and poured himself another rum and Coke so as not to waste the last half of the can, his third of the evening. There was just enough Bacardi left in the second half-pint bottle. Then he replayed the answering machine tape and used his Walkman to add tonight's message to the anthology of her other messages. Tonight's was surely one of her finest, especially the suggestion that *he* was the only one who could reveal her dark secret, her Alzheimer's having wiped the slate of *her* memory clean. Neat.

He wondered if elderly lifers in penitentiaries came down with Alzheimer's and had to ask guards or cellmates what they'd done to be there. He also wondered, as he had other times, if his mother was quite as fuzzy-headed as she made herself out to be. Sometimes she just seemed devious. Of course, it was possible she was both fuzzy-headed *and* devious. Devious could become a habit, like drinking, that a person maintained in a variety of circumstances. Richard III was devious and physically challenged, so why not devious with Alzheimer's? Peter was devious himself, and as he approached the end of his rum and Coke he had a genuine brainstorm of deviousness.

If he'd been sober he wouldn't have succumbed to the temptation. But he wasn't sober and he did succumb. He dialed his brother's number at the rectory. He knew Pat's habits, which weren't that different from his own, and sure enough, instead of his answering the phone himself, the answering machine came on.

"Hello," said Father Bryce in a tone of professional warmth, "and thank you for calling. I'm sorry I can't come to the phone right now, but if you'll leave your name and number and a brief message, I'll get back to you as soon as I can. Meanwhile, why not get in touch with God—and say a prayer for me while you're talking with Him. We all need each other's prayers. God bless."

After the beep, Peter played the tape he'd recorded on his Walkman into the phone receiver. If Pat was by his phone monitoring his calls, Peter was sure he would not pick up the phone but just let their mother go on talking, and he'd assume that she'd dialed the rectory by mistake. She regularly confused her sons' phone numbers, or else she'd simply forget which of them she'd meant to talk to when she dialed.

As soon as the tape reached Mrs. Bryce's "Bye," Peter hung up. Now, what would Pat make of *that*? Would he believe Margaret's story about their father not being, after all, their real father? For that matter, did Peter believe it? He would have liked to. He couldn't remember that much about Paul Bryce, who'd died when his sons were in kindergarten, and even the little Peter could remember bore the impress of his mother's recollections, which had varied from maudlin to embittered according to her mood and her narrative purpose. Sometimes Paul had been a model Catholic layman, a regular Sunday communicant and keeper of Lenten fasts; other times he was a drunken brute who'd given his wife black eyes and overturned Christmas trees. Peter could dimly remember a wrecked Christmas tree, though he hadn't witnessed the event. In either case, whether a Knight of Columbus or a standard-issue Irish drunk, Paul Bryce was no prize as a father from Peter's point of view. A mystery father was a much more exciting idea.

The drollest part of the situation was that Peter had no way of knowing whether or not Margaret had told him who his mystery father was, as she claimed, because he'd blacked out the entire three days of his grandfather's wake and funeral four years ago. That had been his first sustained blackout and a very scary experience, though not scary enough to have stopped his drinking. So it was quite possible she had told him and that he'd thereafter dealt with her confidence with perfect discretion, never mentioning it or passing along the information to his twin brother, because it had got misfiled into that part of his memory he couldn't access. There were card files on his hard disk where the same thing had happened. By some glitch in his software he got a message that said IRRECOVERABLE PROGRAM ERROR anytime he tried to access those particular files. They were there, but they couldn't be reached.

The mind was like a computer. It consisted of an infinite number of on/off switches. The cartoonist's cliché of ideas as lightbulbs was not far off the mark. And just as, with a faulty switch, a bulb would sometimes be turned on and sometimes not, so with the switches of memory. You see a face and think, I know who that is, but memory won't yield the name until too late. And some of the switches were faultier than others, for reasons not completely understood, although it was pretty obvious that alcohol did not improve the operation of any of the switches. Somewhere he'd read—was it in Wilkie Collins's *The Moonstone?*—that a person who hides something when he's under the influence of opium can only hope to find it when he is once again under the same influence.

Therefore, another rum and Coke? Why not.

Father Cogling was on his knees before the statue of the Virgin in his office at the rectory, and was on the third decade of his third rosary of the day, when the telephone in Father Pat's office began to ring. Although he knew the answering machine was on, he could not resist the temptation to interrupt his prayers and monitor the phone call. It might, after all, be an emergency that ought to be addressed immediately.

It was, instead, Father Pat's mother, calling from her nursing home, and calling (it gradually became clear) a wrong number. For she'd dialed Father Pat's number, thinking she'd dialed her other son, Father Pat's apostate twin, Peter.

The message she left was appalling. If Father Cogling had known how to operate the machine so as to erase the filth that Mrs. Bryce had spewed out against her husband and herself, he would have done so, but playing back what the machine had recorded was the furthest extent of Father Cogling's capabilities. That much he did: He played back Mrs. Bryce's message, which seemed even more dismaying a second time. The woman was perhaps not responsible for what she said. She was deranged by the disease that had put her into a nursing home. But for that very reason her words might seem more credible to her son, because we tend to suppose those who are deranged have some special relation to the truth, when in fact the contrary is often the case. An exorcist would often be of greater benefit to the insane than so-called mental health professionals.

If only there were some way to spare Father Pat the needless pain of hearing his mother's message. It wasn't, after all, intended for his ears.

And there *was* a way. Really quite an easy one. If the tape were rewound to the beginning, which it was, and someone else were to call and leave another message just as long, or a little longer, the later message would replace Mrs. Bryce's. Father Cogling might make such a call himself, from his own phone line in the rectory, but how could he explain his doing such a thing? No, it would be better to have someone leave a call about ordinary parish business. But whom to ask for such an odd favor? Who wouldn't want to be given some *reason* for what he was doing?

Gerhardt Ober.

Of course.

6

Even in a state of mortal sin, which was surely his condition this morning, Father Bryce found a familiar, antidotal comfort in celebrating Mass. As he lifted the chalice at the moment of consecration, his body felt a single integrated ache that was his hangover, his penance, and his dread, and when he drank the wine from the chalice, his usual doubts were added to the mix—doubts not only as to his own priestly powers but also concerning all things supernatural and divine. But for that very reason he could pray, with the father of the child possessed by the demon, "Lord, I believe. Help thou my unbelief." If one has known (or has been) such a child and seen its convulsions, seen it foaming at the mouth, seen it in its fits of self-destruction, then one must believe in that demon, at the very least. Could he, as well, believe that Christ could and would drive out the demon? That was where he needed help, the help even of this tainted sacramental wine.

He ought not to be celebrating Mass in a state of sin, and the very act of consecration added to his inventory of misdeeds. But to have avoided performance of priestly duties would be tantamount to a public confession. He was entangled in his daily routine as in a net. It was like the dream he'd had last night, when he had fainted from the pain of the tattooing: He'd thrashed on the floor, trapped in his priestly vestments like a fish in a net.

Bowing his head and closing his eyes, he could see it again. So clearly. The fat little man he'd struck and shrieked at in a language he'd never heard before but at once understood. The chill of the stone floor against his cheek at the moment of his complete collapse, like a cold cloth pressed to one's forehead during a bout of fever. The stiff fabrics of the vestments as he tried to pull them off—especially the coarse wool of the pallium. The orphrey work embroidered on the chasuble, at once so painstaking and so crude, the toil of fingers still fumbling at the first tasks of civilization.

He was no archaeologist, but undoubtedly he'd acquired enough visual cues and memories in his years in Rome, during the afternoons and weekends of touring all the antiquities within a fifty-mile radius of the Holy City with his Michelin Guide in hand, that now his unconscious could create, in his dreams, simulations of the medieval past that seemed entirely authentic. In any case, he had brought back no photographs of what he'd dreamt. Only the dreamer knows what his dreams look like, and his memory of them, when he wakes, is evidence of nothing. People have flying dreams, but that doesn't mean that they are able to fly.

Yet it seemed so real. It seemed as if he had actually been there (wherever and whenever that might be) in the flesh. The flesh was, indeed, what the dream—or vision?—had chiefly been about: the bleeding flesh pierced by the enamel pin, the gout of blood staining the white wool of the pallium, the flesh beneath the priestly robes being tortured by the tattooist's needle. Undoubtedly, it had been some kind of psychological mechanism for escaping the pain of the tattooing, a retreat not only through space but through time, to another continent and another century, yet all the while preserving his priestly identity.

And not just preserving but enhancing it. For he'd felt more perfectly a priest in those instants on the stone floor of that dreamt sacristy than even at the moment of his ordination in A.D. 1969. If he knew how to, he would return to the dreamt era, step beyond the sacristy door, and see how large a medieval world his unconscious could construct. Just that little glimpse, despite the horror attending it, had seemed . . . *Beautiful* was not the right word. He did not have the word that would express it. He had only the desire to return.

All the while he entertained these fancies he continued the prescribed rituals of the Mass, and now the inevitable moment had come when he must offer the Host to the communicants. Only two of the six people who'd come to the 7:30 Mass had approached the altar, old Mrs. Smede and Gerhardt Ober. Mrs. Smede received the sacrament from his hand with a furtive smile and averted eyes, as though she shared his sense that the Communion wafer had been sullied by his sins but yet, like him, she could not resist her hunger for it. Gerhardt, by contrast, insisted on making eye contact as he took the Host in his own gnarled fingers and placed it on his tongue, and chewed, and swallowed, as though these were acts that must be performed under priestly supervision.

Gerhardt had left another of his tirades on the answering machine last night, apparently in response to Wilfrid's having relayed Father Bryce's wish that he would stop harassing members of Agnus Dei, a group of laywomen that met at various churches in the Twin Cities— at St. Bernardine's on the first and third Wednesday of each month— to discuss issues peculiar to their sex. The membership included some women who had once been in religious orders, some of whom had spoken out in favor of pro-Choice political candidates, while others were ardent advocates of opening various church offices, and ultimately the priesthood, to women. In some parishes they had managed, briefly, to have girls assist at Mass, a trespass on ancient masculine privilege that had provoked Gerhardt Ober and some few other old-timers into a fury of denunciation. Even now that Bishop Massey had clamped down on the practice and "altar girls" were no longer tolerated in the Minneapolis archdiocese, Gerhardt continued to picket meetings of Agnus Dei and to inveigh against the organization in a steady outpouring of crank letters to parish bulletins, to local news media, and even to the papal nuncio in Washington, who had replied to one of Gerhardt's missives with a form letter thanking him for his frankness and concern. That letter had acquired in Gerhardt's mind the magisterial importance of a papal bull. It had become his license to go on making a nuisance of himself every time the urge came over him. And because he was Father Bryce's parishioner, the leaders of Agnus Dei tended to hold the priest personally responsible for each of Gerhardt's outrages.

Father Bryce had yet to play through Gerhardt's latest tirade from beginning to end. It seemed to take up most of the tape on the answering machine and included a reading of the nuncio's entire letter and of Gerhardt's three obsequious replies. Gerhardt could test one's patience even more than one's charity.

Thinking of such matters was somehow cheering. It returned Father Bryce to his ordinary parish problems and gave him something to fix his mind on besides the larger bind he was in. For years he'd dealt with his guilty mornings-after by acting as though the night before hadn't happened, by turning his thoughts to other matters, by trying to bring a kind of zeal to business-as-usual. He had often observed the same behavior in those who came to confession to him, which afforded a kind of sanction: He was dealing with his sins just as other sinners dealt with theirs. It was humbling to know that he was no better than the most peccant of his flock.

After Mass, he was thankful that there was no altar boy on hand and that he could remove his vestments without having to keep up a stoic front. He could wince and flinch and grimace as the different customary motions of disrobing provoked different uncustomary pains. The wadded gauze bandages taped to his chest and abdomen protected his raw flesh from the direct abrasion of his clothing as he lifted his arm, or bent over, or turned sideways, but the pain was now more than skindeep. He felt as though his flesh were being roasted, as though he were covered with Ben-Gay that had gone nuclear. He knew he was running a fever, but he didn't want to take his temperature for fear of finding out he was dangerously feverish. It occurred to him, for the first time, that medical examinations would be problematical in the future, for he couldn't let a doctor see his tattoo. He couldn't go swimming (but then he hadn't been swimming in several years) or go into saunas.

But his sex life might not actually change that much. It was not something he cared to think about right now (it was his sex life that had got him into this situation), but the thought offered some faint comfort even as he tried to fix his attention elsewhere.

He went to his office in the rectory, where there was a thermos of coffee waiting for him and a plate of four Oreos, as, thanks to Mrs. Daly, there was every morning after Mass. "Give us this day our Daly bread," he would quip when he came upon the housekeeper in the act of putting the plate of cookies by his phone, and she would always pretend to be shocked, as though he'd told a racy story or been caught in a small blasphemy, a "goddamn" or "oh hell."

Just as he'd poured his first cup of coffee and taken the first crisp bite of an Oreo, the phone rang. Not the rectory phone, his private line. He stared at the phone, counting the rings, and when it had rung ten times he answered with his most neutral "Hello."

It was, as he'd known it would be, his tormentor.

"Hi there, Father, it's Clay. How you feeling today? A little tender from the needlework?"

His throat had grown dry, and he was unable to swallow the bolus of thick, sugary paste that the Oreo had become. He moistened his tongue with the coffee and managed to say, "Hello, Clay."

"Is that it? Hello? You didn't answer my question, Father. Or it's Damon now, isn't it? Damon the Demon."

He tried to form a simple statement that yes, he was sore, but it was not just the dryness of his throat that prevented him but a paralyzing constriction of his chest, as though he were in the grip of some huge clawed hand squeezing the breath from his lungs. He knew exactly what he was feeling: lust, intensified by fear. A feeling that Clay had roused in him almost from the moment they'd met at the after-hours club in Stillwater. Now just the sound of Clay's voice could have the same effect on him.

Clay chuckled, as though he'd confessed his thoughts aloud. "So, tell me, I'm dying to know—did you get off on it? Did you and Wolf have a scene?"

"I did just what I'd been told I had to do, Clay. No more, no less."

"There's no hurry. You take your time with Wolf. The two of you'll be clocking a lot of hours together. And I realize he's older than you generally get off on. By how much? About forty years?"

Father Bryce made no reply to the taunt. There was none he could have made. If the taunt had not been true, if Clay had not possessed the most damning and irrefutable evidence of its truth, Father Bryce would not have had to submit to his blackmail.

"To get serious for a moment, Father—I can't seem to get over the habit of calling you Father—the organization isn't doing this to *punish* you. I hope you understand that. It's just the same as the kind of penance you deal out in the confessional. More drastic, but the same basic idea. Reformation. Maybe that's a bad word for Catholics. But the idea is, you've got some flaws of character, and we're going to help you *reform* so you won't have those flaws. You don't want to be a pedophile, do you, Father?"

After a pause, Clay insisted: *"Do you?"*

"No," said Father Bryce.

"Of course not. No one would. It's a shameful and degrading vice. Also rather ridiculous in its way. It obviously represents some kind of arrested development, doesn't it?"

When Father Bryce did not reply, Clay said, "These are not rhetorical questions, Father. When I ask you a question, I expect an answer."

Father Bryce forced himself to take a deep breath. Then he said, "Yes, you're right. All the psychology texts would agree—arrested development."

"Psychology texts? That's just another kind of bullshit, Father. Do you think there'd still be all these sexual perverts around preying on thirteen-year-olds if psychology or psychiatry or Sigmund fucking Freud knew shit about anything? That is how old the Kramer kid was, right?"

Father Bryce closed his eyes as a means of denying his tears. "He was fourteen."

"Yeah, fourteen when he committed suicide, but thirteen when you got your first blow job from him. Right, Father?"

"I stand corrected."

"You sure as hell do, Father. Correction's going to be your middle name. Now, let me ask you this: Have you been reading the literature?"

"Not thoroughly."

"You've been too busy? You've had a fair while now, Father. And you keep saying, 'Yes, I'm going to read it.' Then the next time I call, you still haven't got to it. It's very important for you to become acquainted with the literature, Father."

"I confess I have difficulties."

"That's an understatement, Father. But I guess you meant a different kind of difficulty. Like, you got a problem accepting some of the ideas, is that it?"

"That would sum it up pretty well."

"But you believe in all that Catholic bullshit, right? The Virgin Birth. Jesus coming back to life. Noah's ark. All kinds of miracles. The devil. You'll buy all that, but you can't believe in UFOs? You think we're all there is in the whole universe?"

"Not necessarily. But I have to say that much of what I've read in Mr. Boscage's book strikes me as . . . invention."

"Science fiction is what a lot of his enemies call it."

"That is what he was known for initially, I gather."

"That's because at first he didn't realize where his ideas were coming from. He explains that in chapter one of the *Prolegomenon*. Have you read *that* far?"

"Yes."

"So, how much *have* you read?"

"Up to the point where he learns he was a Roman centurion in an earlier existence."

"And there is *proof* of that, Father. There is a tape that you can listen to. There is a session where Boscage was regressed back to his identity as Gaius Lucius, and he talked in Latin, very clearly, for about ten minutes. And what do you think he's talking *about?* The Lupinids. So how do you explain that away? Boscage never studied Latin. He didn't go to fucking high school."

Father Bryce could think of no reply. Boscage's book, *A Prolegomenon to Receptivist Science*, was a virtual anthology of New Age absurdities and an obvious hoax by a rather unsophisticated hoaxer. To argue against it was as hopeless a task as bailing water out of a ruptured boat.

The problem was that he was a passenger in that boat and the boat was in deep water. Clay was a true-believing Receptivist, and he was determined that Father Bryce was to join him in his folly. If only his blackmailer had been motivated by simple greed, or even malice.

"So, I asked you a question, Father, and I'm waiting for an answer."

He sighed. "There is no explanation that I can think of."

"Hey, now we're making some progress. You keep reading the book. And think about it. 'Cause it is relevant to what is going on with you. These things don't happen by chance. Your little hustler didn't kill himself because you were abusing him sexually, Father. Somehow the Lupinids are involved in this. I don't know how but somehow."

Father Bryce said nothing.

Clay seemed satisfied. "I gotta go now, Father. I expect you got things to do, too. But I'll be checking in same time next week to hear how the tattoo is progressing. Give my regards to old Wolf."

"I'll do that."

The line went dead.

Father Bryce realized that there were tears in his eyes—and, at the same time, such rage in his heart that if Clay had been here in this room with him he would have bludgeoned him to death with the telephone receiver. He would have done it joyfully.

But Clay was not here, and Father Bryce had no idea where to begin to look for him. Murder was not a possibility open to him. And he hadn't the strength for suicide.

He was trapped. There was nothing he could do, if he wished Clay not to send the incriminating videotape to the police and the media, except to submit to his demands, however lunatic, however grotesque.

7

It was a miracle that she was still alive.

For a while she just lay there on the bed blissfully unaware of anything but her gratitude at having been spared. By rights she should be dead. There was the empty pill bottle weighing down her suicide note on the table by the bed, the almost empty water glass beside it. If she were a painter she would have painted them as a still life, and it would have been more beautiful than any painting of a vase of flowers, for the sunlight seemed fairly to explode from them. They were chandeliers of sheer joy.

She was alive. Thank you, sweet Jesus.

She pulled herself out of the bed and knelt beside it and said a formal prayer of thanks, a Hail Mary to balance the Hail Mary she'd said in her last moments of consciousness after taking the pills. Then she had begged only Mary's forgiveness for her terrible sin, and Mary had answered the prayer with the gift of her whole life.

Yet, in a way, hadn't it also been the Virgin who had got her into the pickle she was in?

No sooner had she framed the ungrateful question than the light in the room seemed to dim, and the pill bottle and the water glass beside it shrank into their ordinary geometric shapes and ceased to transmit the message of redemption and hope that briefly had seemed to glow from them like the neon gas inside a bulb.

She knew that heaven worked like that, that you could see it only in glimpses, like a beam of sunlight darting out from clouds and then disappearing the moment you saw it. There was never time to point it out even to someone right beside you. It was there and then it was gone, but *while* it was there you knew that you were in touch with something out of the ordinary. God had touched you.

Now it was gone, and she was in the same situation that had made her want to kill herself . . . how long ago? Her alarm clock said nine-thirty, and she'd taken the pills at two in the morning, after Greg had hung up.

The marriage was off. Greg had said things that could never be forgiven. Worse than that, he'd forced her to say things she couldn't believe she'd said. He'd tried to make her choose between the Church and marrying him. And it all had to do with what the old priest had said two nights ago at St. Bernardine's parish hall about the Virgin Mary and contraception. Greg had said all the Church's teachings were just a way of getting people trapped into marriage and breeding lots of babies, so there'd be more and more Catholics. He'd said he'd never wanted her to have the baby, that they were both too young to be saddled with being parents. And in a way she could agree. She was seventeen, he was twenty-four: They *were* too young, in some ways. It would have interfered with Greg's continuing at the U, where he was getting a degree in business administration, and it would make it difficult if not impossible for Alison to graduate from high school.

But if they had really been too young, she wouldn't have become pregnant. As Father Cogling had told her privately, in the confessional, the pregnancy was God's way of showing her what *He* wanted. It had been just the same when the Angel had come to Mary to tell her she would bear the baby Jesus. Not exactly the same, of course, since Jesus had been conceived without sin—without even sex, according to the Church—while the baby inside of Alison was the result of a mortal sin. But it was the same in terms of her having to accept what God had shown he wanted: a new soul. And what Alison and Greg wanted for themselves didn't matter that much by comparison.

At first Greg had gone along with that idea, but the night after the instruction class where he'd got so sarcastic with Father Cogling, he'd come around to the trailer after Alison's mom had gone off to her night job at the hospital. He was already drunk at eight o'clock, and he had proceeded to get more drunk, and he'd insisted on arguing with her like they were having some kind of debate, and suddenly it was Alison's job to defend every ridiculous thing the Church said you had to believe in, from Mary's being a virgin even after Christmas to birth control being a sin that would send you to hell even if you had AIDS and were wearing a condom to protect your wife—an example that Greg had posed to Father Cogling, which at the time had made Alison wonder if Greg was worried he had AIDS. But he wasn't; it was just his way of arguing. He always looked for the exception to every rule.

Finally, around ten o'clock, drunk and belligerent, he'd given Alison his ultimatum: Leave the Church or forget the wedding.

At that point she'd told him to get out of the trailer. "Does that mean good-bye?" he'd asked, and she'd said, "I can't leave the Church." "So that's that," he said. "Fuck it."

That was the last thing he'd said, and when she tried to phone him at his home two hours later, after he'd had time to cool off, he hung up as soon as he heard her voice.

So that was the end of everything. Of the wedding. Of getting away from the trailer and her mom, whose drinking and drugging had been getting worse every day. The end, almost, of her life.

One good thing had come of it. She knew with absolute certainty that no matter what awful mess she might get into in the future, she would never, ever do such a dumb thing again as try to kill herself. She knew it the moment she'd come to, when her first thought was: I could have gone dogsledding.

All her life, ever since she'd read *The Call of the Wild*, she'd dreamt of going up to the area north of Duluth to go dogsledding. Greg actually had a friend in Boy River who took people on dogsledding trips, camping out overnight on frozen lakes and fishing through the ice. If she had killed herself, she would never have been able to realize that dream. Or anything else she'd ever wanted to do. She would never know how things worked out on *General Hospital*. She would never know what she might look like as a redhead, supposing she could ever get up the nerve to dye her hair. There were hundreds of things she'd never do or know about, and all because she'd had the imbecile idea of killing herself with her mom's sleeping pills. Jesus, she was lucky.

The fact remained that she was also in deep trouble. Never mind the embarrassment of calling off the wedding. That would be no great loss. They hadn't been able to afford anything especially wonderful. No caterers, no reception, not even a bridal gown rental, since there wouldn't be anyone to see her wear it. The ceremony wouldn't have been in the main church, which was also awfully expensive, but in the chapel around to the side—the wedding equivalent to the kind of funeral they give to suicides or homeless people—and in a way Alison was relieved not to have to go through the motions of pretending to be the radiant bride. It would have been like one of her wretched birthdays, with little candles stuck in Hostess cupcakes and her mom woozy with booze and self-pity. Who needs that kind of celebration?

No, her real problem was the one located inside, and not inside her mind. Inside her uterus.

She did not want the baby. Not if it meant living here in the trailer with her mom, instead of marrying Greg and having her own place to live. Not if it meant dropping out of school and wasting all the time she'd clocked in, including the whole summer when she'd taken the makeup course in algebra.

Not if it meant becoming someone like her mom. Alison was grateful to her mom. She'd made real sacrifices in bringing up Alison all by herself. But it had taken a terrible toll. And it would do the same to Alison, because she wasn't that different. After twenty years of unemployment or jobs waitressing or changing bedpans, with boyfriends and booze as the only antidotes to the drudgery, Alison would be another Lila. At thirty-seven, while other women still looked like movie stars, she'd be a fat, bitter, alcoholic failure with a child who couldn't think about her without feeling ashamed.

Abortion? Could she really be thinking of an abortion? Pious Miss Sanders, who'd taken such shit from her classmates when she'd been seen on TV picketing the same abortion clinic on Cedar and Lake she might now be going to herself?

Well, why not? If she'd been that afraid of spending eternity in hell, she wouldn't have kept jumping back into the sack with Greg at every opportunity. Each time they'd fucked was a mortal sin, and the abortion would be only one more added to the tally, with the advantage that once this sin was done, she wouldn't be tempted to repeat it on a regular basis.

The number she needed was in the phone book. She knew because Greg had pointed it out to her when she'd first told him the good news. She dug out the phone book from where it was buried under a stack of old magazines and ran her finger down the first column of names under *A*. There it was: Abortion Central Information. 555-6116.

She dialed the number, and after five rings, a man's voice said, "This is Abortion Central Information. Can I help you?"

Alison sighed and said, "I hope so."

8

The following is excerpted from chapter eight of A Prolegomenon to Receptivist Science, *by A. D. Boscage (Exegete Press, 1984):*

The explanation for the problems I'd been having—the lapses of memory, the motor control difficulties, the phone calls, and the increasing tension between me and Lorraine—became clear to me at the very moment when it might have seemed to an outside observer that I'd finally become certifiably insane. This was in July of 1981, when I'd gone to be Guest of Honor at the annual UFO-Con gathering in Rodez, a city in the south of France that reminded me very much of Poughkeepsie, where I grew up, though it is only half the size. Ever since the famous "Alphane" photographs of 1963, Rodez has been a mecca for UFO investigators hoping for their own close encounter. Because of my long-standing fear of air travel, I had not been to Rodez before; but because I was to be Guest of Honor, the convention committee had kindly undertaken to pay my way aboard the Polish ocean liner *Stefan Batory.* They also paid for Lorraine, on the understanding that she was my secretary. I found the voyage invigorating and provocative, but poor Lorraine was ill the entire six days from New York to Le Havre, partly because of the motion of the boat but also because she was again withdrawing from the amphetamines.

I find there is nothing in my journals about how we made our way to Rodez from Le Havre. I know that neither Lorraine nor myself was in shape to drive a car, especially where we would have had to look up the words on the road signs in our dictionary, a paperback Larousse that I had retained from my days in college in 1964, and which had cost only sixty cents at that time, when it was in its *fifty-sixth printing!* I still have that same book within easy reach of my desk as I write these pages, and it still contains, as a page marker, a receipt from the pharmacy near our hotel in Rodez, Le Comte d'Aveyron, where Lorraine was finally able to fill the phony prescrition written out for her by the homeopathic healer we met on the *Batory*. Lorraine has an incredible ability to meet exactly the people she needs to meet at any given time.

The actual panels at the convention were without surprises. I had difficulty slowing down my speech to allow time for my simultaneous translator to keep up with me. Her name was Héloïse (I cannot remember her last name, which began with either a *V* or an *F*), and she had the most extraordinary jet-black hair, which she wore in a kind of loose chignon that was very becoming. I showed the slides of the Boulder anomalies, which Alyx West had lent me for the occasion, and I told about my own experiences in writing *The Transmentated Man*, more or less as they are set down in chapter four of this book. Interestingly, there were three or four gentlemen in the audience who had had similar experiences. This is no longer surprising to me, though at that time I had not known whether to expect to find others like myself on the far side of the ocean. Though what is the distance of a mere ocean to Beings who have bridged the abysses of Space?

The real significance of my trip to this area of France did not become apparent until after the convention, when my hosts as a special courtesy took me to visit the ruined abbey church at Montpellier-le-Vieux. It was here, Alyx West had told me, that a second series of Alphane sightings had taken place in the early seventies, almost a decade after the original event. Although there is no photographic record of these later sightings, Alyx had been able to examine two of the witnesses under hypnosis and discovered clear evidence of memory alteration.

I realize that some of my readers may not be familiar with—or may not credit—Alyx West's theory of the mnemocyte. For those readers, let me offer a brief explanation here, since I can think of no better explanation for my experiences at Montpellier-le-Vieux and afterward than to suppose that I had been infected many years earlier with a virulent strain of mnemocyte that had blocked all my teenage memories of abduction and replaced them with images of what I believed to be horror movies. When in adult life I tried to rent VCR tapes of these movies, I discovered that none of them existed! Apparently, none had ever been made! Then what, I had to ask myself, had I been watching during those evenings when I had been an usher at the Rialto Theater in downtown Poughkeepsie? Whence came these images of skin being flayed from the breasts of living women, both Negroes and Caucasians? These mutilations, decapitations, eviscerations?

A Freudian would say that these false memories were in fact the diseased by-products of my own bubbling id. A Jungian would say that I achieved some kind of psychic rapport with archetypes of the collective unconscious. And I had thought that I was remembering old Hollywood horror movies. What had really happened? Until my visit to Montpellier-le-Vieux—when I entered the crypt of the ruined abbey church and found myself hurled back through the centuries to the time when that church was being built—I could not know that those recollections of "horror movies" were not really false memories, nor fantasies from my id, nor Jungian archetypes, but *actual events that I had been forced to witness and take part in!*

What a profound relief it has been to realize that I did not "make up" these dreadful images that have haunted me throughout my life and which I have often represented, in modified form, in my fictional writings—to the distress of so many would-be censors and indignant school librarians. No, Mrs. Stevenson, of Champaign, Illinois, I have not escaped from a lunatic asylum, and I am not a serial killer. In point of fact, I so much detest the sight of blood that I have been a strict vegetarian since the age of twenty-four (excepting for the period, noted in chapter five above, when I was living in the Vancouver commune with Valerie Hoover).

It should be noted at this point, in terms of an understanding of the *origins* of Receptivist Science, that I had been fasting for three days before my visit to Montpellier-le-Vieux. In addition, I had taken a megadose of vitamin C. There is no television transmitting station nor any power station within several miles of Montpellier-le-Vieux; the ether is, therefore, exceptional clear, especially in the infrared area of the spectrum. So, as a result of my own internal condition and my external physical circumstances, I was in a state of exceptional receptivity. My nervous system was like a satellite dish newly installed on an Andean peak.

Poets have tried to describe the beauty of Montpellier-le-Vieux, and all have failed. I will make no attempt. It is a scene of uncanny beauty. The ruined blocks of limestone, eroded by the savage weather of the Cévennes, writhe and twist like the souls of the damned, assuming shapes that defy the imagination. Towering above them all are the massive truncated pillars that once supported the lead tiles of the roof of Notre Dame de Gevaudon, their capitals embellished with the curious carvings of Lombard workmen dead now for almost a millennium. Upon one column may be discerned the spread wings of an eagle—or of some creature that antiquarians have called an eagle for want of a more precise term. And the figure on this column? A dragon of some sort? One would really have to ask the mason whose chisel did the work what he had in his mind, and whether his is a work of imagination unassisted by any model.

And you *can* ask that mason—for I am he! I am, or I have been, Bonamico of Lombardy.

It is difficult to believe, I know. It would be months after that first visit to Notre Dame de Gevaudon before I could admit to myself that what I had witnessed that afternoon had not been some trance-induced shamanic vision but rather, a *direct apprehension of tragic historical events.* But at last it could not be denied, for I came into possession of incontrovertible physical evidence of a sort that simply could not be explained away by any other hypothesis.

It is a book. Written on crumbling parchment, the ink on its first pages faded almost to invisibility. A book of only ninety-six pages, but oh, the implications of what is written on those pages! For it was not written by any human agency, and the message it conveys was never intended for human eyes.

Was it, then, the work of aliens visiting this planet at the dawn of our Western Civilization? I cannot surely say, for it seems to me equally plausible that the book was written by a being of supernatural rather than extraterrestrial origin.

All I can say with certainty is that I have read that book, and what I have read therein fills me to this day with a strange dread, which is also (this is its strangeness) a sense of longing that is inexpressibly sweet.

9

"Well, then, cheers," said Peter Bryce, lifting his glass of Diet Pepsi in a halfhearted toast to clink against the glass in his twin brother's hand.

"Cheers," Patrick agreed. He took a sip of the soda and shook his head in a pantomime of wry resignation. "I'm sorry we can't order wine. It didn't occur to me that they wouldn't have a liquor license here. But I've been told it's a good restaurant. If you like Italian food."

"Not to worry," said Peter. "I'll survive." He felt that he was being punished for the table talk at their last two-man family reunion in March, which had got somewhat out of hand as the bar tab had mounted, though at the time Patrick seemed to have no difficulty entering into the spirit of the occasion. With his Roman collar off, Patrick had frisked about like a puppy off its leash, sniffing at all sorts of forbidden ideas and even producing a few of his own. No one eavesdropping on that conversation would have believed one of them was a priest—or if they had, they'd have believed it of Peter. Afterward Peter figured that that evening's heresies were a by-product of their lifelong contest as twins. Patrick couldn't stand to be outshone by his brother, even in a contest to see which of them could be the more complete cynic. Later, Patrick had probably regretted some of his opinions—regretted, at least, the fact that he'd expressed them.

Peter studied his menu with growing discouragement: veal parmesan, chicken cacciatore, spaghetti with Italian sausage, spaghetti with meatballs, spaghetti with Italian tomato sauce. Imagination and novelty were not top priorities at The Blue Grotto. Rather, to judge by the size of the portions he'd seen being delivered to other tables, the place prided itself on offering an optimum pig-out for the dollar.

Fat people had to expect to be treated like fat people. Lots of fruit-cakes at Christmas, and invitations to smorgasbord-type restaurants. Usually, Peter didn't let it get to him, but when it came from a brother who was his identical twin, and who had managed to keep reasonably trim despite the same genetic inheritance, it was hard to maintain his usual pose as the jolly fatso. They say that inside every fat man there's a thin man crying to get out; in this case, Peter could see, sitting across the dining table from him, what that thin man looked like.

The waitress came and Patrick ordered first: spaghetti and meat-balls. Was he mortifying his flesh? Peter wondered. The waitress turned to Peter, and he said, "I'll have the same." She asked them if they wanted garlic bread, and his brother nodded yes. She offered a choice of dressings for their salads, French, blue cheese, ranch, and spicy Italian. Patrick said, "Blue cheese," and Peter said, "The same."

"I saw you on TV," Peter remarked when the waitress had left the table.

Patrick grimaced. "That seems to have become part of the job de-scription."

"The next day three different people at work mentioned it. They know you're my brother."

"Did I get good reviews?"

"You got good marks for style. Content's another matter. You'd need more than a ten-second sound bite to convince any of the women at our office that abortion should be made illegal."

"Well, that isn't the purpose of the protests."

"What is, if you don't mind my asking? It's been two years now, and you haven't closed down the clinic, so that can't be your purpose either. Why keep beating a dead horse?"

"Martyrdom. There's nothing like martyrdom for bringing people together. It's an exalted feeling to be persecuted for righteousness' sake. As Christ remarks, theirs is the kingdom of heaven. It's how the Church came into being originally. Without Rome's inspired persecu-tion, Christianity would have been just another cult from the East. But Rome fed *us* to the lions, and made saints of us. People want to be saints, if it can be done without dieting."

Peter at once retaliated with his own pointed observation. "It's a nice theory, but I don't notice that you ever put yourself in jeopardy of arrest. *You* don't lie down in front of the police cars. *You* don't handcuff yourself to the clinic's front door. Is martyrdom a privilege reserved for the laity these days?"

"The Bishop hasn't required such a sacrifice of me yet."

"And you just follow orders?"

"That's how hierarchy works. To do him credit, I expect the Bishop would see to it that he got arrested before any of us. There is a certain amount of prearrangement in these manners. The police don't like surprises, and neither does the Bishop. So he may opt to be arrested at some point, and not just because he has a taste for the limelight. Though of course it's *all* theater. We want to dramatize our moral position, which is that abortion is tantamount to murder. I shouldn't say 'tantamount': It *is* murder. If indigent parents could take their children under age sixteen to a clinic to have them put to sleep like unwanted pets, most people would allow that that was morally objectionable. Would it seem fanatical to try to save those children by acts of civil disobedience?"

"Yes, I remember—that was your sound bite. And it's a good one. In fact, when you put it that way, the Church's actions don't seem sufficiently drastic."

"Peter, you take the words out of my mouth. And just in time. Here come our salads."

The salads came in large bowls of simulated teak and were just such salads—iceberg lettuce, tomato wedges, slices of cucumber and radish—as most of the customers would have made for themselves at home. The only difference was that the waitress offered to grind some pepper over them.

"How are things at *your* job?" asked Patrick, who tried to allow his brother equal time conversationally.

"The same as ever," Peter grumped. He didn't much like his job as the head of the amortization division of North Central Insurance and much preferred, with his brother, to talk about Church matters, even though he was no longer a Catholic. He was, instead, a fervent ex-Catholic of the sort that keeps tabs on every scandal concerning the Church and has to comment on all of them. "It's a dull job, you wouldn't want to hear about it."

"Most people say that about their jobs when they're away from them. Then at their offices they become obsessed."

"You want to know what we've been obsessing about at my office this week? Tetris."

"What's Tetris?" Patrick asked politely, with a tomato wedge poised before his lips.

"A computer game we all play when we think no one is looking. I used to be the office champion. I was getting scores over twenty-two thousand. But now there's this secretary in personnel who is a pinball wizard. Twenty-five thousand is nothing to her. I swear she has a five-nanosecond reaction time. It's not like I'm even competition for her. And that's the news from North Central. All of it." Before Patrick could change the subject again, Peter went on, "You were saying about the abortion thing—how I took the words out of your mouth."

"Mm." Patrick pantomimed that his mouth was full. "Yes, when you said the Church isn't zealous enough. The Bishop agrees. So, we intend to initiate a more aggressive program of intervention. However, that's something I'm not free to talk about until the formal announcement has been made."

"What a tease you are, Patrick."

"You'll twist my arm? Okay, I'll tell you. We are going to open up a facility for reluctant teenage mothers whose parents can be persuaded to commit them to our care. We've had the lawyers going over the details for a couple years, and with the changes that have just been made in the state laws requiring parental consent for girls under eighteen, we think it'll pass muster in the courts. There have been similar 'tough love' detention centers for teenage drug abusers, but it's never been applied to the abortion situation."

"You mean to say, you're going to put pregnant teenage girls in prison and force them to come to term?"

"You've got to admit that's a more effective way to save fetuses than chanting outside abortion clinics."

"Jesus. That could be a major felony. Not to mention what you could be sued for."

"That's why it will have to be undertaken, initially, by lay groups without the official sanction of the Church."

"More martyrs?"

"We have enough volunteers to fill one or two federal prisons, if it comes to that."

"And will you be building prisons of your own for the lucky mothers-to-be?"

"The Church already has a lot of underutilized real estate."

"Empty convents, that sort of thing?"

"There would be an irony in that, wouldn't there? In terms of the old anti-Catholic canard of convents being filled with the graves of the nuns' illegitimate offspring. Now those imaginary bones can actually be given life. Poetically speaking. But in fact, the first site that's been selected is my old stomping grounds at Étoile du Nord."

"The seminary you went to."

"It hasn't been a seminary for quite a while now. Vocations have fallen off, as you may have heard, and Étoile du Nord has never been considered top of the line. It's my alma mater and all that, but even so. I think my most vivid memories of Étoile du Nord is the mosquitoes. I can still remember how they . . ."

A strange expression came over Patrick's face, and he lifted his hand and pressed his outspread fingers against the breast pocket of his madras shirt. He closed his eyes and took a sharp breath.

Peter thought his brother must have something caught in his throat and feared he would have to attempt the Heimlich maneuver. He prayed a quick prayer to the god of desperate atheists, and his prayer was answered at once, for Patrick took another, easier breath and opened his eyes.

"Are you all right?"

Patrick replied with a weak smile. "All better. It was just . . . nothing at all."

"You know, Patrick, between the two of us there's no need to be secretive. I mean, I've got a vested interest in your good health and vice versa. If you've got some kind of heart condition, I should know about it—for my own good."

"Honestly, Petey, it's nothing like that. It's the skin on my chest. It's, um, sore." When Peter continued to give him a questioning look, he elaborated. "I spilled a hot cup of coffee on myself this morning. The skin developed some kind of blister, and sometimes my clothing rubs against it the wrong way and it's painful. Usually I'm not even aware of it. Okay? Now, about what I was talking about before, I really shouldn't be saying anything more about it. My tongue got carried away. But there is another matter that I wanted to pick your brain about. If I may?"

"You can pick what's there."

"It's about that cult that was having trouble with the tax authorities—the Receptionists? Some name like that?"

"The Receptivists. What about them?"

"I was wondering what you might know about them. Do you still get that magazine about all the crank religions and pseudosciences?"

"*Skeptical Inquirer*. Oh yes, I'm still an addict. And they have had a couple of articles about Boscage in recent issues."

"Boscage is the head of the cult?"

"Maybe. If he's still alive. There seems to be some question about that. It's a very shadowy organization. Not to say flaky. Why do you ask? You know someone involved with them?"

Patrick nodded. "The son of one of our parishioners. And I can't say more than that. They approached me in confidence. And I recalled that I'd heard you mention them a while back. So I thought I'd ask you what you remember about them."

"Basically, you want to know: Should the kid's parents be worried?"

Patrick nodded.

"Well, they probably should. I hate to have to say so, since I was a fan of Boscage as a writer back in the seventies. But when he got to be a guru, then—" Peter rolled his eyes discreetly and did a sotto voce imitation of the *Twilight Zone* theme song.

"What exactly do his followers believe?"

"You name it, they'll believe it. I'm not really exaggerating. Boscage had a fertile imagination as an SF writer, and when he went around the bend, he continued to have a fertile imagination."

"Then you think he was crazy?"

"What's the alternative? Believing he really *was* abducted by dog-headed aliens in UFOs? Believing his soul has been recycled about once a century ever since the sinking of Atlantis? Believing there has been a conspiracy directed against Adolf Boscage, personally, for the last couple millennia, masterminded by clandestine Albigensian heretics who have infiltrated almost every organization and business Boscage has ever bumped against, including the Boy Scouts? Excuse me if I sound like a secular humanist party pooper, but somehow it is easier for me to believe that Adolf Boscage was crazy than to believe all that."

"Of course," Patrick hastened to agree. "What I meant was, he might simply be a con man. A manipulator. A liar who wasn't afraid to tell his lies on the grandest scale."

"Yes, that's a possibility. He certainly was a bullshit artist whose bull got out of control, but I'm inclined to give him the benefit of the doubt as to his being sincere. In that way he's a lot like Philip K. Dick, if you ever read the book he wrote called *Valis*. Boscage's followers are another matter. *They* are scary."

"That's what worries me. I gather there was a civil case against them in California, and the person who was suing them simply disappeared. And in other cases that have been settled out of court, no one will say what was at issue."

"From what I've read, it usually involved abduction in some form or other. Or people being detained against their wills after they'd gone off to what they thought was a rehab center. In fact, Patrick, it occurs to me that you may be inviting exactly the same kind of legal difficulties with the new project you're talking about. That wouldn't be what all this is about, would it?"

Patrick waved aside the question with a look of annoyance. "No, not at all. What I would be interested in knowing, though, is, what is it that's behind their success? What makes people join? What do the Receptivists offer that makes their cult different from other fringe groups?"

"Well, the major difference is that they're the first cult that's been able to turn UFO-abduction mythology into an institution, with its own hierarchy and rites and, I gather, even its own heresies now. What it offers newcomers is a more intense version of channeling. According to the accounts of a few people who've left the cult, the initiates are put through some kind of boot camp at this ranch in the Mojave Desert, and they're regressed, under hypnosis, back to their former lives. And they also relive their UFO-abduction experiences, apparently in a highly persuasive way. Some of those who've left the cult have suggested that these hypnotic 'regressions' have actually been staged, and they claim that they were physically abused in the course of being 'debriefed.' Which is the Receptivist term for their channeling process. No one's been able to prove anything."

"That's all very interesting," said Patrick, "but what I was really wondering is, whom do they appeal to?"

Peter laughed aloud. Then blushed.

"What's so funny?" Patrick asked with an anticipatory smile.

"Because of the answer that came to me the moment you asked the question. The Receptivists' main appeal is to the same kind of people who were fans of Boscage's SF—sexually dysfunctional males between the ages of fourteen and thirty-four. The kind of eternal teenager who joins the Marines to prove his manhood and then fucks it all up. Like me, you might say. I'd have been a perfect candidate back in the days when I was still trying to be Mr. Universe. I was a Boscage fan, after all, right up to the point where he went off the deep end. Even then, I kept reading the books. He's a very subversive writer, the way he can inveigle you into sharing his weirdest paranoid fantasies. I hope that answers your question, because I honestly can't come up with much more off the top of my head."

This was a polite lie, since the most salient feature of the Receptivists' appeal was their peculiar attitude toward homosexuality, a subject that Peter and Patrick, by a tacit understanding, always avoided when speaking with each other. In the summer they'd turned fifteen, they had done things together they ought not to have. Peter had discussed these matters with his psychotherapist, back twenty years ago when he'd felt he'd needed psychotherapy, and since that time he considered the whole thing a closed matter, water under the bridge. He assumed that Patrick felt the same way about it.

A closed matter but also a potential minefield, since they'd never, even when they'd been doing what they'd done, ever discussed it. It was simply too embarrassing, and anyhow, what was there one could say?

Patrick solved the momentary awkwardness by pushing his chair back from the table and getting to his feet. "You'll have to excuse me a moment, Petey. My bowels have been in a peculiar state all this last week."

Patrick was in the bathroom for fully five minutes, and when he came back, the two bounteous plates of meatballs and spaghetti had arrived at the table, and the brothers were able to concentrate on the serious business of eating.

10

Bing Anker was seething with rage. It felt good. He was ashamed of himself, of course—rage is an ugly emotion—but then he was used to feeling ashamed of himself, whereas he was not used to the rage, except in its most repressed and inaccessible forms, when it would curdle into depression or self-loathing. This rage was directed at someone who deserved it, someone he could imagine himself strangling to death with a rope. He'd actually done just that, in fact, at the suggestion of his therapist, Caroline Kean. Not strangled anyone literally, but imagined it, with a real piece of rope in his hands and his own calf substituting for the neck of his desired victim. There was still a rope burn there to bear witness to the strength of his feelings.

"There," Dr. Kean had said at the close of their session. "Now, don't you feel a lot better to have let go of that?"

He'd agreed that he felt a lot better, since he didn't like to say anything to contradict Dr. Kean, who was a jewel among therapists—supportive, nonjudgmental, appreciative of his least little joke, and best of all, that name! Of course, it wasn't *spelled* the same way as the author of the Nancy Drew books, but it *was* a homophone, and that was enough for Bing. Anyhow, he wasn't lying, he did feel better. Only he had not "let go" of his rage. Not while it was still so fresh and exhilarating. He felt he could walk down the street and break the windshield of every car he passed. With just a whack of his ball-peen hammer it would be *Smash* to the Olds! *Smash* to the Toyota! *Smash* to the Cadillac Fleetwood coupe!

Not that he'd ever do anything so wasteful and adolescent. What

satisfaction could be gained from mere vandalism? That was the problem with rage. It flailed about at everything in sight, whereas if it were
focused and directed it could be as precise as a bullet. So here he was,
feeling almost preternaturally focused and directed, by the white marble statue of cute little Bernardino of Siena that greeted the faithful on
their way from the parking lot into the church that bore his name. He
was a very garden elf of a saint, three feet high, in a monkish robe cut
along distinctly Empire lines.

Bing checked to see if anyone could see him and then, having already peeled off the paper backing, he stuck a SILENCE = DEATH sticker
atop little Bernardino's tonsured pate. In its own small way it felt quite
as satisfactory as smashing a windshield.

Bing entered the church by its wheelchair-accessible side entrance,
and stood for a little while lost in admiration. This was the Chartres of
suburbia, the Notre Dame of Middle America, the Mont-St-Michel of
fifties Catholicism when the spirit of the nation and of the Church
were at their most congruent. Everywhere there was blond wood in
softly rounded shapes. The ribs of the ceiling looked like the ailerons
of some vast fifties coffee table. The stations of the cross were bland,
tan bas-reliefs with stylized figures pantomiming the most decorous
distress. And the Christ who was suspended on the blond crucifix
above the simple slab of altar was the most epicene of saviors, with an
upper body that had never been to a gym or done a lick of work in its
life. No nipples and no underarm hair, which seemed to be standard
omissions in liturgical art, but *this* Jesus had even had his navel stylized
out of existence, which, if you gave the matter any thought, amounted
to heresy. It was hard to believe that there'd ever been a time like the
High Renaissance when painters and sculptors had given Jesus a cock
and balls. What would Michelangelo have thought if he could have
seen St. Bernardine's? Would he have wanted to put it to the torch? Or
would he only have laughed?

For Bing's present purpose St. Bernardine's was as empty as could
be hoped. There was one old lady saying a rosary in the pew nearest
the altar, and one confessional in use. Not much of a turnout for a
Saturday afternoon by comparison to what Bing remembered from his
grade school days at Our Lady of Mercy, but perhaps people didn't sin
as much here in the suburbs as they did in the city. While he waited for
the present penitent to be absolved, Bing made a reverent circuit of the
side aisles and the vestibule looking for good places to put the five

other SILENCE = DEATH stickers he'd brought with him. One went on the tenth station of the cross, in which Christ's clothes are torn from his body, a second on the holy water font beside the center aisle, a third on a metal collection canister labeled FOR THE HOMELESS AND HUNGRY, and a fourth as a diadem upon the crown of the Infant of Prague. There was no time to affix the fifth, for the confessional had become free.

Bing entered it and knelt, and waited for the panel to slide open. When it did, he said, at ordinary conversational volume, "Bless me, Father, for I have sinned. It's been quite a while since my last confession."

And he knew from the first syllable of the priest's hushed response—"Just how a long a time, my son?"—that it was him, his target, his sitting duck.

"Years and years . . . Father Pat."

There was a longish silence while Father Pat tried to identify the voice on the other side of the screen that veiled confessor and penitent from each other's sight. When he could not, he shifted out of sacramental mode and said, "I think you have the advantage of me."

"You don't want to hear my confession?" Bing parried.

"If you feel a sincere repentance and are resolved to sin no more, then I will hear your confession. That is what I'm here for—not to speak with you on a first-name basis. Within the confessional I am the same as any other priest."

"The way all cats are the same color in the dark? Excuse me, that's probably not an appropriate remark. As I said, it's been a while, and I've got a little rusty. So, where to begin? There's a lot of territory to cover. *Some* of the sins you're already familiar with, though that was a while ago, and you probably hear so many confessions that all the different sinners' sins must get muddled up. Though I do like to think that mine were special."

"You need not confess any sin that has already been absolved," the priest said coldly. "And try to keep your voice lower. The confessional is not soundproof."

"Oh dear, I always do that. I'm a little hard of hearing myself, and in a restaurant I will gradually keep raising my own decibel level until I sound like a PA system. If I whisper, like this, can you hear me?"

"Not very well. Try to speak *softly*. And to begin your confession, tell me—what is the particular sin that brings you here today? There is usually one sin for which we feel a special remorse, and that would be a good place to begin."

"Right! The sin that brings me here is anger. I'm not usually an angry kind of person, almost the opposite, at least in terms of my personal life. I don't have that much to be angry *about*. Although I have friends who say that's my denial, and denial isn't just a river in Africa."

"Anger is not a sin in itself. Did it lead you to some sinful action?"

"It *isn't* a sin in itself, is it? I mean, sometimes it can be justifiable. Sometimes you read of things in the paper that can just get you furious for a good reason. I mean, I've seen *you* on the TV news, talking about abortion, and you certainly came across as angry."

"Even Our Lord was known to express anger at times."

"Yes!" Bing exulted. "With the scribes and Pharisees! And the moneychangers in the *Temple!* You see, I haven't forgotten it all. So, where was I? The newspaper. About a week ago there was a story about this priest in Massachusetts, a Father Porter, who sexually molested an *enormous* number of altar boys. It had been going on for decades, and it only came out just lately, I suppose because people used to be too ashamed to *talk* about such things, but now with Geraldo and Sally Jessy Raphaël, shame doesn't control people the same way. We can realize that we were victims, and that the shame belongs with the blame. So, after I read that news story, and the ones that followed it, I began to be *obsessed*. I wanted to *do* something. I wanted to wreak vengeance."

There was a significant silence. At last the priest said, with lawyer-like caution, "Scandals of this sort are a source of pain to everyone who loves the Church. But I'm sure this priest . . ."

"Father Porter," Bing said helpfully.

"I'm sure that he is going through quite enough suffering right now without your needing to add to it yourself."

"Did you know that he's living here in Minnesota now? And that he went through another harem of altar boys while he was an assistant pastor in Bemidji? And that was *after* the Church had sent him off for treatment to their own special pedophilia center in New Mexico. So the Church *knew* what he was doing."

"I've read these allegations and speculations in the paper as well. And they are distressing, surely. But how does this matter affect you, directly?"

"That's a good question, Father. And the answer is, yes, *very* directly."

"Did you know the man when he served in Bemidji? I say 'man' advisedly, for he's left the priesthood, you know. He's married and has four children of his own."

"No, I didn't know *him*. But I had a somewhat similar experience myself. When I was an altar boy."

"Similar in what way? Be more specific."

"Well, in terms of *oral* sex, I think there were five times that he blew me. How often I did the same for him I really couldn't say. For about a month it was almost every day. A few times he was wearing his vestments, and that was hot. In terms of *anal* sex, he never cared much for that, either way, though sometimes when I was blowing him, he'd wiggle his fingers up my ass. I don't know if that counts as a separate sin or not."

The priest had no reply.

Bing let the silence lengthen, and then, since there was nothing to be gained by further pussyfooting, he said, "Is it all starting to come back, Father Pat?"

"I don't think there's anything to be gained by continuing this discussion. Obviously, you did not come here to confess."

"For goodness sakes, what would you call what I've just been doing if not confessing!"

"I'd say you were playing a game of cat and mouse."

"Well, there's been that side to it. But now here we are out in the open, so to speak. And I'd appreciate the opportunity of having a serious discussion."

"If you like. But not *here*."

"Here is best for me, Father. Here and now. Let me ask you something. Do you know who I am at this point? Do you remember my *name*? Or have there been so many of us over the years, as there were for Father Porter, that we've all just blended into a single generic fifteen-year-old altar boy? I like to think that I was special. I was pretty cute back then. And short for my age. I looked more like thirteen at the point we had our fling. Maybe even twelve. Is that enough to go by? Can you answer the riddle and say who I am?"

Another silence.

"It's a blow to one's pride, of course, not to be remembered. But in all fairness, I've had my share of tricks that I'd be just as hard-pressed to assign a name to."

"Please," the priest whispered earnestly, "if you insist on speaking, try to whisper. There is someone who's entered the other side of the confessional."

"I'll tell you what, Father. Open the window on their side and tell them to come back later. But leave this window open. I want to hear what you say. I wouldn't want you asking them to send for the police."

"Believe me, there's no danger of that."

"That's as may be. In any case, do what I said. Get rid of them. We've got more to talk about."

While Father Pat was explaining to the other penitent that it would be some while before he could hear anyone else's confession, Bing slipped out of the confessional and hastened to the side door of the church, which was now (he was pleased to see) entirely deserted.

However, just as he put his hand on the brass handle of the door, it was opened by someone on the other side, an elderly priest, who stepped back when he saw Bing and said, with a smile and a nod of his head, "Madam."

Bing favored the old priest with a grateful smile and murmured a tremulous "Thank you, Father" without breaking stride. He resisted making any gesture that might have called attention to his clothing, which was always a dead giveaway. Real women did not run their hands over their haunches to enjoy the feel of layered silk. They didn't keep patting their coiffure. A true drag artist should seem as oblivious of what he's wearing as a bird is of its feathers, a fish of its scales.

Once seated behind the wheel of the car, Bing took off his heels. He had no difficulty walking in high heels—indeed, he enjoyed it—but driving was something else again. He backed the car out of the parking space and waved a mocking, unseen bye-bye toward the side door of St. Bernardine's.

He must be shitting in his cassock, he thought with satisfaction. He must be in a state of total panic.

Is revenge sweet? Revenge is sweet.

11

As a young woman, in the late forties and early fifties, Hedwig Ober had hoped to become a Servant of the Blessed Sacrament, the order of nuns that served at the Shrine of Blessed Konrad of Paderborn, but that privilege was denied her. Like her namesake, Saint Hedwig of Dalmatia, she had submitted to her father's authority and married young—at the age of eighteen, to her second cousin, Wolfgang Ober, who was then a vice president in the Ober and Ober Chemical Corporation, the Midwest's largest manufacturer of fertilizer and pesticides. Her life also resembled that of her patron saint in that she had borne six children to her spouse, but there the similarity ended, for Hedwig Ober's children had been a source of sorrow rather than of joy in her life. All of them had died within a few months of birth due to severe myotonic dystrophy, a disease they had inherited from their father, though in Wolfgang's case its symptoms had been inconsequential: a tendency to be unable to relax his grip when shaking hands and, later in life, cataracts. The six infants simply could not breathe, and they'd been born in an age when respirators were still uncommon in delivery rooms.

After the second child, Wolfgang junior, died, Hedwig's gynecologist advised her to practice birth control if she did not want to experience the same tragedy again. Dr. Vogelman explained that the disease was "dominant" in a hereditary sense, and that all her children by Wolfgang would be afflicted to some degree or other. Hedwig, as a good Catholic, did not oppose herself to God's will or her husband's, and she continued to fulfill her conjugal duties without violating natural law. Four more children were born and baptized and taken directly to heaven, and so, at last, was Wolfgang, who died of a stroke on the golf course of the Minnetonka Athletic Club in 1975.

Now might Hedwig have fulfilled her lifelong wish and become a Servant of the Blessed Sacrament, but once again it was ordained otherwise, for the Church had disbanded the order after a long controversy concerning the alleged anti-Semitism of its founder, Blessed Konrad Martin, the Bishop of Paderborn (in Germany). The good Bishop was noted for his pious life and especially for his devotion to the Eucharist, and so when it was discovered that the Jews of Deggendorf had stolen and tortured a consecrated wafer and that, when this abomination was committed, a lovely little child had emerged, miraculously, from the wafer, it was natural for the Bishop to have preached against the perpetrators of the deed. It was also natural, albeit a sin, for the townspeople of Deggendorf to have risen up against the Jews of that town and slaughtered them, which they had done on September 30, 1337. But Blessed Konrad could scarcely have been held responsible for the crime of those avengers of the honor of the Eucharist, given the considerable distance between Paderborn and Deggendorf. Despite this, Jewish protesters had made such a fuss about the efforts of the Servants of the Blessed Sacrament to secure the canonization of Blessed Konrad, who had founded their order, that instead of declaring him a saint, the Vatican had stripped the Bishop of his beatification—an almost unprecedented action and one that had caused Hedwig and others who'd hoped for Konrad's canonization grave distress.

Indeed, she had come close to leaving the Church over the matter. Providentially, she had been strengthened in her faith at that moment by the Supreme Court's decision to legalize the crime of abortion. Hedwig could scarcely leave the Church at such a juncture, when the souls of thousands of innocent unborn children were in peril. It took humility to ignore the slight that had been done to the honor of Blessed Konrad, whose beatific status—indeed, whose sainthood—would never be questioned by Hedwig Ober.

And now—such are the mysterious ways of Providence—here she was, just as she might have been if she had joined the Servants of the Blessed Sacrament all those years ago, the chief caretaker, in a day-to-day way, of the Shrine of Blessed Konrad. Of course, it was no longer officially *his* shrine. After he had been de-beatified, it had become the property of the neighboring Étoile du Nord Seminary. Then, because of diminishing vocations, the seminary had been closed down, and for a while the Shrine had served the few Catholic families in the area as their parish church, with a single Sunday Mass conducted at eleven a.m. by a visiting priest. But the patience and humility of Blessed Konrad's devotees were ultimately rewarded, and now his shrine, because of its peculiar physical character, was to serve in the vanguard of the fight against the forces of abortion.

For the Shrine had been built by its founder, Monsignor O'Toole, as literally a bastion of the Faith, its crypt dug so deep into the earth that those taking refuge within it could survive the shock of a nuclear blast. It had been among the first bomb shelters of the Cold War era, and was still one of the largest to be owned by a religious denomination. Every ton of concrete had all been paid for by the contributions of millions of viewers of Monsignor O'Toole's television program, broadcast nationally for years every Thursday evening at seven p.m. *The Ave Maria Hour* commended itself not only to the religious faith of the TV audience but to its patriotism as well. In the heyday of *The Ave Maria Hour*, from 1949 to 1958, the threat of Communism had been taken seriously, and the Shrine—with its enormous ferroconcrete dome (the fifth largest in the nation) and its immense subterranean complex of crypts, chapels, catacombs, and nuclear contingency command centers—was arguably the most imposing nonmilitary monument of the Cold War era.

Monsignor O'Toole had been a good friend of the Republican Senator Joseph McCarthy, and in the years of the Senator's decline from public favor, the Monsignor's Nielsen ratings had suffered a similar fate. *The Ave Maria Hour* was canceled. Contributions to the Shrine dried up, and the work of construction ground to a halt. The Bishop of Minneapolis was quoted in the press as saying that he was happy that "O'Toole's Folly," as he called it, had finally stopped draining the wells of legitimate charity. Monsignor O'Toole had replied, in a spirit of humility, "All the great Gothic cathedrals were the work of many centuries—and Rome itself was not built in a day. Others will come to complete the work this servant was able to begin." These words, cast in bronze, could now be read on the plaque mounted on a rough-hewn boulder that stood before the west portal of the Shrine.

It was to the little flower plot encircling this boulder that Hedwig came each morning at precisely six a.m. to water the petunias, pansies, and marigolds she had planted here. Then she would raise the flag to the top of the flagpole, offer a respectful salute, and retire within the vast Shrine to pray at the modest side altar devoted to the memory of Monsignor O'Toole. It had not always been so modest. At the Shrine's inauguration in 1954, a precious reliquary containing the hair, the metacarpals, the cranium, and three ribs of the Blessed Konrad had stood here in all its glory. Hedwig and Wolfgang had been joined in holy matrimony at this altar. But then the Blessed Konrad had suffered his posthumous disgrace, and the reliquary had been removed at the order of the Bishop. When Monsignor O'Toole died, the Bishop compounded Konrad's dishonor by decreeing that the altar that the Monsignor had erected in anticipation of Konrad's sainthood should be rededicated to the memory of the Monsignor, which was accomplished by the plainest of marble plaques cemented to the wall behind the altar.

On the same wall, some few feet to the left, another plaque (which had *not* been placed there by the direction of the Bishop) quoted from Isaiah, chapter 66, verses 5, 6, and 7:

> Hear the word of the Lord,
> you who tremble at His word:
> Your brothers who hated you,
> who cast you out for My name's sake,
> have said—Let the Lord be glorified.
> But the Lord will appear to bring you joy,
> and your brothers will know their shame.
>
> There is an uproar in the city
> and a tumult in the Temple—
> it is the sound of the Lord
> dealing retribution to his enemies.
>
> A woman brought forth issue
> without travail; without the pain of labor
> she gave birth to a Son.

It was a never-ending source of wonder to Hedwig that there could be such directly and unmistakably prophetic words set down, and that their import was simply lost on ninety-nine out of a hundred people. She'd known tourists to visit the Shrine and stand before this altar and read these verses aloud, and then profess to be puzzled as to what they might mean. Of course, even those tourists who were aware of the tragic past history of the Shrine, even those who knew how Monsignor O'Toole had been set about by enemies in his last days, even those faithful souls could not be aware of the Shrine's appointed future, and so the peculiar relevance of the final verse escaped them.

After saying a rosary before this side altar, she crossed the nave— each footstep was wonderfully magnified by the remarkable acoustical properties of the dome—and then took the elevator down to the third subbasement, where she began to prepare a wholesome breakfast of oatmeal, bran muffins, and hot chocolate for the four young women under her charge. She cut two grapefruits in half and sectioned them carefully. Then, loading these things onto the serving cart, she took the elevator down one floor deeper. For security reasons the prenatal ward was not directly accessible from the main corridor. There were further doors to be unlocked, and relocked behind her, but when she did reach the row of individual cells where the girls were lodged, their breakfasts were still piping hot.

In Cell 1, Mary Tyler was still in bed, though the PA system had been playing an LP of peppy polkas ever since reveille at six a.m. She was given to apathy and listlessness, but she was not really trouble-some, and she never left any food on her tray. It seemed certain that Mary, now in her seventh month of pregnancy, would be the first to bear a child here—a child who would have the Shrine of Blessed Konrad of Paderborn to thank for the gift of life.

Hedwig retrieved the tray that had contained last night's dinner and replaced it with the breakfast tray, which she slid into the cell through the security hatch. When the hatch was opened on Hedwig's side, it was automatically locked on the inside, and vice versa. Hedwig's brother Gerhardt had designed and installed the security system, which occupied that part of the underground complex that had origi-nally served as a convent for the Servants of the Blessed Sacrament. As a result, Hedwig never felt the least concern for her own safety. As Gerhardt had said, even if the cells had housed wild animals, Hedwig would not have been in jeopardy.

The detainee in Cell 2, Janet Joyner, seemed to Hedwig no more than a child, though obviously in a biological sense she was a woman. How Janet, who was only twelve years old, had become pregnant was not something Hedwig wished to discuss. Indeed, she often had to ask herself which was more shocking: that a child so young should be pregnant, or that she should have, on her own initiative, tried to secure an abortion? Fortunately, the girl had called the Abortion Information Hotline, which she and Gerhardt had set up, and so it had been possible to intervene by having Father Cogling approach the girl's parents. They had been horrified when they'd been informed of their daughter's condition and of her sinful intention, and had agreed at once to Janet's transfer to the facility at the Shrine. Not all parents were so immediately cooperative.

Temperamentally, Janet was the opposite of Mary. She was a kittenish child, pathetically eager to chat, or play games—or even to say the rosary along with Hedwig, though she had obviously not been brought up with a proper sense of her religious obligations. Hedwig felt sorry for the poor little creature. No girl of twelve wants to spend all her time with no companion but a woman of sixty-three. Later, when there was a larger staff at the Shrine, and other girls as young as Janet, it should be possible to allow the more trustworthy girls to spend a certain part of each day together in the recreation room on the floor above. But with only Hedwig here through most of the week, that was not yet feasible. For now, little Janet would have to learn to develop her own inner resources. There was a wide choice of good books from the library that had belonged to the Servants of the Blessed Sacrament, not to mention that most sustaining inner resource, prayer. The times that try our souls most sorely are also those that give us the greatest strength. Hedwig had learned that lesson as often as she had brought her own unfortunate children to birth, then seen them taken from her. Now she could be at hand to help others learn the same lesson and to show them by precept and example how to embrace their own crosses joyfully and with thanks.

Of the four detainees, Hedwig was fondest of the girl in Cell 3, Tara Seberg, who appeared to feel a sincere remorse for the sins that had led to her forcible detention. She prayed a great deal, and often wept while she was at her prayers. Many girls possess the gift of facile tears, of course, but Tara wept when she supposed herself unobserved, so it wasn't likely that she was feigning. She had read the books Hedwig had urged her to read, *Unto Us a Child Is Born!* and *Accepting the Gift of Life*, and she had taken their message to heart. While the other three girls fretted about the constraints of their life at the Shrine, Tara's most urgent concern was that she might see a priest and be able to go to confession. It did Hedwig's heart good to be able to minister to Tara's needs, not just her physical needs but her spiritual needs as well. For man lives not by bread alone, and woman doesn't either.

It was the girl in Cell 4 who was the bane of Hedwig's existence. Her name was Raven Peck—an absurdity, but it was actually her legal name and appeared on her birth certificate. Not only was the girl wholly unrepentant, but she seemed determined, even now, to induce the miscarriage of the five-month-old child in her womb. Consequently, she had to be kept almost completely immobilized, with padded leather restraints buckled around her wrists and ankles and a kind of harness about her shoulders and rib cage that kept her confined to her bed. She had to be spoon-fed and, what was nastiest, assisted in going to the bathroom. And all the while Hedwig would be caring for her in these intimate ways, the girl would say the most blasphemous and insulting things, using such foul and abusive language that sometimes Hedwig could not even comprehend the meaning of the obscenities.

Christ commanded us to love our enemies, and to do good to those who intend us ill, and to turn our other cheek, but had Christ ever had to deal with Raven Peck? That was a foolish question, of course. He had been reviled, and whipped, and crowned with thorns by His tormentors, while Raven Peck had done nothing more harmful, physically, than to spit gobbets of warm oatmeal into Hedwig's face. And Hedwig *did* return good for evil. She read aloud to Raven from *Accepting the Gift of Life*, ignoring the girl's jeers and blasphemies and simply wearing her down until she listened, unprotesting, to the message that must, eventually, change her life. Hedwig fed her—*and* the life within her—anything she asked for that was within Hedwig's power to prepare. And Hedwig prided herself on her cookery. If Raven had an urge for gingerbread with mounds of whipped cream, Hedwig made fresh gingerbread. If she fancied Belgian waffles, Hedwig made Belgian waffles. Lentil soup? Hedwig had an excellent recipe for lentil soup. Raven only had to ask, and each time she did ask, Hedwig felt she had won another small victory. She was the rain and Raven was the stone, and gradually the rain will wear away the stone.

12

He felt as though he were being buried alive. As though he were in a pit dug deep in loose, sandy soil, and when he would try to shore up one side of the pit, the opposite side would cave in on him. At the first crisis, two years ago, when Bishop Massey had called him on the carpet about the lawsuit being threatened by the parents of the Petrosky boy, he had marveled at his own coolness and composure in the face of what had then seemed certain disgrace and a possible criminal prosecution. Eventually, the boy's father had come around—or, more accurately, the diocesan attorneys had come up with enough money for the out-of-court settlement—and Father Bryce was let off the hook. But that had really been a transfer from frying pan to fire, for though the Petroskys' silence had been secured, Father Bryce found himself at the mercy of a much shrewder and more ruthless adversary, Bishop Massey himself.

As teenagers they had attended minor seminary together, vying for the same honors and the same teachers' favors. They had played on the same basketball and baseball teams. They had completed their theological studies at the North American College in Rome in the heady aftermath of the Vatican Council. Upon ordination, they had been considered among the likeliest candidates for advancement to high office within the diocese. In the way of such rivals, Father Bryce and Father Massey had maintained a fiction of being the best of friends while doing all they could to avoid each other's company. Their first assignments made that easy, for Father Bryce was appointed assistant pastor to the rural parish of Leech Lake, with teaching duties at nearby

Étoile du Nord Seminary, while Father Massey had been appointed to a post in the Chancery with the duty of developing a new, post-Conciliar liturgy for the entire diocese.

It was clear to Father Bryce, even then, which of them was slated for rapid advancement. Was it uncharitable of him, or merely realistic, to think that Massey owed his greater success to the fact that he was black? That he was personable, a good politician, and black after the café-au-lait manner of Harry Belafonte rather than in the Sidney Poitier style—these were also advantages. To be fair, Massey did all he could to emphasize his ethnicity. He wore his hair in an Afro long before Afros became respectable. He favored civilian clothes, and even vestments, with an "African" flavor, wearing long-flowing dashikis even as other priests were abandoning cassocks. He cultivated a style in his sermons that called to mind the Reverend Martin Luther King, Jr., though he'd grown up in Shakopee, Minnesota, and had no direct experience of charismatic black religion until he went to Rome and became friends with African-American seminarians studying there.

During the seventies Father Massey had moved up the ladder of promotions at a rapid clip, alternating service at the Chancery with increasingly prestigious pastoral appointments. Father Bryce, in the same period, was involved in the decline of the Étoile du Nord Seminary, as vocations diminished and a new breed of seminarians began to set a new tone. That tone was gay, and Father Bryce did not like it. He did not like the word itself, which was just then becoming the accepted euphemism for *homosexual*, as *black* was replacing *Negro*. And he did not like what the word stood for—a tolerant, smiling acceptance of sodomy as an accepted "lifestyle." Of course, the new breed of seminarians did not come right out and declare *themselves* gay. They used other code words for their own transgressions. They spoke of a need for intimacy, of the joy to be realized by becoming "available" to others. Father Bryce himself was not beyond the reach of temptation, and sometimes, when he had exceeded his three-cocktail limit, he would succumb to one of the seminarians who'd made himself too readily "available." But he'd always repented afterward, and he'd never allowed such falls from grace to become "relationships." Indeed, he did all he could to avoid the young men who had led him into sin, though this could prove difficult when they were students he had to encounter on a weekly basis.

At last, at his own request, he'd been transferred from Leech Lake and his seminary duties and become an assistant pastor at one of the largest parishes in St. Paul, Our Lady of Mercy. It was there that his desire for young men had become his scourge. Indeed, the objects of his lust were no longer, properly speaking, young men but, rather, youths, generally between ages eleven and fourteen. Usually, they were altar boys who attended the OLM parochial school, but there were also a few who attended public schools, whom he came to know through the confessional. There was nothing that so transfixed him as hearing the voice of a boy who had never come to him before for confession haltingly explaining that he had been guilty of sins of the flesh. What sins *exactly*, he would have to know, and how many times, and where, and what acts had the boy *imagined* as he'd masturbated? Had he ever thought of doing such things with other boys, or with men? Had he thought of touching them? If he were to touch his own private parts, at that moment, in the darkness of the confessional, would sinful thoughts take hold of him? He would lead his young penitents along the path to where he lay in wait for them, in his own little darkness so close by, and it was rare that one completely escaped him. Some might not be given to feel the actual pressure of his flesh on theirs but, really, the most exciting part was stimulating their imaginations. He had read that an exhibitionist achieves orgasm at the moment he makes eye contact with the person to whom he's exposed himself. For Father Bryce the moment of release was the moment he could feel a boy's will yielding to his. It was not necessarily a carnal moment, though carnality might well be the end result.

It was, however, always a *priestly* moment, for a priest is also a bender and shaper of wills. He is someone called on to exercise authority and to lead souls toward the condition Saint Paul speaks of in First Corinthians, when he tells of the two kinds of bodies, the corrupt and the incorruptible, and how we are able through Christ's love to change the one kind of body to the other. The nature of the incorruptible body was a mystery of the Faith, but there were moments when Father Bryce had felt as though he stood before the very Tabernacle of that mystery and saw the veil begin to be parted, and then—

And then the veil would close and he would discover himself to be a sinful beast, guilty of acts that even the lavender priests of Étoile du Nord and Bishop Massey's Chancery considered shameful and regarded with contempt and even horror. It galled him that such men— effeminate, epicurean, hypocritical—could think of themselves as pillars of the Church and of Father Bryce and those who shared his fleshly needs as diseased members fit only for amputation. They were the sheep, and he was a goat. Their love was holy and redeeming, and his stank of shit. And there was a part of him that agreed with them, that shared their contempt for and horror of the acts he was compelled to perform.

With the Petrosky boy he began to feel the madness of love. Before Donny his sexual feelings had been like the weather, with longer and shorter stretches of calm and of stormy weather. Once he had initiated a boy into the rudiments of sexuality, Father Bryce tended to lose interest. Their innocence was the wine for which he thirsted; once he'd slaked his thirst, the boys were like empty bottles, an embarrassment to be tidied away. He would insist on hearing their confessions and then, under the seal of the sacrament, swear them to a secrecy they were usually all too eager to agree to.

But Donny Petrosky had been different. Donny would not be coerced into postcoital shame. He declared himself to be in love with Father Bryce, and called him on the phone at all hours, and appeared as a communicant each morning at Mass, even after Father Bryce had told him he could no longer serve as an altar boy. At first Father Bryce had been alarmed and angered, but then the boy's obsession began to kindle similar feelings in himself. He invented reasons why Donny had to spend the night at the rectory. He took him on fishing trips to Rush Lake. He bought clothes for him and helped fabricate lies that would account for his frequent absences from the Petrosky dinner table. He interceded with Sister Fidelis, Donny's seventh-grade teacher, so that Donny would not be required to take a summer course in remedial math as a condition of advancing to eighth grade. Donny began to speak of the possibility that he might have a calling to the priesthood, inspired by his mentor's example. Father Bryce felt a strange joy at the thought of Donny's vocation, a feeling that was at once priestly and paternal.

And then Donny Petrosky exploded. Father Bryce never knew what triggered the outburst, for there had been nothing amiss between them. The boy had had an argument with his parents, who'd told him he would not be allowed out of the house after dinner for the rest of the summer. Donny set the Petrosky house on fire the same night. Fortunately, the fire department prevented any serious damage, but Donny was sent by a family court judge for psychiatric evaluation, and the cat was out of the bag. Donny told the psychiatrist about Father Bryce, the psychiatrist told Donny's parents, they hired a lawyer, and the lawyer went not to the OLM rectory but directly to the diocese of Minneapolis. Only a month earlier Father Bryce's erstwhile friend and longtime nemesis, Father Massey, had been appointed Bishop of Minneapolis.

Massey made the most of his opportunity. He was all love and concern and prurient interest. He did not pry directly into the sexual details, but delegated that task to his vicar-general Alexis Clareson. Father Clareson was the most openly gay member of the Chancery staff, but was probably true to his vow of celibacy, being quite obese and confined to a wheelchair. Though Father Clareson displayed an avid curiosity about everything Father Bryce had done with Donny, he never tried to ferret out the names of other boys who might have led the priest into the same temptations, for had he done so, the diocese would have been obliged to seek out the victims and offer, at the very least, to pay for their therapy.

Once Father Bryce had returned to the diocese from his mandatory term of treatment at a Church-run clinic in Arizona that specialized in the rehabilitation of pedophile priests, Bishop Massey astonished him with his new assignment: He was to become the pastor of St. Bernardine's Church in suburban Willowville. St. Bernardine's had been Massey's last pastoral appointment before assuming the episcopal throne. It was one of the most prosperous and active of the diocese's parishes, a plum among parishes. There had to be a catch.

"Yes," Bishop Massey had admitted, with a playful smile, "there is. You must be prepared for martyrdom."

"Believe me, Your Eminence, I have been."

"Of another, and more honorable, sort than would have been the case if the Petrosky matter had become public. The Church has a problem with abortion. Perhaps you're aware of it."

Father Bryce replied with an ironic smile.

"The Church," the Bishop qualified, with his own ironic smile, "in the sense of its hierarchy. In the sense, really, of the Vatican. I believe that even many of my fellow bishops here in America are not much troubled by the issue. It is an evil that must be deplored ritually at regular intervals, but it is of as little personal concern to them as the propriety of clitorectomy. The failure of the American clergy to form the conscience of their parishioners and to stir them to effective action is a matter of much concern in Rome. We all know this, but what do we, the clergy, *do?*"

The Bishop waved his hand to forestall an answer. "A rhetorical question, Patrick. No need to dredge up one of our usual pieties, for the answer is, we do nothing."

"I take it, Bishop, that where you are leading is that I *am* to do something."

"Yes, Patrick, you are to take a bold new initiative. You are to venture where none has ventured before."

Then he'd explained his plan for adapting the derelict Shrine of Blessed Konrad of Paderborn into a detention facility where reluctant teenage mothers could be forced to come to term. According to the diocese's lawyers, the plan's legality was questionable, not to mention its practicability. That is why the Bishop wanted Father Bryce to operate the facility for a time in a quiet and not quite official way—testing the water, so to speak. He could use his own experience of the therapeutic environment of the facility in Arizona where he'd just been as a kind of model, though in the initial stages of the home for girls it would not be possible to supply a professional psychologist for the staff. There was, however, a qualified midwife, Hedwig Ober, who could be trusted implicitly. She was a fervent pro-Life crusader, as was her brother, Gerhardt Ober, a professional contractor who had already almost completed the adaptation of the Shrine's physical plant to its new purpose. In fact, the idea for putting the Shrine to this new benevolent use had to be credited to Gerhardt and Hedwig, and to their old pastor, Father Wilfrid Cogling, whom they'd approached with the idea when the Shrine was put into mothballs some years ago. Father Cogling had been skeptical at first, but the Obers' enthusiasm proved contagious.

What was wanted now, the Bishop had explained, was a cooler head—someone of an executive temperament, who could be counted on to exercise prudence and discretion. In a way, Father Bryce's very sins had schooled him for such a task. Providence was always playing little tricks like that. The Bishop could understand and sympathize with Father Bryce's lack of enthusiasm for the project, but it would not have done to have some firebrand or zealot in charge. Father Cogling was a devout priest who'd done much good service, but the truth of the matter was that he sometimes lacked discretion. He could *assist* Father Bryce quite ably, but the responsibility ought not to be his.

The Bishop did not need to spell out the quid pro quo being proposed. The legal and medical costs that had been incurred in securing the Petroskys' silence exceeded $200,000, which the diocese had had to bear itself, since it was no longer possible, after the debacle of the Gauthe case in Louisiana, to obtain liability insurance that would pay for legal claims brought against pedophile priests. ("As well try to get flood insurance in Bangladesh," the Bishop had quipped.) But that $200,000 was just the tip of the iceberg of Father Bryce's debt. The Bishop's greatest kindness had been his lack of curiosity with regard to other possible transgressions. He was surely not so naive as to suppose there were none to be discovered. And if other such misdeeds were to be brought to light, eventually one would encounter (as had happened in the Gauthe case) a set of parents who would not agree to settle out of court and who would insist on the prosecution of the offending priest on criminal charges. Father Gauthe was now serving a term of twenty years at hard labor with no possibility of parole. This was the Damoclean sword suspended over Father Bryce's head that the Bishop never had to mention. There was never any doubt that he would cooperate.

Father Bryce had learned in Arizona that it was not quite accurate to think of himself as a pedophile. Pedophiles love prepubescent children. He was an ephebophile, from the Greek *ephebos*, which meant "young man." Arizona had not changed him in that respect. Like convicts who learn in prison to refine their skills at safecracking, Father Bryce had learned many things during his group therapy sessions that he was now able to apply in his day-to-day life as the pastor of St. Bernardine's. He took to heart the advice of Father William Laroche of St. John de Matha Church in Opelousas, Louisiana, who testified to the effectiveness of foot massage and shiatsu in overcoming a boy's initial shyness. He bought a video recorder that used a peculiar kind of tape that could not be played back on ordinary equipment, thus insuring against his private videos becoming mixed up with ordinary VCR tapes in the rectory—a confusion that had got more than one of his fellow priests in hot water. He even learned of two pickup places in the Twin Cities area that he'd never heard of before. One of them was Papa Bear's, the bar near Stillwater where he would later meet Clay.

The other was the Fun Fun Fun video arcade, where he discovered

Lance Kramer, the boy for whom Donny Petrosky had been merely a warm-up session, the boy he knew, almost from the moment he got into the car, would be his undoing. Father Bryce had never patronized male prostitutes before. He thought it demeaning to pay money to someone in order to have sex with him. Wasn't it the same as admitting (he'd asked those priests in therapy who favored sex that could be bought and sold) that one was simply too old, or too fat, or too homely to be desired for one's own sake? Those who favored "fast food" as against "home cooking" had protested that paying for sex was part of the excitement. Of course, its primary advantage was the safety and convenience. The boy got in the car, he blew you, he got out, you drove away. Whereas, when you seduced children from your own parish, there was always the possibility that you might wind up repenting your sins and biding your time in a rehab in Arizona's 105-degree heat. Such counsels had made sense, and so Father Bryce, without completely abandoning the children of Willowville, had tried out the Fun Fun Fun arcade.

At first Fun Fun Fun had fulfilled the promise of the advocates of fast food. For a modest twenty dollars a pop, Father Bryce was able to get his rocks off a couple of nights a week without the risk of exposure (if also without the excitement that came with the risk). Then he met Lance. With his corn-silk, summer-blond hair; his newly minted swimmer's physique, plumped with steroids. The smoothness of him. The coltish ungainliness. The intensity of his need to please—and his facility in doing so. The fast-food advocates had certainly got that part right. Young as he was, the boy knew his business.

Father Bryce could not get enough. When he returned to Fun Fun Fun it was only for Lance's sake. If Lance was not there, he would wait in his parked car, fuming. Lance claimed to have no phone number he could be reached at. He would not give Father Bryce his address. He refused to go to motels. "If you want to do it in a bed," he told Father Bryce, "we can do it in your bed, at your own home. Otherwise, the car's okay." Neither liquor nor pot could change the boy's mind in that respect. At last, one night when Father Bryce knew that Father Cogling had driven to the Shrine and would be staying there overnight, he brought Lance to the St. Bernardine's rectory. Lance already knew he was a priest, but that fact had not impressed him. "You're not the first priest I've had," the boy declared, with his air of being the world's weariest sinner. "There was three before you. That I know of." Even so, Lance got off on it. They had sex in the confessional, and in front of the altar. Lance loved to see himself on videotape wearing one of his silly heavy-metal T-shirts while Father Bryce, in full clerical rig, gave him a blow job.

Lance considered himself a Satanist, and was surprised when Father Bryce professed to have no interest in the occult and its mysteries. "I mean, you dig us fucking right there in front of the big crucifix. And you did that thing with the wafers—that was your own idea."

"Well, yes. But I thought it was something that would turn you on. It did, didn't it?"

"You know what your problem is, Father—your problem is you don't have faith. And I got the solution to your problem."

"Yes, I know you do," Father Bryce said, ruffling his hair.

"No, seriously," the boy said, pulling back from his caress. "Acid. That's what's going to do it for you. You've never tripped, have you?"

Father Bryce shook his head. The idea of using hallucinogens did not appeal to him. But Lance had persisted, assuring him that the sex that you had when taking acid was like no other sex in the world.

A week later they had their trip, and it was a disaster. Father Bryce's misgivings had not been without foundation. Usually, even when sex wasn't the top priority, Father Bryce was able to turn in a creditable performance. But the acid seemed to short-circuit his sexual capabilities. He couldn't get an erection, and couldn't get interested in making the effort. Everything started to turn sinister, including Lance, whose acne suddenly became not just noticeable but increasingly a source of dismay and then of alarm. It had not occurred to Father Bryce until just this moment that the boy, with all his sexual contacts, probably was HIV-positive. He had to get Lance out of the rectory, but Father Bryce was in no condition to drive the car, and he couldn't phone for a taxi to come and take Lance away, and Willowville was a good thirty miles from the video arcade, so Lance couldn't simply be turned out onto the street.

They reached a compromise. Lance was mollified with a sundae of vanilla ice cream swimming in crème de menthe and was given the use of the VCR and Father Bryce's library of tapes while the priest went into the bathroom, poured himself a tubful of hot water to calm down, got into it, and promptly blacked out. When he came to five hours later, Lance was gone, along with the VCR, four of the tapes, and an expensive ivory crucifix from the vestibule. Lance had also drawn a pentagram in crème de menthe on the felt of the billiard table in the rec room.

Father Bryce waited for the blackmail note that he was certain would be the next penalty to be exacted for his sins, but there was only silence. He considered returning to Fun Fun Fun and demanding that Lance give back the things he had stolen. But his was not a confrontational nature. He preferred to let sleeping dogs lie.

He vowed to reform. In the future he would satisfy his sexual needs without taking the risks inherent in pursuing minors. He'd been assured that Papa Bear's, the bar in Stillwater, was a virtual harem of hunky, available collegiate types. Not hustlers, necessarily, but young men who had a sense that there could be some long-term advantage to be gained by associating with those more mature. Networking, it was called nowadays.

Papa Bear's was not quite as agreeable as its admirers in Arizona had claimed for it. If one was not known to its regulars, one could spend a great deal of time drinking alone. The collegiate hunks seemed mostly to prefer the company of other collegiate hunks. There was also a large population of types Father Bryce found distasteful—the fat, the fruity, and those with bad skin or bad teeth or shabby clothes. He had just about given up on Papa Bear's—indeed, he'd exited to the parking lot late on a slow Wednesday night—when he met Clay.

He was sitting propped against the fender of Father Bryce's car, smoking a cigarette. Even at that first glance the priest thought: It's Lance, ten years older. Lance, aged twenty-four, with his acne cured, and the blond hair already thinner, and the body-builder muscles gone a little soft, like August tomatoes. In terms of the charms peculiar to youth, he might as well have been forty-eight as twenty-four, but he was there, leaning on the car, and there was something in the way he looked at Father Bryce—the long, cool, Clint Eastwood gaze—that signaled a different kind of danger, risk, excitement. Not until he thought about it later on did it seem strange that Clay, a stranger, should have been waiting for him there. That was somehow the assumption everyone made when they came to Papa Bear's, that there would be someone there who would consider you his destiny, if only for that one night.

"I'm Clay," he said, flicking away the butt of his cigarette. "And you're . . .?"

"Damon," said Father Bryce. Damon was the alias he'd been using with pickups since his first summer vacation away from the seminary.

"Damon," Clay repeated thoughtfully, as though it were a clue to be unriddled. "You want to—" He tilted his head toward the shrubberies bordering the bar's parking lot.

"Sure. Why not."

They went behind the shrubberies and had a quick, vigorous screw. When Clay was zipping up the fly of his jeans, and while Father Bryce was still enjoying the sweetness of the collapse that comes immediately after orgasm, Clay said, "I'll be getting in touch with you again soon, Father."

Only after he'd walked off into the darkness did it occur to Father Bryce that he had not told Clay he was a priest. Clay must have known it beforehand. Which in itself was not too alarming. He'd had some embarrassing moments of mutual recognition in other gay bars. Usually the men who recognized him were married parishioners who were more embarrassed at having been seen in a gay bar than Father Bryce was. More than once he encountered men who had enjoyed their sexual initiation at his hands, but in those cases as well, the result was usually mutual embarrassment. One such no-longer-youthful young man, who was quite drunk, splashed his drink in the priest's face before Father Bryce was able to recognize him as someone who'd served Mass for him at OLM almost twenty years earlier. The man became verbally abusive, and his friends had to drag him out of the bar to keep him from attacking Father Bryce with his fists.

So he did not give much thought to the fact that this Clay knew him to be a priest. If all the priests in the diocese of Minneapolis who'd been seen cruising gay bars were to be defrocked, there'd be a lot of empty frocks and a lot of priestless parishes. By Father Bryce's own estimate, something like forty percent. Indeed, in his own case, a videotape of his five minutes in the bushes with Clay would have actually been accounted to his credit, could it have been seen at the Chancery, for it would have indicated a preference for sexual partners of mature years—genuine consenting adults.

The very next morning he received an Express Mail package that contained the ivory crucifix that Lance had stolen from the rectory six weeks ago, together with a brief handwritten note—"Thought you would want to see this. Clay"—paper-clipped to an undated newspaper clipping stating that the corpse of a teenage boy had been recovered from the Mississippi. The boy had been tentatively identified as Lyle Kramer, age fourteen, who had been missing from his home in San Diego for nearly a year. The boy had died by drowning and was believed to have committed suicide. Readers who might have information about the boy's presence in the Twin Cities were asked to call a number at the St. Paul Police Department.

Clay let Father Bryce think about this for two days before he phoned and told him to meet him at the Coon Rapids Econo-Motor Lodge in two hours. He refused to give any explanation over the phone. Father Bryce drove directly to the motel, and went to the room he'd been told to go to. The door was unlocked, and the room was empty. He'd been told to get undressed and he did. Then, also as per his instructions, he blindfolded himself and waited. He did not know how long he waited until Clay came to the room and told him what he would have to do. He had protested, but with a sense, from the first, that his protests would serve no purpose.

"Here's the situation," said Clay. "We've got the videotapes you made with Lyle Kramer. And we've got his suicide note, which mentions you by name. There's no way a jury wouldn't send you away for a good long stretch. So that's your alternative, if you refuse to do what we tell you. And don't think you can negotiate the price. We don't want your money, Father. We want your soul."

13

"How am I feeling?" Bing held the telephone receiver away from his ear so that it could see the expression of incredulity on his face. He echoed Father Mabbley's question a second time, with a deadlier sarcasm: "How am I *feeling?* Furious, that's how I'm feeling—epileptically furious. The whole thing obsesses me. I can't think of anything else. I'd like to see *demons* drag him down to *hell,* and then I'd like to sit in the audience and watch him suffer eternal torments designed by Dante just for him. Though he wouldn't be there by himself, of course—I realize that. There'd be a throng of other pedophile priests there with him, a thousand strong, with snakes in their fucking asses." He took a deep breath, and then, in a tone of cool inquiry: "Does that answer your question?"

"You do sound upset," Father Mabbley replied. "And upset is a reasonable response to the situation. Hysterical isn't. It won't serve your purpose. If you've formed one. Have you?"

"I want to make him pay."

"You couldn't just leave him to God's judgment?"

"What I figure is that I *am* God's judgment. For all these years I'd never given a thought to the loss of my cherry. And if I *had* thought about it, I probably wouldn't have got riled. I wasn't going to be a virgin all my life, so somebody had to get there first, and the fact that it was a priest seemed just the luck of the draw. The guy wasn't cruel, he didn't *abuse* me, except in the technical sense. Sometimes I did look back and wish I'd had a chance to fall in love with someone my own age and lose my heart and my cherry *together*, the way it happens in movies. But how often does that happen?"

"It's rare," Father Mabbley conceded.

"And it's not the fact that he's a priest that gets me fussed."

"I should hope not," said Father Mabbley, who'd had a lot of cuddly sex with Bing over the years they'd been friends.

"What gets me fussed is the fact that he's a priest *and* a pedophile *and* this holier-than-thou *crusader* against abortion. The last straw was when he was out at the Catholic cemetery dedicating this memorial to the Unknown Fetus, which took place on the same day there was the story in the news about the Vatican's latest mortar attack against gays. So the reporter at the unveiling of the memorial asked him whether he agreed that gays shouldn't be allowed to teach in schools—not just parochial schools, but schools anywhere, public schools, universities, schools across the board—and he said yes, he agreed, that there should be laws to keep gays *out* of teaching jobs and *out* of public housing. *He* said that, on the TV news—the man who'd wiggled his fingers up my fifteen-year-old ass and told me that Jesus Christ is a god of love and so please, baby, give me some. I would submit that that has to be considered hypocrisy."

Father Mabbley sighed. Then there was a pause just long enough for him to take a sip of the wine that Bing was sure was there at hand beside his recliner. "Of course it is, Bing. But we're all hypocrites nowadays. The Vatican has made it a condition of employment, so to speak. If we're not hypocrites about being gay, then we're hypocrites about birth control or abortion. We preach one thing in public, but in the confessional it's another story. If every priest in every parish in the country were to insist that all his parishioners refrain from birth control if they wanted to receive the sacraments, instead of quietly letting people go their own way, we would soon solve the problem of the priest shortage by creating an even more impressive shortage of laymen."

"I don't want to destroy the Church," Bing insisted. "I just want to destroy *him*."

"Destroy him legally?"

"Wouldn't that be a good place to begin."

"If it were possible, but I doubt that it is. The statute of limitations ran out a long time ago."

"I realize I'm not an altar boy anymore. But I've read about cases where people suddenly remember things they've repressed for years and years because they were so traumatic."

"I'm not sure but I think it's only murder where charges can be brought so much later. You'd have to consult a local lawyer."

"Even if there weren't criminal charges, couldn't he be sued in civil court?"

"Again, you'd have to ask a lawyer. But the Church has a great advantage in cases like that. They have lawyers who do nothing else but pile up paperwork in order to make the cost of any litigation ruinous. You'd be bankrupt in a twinkling."

"So forget the law. Suppose I just went to the newspapers and told them what happened?"

"They probably wouldn't touch it. Unless you had some kind of proof to back up your charges. Letters, photographs. Do you?"

"*He* may. I don't."

"Did you ever tell anyone about it, when it happened?"

"Are you kidding?"

"So it would be just your word against his. And what the Church would do is hire detectives to dig up everything that could be used against you. They'd find out you were active in Act Up. They'd say you are unbalanced and have a vendetta against the Church. *And* Bryce's lawyer could sue you for defamation of character. That's often done. The best defense is an attack."

"Whatever happened to turning the other cheek?"

"I think that went out with the invention of gunpowder."

"So you're telling me not to do it."

"I'm telling you how the Church deals with those it perceives as its enemies."

"But I *love* the Church. I need the Church. And I feel sorry for the priests in your position, who get caught in the gears of the machine. And I don't believe in outing *every* gay priest in the country. Although, the way things are going, that may happen."

"A lot of the older hard-liner types among the priests I know are praying for exactly that. They'd love a witch hunt. And sometimes I wonder if it wouldn't be a good thing in the long run. For *us*, the forty or fifty percent of priests who are gay. It wouldn't be an unbearable martyrdom: They don't burn heretics at the stake anymore. Though, speaking of martyrdom, I had *such* a nightmare the other night . . . did I tell you? It was a lulu."

"So tell me," said Bing, who realized that he'd been hogging the conversation, even though it was Father Mabbley who was paying for the long-distance call all the way from Las Vegas.

"Well," Father Mabbley said, easing into storytelling mode, "it started with me delivering a sermon in this really creepy Gothic chapel. It was a Hammer horror film's idea of the High Middle Ages, with a gigantic polychrome crucifix over the altar with a Christ all ripped to pieces and writhing in agony. I'm in this pulpit at the top of a windy staircase, and I'm preaching to this congregation that looks like the Living Dead, and the subject of my homily is the unspeakable sufferings Hell has in store for anyone who masturbates. And then, this is so ridiculous, someone starts playing the *organ*—"

"Oh, Mabb, come on, you're making this up."

"No, I swear to God. The organist was a cross between Lon Chaney in *The Phantom of the Opera* and the evil monk in *Alexander Nevsky*. I became petrified. Then out of the darkness at the back of the church comes this very solemn procession of figures in pointy hoods, like Klansmen, but also like heretics being led to an auto-da-fé. Some have whips, and others have torches, and as they come down the center aisle, the zombies in the congregation get up out of their seats—which is a terrible anachronism, since medieval churches didn't cater to creature comfort with furniture—"

"That's okay," Bing assured him. "We're not responsible for what we dream."

"Well, the dream starts to blur at this point, and the Klansmen start using their whips and torches on the Christ up on the crucifix, but it's not a crucifix anymore. It's like a suspension harness in some very kinky after-hours club. I'd been reading that book about the Crispo murder case, you know the one?"

Bing nodded, and then had to explain, "Yes, I nodded my head yes. I haven't read the book, but I read about *him* in the papers. The boy who got picked up at a bar and was tortured to death. There but for the grace of God, and all that."

"Exactly," Father Mabbley agreed. "It's a very distressing book that way. So in my dream I expressed that distress and tried, from the pulpit, to stop the Inquisition that was going on, with predictable results. The Klansmen stopped torturing the crucified man, who wasn't Jesus anymore, just some trick from a bar—and came over to the pulpit. And I realized they were going to set fire to it, and I was going to be burned at the stake."

"Just like Joan of Arc. But in which version? Preminger's? Or the one with Ingrid Bergman?"

"Bing, really! There's only one Joan. Maria Falconetti in Dreyer's *Passion of Joan of Arc.*"

"Oh, another one of your musty old silent movies. I've never seen it."

"Then do yourself a favor and *rent* it. It's one of the great movies of all time. If it's available at video stores in Las Vegas, they must have it in Minneapolis someplace."

"You're always putting down Las Vegas and making out the Twin Cities to be some kind of Athens. Believe me, when it comes to entertainment, it's more like Sparta here. Anyhow, don't keep me in suspense. Were you burned at the stake?"

"That's when the dream turns into something out of George Romero."

"Now you're in my century. Oh damn, wouldn't you know it? I've got another call. Can I put you on hold? I told you I volunteered for this suicide hot line, and though I've never had a single call (which is a blessing), I should pick up. If it's not something important, I'll ask them to call back. Okay?"

"I think call-waiting is destroying American civilization, but what can I do? I'll wait."

Bing pressed the appropriate buttons and said, "Hello?"

A voice said, "Bing Anker?" and there was no doubt whose voice it was.

"Father Pat! After all these years. My goodness, what a surprise. Could you hold on just a moment? I've got someone else I have to say good-bye to." Without waiting for an answer, Bing switched back to Father Mabbley's line. "Mabb, you won't believe who just called. Bryce. I've put him on hold. Do you want to listen to what we say? Be the good angel on my right shoulder?"

"Without his knowing?"

"My telephone can do that. It's Japanese and very clever. Come on. He may say something indiscreet."

"And then I'd be a witness to it. I'm not sure I like that idea. How did he get your number? I thought you said he didn't know who you were when you were in the confessional."

"I don't know. He probably racked his Rolodex. I gave him enough clues. I'm going to press the button now, so it's a conference call and you can eavesdrop. But don't sneeze. Please?"

"Okay, hide me behind the arras."

Bing switched back to Father Bryce. "Father Bryce. My goodness, how long has it been?"

"Since yesterday afternoon."

"You didn't seem to know who I was in the confessional. But I guess I jogged some memories?"

"Why did you come to church dressed in women's clothing?"

"Now, how did you know that? Is there some kind of camera system for spying on people inside the confessional?"

"You also vandalized church property."

"The stickers? You call *that* vandalism? I guess it's been a while since you were in an inner-city parish."

"This is intolerable and aberrant behavior. I will not allow it."

"Intolerable and aberrant behavior. That sort of gives us something in common, doesn't it, Father?"

"I will also not allow you to taunt me with accusations and innuendos under the guise of going to confession."

"You seem much more sure of yourself today. I guess you must have been talking to a lawyer? And he explained about the statute of limitations. My legal counsel went through all that stuff with me, too." Bing paused a beat to let Father Mabbley appreciate his tip of the hat. Then, in an icier tone, "But I explained that I don't care about *winning* a legal case. My interest is just in exposing the Church's hypocrisy. And there'd also be the excitement of being in the media limelight. I'd probably be on TV. Who knows, the story might go all the way to Geraldo, or Sally Jessy Raphaël. It's a hot topic these days. And to be perfectly honest, I would get off on a little limelight. You do, don't you? Whenever I see you on TV, like when you were at the unveiling of that tacky Tomb of the Unknown Fetus, you seem to revel in it. Your voice goes down about an octave. Your brow furrows. It's just like when we said Mass together. I remember it so well. *You* would say, '*Introibo ad altare Dei*,' I will go unto the altar of God. And I'd reply, '*Ad Deum qui laetificat juventutem meam*,' To God, who gives joy to my youth. And I would smile to myself at the idea of what they would have thought out there in the audience if they'd known it wasn't just God who gave joy to *juventutem meam*. If you know what I mean, and I'm sure you do. You studied Latin at the seminary. And a little Greek?"

"You disgusting little faggot."

"Oh, Father Bryce, you do know how to get a boy excited. You might even say that that has been your tragic flaw."

There was a silence, and the silence lengthened. Bing had worked as a dealer at various Vegas casinos, and he knew that when you're playing poker against a desperate and inept player, the best strategy is to stand pat and wait for the person to do something stupid. He didn't have to wait that long.

"Are you after money?" Father Bryce asked. "Is that what it is? Because if you are, I can't help you."

"Father Pat, are you suggesting that I have been trying to *blackmail* you? Have I said one thing to make you think that? Have I *mentioned* money? When I came to confession, did I speak of anything but the *sin* we committed?"

"Bing, if there was any sin, it was long since forgiven."

"By the confessions I went to right after we'd had sex? Do you really suppose those were valid sacraments? I can't believe that. In fact, it's a wonder I can believe anything at all, that I didn't lose my faith then and there. That's what usually happens, and it happens a lot. When I first shared my experience with friends, in a consciousness-raising situation, I was just astonished at how *many* other gays had had the same thing happen to them. If it wasn't their parish priests, then it was a brother at the high school they went to. The *drama* coach, nine times out of ten. Especially if it was an all-male school where the younger boys did women's roles in drag. I guess that hasn't changed since Shakespeare's day. There was even a standard pattern for the *way* we had sex—very gentle, very quick, with the lights off, then sweep it under the carpet and pretend it never happened. But always the open invitation to come back soon. Until we got too tall, or too hairy, or too clingy, or someone cuter came along, and then God would revise his opinion of the gravity of the sin we'd been committing and issue a call for repentance. In other words, we got our pink slips. Does the pattern sound familiar?"

Another silence. Bing didn't think the man was about to fess up at this juncture, so he went on:

"I'll tell you what I do want. I want the Church to treat me like a human being. Not like a pariah. You know, a while ago I used to run the Las Vegas night at Our Lady of Mercy. On the nights I ran the bingo operation and called the numbers, the church brought in nearly half again as much money. But *somebody*—I will never know who—complained to Father Youngerman that I was queer. And I got canned. No discussion. They'd never tell me who complained. And it wasn't as though I'd been trying to *conceal* who I am. You're queer, that's it, good-bye. How do you suppose that made me feel? I'll tell you: bitter."

Father Bryce had gathered enough composure to be able to say, "I'm sorry. It's not a perfect world. It's not a perfect Church."

"So we must ask ourselves, mustn't we, how could *I* help to make it a better world and a better Church? And I'll offer a suggestion. St. Bernardine's could institute its own Las Vegas night. And I could be your bingo caller. There'd be a certain poetic justice in that, don't you think?"

No reply. This time Bing did wait him out.

"I'm afraid it wouldn't be feasible," Father Bryce said, audibly walking on eggs. "St. Bernardine's has never had bingo nights. A lot of the parishioners would be strongly opposed."

"They're too upscale for bingo? Well, chemin de fer is okay with me, if they'd prefer that."

"I'm sorry, I have to hang up. This has become an impossible conversation. I can't say anything without your twisting it into something ludicrous. I shouldn't have phoned at all."

"Oh no, Father, it's a good thing that you did. It shows you have some sort of conscience. A *guilty* conscience, needless to say, but that's better than none at all. If you hadn't called me, I would surely have gotten in touch again. I'm not letting you off the hook. Which is a very Christian idea, isn't it—being on the hook? The apostles were supposed to be fishers of men. Have you noticed how often Christ spoke of the soul as basically a source of protein? We're all just lost sheep or fish to be caught or wheat to be harvested and threshed. Christ must have been hungry a lot of the time, don't you suppose?" Bing paused, not for a reply, but to give Father Mabbley a moment to appreciate his little homage, for what he'd said about the soul as food was a direct plagiarism from one of Father Mabbley's sermons on the Sunday he had to pass the basket for famine relief.

"Seriously, Father," Bing went on. "You asked if I wanted money. No, that's not what I had in mind at all. I just want to be able to help you do what has to be done. And I'm glad you felt the need to call me. The first step is the hardest. Your getting in touch with me shows that you understand you can't do this all by yourself. You have to surrender, to ask for help, and for a priest that must be *so* hard. There's another Latin saying, which I can't quote in Latin, but the gist of it is, 'Who'll put the custodians into custody?' That's your problem, isn't it? And I'm the answer. I can show you the things you have to do to *atone* for what you've done.

"First off, you've got to make a *list* (if you don't have one already) of all your conquests. I'm sure there were lots before me, and I *know* many came after, because for a while I was a monster of jealousy, and I would come to your early weekday masses at OLM to see how you were relating with whoever was serving Mass for you that day. And I could always tell if you had your eye on him, and if you'd got to first base, and whether he was confused about it or gaga, like I'd been. It must be quite a list by now. *Then*, when the list is done, you can track down each person on it and arrange a tête-à-tête-à-tête for the three of us, so you can make amends. You may feel awkward at first, but I'll be there and able to help you through it. You'll be amazed, once you begin really to deal with all the ghosts in your past, how much better you will feel. Truly, this will be an emotional and spiritual *adventure* for you. And for me, too."

"You're crazy," said Father Bryce, trying to maintain a neutral tone.

"It is a challenging idea, isn't it? And not without some risks. Who knows how each of the people you'll contact will react? Some may have very strong feelings toward you still, as I do. Yet there's no other way to reestablish a sense of honesty and fair dealing in your life than by squaring away those old accounts. *Then*, with the strength you've gained from that process, you can begin to use your position in the Church in a positive way. Instead of seducing teenage boys and preaching hatred toward gays, you can direct the homosexual component of your character toward affirmative, life-enhancing goals. Such as? you must be asking yourself. Such as opening a chapter of Dignity at St. Bernardine's, somewhere gay Catholics can get together and feel they have a place in the Church. And if Bishop Massey tries to put a stop to it, I'll bet we could find one or two young men who could help persuade the Bishop toward a more charitable attitude, in the same way I'm persuading you."

"This is blackmail," said Father Bryce, "pure and simple."

"Well, it may be *emotional* blackmail, but I don't think there's a law against that. The Church does it all the time, doesn't it? Standing outside abortion clinics and screaming at women that they're killing their babies. Sometimes it takes drastic measures to awaken the sleeping conscience."

"Clay got you to do this, didn't he?"

"Clay?" Bing asked.

"I knew he'd try something else. I knew he wouldn't be content to torture me just one day a week."

"I'm sorry, but I don't know the Clay you're talking about. He sounds like my kind of guy, though. Maybe you can arrange for us to meet."

"This is unbearable. I can't go on like this. Tell him that. Goodbye."

Father Bryce hung up.

"Well," said Bing. Then he explained to Father Mabbley: "He hung up."

"I gathered that, but I didn't want to come out from behind the arras until you'd sounded an all-clear. What was that last thing about 'Clay'?"

"I don't know. It sounds like I may not be the only person he's having a problem with."

"Candidly, Bing, the guy sounds a bit flaky. I was happy to see you were able to resist his virtual invitation to blackmail him. And the way you did eventually put the screws on him would have delighted any Grand Inquisitor. But I don't think you should push him any further."

"What can he do—murder me?"

"Well, he could, couldn't he?"

"Or hire a hit man, though I don't know if they have hit men in Minneapolis."

"It sounds, Bing, like Minneapolis has a good supply of *all* the latest vices. I'd be careful."

"I will be extremely careful. If I see any hit men, I will immediately cross to the other side of the street. Now, you still haven't told me what happened in your dream. They were just about to burn you at the stake."

Father Mabbley finished his dream, but his heart was no longer in it, and when it came time at last to ring off, he repeated what he'd said earlier, "Be careful, Bing." But he might as well have offered his advice to a roulette wheel or a slot machine. The machinery was already in motion, and the laws of physics were in charge of the result.

14

"There may be photographers there from the newspapers," her escort explained as they waited for the traffic light to change, "but they're not there to photograph *you.* They have a commitment to respect your privacy. They're there to shoot the protesters. And I'll tell you, sometimes I'd like to shoot the protesters myself."

Alison knew it would be polite to laugh at the woman's joke, or to say something bright and sarcastic herself, but she just didn't have it in her. If someone had asked her what her name was, she'd have had to think.

If she'd said what she was actually thinking, she would have asked the woman, whose name was Ms. Stern, to please stop talking every minute. She regretted now having agreed to have an escort bring her to the abortion clinic. She could have taken the Lake Street bus by herself and avoided all of Ms. Stern's worries and opinions, such as whether the protesters would be spraying people with red paint symbolic of blood as they'd done in the past, in which case Alison should have worn something easily washable, like the blue jeans Ms. Stern was wearing. She also made several rude remarks about President Bush. Not that Alison cared anything at all about the President. She'd never been able to get interested in events on news programs, and she'd hated it in civics class when she had to come up with her own opinion about some controversy or other. We should not be exporting U.S. jobs to Mexico: Discuss. Mr. Bard had made her look like such a fool during that discussion, asking her if she didn't think this, and then if she didn't think that, and then pointing out that she couldn't think *both* things, because you couldn't have your cake and eat it too.

And here she was on her way to becoming part of the news. Having to wear a scarf, on a hot summer day, so she wouldn't be recognized in case they did, after all, show her on TV.

"Nervous?" Ms. Stern asked.

Alison shook her head. "No. I just wish it were over."

Ms. Stern patted her thigh and said, "That's the spirit," and then they were turning left on Cedar, and there were the protesters, a great crowd of them with posters mounted on sticks, and every one of the slogans was familiar to Alison. There were even *faces* she recognized from when she'd been recruited to come here on weekends last summer. Till this moment it hadn't occurred to her that there might be people among the protesters who *knew* her. People she'd had coffee with at The Embers. She wanted to tell Ms. Stern to drive on past, she wanted to rethink things, but it was too late. Ms. Stern rolled to a halt at the entrance to the clinic's driveway and waited for two policemen to push back the protesters who'd stepped forward to try to keep the car from entering the parking lot. They were chanting, "Let your child live! Let your child live!" A girl who seemed no more than twelve managed to slip past the policemen and throw herself across the hood of Ms. Stern's Toyota on Alison's side.

Ms. Stern honked vigorously, and the girl screamed, "Stop the murders! Stop the murders!" Her face was just on the other side of the windshield from Alison. She could see the tears in the girl's blue eyes.

A photographer came around to the driver's side of the Toyota and began snapping pictures of the police as they lifted the girl from the hood of the car. The girl struggled until one policeman put handcuffs on her, and then she smiled a smile of beatific martyrdom, holding her cuffed hands above her head like a boxer proclaiming his victory.

When the driveway had been cleared, Ms. Stern drove into the parking lot and took a space between a van and a police patrol car. "I hope that little bitch didn't dent my hood," she grumbled as she removed the keys from the ignition and tucked them into the pocket of her Levis.

At just that moment, Alison had been thinking: That could have been me. Throwing herself on the hood of the car. Screaming. Tears in her eyes. And being called a little bitch by Ms. Stern.

Probably Ms. Stern felt the same way about Alison, though she wouldn't have said it out loud. The little bitch couldn't keep her pants on. The little bitch doesn't have enough sense to take the pill.

"Well, how about it?" Ms. Stern asked, already out of the car and bending down to peer at Alison.

"Right," said Alison, reaching for the door handle. "Let's get it over with."

All she had to do was get from here to the door of the clinic, and after that it would all be out of her hands. She'd be like a car going through a car wash. It was just a matter of walking past the protesters, keeping her head down, and not listening to what they were screaming at her.

But then, just as she took the hand Ms. Stern held out to her, one of the protesters recognized her and called her name aloud: "Alison! Alison, don't go inside! Don't kill your baby!"

The other protesters took it up at once: "Alison, don't go inside! Alison, don't go inside!"

As she passed by them, she tried to keep her eyes on the cement slabs of the sidewalk, only looking, as Ms. Stern had advised, at the next step she must take. But then a voice deeper than the others pronounced her name, and even before she looked up, from seeing the hem of his cassock swaying over his black shoes, she knew who it was.

The priest raised his right hand, and the protesters fell silent.

"Alison," said Father Cogling earnestly. "My dear child. Can't we talk together for just a moment before it's too late?"

"Just step out of the way and leave her alone," Ms. Stern said, tightening her grip on Alison's hand. "She doesn't want to talk to you."

"Then why not let her tell me so herself?" Father Cogling said softly. He turned to Alison and took her free hand in both of his. "Five minutes, my dear. That's all I ask. A chance to speak away from the crowd and the cameras. No one can be expected to reach a wise decision in this carnival atmosphere."

"I like that," Ms. Stern said, addressing the cameraman from WCCO who stood right in front of her. "He brings in his crew of hysterical teenagers ready to riot on command and then *he* complains about the carnival atmosphere. As for reaching a wise decision, my friend has already *made* her decision, thank you very much. And now if you would, please, step out of the way?"

"Alison?" Father Cogling asked, tightening his grip on her right hand.

At the same moment, as though she were in some kind of telepathic linkage, Ms. Stern tightened her own grip and said, "Well, Alison?"

It seemed almost ludicrous, as though they might begin a tug of war. As though her body was the prize in a contest, and the way to win the contest was simply to hold on and not let go.

Father Cogling let go of her hand. "It's up to you, Alison," he said.

Ms. Stern kept her grip on Alison's hand and began to walk forward, but Alison resisted. Ms. Stern looked at her quizzically.

"I will talk with him," she said. "For just a minute or two."

"Thank you, my dear," said the priest.

"Do as you think best, my dear," said Ms. Stern, letting go of her hand and, in the same instant (Alison knew), writing her off as a lost cause. Alison couldn't blame her. She was exactly the kind of person that women like Ms. Stern had no use for. She was weak and passive and couldn't stick to her guns. That's why she was in the fix she was in now, because she hadn't been able to say to Greg, "No, not tonight."

She followed Father Cogling away from the crowd and in the direction of Lake Street with a feeling that she didn't have an ounce of willpower of her own. She hated the feeling, but at the same time there was a kind of comfort in letting someone else take charge. The way, when you're sick and someone tucks you into bed, you're almost grateful for being sick, because it's brought you somewhere that's momentarily so much kinder and warmer and motherly.

She didn't even have to listen to what Father Cogling was saying to know that she'd agree to have her baby. Wasn't that what she'd really wanted to do all along? Wasn't this the reprieve she'd been hoping for?

15

On Wednesday night, an hour before Father Bryce was expected at Knightriders Kustom Ink, Clay called him at the rectory. "Hey there, Damon, shouldn't you already be on your way to Little Canada? Wolf can't do nothing with his needle till he's got some skin to work on."

"It's all off," Father Bryce said.

"Now what in hell has got into you?" Clay said in just that tone of humorous indulgence that a sitcom husband uses with his wife when she gets whims.

Father Bryce, with only a little prodding, explained about Bing Anker's visit to St. Bernardine's and the threats he had made on the phone.

"You say he came to the church dressed like a woman, but then you say you never actually saw him. That doesn't gibe."

"He left the confessional suddenly, and I couldn't immediately go after him. But my assistant, Father Cogling, came into the church just then, and he remembered seeing a middle-aged woman leaving. So that had to have been him."

"What a perverted thing to do," Clay said with conviction. "Going into a church in drag! That takes the cake."

"Don't pretend you didn't know about this. Some of the things he said on the phone were exactly the same as things I've heard you say."

"Such as?"

"He said he wasn't interested in money, that he didn't want to blackmail me, that he had me on a hook, which was an expression you've used, and that I would have to make a list like the list you had me make, with the names of all the kids I've ever fooled around with. Then he was going to have me *contact* everyone on the list and make *amends.*"

"Shit," said Clay, "he might as well ask you to commit suicide. So, what's the guy got on you? Are there pictures? Did you write letters to him?"

"He's only got his word. But he seemed very . . . determined. And confident. He seems to feel no shame about the idea of a public scandal. He's probably openly homosexual."

"If he's a transvestite, shame is probably a turn-on for him. You said his name was Bing? What's his full name?"

"Oh, don't pretend you don't know. I'm sure this is just your way of turning the screw on me."

"Quit fucking around—tell me his name."

"Bing Anker. With a *k.*"

"Where's he live?"

"In St. Paul. Calumet Avenue."

"Okay, you leave it with us to deal with Bing Anker, with a *k,* and get your ass out to Knightriders. Now."

Father Bryce did not at once reply.

"Did you hear?"

"I heard."

"Because you are on *our* hook, and no one else's. So you do what *we* say, and you do it like you were getting your orders from Jesus Christ. What we are doing is, we are taking charge of your *soul.* You may not believe we can do that. But you just wait, and do what we say, and the belief will come. We will own you. Not all of you, all at once. But piece by piece, in increments. And the more of you that we take possession of, the more *you* will enjoy surrendering the properties you've still got left. It is a fascinating process."

"My damnation."

"You can call it that, if that makes it sound like more fun. Enough chitchat. Go get more ink."

In some ways Clay figured he knew more about the priest than the priest knew about himself. He knew what Father Bryce was afraid of and what turned him on and the way the two things connected. For instance, his panic attack when Wolf's latest dragon lady came into the back room of Knightriders just as Wolf had moved into high gear and Father Bryce's midriff was all slicked with sweat and blood. "Hey there, Delilah," Wolf said, not even looking up or bothering to perform introductions. "How's tricks?"

Delilah just nodded in her usual luded-out, lazy way and let her jaw drop preparatory to words that never got spoken. When her mouth was open you could see her dental problems, which were major. She went over to stand beside Wolf and watch the work-in-progress, blocking Clay's view of Father Bryce. But Clay didn't need to see the priest to know he'd be freaking. This was probably the first time in his life any woman had seen him with a hard-on, much less handled it. For Delilah's first slurred words were "You like that?" And then, to Wolf, "I think he likes that."

"Easy with those fingernails," Wolf told her.

"Sure," she said. "If you let me have the needle a minute instead."

"That's my job, beautiful."

"Aw, come on. I'll just put a little heart right here on the end of it. Come on."

"She's got a real sense of humor, don't she?" the tattooist said to Father Bryce.

The priest replied with a noncommittal grunt, and the tattooing continued, complicated now by Delilah's inputs. Wolf regarded her casual tweaks and squeezes with an indulgent half-attention, the way a parent keeps half an eye on an infant crawling about on a rug. How Father Bryce regarded her, Clay could only imagine. Wolf had done a lot of work on her, great sweeping curves of flowers and serpents twining up her bare legs and wreathing around her midriff and over her shoulders. There were even tendrils of the design encroaching past the leafy collar circling her neck, like a vine that is always exploring, testing, reaching out. Delilah's hands were like her own tattoos in that way, restless with a slow-motion inquisitiveness.

Father Bryce endured it without protest until she began to scratch at the hairs of his false mustache with one of her false fingernails, at which point he lifted his hand, signaling a break, and Wolf took his foot off the tattoo gun's on/off switch. "I think I'll have some of that whiskey after all."

"Whatever you say, Damon." Wolf handed him the uncapped but still untasted pint bottle of Jack Daniel's, and Father Bryce tilted his head forward to meet the neck of the bottle. Even so, some of the liquor spilled down the side of his mouth. He took a second swallow and then, with a sigh, relaxed.

The tattooing continued for a few more minutes, and then Wolf handed the tattoo gun to Delilah, stood up, and turned to face the peephole through which Clay was watching. "He's out. And down for the count. No need for you to be holed up in the can."

Clay got down from the plank he'd been standing on, which was spread across the cracked tank of a defunct toilet. As soon as he was out of the closet-sized bathroom, he lit a cigarette. He'd had one smoke in there just as the tattooing session had started, almost an hour ago, and the air had got so smoky he'd almost had a coughing fit.

He went over to the barber chair that served Wolf as a drafting table and took a closer look at Father Bryce's tattoo. The outline had been completed at the first session, and now Wolf was darkening the wreathing clouds of smoke that defined the recesses of the Satanic face, the eye sockets, cheekbones, and open mouth.

"It's starting to look three-D," Clay commented.

"It's gettin' there," Wolf agreed. "I'm surprised the fucker lasted as long as he did tonight. When the work is concentrated in a single area, the pain is more intense than when the outline is laid in. I thought he might go through the whole session without asking for a drink."

"You going to let me use the needle on him or not?" Delilah wanted to know.

"What difference does it make if he's out cold?"

Delilah gave an impatient shake of her tangled black hair, as though Wolf's words had been a fly bothering her. "I just want to put *my* mark on him. The same as you. Okay?"

Wolf turned to Clay. "You mind?"

"On his cock?" Clay asked her.

She grinned, offering a full view of her dental problems.

"Sure, why not. As long as that won't wake him up."

"No problem," said Wolf. "Just with what he's got in him now, he probably won't come around till early morning. And if you need longer, I'll just administer some more of the same medicine."

Clay went over to the chair where the priest's clothes lay in a heap. He got a ring of keys from the right-hand pocket.

"I should be back inside of three hours. Don't let Delilah get carried away, okay? And, um, what I was asking about earlier?"

Wolf went to a decrepit filing cabinet, unlocked the top drawer, took out a brown paper bag, and handed it to Clay.

Clay hefted the bag with satisfaction. There was something in just the weight of a gun that was like shooting up. You could feel it moving through your bloodstream, effecting changes. It was like walking through an empty house and turning on the lights each time you entered another room.

"The clip's already in it?"

Wolf nodded.

"Well, see you later."

The priest's car was parked along the curb a block north of Knightriders Kustom Ink.

On the floor of the car behind the driver's seat was the priest's suit coat, folded up on top of an Adidas bag. His pants and a shirt with a built-in Roman collar were inside the bag. He must have had to drive to the tattoo parlor directly from some official business that had required him to be in uniform.

Just for the hell of it, Clay tried on the whole getup. The pants were a little baggy, but the jacket was a good fit. He checked out the effect of the collar in the rearview mirror. He looked genuinely holy. The gun fit comfortably into the inside breast pocket of the jacket.

Finding Calumet Avenue wasn't that easy, even having checked the map in advance. He took the wrong exit off 35W and had to detour several blocks to find an overpass that would let him get to the other side of the thruway.

The house he was looking for turned out to be on the corner. A garage with a driveway connecting to the side street. One car was already parked in the driveway, but there was room for Clay to park beside it.

No lights on anywhere in the house, and the back door unlocked. Could anything be easier?

There were ways in which walking through a dark house you had no right to be in was more exciting than armed robbery or even rape. In those situations you had to be able to react so fast there was no chance to savor what you were up to. But this was like being in a movie. Each dark, indefinite shape posed a separate riddle. From the back door there was a short flight of steps up to the kitchen, which had a vague cabbagey stink of home cooking. Then a right turn into the dining room, with its ceremonial Sunday-dinner table, and on the table a centerpiece of dried flowers, all gray and ghostly in the light that seeped though sheer lacy curtains from the streetlamp at the corner. For a faggot, this Bing Anker seemed to have some very traditional family values. If you thought about it, Clay would have done better getting rid of the priest, who was a total shithead, instead of this Anker guy, who sounded pretty harmless. But it was not Clay's job to think about such things. His job was to do what his handler told him.

He figured the guy must be asleep in one of the upstairs bedrooms, so when he went through the living room, heading straight for the stairway, he almost didn't notice the body slumped sideways on the couch. But the moment he did notice it, he realized that someone had done his job for him.

Clay turned on one of a pair of end table lamps, and then thought to draw the drapes. As he turned away from the living room window, he saw himself in the mirror mounted over the sofa: a priest who'd arrived to deliver the last rites. He made a little sign of the cross at the mirror and furrowed his brow. Very priestly, he thought. The uniform suited him.

Then he checked out the corpse. There'd been two shots, one a little above the heart, the other through the gut. The gut shot had soaked the guy's jeans and the cushion of the sofa. He must have died right away, because all the blood was concentrated right where he was sitting. The blood on his jeans was dry, but the cushion was still slightly damp. Clay was no forensic expert, but he figured the guy had been shot three or four hours ago.

Surprise: Father Bryce was not entirely the dink he had thought. Because who else could it have been? He must have come here on his way to Knightriders.

Maybe it was the tattoo. Maybe it was changing him.

Clay would have to phone his handler to acquaint him with the altered situation, but not from the phone here in the house. He switched off the lamp and retraced his steps to the back door. Just as he was about to get into Father Bryce's car, a dog walker appeared in the alley behind the garage.

"Good evening, Father," said the dog walker.

"Good evening," Clay answered as he got into the car. Inside the car, he almost had to laugh out loud at the weird good luck that had led him to put on the priest's uniform. It was dark by the garage. The woman walking the dog had seen a man in a Roman collar getting into a black Lincoln. If the woman thought to tell the police about it, that's all she'd be able to tell them.

It really was as though God were looking after him. There was no *reason* he'd changed into the priest's clothes. He just liked trying on different kinds of costumes, and this was one kind he'd never tried on before.

Just to be on the safe side, he changed back into his own clothes before he returned to the thruway. No one saw him. Everything was going to be okay. Even so, as he drove back to Little Canada, he felt edgier and more strung out than he would have been if he'd made the hit himself.

XVI

The whirring he had thought, as he woke, to be the sound of the tattoo gun was, in fact, the buzzing of many bees. He was outdoors, on his back, looking up through branches of white blossoms at an overcast sky. When he tried to shoo away the bees that hovered inches above his face, he found his arm encumbered by a kind of thick blanket or cloak. And on the middle finger of his right hand was a ring with a preposterously large green stone.

He thought: It's happened again. The pain of the tattooing had tipped him back into this other world.

A garden this time. Fruit trees in blossom, but the day so cloudy the petals seemed to have no radiance. Nor perfume, for the air was rank with the smell of composted waste. Father Bryce had stood in for a convalescing pastor, briefly, in a town near the Iowa border that suffered, when the wind was from the wrong direction, from a similar stench, which had been generated by a fertilizer factory. The garden abutted a meagerly windowed building built of massive blocks of cut stone, and it was enclosed on the other three sides by a high wall of the same cyclopean stonework. A large, lichen-crusted calvary formed the centerpiece of the garden. The figure of the crucified Christ was almost ludicrously primitive, goggle-eyed and eagle-beaked, like some African ceremonial mask.

He was not alone in this garden. A monkish figure fidgeted in the recessed doorway of the building, glancing toward Father Bryce and then averting his glance, like an anxious waiter in a restaurant with few customers. It was the same fat little priest he'd struck, and screamed at, in his earlier dream. But he was also, Father Bryce realized now, a metamorphosed version of the tattooist, Wolf.

Alert to Father Bryce's glance, the fat priest took a few hesitant steps forward and asked, with a reverent cringe, "Are you recovered, Your Grace?" He spoke in a language that Father Bryce could not identify—not Latin, not Italian, not French, but with a flavor of each—though he was able to take in the sense of it without difficulty.

To reply was difficult until he stopped trying to think of the particular words he meant to say and aimed simply for a certain tone of voice, one that might elicit an explanation of his situation without betraying his entire estrangement, the fact that he had no notion who he was or what was expected of him. He found the tone, and the words came: "I am still . . . a bit confused."

"Naturally, Your Grace. You are unaccustomed to the close air, and the fetor, of the crypt. Not to mention having to witness those things being done. If one is not used to the methods that must be used in interrogation, the sight can be unsettling. Even though one understands that those being put to the question have brought on their own sufferings by the sin of heresy, one feels an instinctual compassion. A revulsion, such as one might feel in a slaughterhouse if one were not schooled in the work of butchering. You will recall that I advised against your accompanying the Legate into the interrogation cells. He is inured to these things. You might even say it is his trade."

"And the Legate . . . where is he now?"

"Still below, Your Grace. Examining the woman."

Your Grace. He was always Your Grace, which implied the rank of bishop or archbishop. The coarse, scratchy robe in which he was dressed (*it* was the source of the stench) would seem to contradict such a high self-estimate. But then there was this extraordinary ring. He looked at the stone intently, but knowing nothing of the craft of jewelry, he could not tell if it was a genuine emerald or . . . whatever. Of course, in dreams bishops and beggars are all one.

"Would Your Grace care for a cup of water? Perhaps a sip of red wine, as a tonic?"

"Some wine, yes."

While the fat priest went to fetch the wine, Father Bryce pushed himself—with a flash of pain in the small of his back—up into a sitting position, resting his shoulder against the knobbed bole of a fruit tree. A few petals fluttered down from the branches above to settle on the rough fabric of his robe. He fingered the robe's stiff, dirt-encrusted sleeve. His fingernails were grimed, and the skin about the knuckles was cracked and caked with dirt.

He was filthy, in the way that some derelicts become filthy, as though his flesh, unbathed for months, had made an insectile exoskeleton, a mortar compounded of dirt and its own exudate, not to be removed except by surgery. Had even the bishops of the Middle Ages been so unsanitary as this? But no, he was dreaming—with an uncanny verisimilitude, truly, but all this was a product of his own unconscious mind. His filth-encrusted skin was his mind's metaphor for the tattooing, and all too apt.

The fat priest returned, accompanied by a boy who appeared to be eleven or twelve years old. The boy knelt beside Father Bryce and offered him a large goblet of crudely wrought silver, filled almost to the brim with red wine. He received it with a nod, and the boy stood up and took some steps back.

He tasted the wine, which seemed at once raw and exquisite, like a fine St-Émilion decanted too soon. Yet even in its rawness there was a grace, a flavor of grapes still warm from the vineyard. Did all his dreams have such sensory authority as this, which the waking mind at once forgot? It was not just the tang of this wine. Every detail of the scene about him had the texture of reality intently observed. Everything in the garden seemed to exist with a fullness and vibrancy that brought back those first delicious minutes when he'd taken the LSD with Lance. The petals on the trees were whiter and lighter, the wine server more exquisitely youthful, the wine more savory, while all that was unpleasant was, similarly, more acutely unpleasant: the coarseness of the wool, his scaly skin, an incipient toothache triggered by the wine, and, underneath it all, its ground bass, a panicky feeling that he was trapped within the stone walls of the garden. He could feel the same undertow of paranoia that had taken over during his acid trip. Perhaps the tattooing had reactivated the drug. Perhaps there was a room within his mind where the drug continued to exert its force, like a lamp left switched on in a basement closet, its light invisible until the door has been opened.

"Silvanus."

Unthinkingly, as a dog might look upon hearing someone speak its name, he turned his head, and there beside the calvary was a man in the white habit of the Dominican order. He had a tonsure of the sort one saw in old paintings of saints, but his face was anything but saintlike. He seemed, as much as any actual human being could, to have been the original for the bug-eyed, bird-beaked Jesus of the calvary. A death-camp face—cheeks hollow, a bony chin, the lips retracted from the unhealthy teeth not in a smile but from a simple insufficiency of flesh.

"And *your* fear was that *I* should lack fortitude if I accompanied you to the crypt," the skeletal monk said in a whining, nasal voice and in another language than the fat priest had spoken. In Latin, Father Bryce realized as the man went on—a Latin not much different from the scholastic Latin in which his theology classes had been conducted when he was studying in Rome; a desiccated, flavorless language from which anything specifically human had been effaced.

"I did have some trepidation beforehand, I will admit. In Rome, God be praised, we do not have a large population of heretics. Of sinners, a sufficiency; that is to be expected. The sinners of Rome sin after the flesh, like the offspring of the bondwoman Hagar, but the sinners of *these* lands—of Toulouse and Carcassonne, of Montpellier and Rodez—sin not after the flesh, but in their very souls, which is more terrible. Aware of this, how should we feel compassion for their fleshly sufferings? They will enjoy worse torments hereafter than any that the civil arm may exact. I think I would feel more pity for a bull being baited for the amusement of a mob, which I understand is a custom of these parts, than for the woman whose interrogation we took part in so briefly."

"Indeed," Father Bryce murmured. "I cannot account for my weakness, but it has passed. I am better now." To testify to this he tilted the silver goblet to his lips and drank a deep draught of the wine.

"Yet there is a lesson to be learned from your very weakness, just because it was a fleshly weakness. You surely did not *wish* to faint away the moment the knife was put to the woman's breast, and yet your animal nature rebelled. As mine did, I must admit. Though I did not faint, salt tears came to my eyes, just as might have been the case if I'd walked into a bitter winter wind. Were they tears of pity for her suffering? No, I cannot pity a heretic. They were tears after the flesh. And were we to let the rabble witness the work of interrogation, they would feel the same *animal* pity, and they would say these Albigensians were martyrs to their faith, and for every heretic that we exterminated, seven more would spring up in his place. The Church, in her infancy, grew by just such means. The martyrs who were thrown to the lions in the Colosseum were the Church's most effective missionaries. The Roman Church must not repeat, here, the mistake made by the Roman emperors. Some few heretics, to be sure, must be burned before the public, as an example and a warning, but it must be done in such a way that the mob will see their execution as a kind of sport. They must be made to be figures of fun, fitted out with peculiar hats and donkey ears. Or they may be offered to the crowd, like the bulls butchered in the arena, as objects of a communal blood lust. I have noticed that older women, such as the one we were visiting just now, produce the most consistently gratifying response."

As he spoke, the Legate would twine his bony fingers nervously, flexing and loosing them, playing brief arpeggios on an imaginary keyboard, and then, of a sudden, clasping his hands tightly together, as though they'd been caught in some guilty act and had to be restrained.

"Could I offer you some wine?" Father Bryce asked, not at all certain of what decorums he must maintain with the Legate. He felt like an actor called on to perform in a play whose script he's never seen, having to improvise from moment to moment on the basis of the hints thrown out by the other performers. It was only a guess that this garrulous cadaver was the Legate the fat priest had mentioned.

As for the time and place in which he found himself, he supposed the earlier Middle Ages and (from the towns cited as heretical) southern France, where the Church had, indeed, proclaimed a crusade against Albigensian heretics. Exactly when that crusade had taken place Father Bryce had no very clear idea. Though he'd often had to study Church history, those courses had not examined such episodes in detail. There'd been a sense that to do so was tantamount to assisting the Church's secular enemies in their work of mockery and muckraking. What need to examine such embarrassments as the Inquisition, or the Church's opposition to the Copernican universe, or the wars against the Protestant states of Europe? If errors or excesses had been committed at such times, they had long since been regretted, corrected, and expunged.

It seemed strange, therefore, that his dreaming mind should have transported him to an era and a place concerning which he was so ill-informed; even stranger how vivid an illusion had been conjured up. For it did not *seem* like a dream. It had not the accelerated pace that a dream has; it seemed to be happening in real time, at the pace of a Casio watch, with each second numbered and accounted for. This

Legate (as he supposed him to be), though somewhat grotesque physically, spoke plausibly and persuasively and with a logic not the logic of dreams. Even in his grotesqueness he was plausible enough, for Father Bryce had had parishioners quite as ugly as he. For instance, that latter-day crusader Gerhardt Ober bore a pronounced resemblance (now that he thought about it) to the Legate. Were the Legate some thirty years older, and naturally bald instead of tonsured, and if he'd had a bit more meat on his bones, he'd have been Gerhardt's brother, if not quite his twin.

The Legate/Gerhardt accepted the offer of wine, and after Father Bryce had managed to get to his feet with the help of the cupbearer (now the problem wasn't his back but his knees), the two men entered the building. At once, the fat priest came up to him and suggested, "If Your Grace does not intend to return at once to the crypt, he will want to divest himself of these rags?"

Grateful for this chance to explore other parts of his dreamworld, Father Bryce excused himself to the Legate and followed the fat priest up a narrow, steep stone staircase that taxed his bum knees and back with equal cruelty. He was taken to a large room furnished, it seemed, only with coffins embossed with brass studs in geometric patterns. The fat priest opened one of the coffins, and it proved to be a kind of wardrobe.

"I should like to bathe," Father Bryce declared, "before I dress. Could you have . . ." The word did not come to his tongue. Perhaps the concept of a bathtub did not yet exist. He reformulated his desire. "Could you have water heated for that purpose?"

The fat priest regarded him with astonishment. "You wish to bathe? This soon before Easter?"

"As soon as possible."

The priest bowed his head. "As Your Grace commands."

"And I should like to be assisted by the young man who brought the wine to me in the garden."

"You wish Ansiau to assist you in *bathing?*"

Clearly, there were limits to what even a bishop might ask for in this dreamworld, and Ansiau was outside those limits. Well, he thought, another time. "Let him pour the water into the . . ." Again, the word would not come.

"Into the lavabo, Your Grace?"

"Yes, exactly."

"I shall so instruct him, Your Grace. Meanwhile, what are Your Grace's intentions?"

"I shall wait here, or"— he waved his hand—"in one of the rooms close by." Then, to be sure the priest got his message: "You may leave."

As soon as he was alone, Father Bryce went to the room's single window and only source of light, a squat pillared arch, unglassed and placed so high on the wall that he had to pull over one of the coffin-shaped chests and mount it (careful of his back) in order to see the view. Which consisted only of foliage, some close to the window, some at a distance, and a stretch of untrafficked dirt road. It was a prospect that stood outside of time—a summer afternoon (or morning) in the century of one's choice. He was about to get down from the chest when, as though to mock his curiosity, he heard, off in the distance, someone whistling a familiar tune. At first he couldn't place it, for the whistler had subtly warped the melody, making something faintly liturgical of it. But then his memory filled in the unsung lyrics: "Oh, I believe in . . ."

"Yesterday": the perfect anachronism. Yes, indeed, here was a yesterday as far from his troubles as any yesterday could get. He listened to the song with the same sense of dreamy comfort it had given him when he'd listened to it, late at night, on the illicit transistor radio in his room at Étoile du Nord. The whistler continued for about as long as the song might have played on the radio, and then fell silent. But the song had delivered its message; Father Bryce felt comforted.

Getting back down to the floor was more difficult than getting up on the chest had been. Was it arthritis? That's what his brother worried was happening to him. Did his own future have these pains in reserve for him? Did one's body know in advance the ills encoded in its genes? When he got to be sixty, would he stifle a groan each time he had to genuflect, as Father Cogling did?

The adjoining room offered the same uninformative view from its pair of windows, but its appointments were ampler, if still rather spare. One large chair of carved wood, flanked by two benches. The walls hung with tapestries that had been hand-embroidered (rather than woven) with stiff, wide-eyed figures of saints and clerics brandishing croziers and crosses and sundry emblems of their martyrdom. A large fireplace with the charred remains of what must have been a considerable fire. There were also sconces on the walls, some with candles in

them, others simply crusted with the drippings of candles that had illuminated some earlier dream he did not remember.

He began to feel uneasy, as though the dream were something
other than what it seemed; as though he'd been caught in some kind of
trap. He would have wished himself awake, even though that would
have meant returning to Knightriders Kustom Ink, but wishing did not
accomplish anything. In that respect, at least, his dream was properly
dreamlike. What was undreamlike about it was its prosaicness. One
didn't voyage back through the centuries and across oceans in order to
savor a young St-Émilion and to tour empty episcopal palaces. But no
doubt his dreamworld was so tame precisely because the world he was
escaping from was too exciting, too dangerous, too terrible. Here he
could be an archetypal priest of the Middle Ages, speaking in Latin,
going unbathed for the forty days of Lent, tippling from a silver goblet,
taking his ease on an episcopal throne carved with acanthus leaves.
Though not taking much ease from it, for the idea of comfort seemed
not to have been invented yet.

He had to wait some time for the water to be readied for his bath.
And that seemed the oddest thing of all, to *wait* for something in a
dream. Dreams are generally excessively eventful, but not this dream.
When he went out into the corridor to explore other parts of the episcopal palace, he found the fat priest hovering in attendance, and he was
assured that his water would be ready presently, that he must wait only
a few moments more.

"What time is it?" he asked the fat priest, who lifted his hands to
pantomime his incomprehension.

"The hour of the day," he elaborated.

"It is approaching terce."

Father Bryce knew that terce was one of the canonical hours, and
that it came before sext and after prime, but none of that was any help.
He still had no idea what o'clock it might be, except that it was not yet
evening.

The water was brought, a ceramic basin containing about four
quarts of tepid water. There was no soap, but a large towel of coarse
linen was placed beside the basin. As he began to pull the filth-stiffened
robe over his head, the fat priest grabbed hold of the boy who'd
brought the water and hastened out of the room with him. And truly,
the state of his naked body, unwashed for weeks, was not a pretty sight.
"Bring *more* water!" he called out after them.

By the time they had returned with a second basin (he draped the linen towel about himself, toga-fashion, so they might enter the room, which they did with eyes downcast), he had managed to clean off just those parts of his torso that had been covered by the tattooist's blasphemous design. The symbolism of his action seemed transparent: He was washing off the tattoo. But it seemed *wrong* (in the sense, once again, of being undreamlike) that he should be conscious, as he dreamt, of the symbolism of his dream.

By the time he'd gone through a third basin and the terra-cotta floor about the basin was puddled with the filthy water, he was simply too exasperated and too chilly to think about such logical niceties. He wasn't really clean yet, not by the standards of his own century, and his skin, stripped of its exoskeleton of dirt, itched terribly (he was certain he had lice), but he wanted to be dressed and busy about some more exciting purpose.

Maybe he should suggest returning to the crypt, where the heretics were being tortured. But despite the fact that his dream presented such a possibility, he wasn't really that keen to witness such things, not even if they were phantasms. The Legate had said something about a knife being put to a woman's breast. Father Bryce had had no very great interest in women's breasts in the twentieth century, whether bared or bra-ed, and the thought of threatening a naked breast with a knife was distasteful and disgusting.

Then it came back to him: the woman who'd entered the back room of the tattoo parlor after Wolf had begun his work. She'd worn a tank top that exposed both her breasts, which were elaborately tattooed. Her arms were tattooed as well, and her shoulders. She had ridiculously long, cherry-red fingernails. She had touched his penis. She'd asked Wolf if she could take over his tattooing. That's when he'd fainted. That was why he'd come here.

"Will you dine now, Your Grace?" the fat priest asked.

"I guess there's nothing else I *can* do at this point, is there?" He smiled oddly.

The priest gestured toward the clothes that had been laid out for him atop one of the coffin-shaped wardrobes. "Then I will tell the Legate that you are dressing and will join him shortly."

17

Silvanus knew almost as soon as he opened his eyes that he was in hell. One minute he had been witnessing the interrogation of the heretic Aielot de Gaillac in the crypt of Notre Dame de Gevaudon, and the next he found himself strapped down to a pallet, much as Madame de Gaillac had been, while she, by a kind of infernal symmetry, had been transformed into a succubus or a female demon and was using an instrument of torture upon the exposed and anguished flesh of *his* male member. Her unbound breasts, which the interrogator had been about to cut from her body, remained intact, and now were covered with Satanic embroideries—images of serpents and flowers twined together, illuminating her flesh as if it were a living parchment. Her very flesh had become an emblem of an Eden fallen into the power of hell, where the serpent might live among the roses without the fear of God.

To his amazement, when he had seen the knife pressed against the heretic's flesh, he had fallen into a swoon. It had not been the thought of the butchery that had unmanned him, nor yet his animal response, which had been one of arousal—an arousal he had not encouraged by any act of self-stimulation and which was therefore guiltless. His distress had sprung, rather, from an intense, unreasoning pity for the heretic and, correlative to that, a doubt as to the necessity, even the justice, of her being put to the question in this manner. That doubt had passed beyond a scruple to a conviction that the interrogation was a sinful act and that his motive for having Madame de Gaillac examined by the Inquisition was not a godly abhorrence of heresy but, rather, a carnal pleasure in witnessing her tortures and a further satisfaction in thinking that the Church would soon attach her properties, which were among the most considerable in Montpellier-le-Vieux. It was just as he had formulated these misgivings that he had swooned, and been transported to this chamber of hell. But had he been brought here in the flesh, as the pain of his torture seemed to suggest, or was this a vision?

He had had one such vision before, on the feast day of Saint Macarius, following the accident in the sacristy when Abbé St-Loup had bled onto the white wool of the pallium, and he had found himself in this same chamber with his flesh being covered with the heraldry of hell. The man, or demon, whom he'd seen then and who so much resembled St-Loup, was present again, standing behind the succubus who was torturing him. The man's hands played with silver rings that hung from the pierced nipples of her painted breasts, like the rings placed in the snout of the pig, an animal symbolizing female lust. *Her* snout was beringed, as well, and each ear was a little marketplace of finely crafted silver. The Bishop almost forgot the pain he was suffering in the amazement of seeing Madame de Gaillac so bizarrely transfigured.

"Hey," said the hellish version of St-Loup, "better ease up. He's awake."

"Yeah, but I think he's like me, I think he grooves on it. His dick is sure as hell hard as a rock."

Madame de Gaillac laid down the instrument of torture while continuing to grasp his male member in her other hand. Both hands had bright red claws instead of fingernails. She smiled at him. "Hi. We were never formally introduced, but I know you're Damon. I'm Delilah."

It seemed to make much more sense that one would meet the Philistine whore Delilah here in hell than an Aveyronaise heretic who had yet to be dispatched to her reward. Did that mean that the succubus was *not* Madame de Gaillac, despite the strong resemblance? Or could she somehow be both women, Delilah *and* Aielot de Gaillac? He remembered that St-Loup, in the earlier vision, had addressed him then too as Damon. Perhaps in hell one's Christian name is forfeited and one assumes a new name reflecting the fact of one's damnation. Thus, Madame de Gaillac had become Delilah, as he was now Damon.

"Hail, Delilah!" the Bishop said, speaking the language of hell with an uncanny fluency, as though it were indeed his native tongue. And then, from a conviction that it was always politic to render obeisance to one's liege, he declared: "All praise to the power and glory of Satan!"

This provoked the mirth of both the succubus and the demonic St-Loup, who, even so, added his own oath of fealty. "Yeah, right on, man—hail fuckin' Satan."

"You're really into that devil shit, aren't you?" Delilah asked respectfully.

There was no help for it. Hell set the terms here. So he followed her prompting and said, "Yes, praise to Satan's shit. Praise to his piss as well."

"Hey," Delilah said with a snaggletoothed smile, "you are one weird motherfucker."

The Bishop was too shocked to respond at once. Needless to say, he had never committed incest with his mother. That was an outright lie—but then in hell lies would be the order of the day. Moreover, to be accused of incest would be a compliment. So, after thinking this through, he said in a tone of modest pride, "Thank you."

"Well, Satan can be real proud of you tonight, Damon," St-Loup said with a chuckle. "Here, I'll show you."

As in the earlier vision, St-Loup held up a silvery speculum large enough that Silvanus could see his entire torso in it. The horned face of Satan was now inscribed there with a clarity and precision surpassing the best illuminations the Bishop had ever seen. The leering face itself, with its hollow eye sockets and snarling mouth, was formed from roiling clouds of smoke, but the smoke had thickened, darkening and becoming more convoluted, and colored flames now shot up all about the face like fiery hair. There had also been added, on his abdomen (or else he'd not noticed it during the earlier, more fleeting vision), the figure of a Norman horseman carrying a flaming brand, whence issued the smoke forming the Satanic face. Interpreting this allegorically, the Bishop took it to mean that it was the Crusaders at war *against* the Albigensians (who had been summoned from Normandy and the Ile de France, and ultimately from the far north of Europe) who were the true vassals of Satan, just as the Albigensians maintained. Could it be that in assisting in the extermination of their heresy he had actually been assisting in the work of Satan? Unthinkable—but how else to interpret this allegory branded on his very flesh?

"Well," St-Loup insisted, "whadaya think?"

"It is"—he had almost said "very good," before he remembered he was in hell—"evil. It is truly evil."

"Another satisfied customer," St-Loup said, putting aside the speculum, and beginning to loosen the knots of the ropes by which the Bishop's arms were bound to the pallet. "Sorry we had to tie you down like this, but a couple times your muscles started spasming. Nothing serious, but it made it hard to work. You was out a long time, so I was able to get a lot done. One more session like this and we'll be through. Unless, of course, you've got some other ideas for more shit you want done. Like, why not a full bodysuit? If you dig that idea, I'd be happy to lower the rate, if that would make it easier for you financially. When I first set the price over the phone, I figured we'd need more sittings, but your blanking out the way you do makes it a whole lot easier for me to concentrate on the needlework. So think about it, okay?"

"Okay," said the Bishop. Unbound, he was able to look at his own hands, which were as he remembered them. He'd thought that his fingernails might have been turned into claws, like Delilah's.

"I'm sorry I can't offer you any more booze. Delilah killed the bottle that was here. But I know an after-hours place that's still open. It's a little late to get polluted, but a couple brews would hit the spot right now. Whadaya think?"

"Okay," said the Bishop. *Okay* seemed to be the most acceptable form of obeisance. It was strange how St-Loup dealt with him—not as a new arrival in hell but as one of its regular denizens, familiar with its customs and leal to its liege. Undoubtedly it behooved the Bishop to continue to act as though this were the case, as though he were the willing companion of these demons. In that way, disguised as a demon himself, he might be spared the worst of hell's tortures. Why he had been assigned the role of one of hell's familiars he could not imagine, unless it was that in the afterlife our worst punishment will be to commit in a perfected form those sins that earned us our damnation, that hell's cruelest punishment is just to be ourselves, the selves our sins have formed. He had heard theologians maintain this, but he'd felt only contempt for such doctrines, which seemed designed to minimize the terrors of hell. Who would cease sinning if the only punishment threatened were to reenact one's sins throughout eternity? The heaven promised to Mussulmen was precisely that—a harem where the lustful might gratify their lust forever. Perhaps *this* was the heaven of the infidels! Perhaps the infidel heaven and the Christian hell were the same place, like cities whose peoples speak two languages and which are called sometimes by one name and sometimes by another.

"We can take my Jeep," St-Loup said, "if you don't mind Delilah sitting on your lap. Come to think of it, you must be a little sore down there."

"I like the pain," the Bishop assured him. "The pain is evil." He had noticed, observing the interrogations of heretics, that any expression of fear of the torture continuing, any visible trepidation, would excite the torturers to inflict new pains. Ergo: To avoid pain, he must accept and even praise it.

His calculation seemed correct, for Delilah gave a final pinch of her talons to his male member, and said, "Hey, you're my kind of guy."

The Bishop pushed himself up into a sitting position and then got off the pallet and stood upon the actual floor of hell. Where he had been tortured, his flesh was sore, but the customary pains of his body had been intermitted. He could twist his back freely, and flex his knees. His toothache was gone. How long had it been since he'd been without his toothache?

"Well," said St-Loup, opening a finely carpentered door, "shall we go?"

"Okay," said the Bishop. He walked through the opened door and entered another larger, and noticeably hotter, chamber of hell, lighted, like the room where he'd been tortured, with long cones of unwavering brightness, candles that burned without flame or smoke.

Ahead of him was another door, and he walked toward it, feeling something almost like eagerness to see more of hell.

Behind him, Delilah and St-Loup laughed in a gleeful way, not maliciously as one would expect of devils, but as parents laugh at the antics of a favored child. He turned around to know the source of their merriment.

"Aren't you forgetting something?" St-Loup asked.

"Am I?"

"Your clothes?"

"Oh."

Even though his two companions were wearing clothes, it had not occurred to him that he must dress to promenade through hell. Admittedly, their tailoring was quite indecent—each of them in breeches of black cloth that was molded to the contours of their legs and loins and each wearing, above their waists, doublets imprinted, like their flesh, with heraldries of hell. On St-Loup's doublet, a snarling wolf, punning on his name, as heraldic devices so often do; on hers, a single word declaring her shame, BITCH.

St-Loup pointed him to where his clothes lay in a heap atop a chair wrought (it seemed) from armor plate. Hell was better furnished than the episcopal palace in Montpellier-le-Vieux. Indeed, even this torture chamber boasted a superfluity of furniture, with several steel chairs (not stools), other chairs of wood, and two thronelike chairs built of cushions, as though meant for sleep. There were shelves and cupboards to house the instruments of torture, and even a small library of thin illuminated manuscripts. Two of these were placed on a low table, and by the same occult gift that enabled him to understand the demons' speech, he could read their titles: *Outlaw Biker Tattoos* and *Tattoo Digest*. The illuminated binding showed other succubi like Delilah, painted with such artistry that one might think them alive.

There was no time to examine these manuscripts. He must dress in order to accompany St-Loup and Delilah to their infernal revels. First, he pulled on the breeches, which were made of a blue fabric as sturdy as drugget yet as yielding as the softest muslin. There were shoes that bore some charm or demon's name unknown to him: ADIDAS. When he sat upon the chair to put the shoes on, he noticed that his feet had been scrubbed as clean as the skin of a suckling infant, the nails trimmed and calluses removed. Indeed, all his skin had been similarly cleansed and softened, no doubt to make it more receptive to torture. With each movement of his body as he fit his feet into the shoes, he could feel the fabric of the breeches caressing his legs.

Now the doublet. He studied it, uncertain if it was to be put on so that it opened to expose the chest or the back. He decided that he would be expected to display the torture that had been done to him, and when he wore the doublet so, St-Loup gave him a nod of approval.

"Gonna fly your colors tonight, huh?" Delilah said.

The Bishop nodded, and then, just to be on the safe side, repeated the oath of fealty that St-Loup had spoken earlier: "Hail fucking Satan."

St-Loup chuckled. "A week ago," he said, "I wouldn't of believed this, Damon. You're a changed man. I guess it's like I said about how the tattoo's like a door. Except I never seen *anyone* come out of that door at quite the speed you're going. Maybe a bull at the rodeo coming out of the chute. But hey, that's okay. I like it. I think Delilah likes it, too." He winked at the succubus. "Am I right?"

"Fuck you, Wolf," she said amiably. "And you," turning to the Bishop, "should zip your fly. Here, let me." She came up to the Bishop and reached inside the front opening of his breeches to nip his male member one last time, then sealed the cloth together by a quick motion of her talons.

St-Loup—or Wolf, to call him by his hellish name—touched an ivory plaque on the wall, and at once the flameless candle overhead was extinguished. The Bishop followed the two demons through the door and beheld, above the quivering silhouettes of windblown trees, a sky full of stars. He could even recognize the constellations—Lyra, Cygnus, Cassiopeia. They shone but dimly, as though obscured by smoke or mist, but that they shone at all astonished him. Was he, then, *not* in hell? Could hell have a sky with constellations identical to those of the earth?

"They're bright out here, ain't they?" Wolf said. "Closer in to the city, you almost forget there's stars up there."

A brighter light than the stars appeared suddenly at the horizon— not singly, but paired with another of equal brightness—and swooped forward like a double comet, threatening destruction. Wolf and Delilah gave it no heed, and as it sped by, the Bishop realized that what he'd thought an aerial phenomenon was in fact a very small armored house much like the one that Wolf was entering now. It moved on wheels by its own power, or else by the power of the demons within. The Bishop had always supposed demons were winged, but then he'd supposed that hell was beneath the earth and had no view of the stars.

Wolf bade the Bishop take the seat beside him within the armored house, opening a second door that he might enter. Delilah followed him into the house and seated herself on his lap, which was a source of excruciating pain to his tortured flesh. Pleased to inflict new pain, Delilah smiled and pressed her mouth against the Bishop's in an obscene kiss, her tongue acting as only lips may be allowed, even between spouses. Yet, just as his tongue had pronounced Satan to be its liege, and would speak any other words that hell required, so now it shared in Delilah's carnal transgression. He received her tongue in his mouth and protruded his into hers, tasting her spit. Was it only minutes ago that he had seen the Inquisition's servitors begin to amputate this woman's breasts?

As though he'd spoken this question aloud, the succubus took his left hand and guided it beneath her doublet to grasp the pliant tissues of her right breast. Hesitantly at first, and then greedily, like a suckling babe, he palpated the complex flesh, aware of structures beneath the skin that eluded his touch and his understanding. The Bishop was not without all carnal knowledge, but such times as he had taken women in his arms, their breasts had not been unbound, nor had he placed his hands directly upon them. The experience was arousing, in an animal sense, but also physically distressing, a sensation that combined a sense of famishing hunger with a wrenching disgust and nausea.

Delilah pulled her tongue from his mouth and whispered in his ear, "Hey, come on, *twist* it!" Her talons guided his fingers to the pierced, beringed nipple as her tongue pressed into his otic orifice. He groaned with a pleasure that expressed, in a language that dogs or cattle would have understood, his complete surrender to the requirements of hell. Just as Esau traded away his father's estates for a bowl of porridge, so the Bishop for the sigh and the shudder of this single ravished moment was ready to cede an eternity of heavenly bliss. He had no desire beyond the pleasure of this instant.

Even as his flesh gloried in its own damnation, the armored house flew forward through space with inconceivable velocity. Had he doubted, seeing the stars above his head, that he was in hell, he could have doubted no longer, for only supernatural forces could have propelled a house and inhabitants at such speeds. And now, as Delilah's tongue resumed its first indecency, the lights of other such houses as theirs flared up in front of them and then were swept away. They joined a river of such houses (two rivers, in fact, flowing on a parallel course but in opposite directions), some as large as the Bishop's stables. The beauty of that double river of lights hurtling through space, combined with the carnal pleasure of Delilah's embrace, was such that the Bishop wished he could sing hell's praises aloud. He was in ecstasy.

Unbidden, he took Delilah's other breast in his right hand and squeezed it as though crushing juice from a large lemon. She writhed about, responsive to each increase of pressure, and raked his back with her talons. She withdrew her tongue from his mouth and began biting his face, wherever her teeth could obtain purchase, clamping down and then moving her head from side to side like a hound trying to tear meat from a fresh carcass.

Delilah bit down on his upper lip. There was a sudden, sharp pain, and then the succubus drew back, spitting something black into her hand. "What the fuck!" she said, looking at what was in her hand and then at the Bishop's face.

"What's the matter?" Wolf asked, looking sideways, and then, looking again, he laughed aloud. "You bit off his fucking mustache!"

Delilah began to laugh as well. Her laughter was precisely the same as Madame de Gaillac's, a low chortle full of phlegm.

The Bishop felt relieved. Not knowing that he *had* a mustache (what bishop ever was adorned so?), he had thought the demon had actually bitten off a part of his lip. Her hunger had seemed equal to the task. He curled his tongue up to be sure his lip was intact. There was only a trace of blood, such as might have resulted from being shaved by an inept barber. It was fitting, for had not Delilah acted as a barber to Samson as well? At this thought, he found himself joining in their laughter.

As is so often the aftereffect of laughter, the Bishop felt his carnal impulses waning, and the succubus seemed less eager to tempt him as well. In any case, the little house they were in had reached a new and more amazing precinct of hell, a roadway as wide and smooth as the southmost Rhône as it nears the sea. On both sides of this teeming thoroughfare were buildings, some of ordinary scale, others towering to heights of seven or eight stories, and all of them ablaze with lights of various colors. Many of these lights took the form of messages the Bishop was often unable to interpret, such as XXX HOT PORN XXX or SAUNA HOT TUB BODY RUB. Others served to indicate the presence of a pothouse or stews. It was on a dark plaza behind one of these, the Limbo Bar and Grill, that Wolf brought the armored house to a stop. He touched the wheel by which he had guided the house's motions, and the rumbling sound that had accompanied their flight through hell fell silent. Wolf opened the door beside his chair and stepped into the dark plaza. Delilah did the same.

She pulled down her doublet over her breasts, so that the declaration of her shame was once again clearly legible. Then she said, "Let's party, dudes. Whadaya say?"

The Bishop said, "Okay!"

XVIII

Three days had gone by. Three days and three nights—the days measured only by the gradual lessening and then deepening of the gloom within the episcopal palace, the nights by the slow wasting away of candles until he fell asleep or had become so drunk as to amount to the same thing. But when he woke, it was always to these same stone walls. Could a dream go on so long, at such a humdrum pace? Could one dream a toothache that would not let up? Or kidney stones? He knew what kidney stones were like, having had two large ones taken out, and this pain was the ghost of the kidney stones he remembered—but no pale ghost, a ghost with teeth.

But suppose it was not a dream.

Suppose that in some way he could not explain he had been catapulted back into an earlier existence to become Silvanus de Roquefort, the Bishop of Rodez and Montpellier-le-Vieux, slipping into his life as if it were a tailored suit. The bishop's face, when he saw it reflected in a basin of water, was more or less the face he knew from the bathroom mirror. The teeth were in sorry condition, the skin was mottled with the scars of some childhood disease, but any of his parishioners would have recognized him, even so, as Father Patrick Bryce, the pastor of St. Bernardine's Church in the archdiocese of Minneapolis. Father Bryce and the Bishop were the same person in two different centuries.

Intellectually, even theologically, this was an unacceptable idea. He did not believe in reincarnation—or, for that matter, in time travel. These were the realms of New Age airheads like Shirley MacLaine or, God help us, of A. D. Boscage. After Clay had browbeat him about it, he'd made himself skim Boscage's ridiculous *Prolegomenon*, but he could remember few details, only his general sense of contempt for the man's zigzagging, self-contradictory flights of fancy. But he had a vague recollection that in one of the middle chapters Boscage had traveled to southern France and had one of his time-traveling raptures when he'd visited some ruined cathedral. Then he'd "transmentated" and become some kind of workman at the time the cathedral was being built. Dipping into Boscage's tale, a paragraph here, a paragraph there, Father Bryce had never once been tempted to give any credence to his fabrications. He'd just become more and more impatient with Boscage's incompetence as a writer and with the crudeness of his hoax. As a work of historical imagination, Boscage's account of the Middle Ages was on a par with Prince Valiant in the comics section of the Sunday paper. But suppose something of this sort had really happened to Boscage. It would not have made him a better writer, necessarily. He sounded just as flaky writing about the details of his daily life in the seventies and eighties—the girlfriends, the parties, the hangovers—as when he went into ecstasies of paranoia about his UFO abductions. That was probably one of the secrets of his success. The weirdness of his theories wasn't any weirder than Boscage's everyday life, as reported by Boscage.

And no weirder than Father Bryce's own life here and now. Though *weird* was the wrong word, for on an hour-to-hour basis his life had become a limbo of monotony. Once, on a flight from New York to Rome, bad weather had forced his plane to land at the airport on Malta, where the plane itself had developed mechanical problems, so that he'd had to spend almost two days in the airport waiting room as the promised time of departure was postponed again and again. Malta itself might have been strange, but the waiting room at the airport was like all waiting rooms, with the barest amenities and nothing to distract him from the single question, the same that obsessed him now: When would his plane leave? When would he get back to his own life? Only in the present case, there was not even an airfield in sight beyond a wall of plate glass, with its assurance that the machinery existed that would, sometime or other, effect his release. He didn't know how he had been brought here and could do nothing to expedite his departure. There was no ticket window, no information desk. Perhaps—this had become his worst fear—there was no exit.

That basic anxiety had made it hard to take a disinterested, tourist-like interest in the thirteenth century. In some ways, he realized, he was reacting in classic tourist fashion. During his first visit to Florence he'd gone into a state of culture shock, holing up inside his hotel room, ordering his meals from room service and reading Perry Mason mysteries. He'd wanted nothing to do with the great stone heap of the past, its cathedrals and museums and palaces. It hadn't seemed real to him. The real life of Europe was hidden away somewhere else, where tourists couldn't get to it.

It was like that again. He was a tourist once again, but there were no guides and no guidebooks. He was able, in this case, to speak the language, but he didn't dare to ask directions. The people around him assumed he was their bishop, and it was not an assumption he wished to challenge. His identity was a kind of camouflage. As it had been (it dawned on him) throughout his life as a priest. The collar had always exacted a certain deference and respect from others, even those not of the Faith or at odds with the Church. Like the Pope when he appeared in a motorcade, there had been a barrier of protective glass between Father Bryce and a world that is always potentially hostile. That had made his occasional forays out of uniform, whether cruising the gay bars or just shopping at a mall, seem so enlivening. But he had always had the collar to return to, and when his affair with Donny Petrosky had been discovered and he had faced the prospect of being defrocked, he'd experienced an unbearable dismay. When he'd submitted to the demands of his blackmailer, it wasn't just to save his ass from jail. It was to keep the collar around his neck.

And now that he was the Bishop of Rodez and Montpellier-le-Vieux, he felt the same determination to preserve appearances, even if they were *only* appearances. It would not do to ask too many questions to which the Bishop would be assumed to know the answer, even such a plain question as "Who is that?" or "Where is the bathroom?" Indirection sometimes served. Of someone he had not seen before, he could ask St-Loup, who was a constant hovering presence, "Why is *he* here now, do you think?" Such questions sometimes yielded a forthright answer ("The Deacon, Your Grace? He's come on chancery business, I presume"), sometimes a comment too terse to decode ("It must be that time of the week"), and sometimes one guardedly puzzled ("Why do you ask, Your Grace?"). He could always take refuge in "Never mind" or "I was just curious," but it would not do to be a frequent questioner of matters usually taken for granted.

He was similarly stymied in what should have been the simple matter of reconnoitering the world he'd arrived in, for he was a prisoner not only of his role as a bishop but of the episcopal palace as well. Even there he could not explore at will without causing alarms that often seemed to verge on genuine terror. Silvanus de Roquefort, whom Father Bryce now served in some sense as deputy, must have been a formidable tyrant to those who dealt with him daily. The servants watched him with the transfixed attention that small mammals accord to a roving predator, the ones that have wagered that there is more safety in immobility than in panicked flight. The canons of the cathedral, whose liturgies and rituals defied the clamor of the masons with a steady, solemn din of hymns and chanting, did not react to his unannounced visits with quite so candid an alarm, but they did perform their rites with increased unction and gravity. It was instructive to note the differences in performance style between the thirteenth and twentieth centuries. Here, broader and louder seemed to be the rule. Genuflections were balletic, and the anthems operatic. The dean of the canons, when he led the antiphon, belted out his lines like a Verdi baritone. But so slow. All tempos seemed retarded here—music, speech, the plodding way that people walked—as though someone were holding a finger against the revolving record of reality.

But the palace and cathedral and their grounds represented the limits of the world he could explore. Of the life people led beyond the precinct of the cathedral he knew only what could be inferred from the faces, clothing, and comportment of those who came to worship. He had yet to walk down any street of Montpellier-le-Vieux, for the soles of a bishop's feet were not suffered to tread upon the common cobbles; he must either be borne aloft in a gilded, unsteady episcopal throne, a kind of gargantuan sedan chair, or his carriage must be summoned, and the social world visible to him from either of these conveyances was not much different from the one he knew within the cathedral precinct—gapes and cringes, doffed hats, genuflections, grimaces, and hands stretched out to implore his episcopal blessing. Most of the citizens on the street wore ragged clothes and seemed diseased or stunted or clinically insane—and all but a very few were so gaunt and spindle-limbed within their bulky, stinking clothes that you would have thought a canvasful of Brueghel peasants had been sent off to Buchenwald. Two such expeditions outside the cathedral precinct and his urge to see the larger medieval world was no greater than had been his desire to tour the prisons and AIDS hospices in Minneapolis. His curiosity about extraclerical realities had never been large. He was not the sort to look under the engine of a car or go down into the basement when there were plumbing problems. Rarely had he strayed from the orbit determined by his professional duties—the church, the rectory, various school basements; hospitals and funeral parlors. When President Bush was ridiculed for his naiveté concerning supermarket bar code scanners, Father Bryce had blushed in sympathy: He would have been just as surprised. To have shopped for his own groceries would have been inappropriate and unpriestly. Seven centuries had not changed him much in that respect.

The one way he would customarily have informed himself about an unfamiliar situation was not available to him here. He could not read. There were no newspapers, no bulletins, no files of old letters and memos. Such records as he could discover were the barest inventories of the diocesan holdings in real estate and church furnishings. There was a ledger of rents and tithes that could be expected, parish by parish, and another ledger of expenditures, but Father Bryce could glean little useful information from these sources. Beyond this, the Bishop's library consisted of Psalters, ordinaries, breviaries, and three volumes of the Bishop's own sermons, the parchment still as supple as glove leather.

On the evidence of these sermons the Bishop seemed to have a limited homiletic range. He preached hellfire and damnation and was the scourge of heretics, meaning Albigensians, against whom the Church must show no mercy. The Bishop's diocese—and Montpellier-le-Vieux in particular—was declared to be a hotbed of heresy, and the faithful were regularly exhorted to denounce anyone they suspected to be harboring heretical beliefs, even if the heretics should be their closest kin, for by his own report Christ had come to set son against father, daughter against mother, and so forth. Father Bryce had never had any argument with that. He'd often preached from the same text—Matthew, chapter 10, verses 34 through 39—both on Sundays from the pulpit and on Saturdays, using the confessional as a kind of prompter's box from whose shadows he'd been able to cue a variety of family showdowns and crises, engineering the scripts of dozens of soap operas large and small every week. "My dear child, you must not allow your husband to practice any method of contraception except the rhythm method." Or "The Church does not recognize divorce and certainly does not tolerate remarriage. Your son's children by his second so-called wife are not properly your grandchildren at all, and you must not recognize them as such."

But those dramas had been insignificant compared to what was possible here. Heresy upped the ante exponentially. Here heretics were tortured and burned at the stake. A crusade had been declared against the Albigensians, and the army summoned by the Pope had lately put all the inhabitants of Béziers, just south of Montpellier-le-Vieux, to the sword. That army now was garrisoned in the ruins of the city it had depopulated, and all of Languedoc—from the mountain fastnesses of Toulouse in the west to the barren massif of the Cévennes, where Bishop de Roquefort held his see, waited to know where the army would next turn. It was as though the terrors of hellfire had been summoned from their mythic realm beneath the earth's thin crust and flamed now in plain sight. Heretics had reason to tremble.

It was needful, therefore, for the local clergy to demonstrate to those who represented the papal authority that they were doing everything in their power to root out all known or suspected heretics within each parish and diocese. Without a conspicuous show of zeal, one's own diocese might be fated to become the next target of the Crusaders' restless and ill-provisioned army, which could not sustain itself much longer on the corpse of Béziers. The need for such zeal and how best to display it were presumed to be the Bishop's overriding concerns by all those admitted to his presence, from the lowly but ever-present Abbé St-Loup to the Abbot of Notre Dame de Gevaudon, who served as a kind of deputy bishop at those times when Bishop de Roquefort moved his residence to the collateral diocese of Rodez.

The city of Rodez was not in the same jeopardy as Montpellier-le-Vieux, for it lay outside the area infected by heresy. The invisible line that divided the realms of *langue d'oc* and *langue d'oil*, the southern and northern dialects of the language that was not yet French, bisected his double see, and the Albigensians had taken root only in the hill towns and mountain fastnesses of Languedoc. High altitudes seem to breed a spirit of independence, and in this age independence was synonymous with heresy.

It was impossible, from listening to the talk about him, to determine the particulars of the heretics' faith, only that they denied the efficacy of the sacraments except for one, the *consolamentum*, which could be received only once, at the point of death. Some of the priests—or *perfectas*—who administered this sacrament were women. Abbé St-Loup maintained that if there had been no other proof that the Cathars were in fealty to Satan, that fact alone would have sufficed. Much of what was charged against the heretics struck Father Bryce as generic vilification of the sort that all the Church's enemies have been accused of at one time or another: They desecrated the Host; their women were unchaste, and both sexes practiced abominations (this, despite the Cathars' avowed rejection of *all* forms of sexual congress, even that between man and wife); they were atheists *and* they worshiped Satan; they violated graves.

This last imputation was a classic example of the pot calling the kettle black, for one of the chief activities of the entourage of the Papal Legate and Inquisitor, Durand du Fuaga, had been the exhumation of the corpses of accused heretics; even death was no protection from the attention of the Inquisition. Often those suspected of heresy, when they were examined and threatened with torture, would denounce those already safely dead rather than betray the living, whereupon the Legate would order these dead heretics to be disinterred and have their corpses dragged through the streets on sledges and posthumously burned at the stake. The heirs of these heretics would then be dispossessed of their inheritance, and the expropriated property would be razed to the ground and the very ground declared anathema, never again to be built upon or tilled. Already, in the little time Durand du Fuaga had been at work in Montpellier-le-Vieux, several of the city's most prominent citizens had been dispossessed in this fashion. It had begun to seem that even if the city were to be spared wholesale destruction by the armies of the Crusade, the Inquisition might accomplish the same essential purpose on a piecemeal basis.

For the process of discovering heresy worked like a chain letter or similar pyramidal schemes. First there had been the Legate's proclamation, offering a week's grace period in which any citizens guilty of heresy or with knowledge of a neighbor's heresy were to present themselves to the Holy Office and confess their errors. Those who answered this summons could be meted out only canonical punishments; at worst, they might be sent abroad on a pilgrimage. Then those who had been denounced were summoned and put to the question in turn. Eventually a confession would be obtained, and more names would be named, more summonses issued, and so on, *in saecula saeculorum.*

"And where will it stop?" asked the Abbot in a querulous whisper.

"Can we be sure that all those who are denounced before the Holy Office are truly guilty? What easier way to revenge oneself against an old enemy?"

"Ah, but there are safeguards against that," Abbé St-Loup had countered, with a smile of smug orthodoxy. "There *must* be two accusations, independently obtained."

"And if a man has *two* enemies? And they collude against him?" The Abbot clearly was thinking of his cousin, Guilhabert de Beaujeu, a petty nobleman who had been summoned before the Inquisition and was sequestered at that very moment somewhere in the cathedral's catacombs, awaiting questioning.

"In that case," said Father Bryce, "we must trust in the wisdom and discretion of the Holy Office itself."

"Amen to that, Your Grace," the Abbé concurred, and the discussion was ended before the Abbot had compromised himself any further.

The old man gave Father Bryce a smile of resentment commingled with gratitude, a smile not unlike the wine they had been drinking, its sourness masked with honey and spices. He excused himself from the table, and Father Bryce had only to nod to the Abbé for him to take the hint and follow the Abbot from the room.

At last Father Bryce was able to help himself to the wine without feeling each cupful monitored and tallied by St-Loup and the Abbot. It was a familiar moment of relief, as when loosening an uncomfortable belt or slipping out of too-tight shoes. After the first unobserved full-throated guzzle of the night, it almost didn't matter where he was, Minneapolis or Montpellier-le-Vieux. All that existed was the tang of the grape on his tongue, the quick *ping* of pain as the honey connected to nerves in his rotting teeth, and then the assuaging and solace of the wine sliding down his throat and into his blood. *This* is my body, he thought, and this is my blood. He would drink until there was nothing left in the ewer, and when he had drunk enough to be able to sleep, he would collapse, still clothed, onto the lumpy pallet that was the best mattress this wretched century had to offer for a bishop's repose.

19

"Well, I'm not sure," Mrs. Sanders said, not so much because she wasn't sure—Alison could tell she was delighted at the idea of having her pregnant and unmarried daughter shipped off to limbo for the next many months—but because she had a feeling that Father Cogling was applying sales pressure. Her instincts as a consumer told her that if she showed a little resistance to his sales pitch, he might sweeten the deal with a rebate or some kind of premium.

"And can you say *why* you're not sure?" the old priest persisted. "Do you count on Alison for helping with the upkeep of your home? Is that it?"

Mrs. Sanders succumbed to his lure. "That's part of it," she fibbed, with a nervous glance toward her daughter. When Alison showed no inclination to contradict her, Mrs. Sanders voiced her age-old grievance. "It's been years since I've seen a dime from Alison's father. He owes me thousands of dollars by now, but I doubt I'll ever see any of it. And now *she's* going to be in the same damn situation." She heaved a sigh and examined the lighted tip of her cigarette, as though the answer to her dilemma might be there, coded into the smoke.

"We understand that an unexpected pregnancy often entails hardships, and not only for the young mother. For everyone. If it would be any help, Birth-Right is willing to offer you a small monthly gratuity."

"Such as?" Mrs. Sanders asked.

"Fifty dollars?" the priest suggested.

"Fifty dollars doesn't go very far these days."

"That's true. But our resources are limited."

"It's not just the money."

"Of course not. The main consideration is Alison's welfare. And the child's."

Mrs. Sanders could see that she wasn't going to be able to strike a better deal. "It would be a help. And I can use any help I can get these days." She looked up at Alison, but then her eyes shied away from making contact. "You're sure you want to do this, honey? I don't want you to think you're not welcome in your own home."

"I know that, Mother. And I'm sure. It'll be like a long vacation. I never get out of the city. There's woods, and a big lake."

"You'll be missing your classes. And graduation."

"If the baby's coming around Christmas, I would be anyhow."

Mrs. Sanders stubbed out her cigarette and picked up the Bic pen that Father Cogling had placed on top of the papers she had to sign. She signed each of the three copies without bothering to read them. Once, drunk, she'd bought a set of the *Junior Universe of Knowledge Encyclopedia* the same way. They'd been a present for Alison's eighth birthday, and they'd sat at the foot of Alison's bed, in their own walnut-veneer bookcase, for six months, until the salesman came back to repossess them. Mrs. Sanders hadn't been able to meet the "easy-to-meet" $25 monthly payments. Alison had known she wouldn't, even at the age of eight. She'd missed the walnut-veneer bookcase. It had been the nicest piece of furniture in the trailer.

Alison didn't think she'd miss her home life either, such as it was. For as long as she could remember, she'd felt ashamed of living in a trailer. She didn't know what the place was like where she was going, but she figured it had to be an improvement. She'd asked Father Cogling if he had pictures of it, and he'd shown her a postcard of a weird-looking church you wouldn't have thought was a church at all. It looked more like the top part of a castle. Father Cogling explained that where she'd be living was underneath the church, but it wasn't like a basement, more like a luxury hotel. Each of the girls at Birth-Right had her own apartment, he told her, nicely furnished and roomy.

She liked the idea of "roomy." She'd never lived anywhere that could have been called roomy. The only thing she didn't like was that it was all underground, and there wouldn't be windows anywhere. But then what did the window of her room in the trailer look out on? An alley with the old Oldsmobile that hadn't been driven anywhere since her mother's license was revoked two years ago. All four tires were flat. No, she wouldn't miss being away from home.

The papers were signed, and then it was time to go. That came as a surprise. She'd thought she'd have a week or two to get ready, but no, Father Cogling wanted her to pack a suitcase and be ready for the car that was coming to pick her up in half an hour. "I don't *have* a suitcase," she'd protested, but her mother said, "You can use the trunk." There was a trunk in her mother's bedroom, beside the bed, that she kept old clothes in. So they took the old clothes out of it, mostly her mother's, from when she'd been at Weight Watchers, and Alison packed her own things into it.

It only took five minutes, and by the time she was done, the car had come for her.

"It's a Cadillac," her mother said, parting the curtains of the front window.

Alison wanted to say, "Maybe *you'd* like to go there," but she didn't. She knew that her mother was as embarrassed about this whole thing as she was. And right then, as Father Cogling was folding up the papers her mother had signed and putting them in the inside pocket of his black suit coat, Alison thought, I don't want to do this! But it was too late. Just as it had been too late when she'd had the same thought the night that Greg had knocked her up. The machinery was in motion. She kissed her mother, once on each cheek, and they exchanged guilty looks, a different guilt on each side, but enough to go around. Then she took up the trunk by its plastic handle. Father Cogling asked, "Could I help?" and she smiled and said, "No, it's not that heavy. I can manage just fine."

20

Father Mabbley had not one drink during the entire nightlong flight from Las Vegas to Minneapolis, including an unscheduled two-hour layover in St. Louis. Not a single complimentary glass of wine—despite his terror of airplanes, despite the fact that the flight had taken them through a thunderstorm that had rocked the plane about dreadfully, and despite the further fact that the young woman sitting beside him was consuming Cuba libres in a spirit of abject, apocalyptic panic. Not that rum-and-Cokes had ever been Father Mabbley's undoing. He considered them beyond the pale, the alcoholic equivalent of Cheez Whiz. If he *were* to succumb to a drink before breakfast (though he might as easily have thought of his personal time zone as afterdinner rather than prebreakfast), it would have to be something more tempting than a Cuba libre. So he did his best to tune out the young woman beside him and tried, without a headset, to figure out what was happening in the movie that was being projected, blurrily, onto the pull-down screen on the wall of the cabin, a low-intensity, low-budget shoot-'em-up with a cameo part for Mickey Rooney, who was evidently still alive and making movies. It was like seeing dear old Bing fast-forwarded into old age, and Father Mabbley had a nice, quiet cry in the dark.

The plane landed just as the sun was coming up on a summer morning that had forgot all about bad weather. Father Mabbley hadn't booked into a hotel, and was hoping he wouldn't have to, but that meant he had three hours to kill before he met with Reese Wiley, the lawyer who'd called to tell him about Bing Anker's death and to announce that he stood to inherit most of Bing's estate, which, it turned out, was not inconsiderable. How not-inconsiderable Wiley could not say when they'd spoken on the phone, nor did he have any information about the murder investigation. Father Mabbley for his part had said nothing to the lawyer about his last phone call with Bing and was feeling a little uneasy about not having already contacted the police. Bing's vendetta against Father Bryce would obviously be relevant to any investigation, and from what he'd heard, eavesdropping on their conversation, Father Mabbley had no wish to *shield* Bryce, who had come across as every bit as unsavory as Bing had painted him. Though, in fairness, who would look their best when they're being put through the wringer by a blackmailer? And that had been the name of the game Bing had been playing. Father Mabbley had even warned Bing, after Bryce had hung up, that he might be putting his life at risk. Now he could address an I-told-you-so to Bing's soul in purgatory.

If Father Mabbley was not immediately volunteering all he knew to the police, it wasn't out of consideration for Bryce but, rather, for the sake of the Church. He had benefited more than once himself from the Church's policy of avoiding any scandal that could be discreetly smoothed over. It was only fair to return the favor, at least till he had more knowledge of the situation. It was Father Mabbley's dearest hope that Bryce had had nothing to do with it. Bing might have brought home a piece of rough trade, though Father Mabbley had a hard time imagining that sort of thing happening in Minneapolis, which he thought of as the Little Megapolis on the Prairie, the hometown of Betty Crocker and Mary Tyler Moore and all things bright and home-baked.

Three hours was not an eternity. He would sit down in the coffee shop, dawdle over an overpriced breakfast, and read a book. Fortunately, he had the ideal book for the purpose: *A Girl of the Limberlost*, by Gene Stratton Porter, which, some incalculable number of Christmases ago, Bing had given him in a mint-condition first edition sealed in Saran Wrap. Inscribed on the flyleaf, in what was intended to be calligraphy (but what calligrapher ever used a ballpoint pen?), Bing had written: "A guaranteed five-handkerchiefer! Toujours l'amour! Bing." Father Mabbley had never managed to get past chapter one: "Wherein Elnora Goes to High School and Learns Many Lessons Not Found in Her Books." In her heyday, almost a century ago, Gene Stratton Porter had been accounted, at least by her publisher, Grosset & Dunlap,

"America's most beloved novelist," but now she was a camp classic at best and intolerably mawkish at worst. When he'd learned of Bing's death, Father Mabbley's first irrelevant and irrational thought was "Oh dear, now I'm going to *have* to read that book." It had been sitting on the shelf specially devoted to books toward which he owed a similar guilty debt, some the gifts of well-meaning friends like Bing but just as many his own stalled good intentions. A garage full of cars whose batteries had gone dead and tires were flat, undriven and undrivable. More than one visitor coming upon this one anomalous shelf (in a library that was otherwise a paragon of rational order) had wanted to know what John Ashbery, C. S. Lewis, the Marquis de Sade, Grace Paley, Daniel Defoe, and Gene Stratton Porter all had in common. "They are my guilts," he would explain, "my little aviary of pet albatrosses."

So now, at a table in the airport's coffee shop, in a spirit of penance and remorse, he would actually sit down and read *A Girl of the Limberlost.* He would *not* buy a newspaper or magazine. He would not work yet another crossword puzzle. (Was there a recovery group for crossword puzzle addicts? There should be, and he should be in it.) He ordered Breakfast Number 3, The Paul Bunyan, and started reading. Despite its years in Saran Wrap, the old paper had a powdery feel, as though the pages were self-destructing as he turned them. But he did turn them, and by the time he'd finished the last syrup-sodden pancake on his plate, he was actually caught up in the plot. Gene Stratton Porter had been a pro, and for all its goopy, goody-two-shoes sentimentality, *A Girl of the Limberlost* was a genuine page-turner. You could almost see Lillian Gish doing the role of Elnora, pluckily smiling down each new adversity, charming every stony heart, always winning through and, despite her poverty, always looking radiantly beautiful. Porter's idea of a major life crisis was not having appropriate and pretty clothes, so Elnora, like Cinderella, was forever getting into the right frock in the nick of time. Father Mabbley could see the special charm the book must have had for Bing—the only middle-aged man he'd ever known who still went shopping for his Barbie doll.

Two chapters after his plate had been bussed away, the nice young waitress with elaborately frizzed hair came by with the carafe and asked if he'd like more coffee.

"Yes, thank you," he said, sliding his cup toward her for a fourth refill.

"That must be a good book," she said.

"It's a real page-turner," Father Mabbley agreed.

"It looks like an antique." She turned her head sideways to read the cover. "Gene Stratton Porter? I never heard of him."

"Her," Father Mabbley corrected. "Though you wouldn't think so from the spelling. She was the Stephen King of her time. Though that time was . . . let me see . . ." He looked at the title page. "Nineteen-oh-nine. The age of innocence."

The waitress blushed and wished him a nice day and fled with her carafe. The collar affected some people that way. Or had it been the tone of his voice, the suggestion that *this* was an age of something other than innocence? The clergy were assumed still to be living in the world of Gene Stratton Porter, a world of positive thinking and happy problems, a Brigadoon sort of world that existed only once a week, on Sundays, when everyone was nice to each other and dinner had to be special.

And really, wasn't that the primary reason he'd become a priest—to live all week in Brigadoon? It *was* a nicer world. When people saw the collar, they switched into Sunday mode—those who didn't just seize up or run away, like Eileen (which was the name sewn on the waitress's uniform). Of course, it made one a magnet for sanctimony and false piety, but it also served as a talisman against muggers. Once, when he'd been impaneled for jury duty, Father Mabbley had been the only person who hadn't raised his hand when the judge wanted to know if any of the prospective jurors had ever been the victim of an armed robbery. There was something to be said for living in Brigadoon, even if it was ninety percent wishes, dreams, and lies. Pretend to be nice for long enough, and you might become a genuinely nice person. Jesus, of course, had thought otherwise. Jesus had no use for whited sepulchers.

Sepulcher: The word was like a bell tolling him back to the sorry, un-Brigadoonish reason he'd come to Minneapolis. He'd frittered enough time away with Gene Stratton Porter, so he settled his tab and left a three-dollar tip for Eileen, out of consideration for the time he'd occupied the table, and lugged his suitcase out to the taxi stand, where a taxi was waiting. Father Mabbley gave the driver the address of McCarron's Funeral Home in St. Paul, and then settled back to enjoy the serenity of the freeways. He liked to think that limbo was full of freeways, all going nowhere, safely and peacefully.

Instead, he fell asleep and had a nightmare that had something to do with an AIDS hospice. "Huh!" he said when the driver woke him. He tried to hang on to the details (he entertained an idolatrous faith in the significance of dreams and fortune cookies), but they'd already vanished.

He felt odd toting his suitcase into the foyer of the funeral home, as though he'd come there to live. It was a modest establishment, nothing like the funeral homes of Las Vegas, which were built on the scale of the casinos, with the same glitz. This was more like a cocktail lounge in an upscale hotel, decorated in lingerie colors with tastefully muted lighting and paintings chosen to be unnoticeable: flower prints, a calm sea, a lobotomized Christ. As though to say: Death? Never heard of him. Were there, he wondered, funeral homes that took the opposite tack and mucked around in the horror of the occasion? Would even bikers and heavy-metal fans want to be buried from such an establishment? No, even they, in the end, would probably opt for Brigadoon.

"I'm sorry, sir, but none of the rooms are open yet for viewing."

Father Mabbley turned around to see who'd spoken.

"Excuse me, Father," said a gray-haired man in a dark suit. "I didn't realize."

"That I'm a priest? I'm not here in that capacity, actually. I'm here to pay my last respects to Mr. Anker. Also, I've been asked to be his executor, and I think there are papers I must sign. Is Mr. McCarron here?"

The man blushed. "There is no Mr. McCarron any longer, I'm afraid. You're Father Mabbley?"

He nodded.

"I'm the director. Lloyd Wells."

They shook hands.

"Mr. Anker isn't . . . with us as yet, I'm afraid. Apparently, the coroner hasn't finished his work."

Twice the man had said he was afraid. It seemed an odd verbal tic for someone in his profession.

"And I'm afraid a problem has arisen concerning the funeral service itself." Mr. Wells fell silent, unwilling to impart the bad news unless pressed to do so.

"Yes?" Father Mabbley pressed.

"It seems that the deceased left a request with his lawyer, Mr. Wiley, that he wished his funeral Mass to be said at St. Bernardine's, in

Willowville, where he is, indeed, a parishioner. At least, some part of the time. And he specifically asked that the pastor of St. Bernardine's conduct the service."

"Father Bryce, that would be?"

Mr. Wells nodded.

"And Bryce has declined to do so?"

Mr. Wells shook his head. "No. Not directly, at least. There seems to be some question as to whether Father Bryce can be reached at all. Mr. Wiley has only been able to speak with his assistant, a retired priest living at the rectory, Father Cogling. It seems that Father Cogling has categorically refused to allow the deceased to be buried from St. Bernardine's. First, he intimated that Mr. Anker might have committed suicide, but Wiley assured him that the coroner had firmly discounted that possibility. There's no doubt that Mr. Anker was murdered. Then Father Cogling declared that Mr. Anker had led an openly sinful life and had appeared in public protests outside of various churches in the Twin Cities. Mr. Wiley naturally refused to be led into an argument on such matters and kept trying to contact Father Bryce. Wiley even went to the eleven o'clock service on Sunday, when Bryce usually conducts the Mass, but it had been taken over by another priest, and there was no explanation for Bryce's absence. Mr. Wiley is certain that Cogling doesn't have the authority to deny the deceased burial from St. Bernardine's—he doesn't even have the standing of assistant pastor—but he doesn't wish to make unnecessary trouble. And since we've had to postpone the date of the funeral in any case, and since Mr. Wiley knew you would soon be here, he hoped you'd be able to straighten the matter out, seeing that you're a priest yourself."

"It sounds like you need a private investigator more than a priest," Father Mabbley commented.

Mr. Wells responded with a mirthless laugh and a reproachful glance.

"I should like to have a chance to talk with Mr. Wiley before I take any initiatives myself. I thought he'd be meeting me here."

"Unfortunately, he's had to appear at a court hearing concerning the release of Mr. Anker's corpse. It seems there was an anonymous phone call to the coroner's office suggesting that Mr. Anker may have had AIDS. If that was the case, some other arrangement will have to be made for his interment."

"And why is that?" Father Mabbley demanded.

"For one thing, our embalmer can't be expected to put himself at extraordinary risk."

"And who is your embalmer?"

Mr. Wells cast down his eyes and made no reply.

"Let me understand you better. If Mr. Anker's corpse tests HIV-positive, you will not handle his funeral arrangements?"

"That *is* the policy at McCarron's. Yes, Father."

Father Mabbley could match the man's prissy smile with one of his own, thinking ahead to the moment he would have the satisfaction of telling him what *his* policy would be with regard to McCarron's. But he would not do that now, he would wait till the man had heard from the coroner as to Bing's HIV status and *then*, when Mr. Wells had graciously agreed to admit Bing into his funeral parlor, Father Mabbley would be able to tell him to stuff it. Or, in this case, not to.

"Well," said Father Mabbley, "it sounds like I have some telephoning to do. Do you suppose I could borrow your office?"

Mr. Wells ushered Father Mabbley not to an office but to a small alcove at the far end of the corridor, where there was a love seat, a telephone, and a small gilt-framed reproduction of a Raphael cherub.

His first phone call was to Reese Wiley's law office, where Wiley's secretary told him that Mr. Wiley would be on his way to McCarron's within the hour and asked would he please wait for him there. Then, after getting the number from Information, he called St. Bernardine's rectory and got an answering machine. "Hello," said a voice he recognized as Father Bryce's, "and thank you for calling. I'm sorry I can't come to the phone right now, but if you'll leave your name and number and a brief message, I'll get back to you as soon as I can. Meanwhile, why not get in touch with God—and say a prayer for me while you're talking with Him. We all need each other's prayers. God bless."

He waited for the beep, and then, as per the machine's suggestion, said a Hail Mary, adding, when he was done, "That's for you, Father." He knew he was being petty, but with an answering machine it's hard to resist such impulses. One has the illusion, as when one throws darts at a newspaper photo, that one is zapping an inanimate object, not a real person.

He made himself say a string of Hail Marys, both as a penance and as a way of composing himself, and then he dialed Alexis Clareson's number at the diocese Chancery. Even though it was supposed to be his direct line, there was someone running interference for Alexis, and then even a second gatekeeper. Alexis was now the vicar-general, so it was not to be wondered at that he should make himself ritually unavailable. At last he did pick up and purred into the receiver: "Mab? Is that *you?* Here, in Minneapolis?"

"*C'est moi*, Alex, yes, indeed. Just off the plane, all bleary-eyed and ill-tempered, so I should probably have waited to call."

"But you wanted to *use* me. Right?"

"You're a mind reader, Alex."

"No, it's the price I pay for temporal power. I am *here* to be used, *cher ami*. Even by my oldest and dearest friends. I remember so well: We shared the same tubes of Clearasil. Go ahead, use me."

"I've three favors to ask. First, do you know a funeral home that doesn't discriminate by HIV status? Second, could you find out who's tending the store at St. Bernardine's?"

"Father Bryce is the pastor there," Alexis said.

"But I'm also told he can't be reached, and the other priest who's there with him—"

"That would be Wilfrid Cogling."

"That's the name. Cogling has refused to let a friend of mine be buried from the church. And as I've been appointed to be my friend's executor . . ."

"I like to be asked a favor I can so easily grant. Wilfrid is an old toad and has *no* authority to make such decisions, and I would find a deep personal satisfaction in telling him where to get off. As to the matter of embalming someone who's died of AIDS, one or two of the local funeral homes have made things difficult. Is it McCarron's?"

"Yes. And my friend *didn't* have AIDS and wasn't HIV-positive."

"But it's become a point of honor not to give McCarron's the job? Bravo, I quite agree. *I* would suggest Schinder's Memorial Gardens. It'll cost a bit more, but it's a lot classier, if that matters."

"My friend certainly would have wanted to exit in style."

"What was the third favor?" Alexis asked.

"I need to pick your brain. Perhaps even your personnel files."

"Concerning?"

"The pastor of St. Bernardine's. Patrick Bryce."

"Oh dear. What has he done?"

"It's something you wouldn't want me to discuss with you, Alex."

"I hope it's nothing serious, but I suppose it is. And I won't ask any more. Hear No Evil is the motto here at the Chancery these days. It's virtually carved on the lintel. I'll take Bryce's file home with me tonight, and you're welcome to come by and look at it. Come to dinner tomorrow night, if you can combine business with pleasure. It will be a buffet with three or four strange casseroles and a few familiar faces. Familiar to me, anyhow, but I think you'll recognize one or two of the faces. Not mine, perhaps. I've gone on gaining weight. What else is one to do in a wheelchair except eat?"

"No need to apologize, Alex. Some of the greatest men in the Church were Xtra-Large. John the Twenty-third. Alexander the Sixth."

"The Borgia pope, yes, I know, whom even Raphael couldn't make look anything but a pig. Will I see you?"

"I hope so."

"And if you should come upon something that I really *ought* to know—shred it, will you?"

Father Mabbley laughed, and gave his word.

21

Silvanus had come to the conclusion, somewhat reluctantly, that he was not in hell, and this for three reasons. *Primus:* The sun rose each morning and cast its light upon a world that was not infernal in a subterranean sense. True, there were teeming hordes of people here, as one might expect to be the case in hell, but few were conspicuously in torment. Indeed, they lived amid unimaginable luxuries and pomp, not unlike the riches of Babylon, whose fall was foreseen by the apostle John, when he wrote: *Alas, alas, that great city that was clothed in fine linen, and purple, and scarlet, and decked with gold, and precious stones, and pearls!*

Secundus: Contrary to his first impression, there were no demons here but only men—sinful men, maybe, with great powers of sorcery, but all mortal men of flesh and blood, like the Bishop himself. For a while he had suspected that the illuminated figures that appeared upon the dark glass of Delilah's Trinitron might be demons, but having pondered them for many hours, he now believed that though they were very often grotesque, indecent, and unnatural, they were not actually alive, but only simulacra, the work of cunning artificers, like the image of the Beast that John writes of, that was given breath and the power of speech, so that all men would worship it. The Trinitron (the very name a mockery of the Triune God) revealed not a single beast but a whole menagerie of unclean spirits: some lustful, like the voluptuous Astrud Gilberto or the preening incubus Marky Mark; some warlike, like Popeye the Sailor Man or the Teenage Mutant Ninja Turtles; some wooing evil like a bride, like the two Moors, Geraldo and Oprah; and still others, kindlier, nameless beings, who appeared in intervals as brief as flashes of lightning to promise relief from various forms of suffering—headaches, stomach upset, hemorrhoidal distress. All of these creatures were illusory, all of them. They seemed to live when one manipulated the Trinitron a certain way; with another motion they ceased to exist. Silvanus found it difficult, now that Delilah was dead and no longer a spur to his lust, to do anything but marvel at these shadowy allegories and try to decipher them. His hope was that if he studied the Trinitron closely, it would reveal to him the nature of this new world and, possibly, the means by which he might escape from it.

But then, in the middle of *The Flintstones*, unable to fathom its allegories, which seemed of a sudden inane and infantile, he became bewildered, disgusted, and despairing, as though all the sins of all the phantasmal figures swirling on the glass of the Trinitron had boiled up inside him. He darkened the Trinitron, and, to be doubly sure its simulacra would be stilled, he removed the small flexible pipe by which the Trinitron's sorceries (and myriad others no less marvelous) were accomplished. Delilah had shown him where the pipe connected to other pipes hidden within the walls of her little house. "You got to plug in the cord, dummy!" she'd explained, whipping his bare thigh with the end of the cord, which was tipped with metal like a scourge, which, at first, he'd supposed it was.

Now she was dead, and that was *Tertius*, for hell like heaven is eternal. One cannot die again in hell and thereby escape its torments. And Delilah assuredly was dead. In the hot air of the little house, her body had begun to stink, and her body, once so very limp, had become rigid. A great quantity of blood had soaked into her bed linens and the mattress beneath, and now that blood had dried and darkened. He had killed her, but not by cutting off her right breast. That had been done *after* he had strangled her, in the hope, that by himself performing the act that had caused him such distress when first he'd seen it done by the Legate's torturer, he might undo the sorcery that had transported him into this nightmarish otherworld, this neither earth nor hell. For it had been at that moment, witnessing the interrogation of the heretical Marquesia de Gaillac, that he had been translated into this other realm. It had seemed somehow congruent that he subject Delilah, who so much resembled the Marquesia, to the same chastisement. A futile experiment. So far from undoing the original enchantment, he had only been inflamed with the fires of a further lust, and in his drunkenness he had yielded to the temptress's final, posthumous seduction and ravished her mutilated and bleeding corpse—an act that now, his passion spent, seemed inconceivably vile. What had he become? What had this woman's sorceries made of him?

Silvanus was no stranger to the sins of the flesh. Often enough in his youth, and in maturity as well, he had yielded to his carnal nature. He was human, after all. A tonsure does not change the essence of a man. But never, never had he acted upon his desires as he had done under Delilah's insatiable incitements. When he had sinned heretofore, it had been done in a manner suited to the act, hastily, in darkness, and when he had spent himself, he'd felt repugnance and remorse. With Delilah one act had followed on another, with a lust that was unremitting and that became, finally, its own punishment. She it had been who'd urged him to tighten his hands about her throat, such moments as their mouths were not united in an unholy kiss. Even now, remembering the moment of his supreme penetration, he was possessed by lust. The woman's very corpse seduced him!

And yet this was not hell. Rather, it was the time foretold by the apostle John, the reign of the Antichrist. Once Silvanus had realized that, the world about him and his own place in it began to make sense. The indelible mark that had been placed upon his flesh, the tattoo that Delilah had praised and anointed with a comforting balm—what else could it be but the Mark of the Beast? Not everyone in this world bore such a mark as yet, but Delilah had assured him that the day was fast approaching when all young men and many women would be tattooed, and she had said he was, by virtue of his tattoo, a warrior in the vanguard of this New Age's army.

Delilah had understood that she was living in the last days and even possessed her own copy of the Holy Scriptures (not in the Vulgate but translated into her own barbaric tongue) and a book of commentaries on the prophecies of Ezekiel, Daniel, and John, *The Late Great Planet Earth*, by Hal Lindsey. Silvanus had never been a skilled reader, and though he possessed the gift of tongues and could speak this alien language, he read it, as he read Latin, haltingly and with difficulty. Even so, he was able to learn much from Lindsey's commentary. For instance, when Ezekiel wrote:

The flaming flame shall not be quenched, and all faces from the south to the north shall be burned therein.

And all flesh shall see that I the Lord have kindled it: it shall not be quenched.

the prophet was describing the arsenals of the Antichrist, which were stockpiled with weapons of inconceivable deadliness, thousands upon thousands of "thermonuclear missiles," each one capable of leveling an entire city with all its inhabitants. Apparently, those who read this book (millions, by the book's self-proclamation) believed that they would be exempt from the horrors of Armageddon. They could not see what was so very plain to Silvanus: that they were all minions of the Antichrist—and bore his mark upon their souls, as Silvanus bore it on his flesh. They could not smell the reek of his dominion in the air. They could not hear it in the obscene incantations that issued from the Trinitron. They were as blind to their own damnation as the heretics whom Silvanus had heard singing the blasphemous praises of their false god even as they were marched to the pyres of their execution.

Silvanus knew himself to be a sinner, so he was not utterly amazed to find himself translated into the realm of the Antichrist. All the prayers and litanies and Masses, the indulgences he'd accrued, the sacred relics and vestments and vessels—none of these had power to blot away the stain of his sins. And if he was not in hell, that was no matter, for surely he was accursed. But did that mean, as he'd first supposed, that all sins were permitted here and all virtue reckoned sin? Even Delilah had had some compunctions about the public display of lust, for when he had tried to engage her in sexual congress at the Limbo Bar and Grill on that first memorable night, she had restrained him. "Later, Damon, you demon!" she'd told him as he tried to enter her. "We can't fuck on top of the fucking bar, for Christ's sake!" So there were limits and decorums even here. A woman might display her breasts; she might blaspheme; she might *enact* sexual congress with an unseen incubus and call it "dancing." But yet she would not publicly perform the act she solicited, for some little residue of shame and decency remained to her even in her depraved condition.

Silvanus inferred from this that her killing, though she had urged him to it, would not be lightly regarded by whatever authorities interested themselves in such matters. In this the Trinitron concurred. One of its most recurrent themes was murder, usually of temptresses like Delilah, and the discovery and pursuit of their murderers by the police and other interested parties. Often, the murderer seemed to be regarded with approbation. He was shown to be virile, prosperous, well-spoken, and meriting respect, but for all that he was judged to be, at last, a guilty wretch, whom the police would shoot down with what Silvanus surmised to be a form of thermonuclear missile, for their weapons had the same wonderful and instantaneous efficacy. These scenes of murder and retribution seemed to be more accurate representations of the world that Silvanus had glimpsed beyond the confines of Delilah's little house than many other things revealed by the Trinitron, but were they, even so, to be trusted? Was not the Trinitron the voice and mirror of the Antichrist? Could anything he witnessed by its agency be accepted at face value? The claims made for Total or Preparation H? For Pepsi-Cola and Miller Lite?

To these questions Silvanus had no answer.

Meanwhile, Delilah's corpse was decaying in the summer heat.

22

The angels were getting on Father Mabbley's nerves. They were nice enough angels in their way—angels, one might say, of the upper middle class. He could identify a few. Two had to be Botticellis, another an El Greco. The one in the corner, with purplish wings, might be a Titian, but he wasn't sure. They were none of them simpering or insipid or otherwise tawdry, but having them grouped together in a single room tended to make the very idea of the angelic a little suspect, as though they were part of some con game that would have simple souls believe that the afterlife was the ultimate children's playground. And that was unfortunate, if one wished to believe in angels, as Father Mabbley did. Admittedly, the angels *he* believed in were of a fiercer sort, like Rilke's angels, demonic and terrible, in the Italian sense of *terribilità*. One admired them, but feared them, equally. Lucifer, after all, was an angel.

Still, this was Bing's party, and Father Mabbley was certain Bing would have been pleased. Certainly, he'd have preferred the ambience here at Schinder's Memorial Gardens to the institutional blandness of McCarron's. This was Minnesota's answer to L.A.'s funereal Disneyland at Forest Lawn, a necropolis in the grand manner and a genuine tourist attraction, with its own restaurant and coffee shop. For all its glitz, Schinder's was not that much more expensive than McCarron's, since the place was selling its atmosphere, not caskets gussied up to look like catafalques. Admittedly, Father Mabbley had opted for one of the less costly chapels, which was decorated with reproductions of art masterpieces rather than the genuine articles. Was that cheeseparing?

Or a sensible economy, in view of the fact that he was not anticipating a large turnout? Aside from inserting a notice on the obituary page of the two Twin Cities newspapers, Father Mabbley had not known how to contact Bing's friends and relations. He might be the only mourner, and that would be a sad thing, but not that unusual for Father Mabbley. People were always coming to Las Vegas to die in solitude, which, after all, is one of the basic facts of death. At the end, every man *is* an island, and there's no one there to talk to but God.

Meanwhile, it was four o'clock, and Wiley's secretary was still conveying his regrets at hourly intervals. Father Mabbley had yet to book a hotel room, since the secretary had thought he *might* be given the keys to Bing's house, though she wasn't certain. Father Mabbley found the notion that he had become, at this late date, a home owner disconcerting in a pleasant way. As a priest, Father Mabbley had always been comfortably domiciled, but the homes he'd lived in had never been *his*, and in that sense they hadn't been homes at all. He felt as he had when, at the ripe age of thirty-four, he'd got his first driver's license: an authentic citizen and a grown-up at last. He would have his own backyard, with his own trees, which he would *own*. He would have a lawn mower. A garage. A basement and an attic!

It was as he was counting these chickens that the first mourner arrived—a young man with a pencil-line mustache and a haircut that ventured in the direction of hip-hop without finally daring to go the whole way. Very Minnesotan.

"This is the Fra Angelico Chapel?" the young man asked.

Father Mabbley winced. They weren't Botticellis at all! They were Fra Angelicos! It was written right on the plaque over the door, and he hadn't even made the connection.

"I think so," he said. "Are you a friend of Mr. Anker's?"

"A relative," the young man said. "You're not Reese Wiley, are you?"

Father Mabbley shook his head. "No, I've been waiting for him myself." He offered his hand. "I'm Mark Mabbley."

The young man took his hand tentatively. "You're a priest?"

"Yes, though I'm not here in that capacity. I'm a friend of Bing Anker's. Did you *need* a priest?"

The young man laughed. "No, no, I said that because you said your name was Mark. I thought priests always said they were Father somebody-or-other."

"I must be the exception to that rule. Priests do come in many varieties. For all I know, *you* could be a priest."

The young man gave him a sideways look. "Do I look like a priest?"

"Yes, in fact. You look a good deal like someone I went to the seminary with, years ago. He didn't have a mustache. We weren't allowed any facial hair in that century. But aside from that, you look a good deal like him. I've forgotten his name, isn't that terrible. But I remember his face, and it's very nearly yours. As for your not wearing a Roman collar, most younger priests tend to dispense with that formality when they're not serving in some official capacity."

"So you were a friend of my cousin's?" asked the young man. There was something in the way he put the question that made it clear to Father Mabbley that what he was really asking was whether he was, like Bing, a faggot. The hostility was uncalculated and perhaps unconscious, but it was there.

"Oh, more than just a friend." He paused, and then added, in a professionally unctuous tone, "A brother in Christ."

"I didn't know he was that religious."

"Then you did not know him well. *Were* you close, Mr. . . . . ? I'm afraid I didn't catch your name."

"Greg. Greg Romero, and no, you couldn't say we were close. In fact, we only met the once. He came to my sister's wedding a few months back and gave her this incredible tree in a ceramic pot. It was huge. At the time she was a bit ticked off. Like, if he was going to spend so much money—and it must have cost a lot—why not get something useful? But she's got so that she likes the thing. It's been growing like crazy in the backyard. Anyhow, at the wedding I remember the guy sitting off in the corner of the hall by himself, so I went over and started talking, basically just doing my family duty, and what happened, we started trading jokes. He'd tell one, and that one would remind me of another, and it went on like that for quite a while. We were both pretty lubricated, so I can't remember that much more about him."

"That sounds like Bing, all right," said Father Mabbley. "Do you remember any of the jokes he told?"

Greg Romero smiled. "None I could tell in mixed company."

"Oh, don't think because I'm wearing a collar, I don't enjoy dirty jokes. The vow of celibacy doesn't stop us from *laughing* about sex. For that matter, it doesn't necessarily stop us from *having* sex, but that's another matter, though in that connection, here's one I heard just last week. How do you get a nun pregnant?"

Greg lifted his shoulders. "I don't know. How?"

"Dress her up as an altar boy."

Greg did a long double take, not because he didn't get the joke but because he didn't believe he'd heard it from a priest. Father Mabbley was used to that reaction and to the way, at last, Greg cracked up, laughing twice what the joke was worth.

The ice having been broken, they proceeded to swap stories, beginning with some fairly old chestnuts on Greg's part, but escalating quickly to those of more recent vintage. Why is it that new jokes always seem racier than those of only three or four years ago? Father Mabbley's favorite was: What's a gay's favorite come-on in a bar? The answer: Can I push your stool in for you? That led to a short string of gross-outs revolving around the use of a bar stool as a sexual prosthesis. (How do you get four gays on a bar stool? Turn it upside down. Etc.) Father Mabbley told some jokes relating to the confessional, and that took them to hillbillies, incest, and bestiality. At one point they got to laughing so hard that the young woman from the reception desk appeared in the doorway to ask them, ever so sweetly, to pipe down or else to continue their conversation in the coffee shop.

"Jesus," said Greg when the young lady had left, with one last cautionary adjustment of her eyeglasses, "I'd forgotten where we were."

"Yes," said Father Mabbley, settling back in an understuffed armchair, "we really mustn't go on. But jokes are such a relief in the face of death, aren't they? I remember when my father died, almost twenty years ago. I flew to Pittsburgh, where my family lives, on a Saturday, and after I'd made a call at the funeral parlor, which was nothing so swank as this, I went home with my older brother, and my two other brothers and two sisters were there, and we all got roaring drunk and watched *Saturday Night Live*. Those were its glory days, but you must have seen some of the reruns. They had Gilda Radner, and Bill Murray, and Steve Martin. And *laugh?* My Lord, we laughed. And I like to think my father would have been laughing just as hard if he'd been with us, though in fact Dad's sense of humor was more in the Bob Hope/Bing Crosby vein. But I'm sure he wouldn't have disapproved of our hilarity. Next to booze, comedy was his favorite indulgence."

"Jesus," said Greg, "I can't get over this. I keep thinking, This guy's a *priest*, he can't be saying these things."

"What that translates to is: Priests aren't people. We are, however."

"Well, perhaps. But I'll tell you, my last experience with a priest wasn't anything like this."

Then, without much prodding, Greg did tell him about his last experience with a priest—none other than the same Father Wilfrid Cogling who'd told the man at McCarron's that Bing couldn't be buried from St. Bernardine's. The story began amusingly enough, with an account of Greg and his fiancée going to the counseling sessions required of couples contemplating "mixed marriages." Conducting such sessions had been the bane of Father Mabbley's existence at St. Jude's, since the non-Catholic spouse-to-be was inevitably resentful. But Father Cogling, by the sound of it, had gloried in the opportunity to rub the noses of his catechists in the Church's most medieval doctrines. He'd certainly made a vivid impression on Greg, who was able to replay enough of Cogling's gonzo theology to have been admitted to Holy Orders. But there was an unhappy denouement. As a result of Cogling's counseling, Greg and his fiancée had broken up. As salt in the wound, Greg had learned just today, from his fiancée's mother, that Father Cogling had spirited the fiancée off to some kind of retreat for reluctantly expectant mothers.

"Well, I don't wonder at your feeling some ill will toward the Church," Father Mabbley said in a placatory tone when Greg had wound down. "Lord knows, I do myself, for all sorts of reasons. But then what employee doesn't bear some grudges against his employer? But I'm sure it's not too late for you and Alice—excuse me, it's Alison, isn't it?—to get back together. It sounds like you should. That's to say, it sounds like you love each other. And that's what counts. In my opinion."

"Jesus," said Greg. "You keep on like this, you're going to turn me into a fucking Catholic."

Father Mabbley laughed. "Believe me," he said, "that has not been my hidden agenda. Though, who knows, God works in mysterious ways."

Perhaps it was God, at that moment, working in one of his mysterious ways, who prompted the young woman with the eyeglasses to reappear and inform them that Mr. Wiley's secretary had left a message for Father Mabbley, to the effect that Mr. Wiley was very sorry, but he would not, after all, be able to get to Schinder's that afternoon, and please excuse him. He promised, absolutely, to be there tomorrow morning.

"Are you, by chance, Gregory Romero?" the young woman asked, turning to Greg.

"Uh-huh," Greg said, startled.

"Mr. Wiley also asked me to apologize to you, and to say that he hoped you might be able to be here tomorrow morning as well. The chapel will reopen at ten o'clock."

"And may we expect the deceased to be here as well?" Father Mabbley asked.

The young lady gave him a dirty look. "You may," she said.

Father Mabbley fetched his suitcase from behind the love seat where he'd hidden it. "And could you call a taxi for me?" he asked the young woman before she'd quite disappeared.

"No, no," said Greg. "I've got my car here. There's no need for you to get a taxi." He waved the young woman away, and then asked, "Where are you headed?"

"I've no idea," said Father Mabbley. "A hotel."

"You can stay at my place if you want to. I've got a couch that folds out into a bed."

"That would be very nice. Would you let me take you to dinner first?"

"Sure." Greg wrinkled his mustache misgivingly. "But there's one thing I should say first."

"And what is that?"

"I'm not gay."

Father Mabbley laughed. "For goodness' sake, I know *that*. But there's something you should know as well."

"What's that?"

"I need a drink. Desperately."

Greg laughed.

They were friends. It's always weird how such things happen.

XXIII

Three weeks had passed.

It was as though the past were a pit into which he'd fallen and from which he could not escape. A pit dug by hunters, and himself the beast trapped within it, unable to comprehend the design of those who'd snared him and then left him to his brutish sufferings. His toothache had been cured, at last, by the desperate remedy of extraction. Four molars had been taken out, an operation performed by the Legate's chief torturer, Bertrand Crispo, who had been accounted (so the Legate had assured him) the ablest dentist in all Lombardy before he'd been recruited to his new profession. Crispo had grinned, toothlessly, as he performed his work. As a child, Father Bryce had been taken to a harelipped dentist, and even then, at the age of ten or eleven, he had sensed a congruence between the harelip's affliction and his profession, as though in becoming a dentist he could revenge himself, on each of his patients, for his disfigurement.

The aftermath of that crude dental surgery had been almost worse than the suffering that had preceded it, and Father Bryce still could only tolerate foods that had been reduced to paps and mushes. But the worst pain had abated. His kidney stones were another matter. There was no remedy for their pain, and so he suffered it, trying as best he could to modify his diet to avoid whatever seemed to trigger the spasms.

The one element of his diet he could not and would not modify was the wine. He subsisted, for the most part, on a priestly diet of bread and wine, *elixir vitae* and the staff of life, which he consecrated before each meal—perversely, ironically, blasphemously, and yet, for all that, reverently. For the strangest thing was that this experience, which was so much at odds with any doctrine known to him, had made him devout, a true believer. In what exactly, he was not sure. Nothing in Holy Scripture or in the writings of the Fathers of the Church could account for what had happened to him. But whatever was happening, of one thing he was sure: It was supernatural in its nature.

He prayed a great deal. He recited rosaries and meditated—on the sorrowful mysteries especially. He tried to recall the counsels of Thomas à Kempis, whom he had not read since his seminary days, and whose *Imitation of Christ* would not be written for another two hundred years. He became obsessed with suffering—not simply his own, often acute, physical suffering, but the idea of suffering, as an agent of transformation and redemption.

And so it was, not from any morbid or erotic interest, that he became curious about the Legate's ongoing work in the cellars and catacombs of the cathedral. Durand du Fuaga himself had been called away by his inquisitorial duties to Toulouse, which was the unofficial capital of the Albigensians. In the Legate's absence, Father Bryce, in his capacity as Bishop of Montpellier-le-Vieux, enjoyed an unquestioned access to the workshops of the Inquisition, where suffering was the order of the day. He was spared direct witness of the heretics' ordeals, since du Fuaga's underlings intermitted their work during such times as Father Bryce appeared on the scene. Even so, he witnessed a sufficiency of suffering.

What he found most disconcerting was the apathy of those who had been put to the question. He'd feared that his appearance among them might awaken hopes, as the souls of those in limbo would have been quickened by the sight of Christ when he had descended into hell in the hours between his Crucifixion and Resurrection. But these sorry creatures seemed to have no souls left to awaken. They scarcely lifted their eyes when he entered their cells. They expected no reprieve from their torments, as Father Bryce had come to expect none from his. In that they were equals. Some had been cruelly disfigured; many more were wasted by fever and starvation; one or two had already died when the light of the torch discovered them. But none complained or thought to ask for mercy or forgiveness.

It was, in the end, a disheartening experiment. What had he hoped for from it? Did he suppose that he would find them transfigured by their tortures? If anything, they had been reduced to the condition of beasts—apathetic, dull-eyed, speechless.

There was one cell to which Father Bryce was at first denied access. The man who barred his entry was his dentist, and he insisted, with another of his toothless grins, that the Bishop . . . And then he simply shook his head, for lack, perhaps, of those auxiliary verbs that serve as euphemisms for the ultimate requirements of arbitrary authority: He must not, could not, should not, might not trespass within.

Father Bryce almost submitted to the man's insistence, but then he heard, within, a song he knew, a song that could not conceivably be sung in this century. Indeed, it was not sung; it was whistled, softly and so slowly that it was difficult to place. Then the lyrics stirred in his memory, only the first three words: "Michelle, ma belle . . ." A Beatles song, again. He still held to the memory of the moment he'd heard someone whistle "Yesterday" as a kind of talisman, as though that simple anachronism were the key that might unlock him from this nightmare.

"Open the door," he demanded with an authority that was not, this time, contradicted.

When the door had been unbarred, he signaled the two torchbearers to precede him, and then he followed them into a fetid cell not much wider than the corridor without. And there, as in a vision from Dante, was every boy he'd ever seduced—though they were not the children Father Bryce had known and caressed. Here were the men who might have grown from those boys, the warped issue of his love. Here was Teddy Hamburg, who'd been an altar boy at Our Lady of Mercy, the very first of them—not thirteen now, but closer to thirty-three and already quite ruined, a cadaver, his hair and beard matted with filth, his pale skin mottled with scabs. There, hugging his scant abdomen, was Johnny Kruger, and beside him, inert and skeletal, Gabriel Owens. Johnny was in his fifties now, Gabriel even older, but Father Bryce knew them, and knew that somehow he was responsible for their presence here, for the chains about their ankles, for the welts and running sores that covered their almost naked bodies.

"Who are these men?" he asked Crispo. "Why are they kept apart from the others?"

"These are the men who were caught trying to return to Lombardy, Your Grace—the masons who had been working on the cathedral."

Father Bryce could remember now the Abbot informing him of the attempted defection of a number of the impressed laborers working under the master mason Bonamico. He had told the Abbot to deal with the men's punishment as best he saw fit, his standard evasion when asked to exercise his authority in matters beyond his ken.

"God forgive me," Father Bryce murmured, turning to leave the cell.

A voice from the darkest recess of the cell responded: "God, did you say? God?"

The question filled Father Bryce with panicky fear, for the unseen speaker had addressed him neither in Latin nor in the language of Languedoc, but in English.

"Do you think *God* hears anything that is said in these tombs? Do you think he forgives anything that is done here?"

"Be quiet, Bonamico," Crispo commanded, "or you'll get twice your ration of the whip when the Bishop leaves." The torturer turned to Father Bryce. "The man is a lunatic, Your Grace. Sometimes he jabbers his nonsense to himself for hours at a time. No one can understand a word of it. I thought at first it was the language of the heretics. Some of them come from countries far to the east. But if it is, none of his fellows understand him any better than our interrogators."

"Let me look at him," said Father Bryce.

Crispo gestured to one of the torchbearers, who picked his way among the prisoners as they hastened to draw up their knees to make a path for him. At the far wall of the cell, he held his torch close to the face of a man who had struggled to his feet. The man was a foot taller than his jailer, and not yet so debilitated as his fellow prisoners, though his body, like theirs, bore the marks of the whip.

"Who are you?" the man asked, trying to peer past the flickering of the torch that was held so close to his face as almost to singe his ragged beard. The face was familiar to Father Bryce, though not in the intimate way the other prisoners' faces had seemed familiar.

"Do I know you?" the man said, blinking against the torch's unaccustomed light. "You spoke in English. I heard you say, 'God forgive me.' No one speaks English here. The language doesn't even exist. Even in England they speak some dialect of French, or else Anglo-Saxon. Who *are* you? And what the fuck is happening here?"

Father Bryce realized who the man must be. He had seen his face, albeit an older version of the face that he saw now, on the jacket of his book. "You're Boscage," he said in English. "You're Adolf Boscage."

Tears filled the man's eyes. "I am," he said. "Oh my God, it's over. You have come to take me away from here, haven't you? I knew it must end some time or other, I knew this could not go on."

Father Bryce turned to Crispo. "I can understand a little of what he says. He speaks in one of the dialects of the Goths. Could you take me to a room where I can examine him privately?"

"Your Grace, the Legate has left firm instructions concerning these men. I am already at fault in having allowed anyone within this cell."

"The Legate need not know," said Father Bryce in a tone of cold authority. He added, more warmly, "And I shall make it worth your while."

Crispo bowed his head with sly submissiveness. "As Your Grace requires."

"And let it be somewhere I can breathe the air."

"Then, in the chief interrogation chamber, Your Grace, on the level above this. The air is much better there."

"Very good."

Father Bryce followed Crispo and one of the torchbearers up a winding flight of steps to another stony corridor. The walls here were of cut stone, not mortared rubble, and the stink of the prison was masked by the smell of burning charcoal. They entered a room that was of the approximate dimensions of Father Bryce's office at St. Bernardine's rectory. There was even a rough trestle with a chair beside it positioned where Father Bryce's desk would be. He seated himself in the chair, and without his asking for it to be done, the prisoner was spread-eagled upon the trestle and secured by his wrists and ankles to bolts fixed to the wood. It was barbaric, yet oddly reassuring. Father Bryce had feared being left alone with the man. Now he need have no fear.

"Leave us now," Father Bryce commanded.

Crispo made no objection. He gave a word to the torchbearer, who placed the torch in a sconce on the wall and then followed him from the room.

"Who are you?" Boscage whispered. "Are you one of them?"

Father Bryce smiled despite himself. "I seem to be, don't I? I seem to have no choice. And you? Are you Adolf Boscage? How is that possible?"

"You're asking *me?* Jesus, this only gets crazier."

"I think you should answer my questions," said Father Bryce. "I think that's where to begin. What did you mean—'one of them'?"

"Aliens? Devils? *I* don't know. Suddenly I'm back in the fucking Middle Ages. Suddenly people are calling me Bonamico, and I'm supposed to know how to build a fucking cathedral. There are these men inside of treadmills way up in the rafters, like squirrels in a fucking squirrel cage, lifting up these humongous blocks of stone, and I'm supposed to be telling them what to do. And meanwhile there are these processions on the streets taking men and women and even goddamned *corpses* to be burned because they're heretics. Albigensians! And now they're telling me I'm one of these Albigensians myself."

"Let's begin again," said Father Bryce calmly. "How did you come here?"

"How did I come here? On a boat, across the ocean. How did *you* come here?"

"Never mind about me. I want to know about you. You're the writer Adolf Boscage. You admit that?"

"What's to *admit?* Yes, that's who I am. But if you know *that,* you know more than I do. Jesus, can't you loosen these ropes? This isn't exactly a natural way to have a conversation."

Father Bryce smiled. He was actually beginning to enjoy the situation. "No, I'll have to agree with you there. It's an unusual way to meet anyone for the first time. Still, here we are. We have our separate roles to play. I must say I don't envy yours, but I'm not about to put mine at risk. If you're cooperative, I may try to help you. If you're not . . ."

"Then what? You'll burn me at the fucking stake?"

"Have you made other plans?"

"You *are* one of them."

"One of whom, Mr. Boscage? You still haven't explained that."

"One of the people who want to burn me at the stake! That's all I know about it! What do I know about being an Albigensian? Am I a heretic? Anyone from the twentieth century would be a heretic if they were brought back here. You tell them the world is *round,* and you're a fucking heretic! Some of those poor fucks in the cell with me, they call themselves Albigensians, and they say the Pope is the Antichrist and all the priests are serving Satan, and at this point I am not about to contradict them. Except maybe I do know a little more than they do, or than you do. Or you wouldn't be asking me what I know, would you? Jesus, I wish I had a cigarette."

"It's a vile habit."

"You think so? I'll tell you a joke. A young priest gets caught by his pastor having sex with a nun in the confessional, and the pastor tells him, 'It's okay this time, but don't get in the habit.' "

Father Bryce smiled. "That's a very old joke."

"I'll tell you another. A nun gets on a bus. It's heading out into the burbs, and at a certain point she's the only passenger still on the bus. She asks the driver, is he married? He says no. Got any children? He says no. So she propositions him. She says she's never had sex, and seeing how he's not otherwise committed, would he do her the favor? He says sure. She says, that's wonderful, but please, for obvious reasons, do it from behind. So he says fine, and pulls the bus over and he fucks her in the butt. When he's done, the bus driver turns to the nun and says, 'I've got something I have to confess. I am married. And I've got three kids.' The nun smiles, and she tells him, 'That makes us square. I'm not a nun. My name is Chuck, and I'm on my way to a masquerade.' "

Father Bryce had not heard the joke before, but he did not smile. "Why do you suppose that I'm gay?" he asked.

"Why do I suppose . . . It's just a joke, for Christ's sake! I don't suppose anything."

"But why that joke? Do you already know something about me?"

"I was trying to break the ice, that's all. You said something about cigarettes are a bad habit. *Habit*, that was the word. So I told a joke, to break the ice. You want to break down barriers, you tell jokes. Right? That's all it was."

"You know something I don't. You know why we're here. One of your people, the Receptivists, is responsible for my being here. How it was done, I don't know."

"One of my *people*?"

"Your cult."

"I'm not a fucking heretic! I don't *know* anything about the goddamn Albigensians. As far as I'm concerned, they're ancient history. All I am is a fucking science fiction writer who wrote a book about fucking UFOs, and you want to know the truth? Okay, it was all bullshit. Does that answer your questions? I made it up, I have a good imagination. And until I went to the goddamn UFO convention in

Rodez, that's the whole story. Drugs, maybe. I took drugs, I had some fantasies. It's how I make my goddamn living. There's men with dogs' heads, and they're checking out my private parts on a flying saucer. It's a fantasy, okay? So, for years I busted my balls writing novels. But then I thought, hey, people want to *believe* this shit. Don't write novels. Write your goddamn memoirs. Tell people how you were abducted by aliens. Make it real. That was the story of my life. Till now. Till I went to Montpellier-le-Vieux and got zapped into this nightmare." There were tears in the man's eyes. "You've got to believe me," Boscage insisted.

Father Bryce took a deep breath. "I do," he said. "Unfortunately, I do."

24

"This is so nice of you," Margaret declared to the fat middle-aged man who was her son. "Peter," she added emphatically, by way of indicating this was one of her good days, when she knew who he was. "This is a real treat. Such weather! What is so rare as a day in June? Someone wrote that, in a poem. Do you have any idea who?"

"Are we playing *Jeopardy*, Mother?" the fat man said, sidestepping her question.

"It was James Russell Lowell. If you *had* been on *Jeopardy*, you'd have lost. It's from 'The Vision of Sir Launfal':

> And what is so rare as a day in June?
> Then, if ever, come perfect days;
> Then Heaven tries earth if it be in tune,
> And over it softly her warm ear lays.

I used to make all my fourth and fifth graders memorize that. Watch out for the beer truck!" She pressed her foot against an imaginary brake pedal.

"I *see* the beer truck, Mother. And it sees us." Then, after he'd pulled out into the passing lane, he said, "But I don't see, 'Over it softly her warm ear lays.' What does it mean?"

"You're just like them. There'd always be someone in the class who'd ask a question like that. Why does it have to mean anything? It's poetry, so it can be a little mysterious. 'Over it softly her warm ear lays.' It's lovely. You *are* driving too fast, Peter."

"We're already running late, Mother."

"And I've apologized for that. I couldn't find my white shoes. If we're a little late, we may miss some of the sermon, but if we're there for the consecration, that's what counts."

Peter pulled back into the slow lane, and Margaret settled into her seat with the contentment, which had become so rare in her life, of having someone do what she'd told him to. The green grass whizzed by on either side of the thruway, and occasionally they drove under an overpass or a pedestrian bridge. Signs announced exits. It seemed one might drive forever without encountering any kind of blemish, nothing but the smooth concrete and the endless valley of neatly mowed grass enclosing it on either side. In some ways the world did improve, and this was one of them.

They exited into Willowville, and drove only a short distance on real streets with houses, and then they pulled into the parking lot of St. Bernardine's Church, which seemed almost as spacious—and full of cars—as a supermarket parking lot. She waited sedately for Peter to get out of the car and walk around and open her door and help her out. Except for its sheer bulk, the church was not that impressive from the outside. Not even particularly churchlike, except for one small white marble statue of a monk at the edge of the parking lot.

But inside, oh my! It was like a continuation of their drive on the thruway, bright and plain and simple, like heaven's own kitchen. "It's lovely," she whispered to Peter, who shushed her. They'd entered at the side of the church, so they were already close to the pulpit, where a woman in ordinary street clothes was reading aloud from a huge book supported on its own pedestal. Margaret disapproved of women butting in on the Mass, but she'd seen enough of it to not be shocked. Peter tried to lead her toward the pews at the rear of the church, but she insisted on going to the front, where she could hear what was being said. If people wanted to stare, let them! She'd stare right back. After a certain age, one had special privileges, and one of them was the right to pretend to be invisible and inaudible in public places. It was your revenge for all the years that other people had pretended the same thing about you.

The woman finished reading and stepped down from the pulpit, and a prune-faced old layman took her place. He put on a pair of bifocal glasses and began to read, in a raspy voice, from the Gospel according to Saint Mark. It was the story of the man possessed by devils, whom Jesus meets and exorcises, at which point the devils enter into a herd of swine, and all the swine—two thousand of them, according to Saint Mark—run down the side of a mountain and jump into the sea and are drowned. Margaret had always thought this one of the more unsavory stories in the New Testament. Why did Jesus have to destroy so many pigs in order to help the man? Couldn't he have just sent the devils back to hell, where they belonged? It seemed almost like an act of vandalism, not to mention cruelty to animals. Then, when the man who'd been exorcised had asked Jesus if maybe he couldn't travel around with him, like one of his disciples, the answer is No, go home, get lost.

God certainly works in mysterious ways sometimes, but the old fellow reading the Gospel didn't appear to have any misgivings about the story. He read it with a kind of gloating satisfaction, like a newscaster reporting on the total destruction of Saddam Hussein's army. She was beginning to wish she'd never let Peter talk her into coming here to surprise Patrick.

Then the priest came up to the pulpit to deliver the sermon, and that was the last straw. He was another old codger, like the layman who'd read the gospel. She leaned sideways and whispered into Peter's ear, "That isn't Patrick!"

"I can see that, Mother. But please don't make a fuss. People can hear you."

"I thought you said Patrick always said the eleven o'clock Mass."

"Mother. Please."

Margaret folded her hands in her lap, and looked up at the priest in the pulpit, who was looking down at her with an identical smile of peeved false patience.

When he seemed satisfied that she'd been shushed, he smiled a benign smile and announced, "Today is Father's Day!" He seemed to be claiming personal responsibility for the fact, as though he were a school principal announcing an unexpected holiday. Then he went on for a while about how wonderful fathers were, and how much we owe them for working hard to support our families, and how if we thought about it, every day ought to be Father's Day. And it was, in the sense that every day was a gift from our Father in heaven, and we should think about how much we owed Him, and that led around to Saint Joseph, and how the angels had alerted him to Herod's intention of massacring the innocents, and you could see what would come next—abortion.

Abortion was a new massacre of the innocents, and a sin that everyone shared in, if they didn't do something to combat it. And that included men as well as women. The protests at the abortion clinics were a step in the right direction, but when you went to those protests, who did you see? Women and children. Perhaps Herod—that is, the government—didn't take the protests seriously because Catholic *men* weren't doing their share. More *could* be done. The priest did not condone the bombing that had just taken place in Edina, but he could understand the anger and frustration that had prompted it. Violence was seldom the right course to pursue, but there might be other steps that could legitimately be taken. Any men—any *fathers*—who wanted to become involved in a positive way were advised to attend the next meeting of the Knights of Columbus, next Thursday evening at eight o'clock in the parish hall.

Margaret felt herself becoming unaccountably angry, an anger provoked not so much by what the priest *said*, most of which she agreed with in theory, as by the man himself. At first, it was more of an irritation, the way sometimes complete strangers can rub you the wrong way—by smoking where they shouldn't or just by a tone of voice. But soon it went beyond that. Soon she began to be all pins and needles. She had to bite her lip to keep from saying something out loud, though what she'd have said she didn't know.

She *knew* who the priest was, up there in the pulpit. Of course, she'd probably seen him other times she'd come here to see Peter's twin brother, Patrick, who was the pastor of St. Bernardine's, and she might even have spoken with him one or more of those times and not remembered. But she was certain that that wasn't the way she knew him. It went back farther. He'd been part of her real life, before she'd gone into the nursing home.

Long before.

She felt like one of those women you read about who'd been sexually abused by their fathers when they were children and then repressed the memory till they were middle-aged, when suddenly it all came spilling back. Or like the people who'd had previous lives in another century. If she closed her eyes and just listened to his voice, it was easier to connect to the feeling. There was a purr to the voice, and a certain rhythm to the words, and a way of falling silent after he'd said anything that might make you feel guilty, as though giving you time to fill in the blank with your own name.

And then he said something that was the key to the whole thing. He'd finished up with abortion and gotten back to Father's Day and the holy sacrament of matrimony, and he said, "There is something holy in the love between a man and a woman, which is only surpassed by the love between man and God." And it was as though he were in the bed beside her, saying the same thing, looking all dreamy-eyed and smelling of sweat and hair tonic.

She opened her eyes and, yes, she could see that the man up there was Willy Cogling, almost half a century older, and his hair gone white, just like hers, and the wrinkles in his face revealing how mean he really was, the way wrinkles can do. But otherwise he was not that much different.

She laughed aloud, one brief bark of recognition, and turned to Peter and whispered, "That man up there is your father."

"Mother," Peter said, with a shocked look. But she could see that he'd taken in her meaning and was already processing it through the computer in his head. He was good at making calculations. They had that in common.

Willy Cogling was glaring at her again, but not with a look that suggested he'd heard more than her laugh. He knew who *she* was all right! And he couldn't have felt that comfortable delivering his sermon on the sanctity of fatherhood with the two of them sitting down there in front of him. So even if he hadn't *heard* what she'd whispered to Peter, he could imagine what it might be.

He smiled, and nodded, and continued: "Marriage isn't all a bed of roses, of course. There are times when it may not seem the least bit holy, and we may want to laugh at the idea. I don't suppose Saint Joseph was that happy to be woken up in the middle of the night and told he had to go to Egypt that very moment. He might have said to that angel, 'You've got to be kidding.' But God's angels aren't kidding when they tell us what we have to do. And neither is Holy Mother Church."

Birth control will be next, Margaret thought, and sure enough, that was the sermon's next theme. There had been a period, after the war, when the suburbs were going up and people were having babies like rabbits, when that's all you heard about when you went to church. The great evil of birth control was right up there with the Communist menace. And when you went to confession, you got the third degree. That was how they'd met, she and Willy. It all came spilling back as though it were yesterday. In fact, much more vividly than yesterday, which was already part of the blur of last week.

It had been an old-fashioned kind of confessional, a big, dark mahogany number that *looked* like sin. Inside it, he had kept cross-examining her about her sex life with Paul until she'd finally confessed to him what she'd never told anyone else, the fact more shameful than any sin she could have come up with, the fact that she lived in a sexless marriage. How sympathetic young Father Cogling had been, how curious, how encouraging. He'd said there could be no annulment, since the marriage had been consummated. He'd advised prayer and patience. He'd said he would like to meet Paul, so he might understand the situation better, and in a few months he and Paul had become good friends while he and Margaret became lovers.

Lovers? Maybe that was overstating it. She'd never loved him in the romantic way that the woman in *The Thorn Birds* had loved Richard Chamberlain. Her biggest satisfaction in having the affair had been revenging herself on Paul, and having the twins was the sweetest part of the revenge. And it had been Willy—with all his talk about abortion being the new massacre of the innocents—who'd tried to convince her to get an abortion before Paul found out she was pregnant. Paul never did find out about Willy, since she'd been able to diddle him into thinking he'd actually performed his conjugal duties one night when he'd got dead drunk. Paul was so gratefully deceived. The twins would be a living proof of his conjugal adequacy.

With Willy it was another matter. Once she was visibly and officially pregnant, that was the end of the romance. Willy was transferred to another parish (probably at his own request) and gradually faded from her life, and she'd been just as glad. If truth be told, she hadn't had much talent for adultery. Once the sex had progressed beyond the point of kisses and caresses, once it got to the parts you never saw in movies (at least in the movies of those days), Margaret could live without it. And so she had, for the next almost fifty years.

Willy wound up his sermon at last, by reading a cartoon from this morning's paper, the moral of which was "Like father, like son." Then, having sermonized for such a long time, he handled the rest of the Mass expeditiously. Margaret, though in no way arthritic, insisted on the prerogative of old age and stayed seated while all the genuflecting and kneeling went on. So, to her annoyance, did Peter. It was his way of announcing he was not a believer, which was fine for him, but it did suggest that Margaret's unbending knees might have the same explanation. *Was* she a believer? Possibly not. The older she got, the less she was concerned with the Church's official teachings. It was not so much disbelief as a feeling that she was entitled, at her age, not to have to pay taxes—even, if it came to that, lip service.

But when it came time for Communion, she had no compunction about joining the line, which, at St. Bernardine's, was not very long. Nor did she lower her eyes when it came her turn and Willy stood in front of her, chalice in hand, to place the host on her tongue. She stuck out her tongue and stared him straight in the eyes, and *he* was the one to blink. Lowering his eyes and reciting the words, so much less magical in English than in Latin, he placed the tasteless wafer on her tongue.

For the very briefest of moments she was tempted to spit it out. But surely no one in the entire history of the Church had ever done such a thing, and Margaret was not about to be the first. On the other hand, she didn't want to swallow it. So, when she was back in the pew, seated beside Peter, she discreetly removed the half-dissolved wafer from her tongue with a Kleenex she took from her purse, then wadded up the Kleenex and put it back in her purse. She was certain that God, if He concerned Himself in such matters at all, would understand.

At last, the Mass was over, and everyone was supposed to give a formal hug to the person next to them—an observance that Peter neatly finessed by an elaborate charade of helping Margaret get to her feet.

The best was yet to come. Willy had stationed himself at the side exit in order to shake the parishioners' hands as they left the church. There was a double flow at the door, a fast and a slow lane, just like on the thruway, and Peter tried to steer his mother into the fast lane, but Margaret insisted, with a decisive shake of her head, that they would be among the hand-shakers.

When it came their turn, Willy didn't miss a beat. "Mrs. Bryce, how *nice* to see you. And your son. Peter, isn't it? Father Pat will be so sorry to hear that he's missed you. He's on retreat."

"You needn't apologize, Willy," Margaret said, matching his tone of formal courtesy. "It was a greater treat seeing you. I didn't know you were still alive."

When Willy didn't have a quick response to that, Peter stepped in, with blundering courtesy: "Mother's memory can be erratic."

"That's just the way it is," Margaret agreed briskly. "Sometimes I don't know my own name. Other times it all comes back. And this morning, Willy, you made it all come back."

"I'm glad to hear that, Mrs. Bryce. And so, I'm sure, will Father Pat be when he returns. Unfortunately, where he is there are no telephones. That is one of the luxuries of a retreat, though some think of it as a penance. I assume you came here expecting him to be saying Mass?"

"Yes, Father Cogling," Peter said. "Then we thought we'd take him out to visit our father's grave. If he could spare the time."

"Father's Day," Father Cogling said, nodding genially. "What a thoughtful idea. Father Pat will be doubly disappointed."

"Perhaps *you* would like to come with us, Willy," Margaret suggested. "There's room in the car."

"I wish I could. Paul was a dear friend, and a good Catholic of a kind that's become all too rare." (This, with a glance toward Peter.) "But"—he lifted his shoulders—"with Father Pat away, my time is not my own."

"We understand, of course," said Peter, laying his hand on his mother's shoulder and shoving her forward, gently.

Father Cogling nodded, and turned to the next parishioner in line behind them. "Gerhardt," he said. "You read the Gospel today with great feeling."

Margaret turned around just in time to see Willy exchange a meaningful look with the man, Gerhardt Ober, who would, only two hours later, murder her.

"Thank you, Father," said Gerhardt.

"Come along, Mother," said Peter.

"Good-bye, Mrs. Bryce," said Willy.

25

A bell was ringing, repeatedly, in the darkness. Silvanus, waking by
degrees, thought at first that he had fallen asleep during a vigil before
the Holy Sacrament. He made his hand into a fist and struck his heart,
praying *Domine, non sum dignus!* O Lord, I am not worthy! Just how
true that was became evident as the bell's ringing continued and he
remembered where he was—in Delilah's little house in the village of
Low Rates Trailer Court, lying beside her corpse. Where he'd struck
himself the inflamed flesh reminded him, with a flash of pain, that it
was not for one who bore Satan's mark to call upon the Lord, even to
proclaim his unworthiness. That had been established beyond all
doubt.

A man rattled the door of the little house and shouted, "Damon, I
know you're in there. I heard you. Stop fucking around and let me in."

He went to the door and unbolted it, expecting to be greeted by the
man who called himself Wolf. But this was someone else, younger, in a
flimsy white doublet that revealed the heraldic emblems on his upper
arms. "I figured I'd find you here," he said, pushing past Silvanus to
enter the house. "Shit—it stinks in here!"

Silvanus stood on the mortar block outside the doorway and considered for a moment simply running away and losing himself in the
maze of the village's unlighted paths. But he had no confidence in his
powers of flight, so he followed the young man into the house and
asked him who he was.

"What's this? Suddenly you got amnesia? The shock of murdering
someone has catapulted you into some new dimension?"

Silvanus stood mute, unable to answer the man's questions.

"I'm Clay, and I'm your personal trainer. Okay, we got that settled? Now tell me what's happened here. Something's gone wrong."

"I did not mean to murder her. I did what she bade me do—but with too great vigor." He held out his hands to be manacled, as he had seen apprehended felons do so often on the Trinitron.

But Clay only wrinkled his forehead and sniffed the tainted air. "Her?" he asked. "Don't you mean *him?*" Then, with great feeling, "Oh shit! Delilah? You didn't!" He went into the next room of the little house and removed the lengths of fine fabric with which Silvanus had shrouded Delilah's body. He turned to Silvanus with a look of in-credulity. "You cut off her fucking *breast?*"

"Only after I knew her to be dead," Silvanus said.

"Have you completely flipped out?"

"I did no more than she asked to have done."

"Have you been here with Delilah ever since you left the bar you went to with her and Wolf?"

"I think so. Yes."

"Was there anyone else here with you?"

Silvanus gestured toward the Trinitron.

"Are you still high on something? You sound spaced out."

The way that the man was looking at him made Silvanus realize that he was naked.

"I'll tell you, if it was up to me, I would like nothing better than just to let the cops find you like this. You would generate some first-class headlines. It's not every pedophile priest who manages to get tattooed and murder a hooker right after he kills the fag who's blackmailing him. You're definitely ahead of the competition now, Father Bryce. But it's not up to me—fortunately for you. I've got orders to get you back to your fucking rectory. Pronto. I got your clothes in the car. You think you can dress yourself?"

Silvanus nodded. "My name is Father Bryce now? I am not Damon?"

The man smirked. "Hey, you learn quick."

"A priest—not a bishop?"

"You were expecting a promotion for what you did?" Clay laughed and shook his head. "Man, you better come down from that cloud. You're in deep shit."

Silvanus nodded. For all the man's expressions of contempt, he seemed to have a clear idea of what Silvanus ought to do—and he himself had none at all.

"You better get washed up," Clay told Silvanus, and made him immerse himself in an immense white basin of heated water to remove the incrustations of blood—his own and Delilah's—from his body. The hot water eased the pain of the Satanic face incised upon his chest and stomach, and Clay found a compartment of balms and unguents hidden behind the speculum mounted on the wall of the cubicle containing the great basin. One of these balms was applied to the inflamed tissues, to their still greater relief.

Then Silvanus dressed himself, with some assistance in the fastenings of his shirt and shoes, in a costume of black wool, finely woven. When he'd finished dressing, the image he presented in the speculum was decidedly priestly.

"Now I am a priest?" he asked Clay.

"It looks like that, don't it?"

"But without a tonsure?"

"A tonsure?" The man laughed aloud. Then, soberly, "You're not joking, are you? You are really *out* of it. Well, that won't be my problem, once I get you out of *here*. Come on, we'll get you back to Willowville. Do you want to kiss Delilah good-bye?"

Silvanus shook his head. "At this moment I feel no lust at all."

"Glad to hear it."

Clay extinguished the flameless torches within the house and stood in the doorway, surveying the dark streets of the village. There was no one in sight. He gestured for Silvanus to leave the house, and then locked the door behind them with a key he'd taken from a small leather purse he'd found in Delilah's bedchamber.

Silvanus now understood, from looking at the Trinitron, that what he'd first supposed to be armored houses were self-powered carriages and were, in the dominion of the Antichrist, more common than horses. Each man seemed to have his own "automobile." (Though no one seemed able to speak Latin, many of the words in use clearly derived from Latin, just as in the vulgar tongues of Silvanus's own era.) There were greater marvels still—self-moving carriages that flew, though with rigid wings. These were not chimeras of the sort abounding on the Trinitron, for he had seen them himself—moving *above* the clouds, traversing the sky from horizon to horizon, just as in the prophecies of Ezekiel.

Clay entered on one side of the automobile, and Silvanus, after fumbling at the latch, entered on the other side and lowered himself, not without difficulty, into the low, cushioned seat. Silvanus watched intently as Clay went through the motions that excited the carriage into responsive motion. In moments they were outside the perimeter of the village and part of the irregular stream of other Fords, Toyotas, Datsuns, and so forth (for there were as many varieties of automobile as there were flowers in a garden, and the distinctive excellence of each one variety compared to all the rest was one of overriding concern to the Trinitron), speeding almost soundlessly along one of the wide, gray, glass-smooth roadways.

Because of the terrible velocity at which they were moving, Clay had to fix his attention on the operation of the automobile, though his eyes would dart from time to time to Silvanus, who, for his part, was transfixed by the prospect before him, at once fearful and wonderstruck.

At length Clay spoke. "What you said a while ago, in the trailer, about how you're a priest now, not a bishop—what did you mean by that? Why would you be a bishop?"

Silvanus did not know how to reply. Clay seemed to have his own idea of an already existing relationship between himself and Silvanus, an idea that Silvanus had no wish to challenge. That he should pose such a question meant that he had no notion of Silvanus's real identity. He believed him to be a priest called Father Bryce, and Silvanus fervently desired nothing more than to step into the priestly shoes of this Father Bryce and to forget the life he'd led as Damon, the slave of Satan and murderer of the temptress Delilah.

So he made a reply as unrevealing as he could devise. "I cannot think why I should have said that. I was in great distress. I was not myself."

"Yeah, that's what I'm asking, shithead. *Are* you yourself?"

"How can I answer such a question?"

"Why not try for honestly."

Silvanus turned sideways and glared. He glared well, being accustomed to authority. "Yes," he said, "I am myself." Then, fearing that Clay's next demand would be for some fuller declaration of his identity, he parried, "Can you say the same?"

Clay was annoyed, but not baffled, by the challenge. "Hey, who *I* am is classified information to *you*, motherfucker. I *ask* the questions, I don't answer them. I thought we established that a while ago."

Silvanus bowed his head, as though in submission.

"Why 'bishop'?" Clay persisted.

Silvanus had recovered his wits to the degree that he could ask in turn, plausibly, "What priest does not think he might become a bishop?"

Clay seemed to give this serious consideration. And then he asked, simply, crushingly, "Does the name Bonamico ring a bell?"

Their eyes met, and Clay knew, and Silvanus knew that he knew, that he had touched a nerve. He had spoken a name that pertained not to this latter-day world but to the diocese of Montpellier-le-Vieux, where Bonamico was the master mason in the Bishop's service, a man whom he detested and suspected of heresy.

"What has Bonamico to do with this?" Silvanus asked, feeling a deeper bewilderment.

"I thought you said you'd read the *Prolegomenon*."

"I don't understand," Silvanus answered, truthfully.

"Boscage *became* Bonamico, when he was in Montpellier-le-Vieux."

The man's pronunciation was so barbaric that Silvanus did not at first recognize the name of his episcopal seat, as Clay's tongue had formed it.

Before he could invent a plausible reply, Clay continued: "And *you* became the Bishop. Right? Is that what happened?" He said it as one might announce that one's opponent in chess had been checkmated.

"I *became* the Bishop?" Silvanus echoed feebly. His sense of the matter was that he had, inexplicably, ceased to be the Bishop and become someone and something else.

"Jesus," said Clay, addressing himself and, for the moment, seeming to forget Silvanus was there. "I've read the book, I've met the man, I've *talked* with him, but somehow I never really *believed* it. I thought this whole fucking business going after you was a damned wild-goose chase. Jesus! Boscage really *was* zapped back to—" He turned to Silvanus. "What year was it, anyhow? Boscage could never quite get that straight."

Though he did not understand most of what Clay had been saying, Silvanus sensed that the man was in some kind of uncertainty that paralleled his own. Each of them knew something the other did not, and each was unwilling to surrender his privileged information.

Silvanus affected to laugh. "What year was *that*? What year is *this*?"

Clay gave him one last sideways look and then gave up. "Shit," he said contemptuously, "you're still stoned out of your fucking mind."

Clay said no more, and neither did Silvanus. The automobile, under Clay's guidance, continued on its path until it arrived at its destination.

"You're home," Clay announced. "You think you can get in the front door by yourself?"

"No," said Silvanus, "I don't think I can."

"I figured as much." Clay got out of the automobile, and helped Silvanus do the same. "I'll have to keep the car to get back to my own. You got a spare set of keys?"

"I don't know."

"Then I'll leave it unlocked in the parking lot of the Grand Union just down the road. The keys will be under the seat. See if your house keys are in your pants pocket."

There was, indeed, a ring of small keys in the pocket of his breeches. He gave them to Clay, who grimaced annoyance, but led Silvanus along a pathway of smooth mortar and up the steps of a house much larger than Delilah's.

"There's no lights on," said Clay, "but if there's anyone who's been waiting up for you, you can say that you were too drunk to drive home yourself, so you had to be chauffeured by the bartender. As for how you explain your absence, the best alibi is always booze. Say you were bingeing and shacked up in a motel and you can't remember any more than that."

Silvanus nodded.

Clay opened the door and handed the keys to Silvanus. "Well, so long—killer."

"When will I see you again?" Silvanus asked Clay.

"I'm not at all sure we should keep meeting like this, and anyhow, the decision won't be up to me. If you was wondering when you're going to get your tattoo finished, I think you can safely assume that you won't be paying any more visits to Wolf. I have a hunch he'll be closing down his shop real soon. You want any more tattoos, you'll have to get them somewheres else."

Silvanus stood in the doorway of St. Bernardine's rectory and watched Clay return to the automobile and drive it away. Then he closed the door and stood there in a darkness that figured forth the darkness within his soul.

Out of that darkness came a voice. "Father Pat, is that you? Thank God you're back! I can't tell you how worried I've been."

"I was drinking," Silvanus informed the unseen speaker.

"That was my fear." There was a pause, and when the man spoke again, his tone was more subdued. "Father Pat, I hate to have to tell you this the moment you're back, but there has been some very, very bad news."

26

The following is excerpted from chapter thirteen of A Prolegomenon to Receptivist Science, *by A. D. Boscage (Exegete Press, 1984):*

What can I say of my period of incarceration in the dungeon crypts of Notre Dame de Gevaudon except that it was inexpressibly horrible! For some months after I had been transmentated back to my own temporal frame, those memories were repressed—whether because of their traumatic nature or through the agency of mnemocytes that erased those recollections and replaced them with others, I cannot presume to judge. Trauma actually seems the likelier hypothesis, since I have no recollection whatsoever of the three weeks I spent in the company of my translator, Héloïse V. (or F.?), who had accompanied me to the ruins of Montpellier-le-Vieux and who discovered me there, after an absence of some four or five hours, in a kind of swoon. Waking from that trance (so Héloïse tells me), I was in a state of great confusion. I knew not my own name. I could not perform simple actions, such as twisting off the cap of a bottle of mineral water. My speech was halting, and it seemed, to Héloïse's professionally trained ear, to have acquired a subtly *French* character, not so much the sound of French, but its *music.* Once I had recovered from my first confusion, I became exceedingly amorous, and Héloïse (she later confided, blushingly) responded to my overtures with enthusiasm. For the next three weeks I lived with her in a state of perpetual rut—of which, alas, I remember nothing whatsoever.

Indeed, I now doubt whether it was I who enjoyed this erotic holiday and wonder if, rather, during the five months I lived and worked as the stonemason Bonamico, he had been transmentated into my own era, for a stay of three weeks. While I suffered in the prisons of the Inquisition, had he enjoyed the favors of the raven-haired Héloïse? Perhaps there are laws for the conservation of spiritual energy just as there are for physical energy, though we do not yet understand them and cannot control them.

Three weeks I lived with Héloïse in unremembered bliss, and then, once again, there was an awakening. One morning Héloïse discovered me curled into a fetal ball at the foot of her bed, whimpering and beside myself with fear. She freaked, and who can blame her? Her pet satyr had become a psychic jellyfish. I was desperate to see Lorraine, and amazed to learn that she had returned to the States without me, in the conviction that I had abandoned her for my French translator, which, to all appearances, I had! Such was my desperation that I possessed the courage to return to the States by plane. My fear of remaining in France was greater than my fear of flying! Yet at that point I had no memory of my experiences as Bonamico.

Even now, as I write this in my Santa Barbara condo, my memories of that experience are erratic—sometimes vivid, sometimes imprecise. I remember the drudgery of the work, the meager rations, the sour wine. I remember being unbathed and the lice in my beard and pubic hair. Worst of all, I recall my dawning awareness that *there was no escape* from my debased condition as a conscript laborer.

Romancers write of the Age of Chivalry and the Age of Faith. Where are the books about the Age of Slavery? The Age of Penury? The Age of Cruelty? Perhaps they are summed up in the single phrase "The Dark Ages"! To my mind, even a pizza delivery boy, working for tips, enjoys a richer and more comfortable life than the nobility and clergy of the Middle Ages. As for those less fortunately situated, forget it! Their lives were a living hell. Or, more accurately, their world was their prison. Not only the serfs were bound to their lords' property; even skilled workers—the men like Bonamico, who built the cathedrals that tourists gush over—were little better than slaves. Bonamico and his fellow masons had come from Turin seeking work in the south of France as workers now migrate from Detroit to Dallas. But once they had found work and shown their competence, the Church decided to requisition their services, the way sailors were once kidnapped from merchant ships and pressed into the service of the British navy. The next time you look at a Gothic cathedral and have lofty thoughts about its "sublimity," consider that its mortar consists of hundreds of men who labored *unwillingly* to raise those forests of chiseled stone.

I have already described, in the chapter before this, how I, as Bonamico, led a rebellion of the conscript laborers of Notre Dame de Gevaudon, how we attempted to flee Montpellier-le-Vieux through the foothills of the Cévennes, and how, after we had been hunted down and put in chains, we were made prisoners in those very crypts we ear-lier had labored to extend. It was in the course of that failed escape that I became acquainted with the doctrines and aspirations of the Albigen-sian "heretics," for many of my fellow masons subscribed to that faith. Indeed, the institution of Freemasonry originated in that period among workers like ourselves, who were, in a sense, the first trade unionists. There are still Republicans who reckon union workers as Albigensians, fit to be burned at the stake!

But *we* were not destined to be burned at the stake. For us a more terrible fate was reserved, a fate so unspeakable that even now, as I struggle to put these words on paper, I am tempted to stay my hand from the keyboard. No one will believe you, I tell myself. You will be reviled! Denounced! Held in derision! Dismissed as a madman!

But what of that! I have been denounced, derided, and dismissed for what I have written already concerning my UFO experiences. I cannot help supposing that these later experiences of transmentation are somehow related to my abduction experiences. Surely it is not incon-ceivable that Entities who have mastered Interstellar Flight might also have mastered the Fourth Dimension of Time? It is not for me to judge or to speculate about such Entities' darkly veiled motives. As-suming, always, that they are the same Entities!

The Shroud of Turin . . .

There, I have written it! Must I now spell it out? The moment I began to read the book about it—*The Mysterious Shroud*, by Ian Wilson and Vernon Miller (Doubleday, 1986)—the memories I had so long repressed were reawakened. I'd found the book on a shelf in the Ana-heim home of my first ex, Barbra Boscage, née Drummond. I was visit-ing my daughters, Lesley and Artemisia, after a court-mandated absence of many years. Finding myself with time to spare (my daugh-ters and their mother had gone to the mall, that cathedral of the twen-tieth century), I picked up the book in a spirit of idle curiosity, but the more I read, and the more closely I examined the seventy-seven black-

and-white and thirty-five full-color photographs, the more vividly I realized that I had chanced upon the key to my erased memories.

For those readers who may be unaware of the significance ascribed to the Shroud of Turin, I will offer a brief résumé. The Shroud "surfaced," scandalously, in the late fourteenth century, when it was denounced as a forgery. It continued to be venerated, and held in suspicion, until late in the nineteenth century, when the new science of photography discovered unsuspected aspects of the Shroud that suggested it could not be, in any ordinary sense, a forgery; the forgers, had they *painted* the image on the cloth, could not have known to paint the authenticating details that were, centuries later, revealed by photographic negatives. The Shroud seemed to be an accurate *photographic representation* of a well-proportioned human male who had been crucified, scourged, and crowned with thorns. It was as though the Shroud had been placed upon the body of the newly crucified Christ and a rubbing had been taken, as nowadays art students make rubbings from the incised brass memorial tablets in English cathedrals. No artist of that period could possibly have accomplished a forgery so perfect in all its anatomical detail.

However—and this is the however that has made the Vatican pause in finally affirming the Shroud's authenticity—the fabric that bears this "miraculous" imprint has been shown, by scientific analysis, to date from a time no later than the thirteenth or fourteenth century and is, therefore, a forgery. But even so, a forgery so well contrived it must be marveled at.

Certainly, when I beheld the photographs in *The Mysterious Shroud*, I had to marvel, for what I saw there were *my own features*—the photographic record of the tortures I had endured and my eventual crucifixion. As I studied the book, the memories returned: the thorny branches twined about my forehead, the whips that imprinted my flesh with their arcane alphabets of suffering, the crude iron nails that were, at last, hammered into my wrists, where they would support the weight of my crucified body, as nails through the flesh of my hands would not— as my torturers, like the Roman legionnaires before them, had learned by trial and error.

Nor was it myself alone who suffered so. Indeed, I am not sure that it is my own features that are represented by the Shroud of Turin. The forgers of the Shroud were perfectionists. Just as later engravers were not satisfied with the first impression of their handicraft, so the creators of the Shroud took pains to ensure that their final image should seem suitably noble and pathetic. They took *many* impressions, for they had a limitless supply of canvas. The creation of some of their work I witnessed.

The last I felt.

27

"Think of the nails," Alison read aloud, "that pierced His wrists. For Christ was not crucified, we know now, as he has always been represented, by driving nails through the palms of His hands. No, the Roman centurions who did the deed were experienced in the craft of crucifixion. They knew, by trial and error, that the weight of the victim might be too great to be supported by the bones and ligaments of the hands. Those engineers of torture drove the nails through His holy wrists!"

"Stop there," said Hedwig, placing her bony hand over the pages of the book, a paperback edition of *The Mysterious Shroud of Turin* by Monsignor Francis O'Toole. "And think, for a moment, that here, just above us, in the reliquarium, we have a relic of that very Shroud, which wrapped His body."

"We do?" little Janet Joyner asked politely. Young as she was, the girl had a canny way of saying just those things Hedwig Ober wished to hear. Alison had sized Janet up at once as a people-pleaser. But was she any different herself? Didn't she do everything she could to suck up to the old frump?

"Yes, indeed, we do," said Hedwig. "It was given to the Monsignor in 1949 by His Holiness Pope Pius the Twelfth, when this Shrine had just begun to be built. Your mother, Janet, would have been no older than you are now when that precious relic was given to the Monsignor. Actual *threads* from the Shroud—just think! Why, it makes this Shrine, in a very real way, a more significant center of pilgrimage than the National Shrine in Washington, D.C. Or it would, if there were any justice. That may seem boastful of me, and it would be, but they are not *my* words. They were the words of Monsignor O'Toole himself, spoken beneath the dome that stands above us, on the day this Shrine was consecrated. Oh my, how long ago that seems now! How much the world has changed since then!"

Hedwig fell silent, and Janet had no further prompting.

"Shall I go on?" Alison asked.

"Yes, please," said Hedwig, and then, at once, "No, no, our time is up. It's so wonderful that we've been able to meet like this, here, together, the four of us." Hedwig cast a significant glance at the fourth member of their party, Raven Peck, in whose cell they had come together for this little celebration.

It was Raven's eighteenth birthday, but Raven was not disposed to greet the occasion in a spirit of celebration. Indeed, she had become very abusive when Hedwig led the two other girls into her cell, Alison carrying the birthday cake that Hedwig had baked, with its eighteen candles already lighted, and Janet bearing the present she'd made for Raven and wrapped in Happy Birthday paper from Hallmark (which she then unwrapped, because Raven could not be trusted to have her restraints removed).

"What is it?" Alison had asked, on Raven's behalf.

"A macramé plant hanger," Janet had explained. "It's the first piece of macramé I ever made."

"And it's lovely," Hedwig had declared.

"Well, you can't really tell until there's a plant in it, but I followed the instructions. It's not like we could go shopping for something."

"Handmade presents are always the best," Hedwig stated primly, without otherwise responding to the girl's veiled criticism.

At this point the candles had burned down very near the chocolate frosting, but Raven couldn't be expected to blow them out, since Hedwig had taped her mouth shut when she'd refused to stop screaming, "Fuck the birthday cake! Fuck all of you! Fuck the Church!" Hedwig proposed that Alison blow out the candles on Raven's behalf, which Alison did, though not all at the first blow, so that any wish that Raven might have been making wouldn't be coming true anytime soon.

Alison was pretty certain she knew what Raven would have wished for. It was what she wished for herself—getting out of Birth-Right. Because for all that it was as comfortable as could be, Birth-Right was more like a prison than anything else, and until you've actually been put in a prison, you don't realize what it means to be free. Alison wondered whether when she'd been here as long as Raven, she'd be just as crazy. So far she'd managed to put on a good front when she was with Hedwig, but that's all it was. On the surface she pretended, as Janet did, to go along with the situation, reciting the rosary along with Hedwig whenever the old lady felt like a rosary, or reading the books that Hedwig supplied her with, which were all about religion and mostly very dull. As a result, she was allowed a little more space to move around in. Not freedom, but a slightly longer leash.

But in her heart she was in hell. It was a hundred times worse than sitting in a classroom waiting for the bell. Because there wasn't any bell. She couldn't leave until she'd had her baby, and that wouldn't be for *months*. She couldn't phone anyone, even her mother. She could write to her, but she was certain that whatever she wrote would be read by one of the Obers before it was mailed, *if* it was mailed, and if a letter did get to her mother, she probably wouldn't do anything to try to get Alison out, because Father Cogling would be able to talk her out of it. So she was really and truly trapped. Sometimes she got to feeling so desperate that she actually thought about attacking Hedwig physically, old as she was. But then what? She would still be down here in this sub-subbasement, in a maze of corridors and locked doors that didn't unlock with keys but with a thing that looked like a pocket calculator. You had to know the right numerical code to open the doors, and only Hedwig and Gerhardt knew the code numbers. And suppose she managed to get up to ground level? This place was in the middle of a *forest* and was guarded by German shepherds, and Alison suspected that the dogs weren't there so much to keep people out as to keep the girls in.

She tried not to think about it. She tried to think in a positive way about the baby she was going to have, and the gift of life, and all that. She even tried to study geometry, and she *hated* geometry, because it was either completely obvious or didn't make any sense at all. But trying not to think about something is the best way to guarantee that you can't think about anything else.

It seemed awful to be eating Raven's birthday cake in front of her when her mouth was taped shut, but Hedwig said that that was the girl's own fault and not to worry, because when Raven got hungry enough, she would eat. She always did. It even seemed a little cruel to be reading aloud from the book about the Shroud of Turin, since the part Hedwig had chosen to read aloud was all about how much Christ had suffered when he was crucified, which was not something anyone would necessarily want to dwell on in Raven's situation, with her wrists and ankles buckled in leather restraints and her mouth taped shut. Hedwig was a very religious person, but religious people aren't always sensitive about what people who are less religious feel, besides which Hedwig's style of religion tended to be on the dark side, not to say morbid. She was an expert on how Christ had suffered and how various martyrs were killed. Also, abortion was a big issue, as you might expect, since preventing abortions was the whole reason she was here at the Shrine of Blessed Konrad of Paderborn, which was what the place had been called when it was built. But Hedwig didn't seem very interested in the bright side of religion, the side that had to do with love.

That was the worst of it. The loneliness. Alison wasn't used to spending so much time all by herself, with no one to talk to, no telephone, not even Mr. Boots, the neighbor's cat who would come to the back door, meowing for scraps. Alison would have given anything just to be sitting beside her mother on the ratty old sofa in front of the TV, watching *Roseanne* and sharing Chinese takeout. Most of all she missed Greg. When they split up, she thought, "Okay, it's over. Too bad. Now get on with the rest of your life." But now that there was no way he could get in touch with her, she felt as though her life were over. Without Greg nothing mattered, not even the baby, even though it was his. She wanted to touch him and to feel his touch, and she couldn't. She wished she were dead, and Greg too, and they were in heaven, making love again.

Janet, seeing that the party was about to be over, asked Hedwig, in her most inveigling whine, "Do you suppose I could have another little slice of cake? Just a sliver? It's *so* good."

"Oh well," said Hedwig, who was vain about her cooking and had every right to be. It *was* a scrumptious chocolate cake. "Why not? Since you've both been so good." She cut two more slices of cake. Then, just as she'd tipped the second slice sideways onto Alison's paper plate, her beeper beeped. "Oh dear," she said, "excuse me," and went over to stand by the door of the cell, as though she'd be more private there, and took out her beeper from the pocket of her gray wool smock and said "Yes?" and then, in a different tone of voice, "No, I can't."

Alison knew right away that Hedwig must be talking with her brother Gerhardt, who had driven Alison to the Shrine in his big

Cadillac. Whenever she talked with her brother, in person or on the phone, Hedwig became a different person. It was like in movies about the army, when the sergeant who is usually such a bully salutes his commanding officer and is suddenly a cocker spaniel. Hedwig clutched the beeper and nodded and said, "No, not now, I'm sorry. Can't it wait?"

Apparently it couldn't wait, because Hedwig finally had to put the beeper back in her pocket. "I'm sorry, girls. I'm going to have to leave you here with Raven for a little. Help yourselves to some more cake if you like. I won't be long."

She unlocked the cell with the little thing that looked like a calculator, and exited, and they heard the door lock behind her.

"I don't believe it," said Alison. "She left us alone. Together."

"But she can still hear us, you know," said Janet. "Every cell has got a microphone or maybe a camera."

"But she won't be listening to us now. She'll be talking with her brother on the phone."

"You're right," said Janet.

Raven was shaking her head from side to side, the only movement she could make.

"She wants us to take the tape off," Janet said.

"But if she starts screaming again . . ."

"She won't do that," Janet said, beginning to peel the white tape from Raven's face. "It's only when Hedwig's around she gets that way. She really hates Hedwig. You can't blame her."

Alison was astonished at the sudden change in Janet, whom she had only seen, till now, in Hedwig's company. She was only twelve years old, a seventh grader, and she didn't seem that bright. Now she was acting like Sigourney Weaver in *Aliens*, full of purpose and determination.

Janet had the tape off Raven's mouth. "Are you okay?"

"Jesus," said Raven, in a fervent whisper, "I hate that woman, I just *hate* her."

"Are you okay?" Janet insisted.

"Yes, I'm okay. Is *she?*" Meaning Alison.

Janet glanced at Alison. "I don't know. I think so. I mean, we can never talk anymore, except in front of Hedwig. It isn't the way it was—it's worse now."

"I figured that," said Raven. "What about Mary? And Tara?"

"Mary is sick. Hedwig lets us visit her, and I don't think she's act-ing. She looks sick. And she keeps asking Hedwig to let her see a doc-tor, and Hedwig keeps saying soon, soon. Tara—I don't know. Maybe they took her away, or maybe she tried to escape."

"But if she'd escaped, she'd have told someone, there'd be police here."

"Maybe she didn't get away, maybe she just tried."

"Maybe they killed her," Raven said.

Janet began to cry. "No," she said, "no, they wouldn't do that."

"Jesus, don't *cry*," said Raven. "Crying can't do any good."

Alison put her arm around Janet's shoulders, trying to give her some comfort, but it's hard to comfort someone else when you feel just as bad. Both Janet and Raven knew more about Birth-Right than she did, and from what she could gather, the situation was even worse than she'd imagined.

"Who is Tara?" she asked, looking up at Raven.

"Tara Seberg. She was the third one to get here. I was the first. Listen, we probably don't have much time till Hedwig's back. You want to get out of here?"

Alison nodded. Raven stared into her eyes, as though she were giv-ing her a lie detector test, and Alison stared back, trying to think of something to say to make Raven trust her.

Janet slipped away from Alison's forgetful embrace. "I'm sorry, I've got to throw up." She went to the lidless toilet bowl in the far corner of the cell and knelt down to vomit.

"That's okay," said Raven, keeping her eyes on Alison. "Let her puke, she'll feel better. I've got to tell you something while I can. The only way we'll any of us get out of here is if *one* of us can get to the police. Right?"

Alison nodded.

"And it doesn't look like it's going to be me. Or Tara, either, by the sound of it. And Mary Tyler can't pick her nose without a handker-chief. Janet? Well, she's a great kid, tougher than any of us. She says when she gets out of here she wants to kill both her parents, and I think she's serious about it. It was her daddy who got her knocked up, and then her mom sends her here, so she can't get an abortion. But Hed-wig's no dummy, she's got the sense not to trust Janet for all the act she puts on like she's still in diapers. But for some reason Hedwig seems to trust you."

"I think it's because when we were driving up here, we got a flat tire, and Gerhardt had to leave me alone in the car. And I didn't make a bolt for it. I mean, it was raining, and where was I going to go? But when he came back with the tow truck, I think he was actually surprised to see I was still there in the car."

Raven nodded. "Hedwig said something, earlier, about how you were up in the church with her, on the main floor?"

"I've helped her with the cleaning. Twice."

"I used to do that. When I first got here, I was like you. Butter wouldn't melt. I was waiting for my chance, but when it came, I messed up. But I did manage to do one thing. Hedwig had this can of Mace in her purse. You know what Mace is?"

"You squirt it at muggers, and it blinds them?"

"Right. She'd left me alone, just long enough to get it out of her purse and hide it the first place I could see. Maybe it's still there. Under the kneeling pad inside the big carved-wood confessional. I don't think anyone ever comes into the Shrine to go to confession, so it could still be there. Unless Hedwig found it, which I doubt, because she still questions me about it sometimes. I wish I'd used it while I had the chance. Anyhow, you better put the tape back over my mouth. She'll be coming back any minute."

Alison nodded and pressed the wide white strip of adhesive across Raven's mouth.

Janet had finished throwing up, but she was still kneeling beside the toilet bowl, looking at the brown mulch still recognizable as chocolate cake. She looked up at Alison, smiling. "Isn't it weird, I'm still hungry. Coming up it tasted almost as good as it did going down." She hit the stainless steel flush handle with the heel of her hand, and watched the cake swirl away into the drain. "You know, a friend of mine told me that in France it's as easy as that to get rid of a baby. There's a pill you take. You bleed a little extra, and it's gone."

"I've heard the same thing. But it's not legal here."

"Sometimes I think I'd like to do the same thing myself. Just whirl around a few times inside the toilet bowl, then disappear. Like one of the rides at the fairgrounds. Have you ever been on the big Ferris wheel at the fair?"

Alison nodded.

"If I ever get out of here," Janet said with determination, "what I want to do is go on the Ferris wheel again, and sit in one of the seats all by myself. I'll probably have to buy two tickets. Do you think so?"

"Maybe if it's not too busy you wouldn't have to."

"That's what I would like to do."

When Hedwig returned, her thin lips were bent into an anxious smile. "Well, I have just had the most wonderful news. We're to have a priest with us here at Birth-Right. We'll be able to attend Mass, perhaps every day. And go to confession, if we need to. To take Communion. Tara, for one, will be delighted."

"What a treat," said Janet.

"Is it Father Cogling?" Alison asked.

Hedwig shook her head. "No. No, it's the director of Birth-Right. He's only been here once before, and that was before any of you girls had come here. His name is Father Pat, and he's much younger than Father Cogling. But a real crusader in the battle for Life. Oh yes, he's been at the forefront!"

"Pat is his last name?" Janet asked.

Hedwig shook her head abstractedly. "I do *wish* they'd given me more notice. There are no fresh flowers on the altar, and I should have something special for his dinner, and a dozen other things. So I'm afraid our little celebration must come to an end. Alison, let me take you back to your room first. Janet, you stay here with Raven, and perhaps she'll let you feed her some cake. But don't take the bandage from her mouth till we've left, or she'll start carrying on again."

"Yes, Mrs. Ober," said Janet.

Hedwig opened the cell door. "Come along, dear," she said to Alison. "I'll get some fresh linen, and you can help me make Father Pat's bed."

28

At ten a.m. promptly Father Cogling rapped on Father Pat's bedroom
door. "Father Pat, you really must get up now. I explained, when you
laid down, that you mustn't get too comfortable. It's imperative that
you set off now for the Shrine without any more delay. You can catch
up on your sleep in the car. Father Pat, are you listening to what I say?"

There was only a groan in reply, but that was better than the silence
of utter, unrousable stupor.

"Gerhardt is waiting for you right now, Father Pat," Father Cogling went on, more loudly. "I've packed two bags for you. You *must* get
up! Do you understand?"

Father Pat produced a groggy "Yes, yes," but that was an improvement on groans.

"The police phoned *twice* yesterday, and once the day before. I'm
sure it's purely routine. It's probably all because the young man I spoke
of had written a new will recently, in which he particularly requested
that *you* perform his funeral service. I told the man at McCarron's that
that would be out of the question, and *he* understood at once, given
what is known about this Bing Anker, which I won't go into. But now
there's another *priest* who's been pestering me about the same thing,
and wanting to talk with you, and it's all become very complicated.
The long and short of it, Father Pat, is that *you must leave now!*"

The door was opened from inside, and Father Pat, unshaven and
bleary-eyed, regarded Father Cogling balefully. He seemed to have
slept in his clothes, and his hair was a fright. Father Cogling took out a
comb from the inside pocket of his suit coat and neatened Father Pat's

hair. Father Pat allowed himself to be put to rights with the resentful impassivity of a four-year-old boy who disdains to comb his own hair or button his own buttons.

"Do you remember anything of what I told you when you got home this morning?" Father Cogling asked, with that tone of resigned, contemptuous solicitude with which the wives of alcoholics address their spouses.

Father Pat shook his head.

Father Cogling found that possible to believe. He'd never seen the pastor of St. Bernardine's looking so much the worse for wear—or so little inclined to assert his own authority. He seemed ready to do anything he was told to, without question or protest. This was gratifying in one way, but also somewhat unsettling. Getting Father Pat to do what needed to be done was like driving a car with a steering wheel that allows too much slip. It went where it was directed, but the driver didn't feel that he was securely in control.

Father Cogling sighed and shook his head. "Then let me explain the matter, as much as I understand it myself. Some days ago—in fact, the very night you chose to go on a binge—a young man in St. Paul was found shot twice. It was in the papers, but I'd thrown them out before the police called here, so I can't give you any more of the details. His name was Bing Anker, and it appears that many years ago, when you were at Our Lady of Mercy, he was an altar boy there. Does the name ring a bell?"

Father Pat shook his head, and Father Cogling could have wished the police had been there to see it. A professional actor could not have given a more persuasive performance.

"I didn't suppose it would, Father. It was so long ago. However, and this is unfortunate, there was a priest outside the house on the night the young man was killed. And there's no possibility, according to the police, that the young man committed suicide. And there was no evidence of a burglary. And that is why they want to talk with you. They'll want to know where you were last Thursday evening, and who you were with. I should have had the presence of mind to tell them, at once, that you were here with me. But I didn't, and now it would be too late. But I did the next best thing and told them that you were on retreat, and that I would tell you to get in touch with them as soon as you phoned here. So, what must be done now is for Gerhardt to drive you to the Shrine, so that you can call the police from the telephone there.

Both Gerhardt and his sister will vouch for your having been there, so there will be no need for you to feel any . . . embarrassment about this. Not that you have anything to feel embarrassed about. However, it's possible that you were . . . with someone else during the time in question, someone who wouldn't want to be involved in this."

Father Pat nodded, and answered guardedly, "Yes, I have been with . . . someone else."

"And there's no reason why *anyone else* need be involved. I really don't think the police have any business in matters that concern the Church. So!" He held out his hand. "Your bags are already in the car, and Gerhardt is waiting."

Father Pat made rather more of the handshake than was strictly warranted. He hesitated at first, and then clasped Father Cogling's hand too firmly and held it too long. It was as though he feared they might be parting forever, and Father Cogling realized, with a twinge of misgiving, that it was not an entirely unwarranted fear.

"God bless you!" Father Cogling said with a final squeeze and then a slipping loose. He led the way to the door, and Father Pat followed with what seemed, under the circumstances, a miraculous acquiescence. No questions, no hesitations, no demurs. Only at the last moment, as he stood in the open doorway, with Gerhardt at the curb, holding open the door of the Cadillac, did he turn to Father Cogling and ask, "I *am* still a priest, am I not?"

"Yes, indeed, Father, you are still a priest. *That* can never be taken away from us. Ordination leaves a mark on the soul that is indelible."

"Like a tattoo," said Father Pat.

Father Cogling nodded. "I would not have thought of that comparison myself, but yes, I suppose it could be thought of as the soul's tattoo. But this is not the time, or the place, to wax poetical. Good-bye for now." He stepped back inside the rectory and, after Father Pat had lowered his head as a sign of parting, closed the door.

The Cadillac had barely pulled away from the curb when the phone rang. If it was the police, Father Cogling could now state unequivocally that Father Pat was not in the rectory.

But it was not the police. It was Mrs. Demain, the manager of the nursing home, who explained that she had been trying for some time to reach Father Bryce but that she always got his answering machine, which was why she was troubling Father Cogling.

"I gather you're calling about Father Bryce's mother?" Father Cogling said. "Is anything the matter?"

"That's what *we* would like to know. Mrs. Bryce was checked out from the Home on Sunday morning by her other son, Peter. The ward nurse was given to understand that they would be going to your church, where Father Bryce would be saying the eleven o'clock Mass."

"Why, yes," said Father Cogling brightly, "I remember talking to them briefly after Mass. Father Bryce was out of town on a retreat that day, and I took the eleven o'clock Mass. Father Bryce is *still* on retreat, which is why you've been getting his answering machine. And I must take the blame for not having monitored his calls for him. Though even if I had, there's not much I could do to help you. There's no phone where Father Bryce is. Is something the matter with his mother?"

"The matter is that she hasn't returned to the Home."

"Well, surely, the person to contact is the son she was with, Peter."

"We've tried. And came to the same dead end—another answering machine."

"Well, it's surely remiss of Peter to have taken Mrs. Bryce off somewhere with no explanation, but I'm afraid Father Bryce couldn't help you any more than I can."

"At this point, we're considering contacting the police."

"That's your decision, of course. Have you tried to call Peter at his place of employment?"

"We did. And learned that he hasn't reported to work since last Friday."

"That *is* worrying. Well, if I hear anything, I will let you know at once."

The woman hung up, and Father Cogling breathed a silent *Laudamus Deo* of relief. If he had had to explain to Father Pat that his mother and brother were missing persons, on top of the business with Bing Anker, it might not have been possible to persuade him to leave for the Shrine. He would have made a nuisance of himself trying to find them, and all in vain. Imagine trying to explain *that* one to Father Pat! My dear boy, I'm afraid I have bad news for you: We had to kill your mother and your twin brother, because they were about to be a source of great scandal to the Church. Father Cogling himself had not taken the matter so calmly when Gerhardt Ober had apprised him of his fait accompli, even though Gerhardt had been acting in this, as in so much else, as Father Cogling's factotum. He'd done unbidden what Father Cogling would probably have agreed to let him do after days of agonized inner debate. Even now, Father Cogling had to ask himself whether he had acted to spare the Church grave scandal or to save his own skin. But, really, that was not a meaningful distinction, since the scandal could only have been averted by saving his own skin.

Now that the deed had been done, by his acquiescence if not by his own hand, Father Cogling found himself wishing that it might have been accomplished years and years ago, before he'd yielded to Margaret Bryce's blackmail demands. Of course, neither of them had ever called it blackmail. She was a poor widow who needed help bringing up her two boys, and didn't he, as their natural father, feel a certain moral responsibility for their welfare? He did not. What he had felt was an abject fear of what might happen to him if she were to go over his head to the Bishop with her self-righteous demands. And so, to placate her, Father Cogling had dipped into the constant flow of donations, and no one had ever been the wiser. God had even performed one of his favorite miracles, producing good out of apparent evil, for the building funds that were pilfered from St. Bernardine's collections box had gone toward the upbringing of the church's future pastor.

Perhaps God might perform the same miracle again and wring some blessing from these later ills. Father Cogling knelt before the altar of the rectory's private chapel and prayed that that might be the case and that God would send some kind of token of his intentions in this regard. Father Cogling often asked for, and received, signs and portents that let him shape his actions in accordance with God's wishes. Christ's prayer at Gethsemane—"Not my will, but thine, be done"—was Father Cogling's as well.

Scarce had the favor been asked than it was granted: The rectory's door chimes sounded their time-honored mi-do-re-sol, sol-re-mi-do. Father Cogling made the sign of the cross, by way of acknowledging receipt of the omen, got up from his knees, and crossed to the chapel's bay window, from which it was possible to oversee anyone standing at the front door.

There were two men there, one of them a priest. The priest seemed unfamiliar, though from the vantage of the bay window his most noticeable feature was the bright pink crown of his bald head, so it was hard to be sure. He kept ringing the bell impatiently, as one does when one suspects that those within are malingering. Father Cogling was quite certain that this had to be the priest from Las Vegas who had already telephoned twice wanting to talk with Father Pat, and then, thwarted in that regard, to insist that Father Cogling allow Bing Anker's funeral services to be held at St. Bernardine's, to which Father Cogling's response had been a polite but categorical no.

Having this priest appear at the rectory was distressing enough (especially if it were to be read as a portent), but what was still more distressing was the fact that the priest was accompanied by a young man whose face was maddeningly familiar, though Father Cogling could not at first put a name to it. And then the young man touched his thin, Clark Gable–style mustache in a particular way and Father Cogling realized that this was the impudent fellow who had been the fiancé of Alison Sanders, the girl whom Father Cogling had rescued from the abortion clinic. Father Cogling could feel his nervous system going on red alert. The priest was trying to find Father Pat, and the boy was undoubtedly trying to find Alison, and both of the people they were looking for were to be found at the Shrine of Blessed Konrad of Paderborn. But *they* could not possibly be aware of this coincidence, so why had they appeared at the door of the rectory together?

Father Cogling was not about to satisfy his curiosity by the simple expedient of answering the door. Indeed, if he'd been living in the Middle Ages and this pair had appeared on the drawbridge of his castle, he would have delighted in dousing them with a cauldron of boiling oil.

Lacking that immediate gratification, Father Cogling returned to the prie-dieu before the chapel's altar and began to say a rosary, meditating on the five Sorrowful Mysteries. His visitors did not leave off sounding the door chimes until he had reached the third decade of the rosary, and the third Sorrowful Mystery, which is the crowning with thorns.

To think that God Himself should endure such torments so that our sins might be forgiven! The wonder of it brought tears to Father Cogling's eyes.

XXIX

It had been unwise, and worse than unwise, to have ventured down into the work chambers of the Inquisition. The torturer Bertrand Crispo lacked all ecclesial authority; he was only the Legate's minion, but in the Legate's absence Crispo acted as though the Legate's powers were his to exercise. And the Legate's authority was virtually supreme throughout Languedoc. He answered only to Rome, which meant, in effect, that he answered to no one. Father Bryce doubted that his borrowed episcopal robes would provide him any protection should Durand du Fuaga come to think he was tainted with heresy. Indeed, there would be a kind of cachet in being able to number a bishop among du Fuaga's victims. Father Bryce understood that now, thanks to a few ambiguous remarks that Crispo had let drop concerning the Legate's zeal to seek out heresy even among the nobility and clergy.

"Perhaps even here in this cathedral, among the canons, Your Eminence, there may be those who have tolerated heresy, though they be not heretics themselves."

Father Bryce had assured him that all the clerics attached to Notre Dame de Gevaudon were of the strictest orthodoxy.

"But, Your Eminence," Crispo had said slyly, "how can you be sure? If a man is a heretic, he will conceal it as long as he can. Unless one has the tools available to the Inquisition, and skill in their use, nothing can be known. One will meet only lies and denials. Take the man Bonamico. He was apprehended trying to escape your service with most of his crew of workmen. We have questioned him many times, but he has been obdurate, when he is not simply speaking that gibberish, and claims to know less about the heretics who surround us than if he were a child of five years. But you will hear another song when we begin his proper examination."

"Yes, I'm sure that's so."

"Perhaps you would like to be present at his examination, Your Eminence? Since I have already acted against the Legate's explicit instructions in permitting you to enter the Lombards' cell and to speak with Bonamico, there can be no harm in your witnessing the work of his interrogation. Indeed, as I recall, you were to have seen the interrogation of the de Gaillac woman, but you were taken ill."

"The spirit is willing, but the flesh is weak," Father Bryce said, avoiding Crispo's gaze.

"The flesh *is* weak. Very true. But this time you may find yourself better fortified. Custom breeds a kind of ease in these matters, as with bad smells. And you may be useful to the Holy Office if this Bonamico begins to jabber again in his strange speech. Is it the language of Egypt?"

Father Bryce shook his head. "No, it is the dialect of a northern people—Saxons, or their neighbors."

"You speak it fluently."

"It only seems so because you cannot understand all my errors."

Crispo flashed his pale gums in a smile. "If there have been errors, Your Eminence, they were Bonamico's, not yours."

And so, unwisely, he had succumbed to the temptation and become the witness to the torture of Bonamico. Or, rather, of A. D. Boscage, though Father Bryce was not so unwise as to translate any of the man's desperate insistences that he was not Bonamico but the transmentated spirit of a twentieth-century science-fiction writer. Instead, Father Bryce had urged Boscage that the only way to bring his torture to an end was to give his torturer what he wanted and confess himself to be a heretic.

Boscage did confess, but his torture continued, until he had implicated all of his fellow masons whom he could identify by name. Still Crispo demanded to know the name of the arch-heretic and high priest of the Albigensians.

At last, when his back was being laid open with a many-thonged whip, Boscage was inspired to take the one revenge within his power. "There is the man you seek!" he declared. "There, beside you. *He* is our bishop and high priest."

Crispo signaled for the whip to be put down. He approached the post to which Boscage had been bound and lifted his sagging head to look into his bloodied face. "You name Silvanus de Roquefort, the Bishop of Rodez and Montpellier-le-Vieux?"

"Yes!" Boscage agreed readily. "That is *your* name for him. But as an Albigensian he has another name. All the *perfecti* have secret names by which they are known to one another."

"The man is lying!" Father Bryce declared with unfeigned indignation. "He would name anyone to have you stop his torture."

Crispo lifted his hand for silence. "There may be truths hidden within a lie, Your Eminence, like seeds in dirt. Let me proceed, please." He addressed Boscage: "What is this other name?"

"He is the High Priest Ammon-Ra of the Ancient Order of Hibernians. And the language you've heard us speak together is Egyptian, just as you suspected. Ammon-Ra has been initiated into the highest levels of Egyptian wisdom."

"These are preposterous lies! You cannot possibly—"

Crispo looked up at Father Bryce. "I think it would be best, Your Eminence, if you were not here to be insulted by the man's inventions. As you say, they must be lies. But it is my work to hear them."

Reluctantly, Father Bryce let himself be led from the torture chamber, and spent the next hour fuming inwardly in the cloistered garden where he'd first found himself when he'd awakened in the skin of Silvanus de Roquefort. How could he have foreseen that A. D. Boscage would still have the presence of mind to ply his trade as an inventor of fabulous falsehoods in his present extremity? The wit, even, to tailor his lies to the appetites and expectations of his audience. Ammon-Ra and Egyptian wisdom! But Crispo's eyes had fairly glowed with the thrill of discovery.

Father Bryce was full of forebodings. But when Crispo joined him in the garden, his manner was more apologetic than threatening. "I beg Your Eminence's forgiveness for my seeming lack of respect. As you understood at once, the man is a liar, nothing but that. Usually I am not so easily deceived. Not that I ever credited what he said with respect to Your Eminence. You must not think so."

"I never supposed you such a fool," Father Bryce replied, in what he hoped was a bishoplike tone of calm condescension. Yet he could not keep from asking, "And does the man still maintain that I am some Egyptian high priest?"

"He maintains nothing now, Your Eminence. He died during interrogation. I misjudged his endurance. The Legate will not be pleased. If I had not been impatient, I am sure that at last I would have worn down his impostures and discovered the truth he thought to conceal with his fabrications. I have no doubt he was a heretic and could have named many others."

"No doubt at all," Father Bryce agreed. "But as you noted, the flesh is weak. Sometimes, perhaps, weaker than we suppose."

"Quite true, Your Eminence. His was. Have you further need of me?"

"No. But—"

"Yes?"

Should he try to strike a bargain with Crispo? Dare he suggest that he would say nothing to the Legate about Bonamico's Egyptian nonsense if Crispo would return the favor? Might that not, instead, reawaken Crispo's suspicions?

At last, he only smiled, and offered his ring to be kissed, and dismissed Crispo with the medieval equivalent of "Have a nice day": *"Pax vobiscum."* Peace be with you.

"Et cum spiritu tuo," the torturer responded, as automatic as an altar boy.

30

Alexis Clareson drove his battery-powered wheelchair across the considerable expanse of what appeared to be a Persian carpet of the first quality, though Father Mabbley was no judge of such matters. Alexis parked beside a wheelchair-accessible liquor cabinet, slid it open, and said, "You'll have some brandy."

Father Mabbley pretended this was a question. "Thank you, Alex. That would top things off nicely. *Such* a meal. I don't think I've ever eaten lobster except in a restaurant. I didn't know it was legal to make it in one's own home."

"It isn't," Alex said. "Unless one has a full-time chef."

"Alex, you're bragging."

"I am, indeed. And *this* is a very special old brandy. You'll enjoy it."

"I'm sure I will. But I fear you won't enjoy what we have to talk about at this point."

"Not yet, please, Mab. Let us enjoy the flowers of friendship a little while longer. You were so droll at dinner—and such a flirt. But you weren't flirting with me, were you? Not that I blame you. Jeremiah is a jewel. Who *could* resist him? But he did rather monopolize your conversation. The rest of us just eavesdropped."

"You flatter me, Alex. As ever. I didn't flirt so much as listen."

"And how better to flirt? But I'm just teasing you. As ever." Alexis handed him a snifter, lifted his own, and said, "Your health."

"And yours."

They performed the rites of the first taste—the hand's embrace of the glass, a slow swirl for the eye to savor, a sniff, then the wetting of the lips and the tongue's astonishment.

"You do live well here, Alex."

"Indeed. Who would have thought?"

"When we were seminarians?"

"A world ago."

"Oh, as I recall, there was liquor then, too. Even brandy. Though it was usually Christian Brothers. Do you miss it?"

"That world? Of course, who doesn't. Everyone misses some fabled Eden of lost innocence. That's why it was the younger Elvis who was elected to be a postage stamp. What a silly election *that* was. Who would vote for being old and fat and corrupt? Which is not to say that I'm corrupt, mind you. Old and fat I must admit to. I've even come around to thinking old and fat a kind of blessing. In the sense of 'Lead us not into temptation.' I think the Church could solve all its present problems if it required not just chastity but *wheelchairs* of all of us."

Father Mabbley laughed.

"So," said Alex, shifting into Chancery mode. "Did you find what you needed to know?"

"I looked through Bryce's files. He seemed, early on, headed for better things."

"Yes, he got derailed. It was more the alcohol than any of his known indiscretions. Of course, the one tends to lead to the other. He's back on the tracks now, I think."

"The abortion protests, you mean? He seems to have become quite active along those lines."

"Indeed, he's our leading pro-Life crusader, and the Bishop is appreciative of his acts of zeal, since he can take credit for them with Rome without having to exert himself unduly in a crusade for which he has, like so many of us, mixed feelings."

"I gather Massey's own ideal agenda would be more liberal than accords with the current temper in Rome."

"Yes, he has all the wrong opinions. Though he takes pains not to express them. Optional celibacy, women in the priesthood, birth control, some kinder accommodation of our gay brothers and sisters. What can I say: The man's a flaming liberal. Which nowadays, of course, amounts to the brand of Cain. But he has two advantages that even Connie O'Connor might envy: He's black, one might even say charismatically black, and his private life and financial life have been irreproachable. So all he has to do is bide his time until the climate changes in Rome."

"Avoiding, meanwhile, any hint of scandal."

"Exactly. And there we come to it, Mab. You've thrown out hints about Father Bryce that were a *little* unnerving. I hope there's no connection between Bryce and the unhappy matter that brings you to Minneapolis."

"I share your hope, Alex, but it's not something we ought to be discussing at this point."

"Oh dear, as bad as that? Well, I trust you won't do anything rash. If it becomes as serious as you seem to think, would you at least talk to one of our lawyers before you go elsewhere?"

"Surely. Unless the whole thing blows up before I have the opportunity. It would help if I could talk to the man. This Cogling person is not exactly forthcoming. In the literal sense that he wouldn't come to the door of the rectory when I called on him there the other day. Oh, and that reminds me. Cogling is stonewalling someone besides me. You may remember my talking to Jeremiah at dinner about the young man I met at Schinder's."

"Yes, the one you traded jokes with over your friend's casket. I liked the one about John Gotti going to prison, though in one form or another it's as old as the hills."

"That young man, yes. It seems that Cogling has spirited away his fiancée and refuses to say where she is."

"I should think Cogling is a little old for *that* sort of thing."

"It may well be she doesn't want to be reached. But Greg—that's the boy's name—has gone to the girl's mother, and she told him that Cogling had her sign some papers—without leaving her a copy, of course—putting the girl in the care of some home for unwed mothers who might otherwise be seeking abortions. Do you know anything about such a place, Alex? I assume it's a Catholic charity of some sort."

Alexis Clareson grimaced into his snifter and answered the question with a significant silence. At last he sighed, and said, "Oh dear."

"Have I stepped in something?"

Alexis laughed. "Indeed, you may have stepped in the same river twice, which is something that's not supposed to be possible. How do you *do* it, Mab? You haven't been here long enough to put your friend in the ground, and already . . ." He finished his sentence by pursing his lips and closing his eyes, as though to say his lips were sealed.

"Is this something else Bryce is involved in?" Father Mabbley persisted.

"Something *else?* Except for his having gone off on an unannounced retreat, I know of nothing Bryce is 'involved in.' And I don't want to. But I would wager that your young friend may find his fiancée and you may find Bryce at the same place. But I don't think I can say more than that, for it's all very hush-hush at this point."

"Oh, I won't reveal my sources, if that's what worries you."

"You wouldn't have to. Massey knows you're dining here tonight. He can put two and two together."

"All the young man wants is a chance to talk to his girlfriend on the phone."

"In order to persuade her to get an abortion?"

"Just the opposite, in point of fact. They had quarreled about it, but he'd understood she meant to have the child. He was floored when the girl's mother told him that Father Cogling had stopped her from entering the abortion clinic. And delighted. You see, his circumstances have suddenly altered in a peculiar way, and it all has to do with my friend Bing Anker. And it involves me, too, in the oddest way. In fact, it's turned my life upside down."

"Really? In a nice way, I hope."

"I honestly don't know at this point. Do you have time to hear the whole story? It's a bit complicated."

"Mab, really! But let me freshen your brandy before you unfold your tale. Mind you, this isn't a quid pro quo." Alexis negotiated his wheelchair to the liquor cabinet to retrieve the brandy bottle, then motored over to his guest to pour a more generous portion than the first into Father Mabbley's snifter. "You may tell me *your* story, but I'm really not at liberty— You understand."

"Whatever you decide, Alex. I can't coerce you. So." Father Mabbley tasted the brandy and thought how best to begin.

"Some long while ago," he began, "my friend Bing Anker came into an inheritance. A double inheritance, in a way. His mother died, and he inherited her house in St. Paul, and he also came into another house, in Willowville, and rather a nice piece of money, from his brother-in-law. That's a *very* long story, which I won't go into, but the upshot is that Bing was able to leave his job in Las Vegas, where I had got to know him, and settle down here, and like the good steward in the parable, he invested the money that had been left to him shrewdly during the go-go days of the eighties. And he died rich. At least, by my standards he died rich."

"How much?" Alexis asked.

"Not counting the houses, half a million."

"That's certainly *respectable.* And are you his sole heir? If so, I expect you'll soon have your sufficiency of lobster—at home or wherever you like."

"Not *quite* his sole heir. That's where Greg comes in."

"The Orpheus of our story," Alexis glossed.

For a moment Father Mabbley was puzzled. "Orpheus? Oh, because his fiancée has been borne off. Rather a sinister simile, Alex. I hope the girl's situation isn't as drastic as all that."

"I'm sorry to interrupt. Go on, I'm all ears."

"My friend Bing was one of those people—thank heaven there aren't that many—who consider the writing of a will a test of their creativity. The writing and rewriting, for according to his lawyer, Mr. Wiley (such a name for a lawyer!), he came up with a new one about once a year. Happily, I always figured prominently. But Bing would add codicils and filigrees, and in the last will he wrote, not long ago, he made provision for his cousin Greg Romero, whom he'd met at a family wedding a short while before and taken a fancy to. He'd always wanted to leave a little something to one of his relatives—in part, at Wiley's insistence, who said it was a kind of insurance policy in cases when one is leaving the bulk of one's estate to someone who is only a friend. It shows that one has given some consideration to the bonds of blood. So Bing provided for his cousin, but with all sorts of provisos. At the wedding Greg had been telling Bing about his problem being torn between wanting to finish up at the university, where's he's studying business, and wanting to get married, and possibly *needing* to get married. So Bing wrote into his will that his cousin should be allowed five years of free rent in the house in Willowville (which then reverts to me), plus a kind of scholarship of ten thousand a year, until he's got his college degree. *Provided* that he gets married. I think it was Bing's not-very-subtle way of getting him to do the right thing."

"It *sounds,*" Alexis commented, "as though he were intending to die the next day. I mean, your friend wasn't on his deathbed, was he? You said on the phone that he wasn't HIV-positive."

"Bing always thought he was going to die the next day. Wiley says that he'd come in every year with some new, similarly fanciful, manipulative codicil. Wiley didn't object. Bing paid good money."

"So now, as a result of the will, this Greg Romano—"

"Romero," Father Mabbley corrected.

"—has a sudden urgent need to tie the knot."

"I must say, to his credit, that he was trying to get back in touch with Alison—that's the girl's name—before he learned of Bing's caprice. But yes, now he is more highly motivated to do the right thing, as I suppose was Bing's intention. In any case, I think he ought to be able to talk with the girl and explain his situation."

"Oh dear," said Alexis.

"There's more," said Father Mabbley. "There were also conditions as to *my* inheriting. One condition, rather—that I leave the priesthood."

"But you can't!" Alex protested.

"Can't, Alex? It's done all the time."

"Yes, of course. I meant the sacrament can't be undone. You'll always be a priest."

"In the sense that I possess sacramental powers, yes. But not in the sense Bing's will intends—that I resign my office."

"But you'd lose . . ." Alexis lifted his hands in perplexity.

"I wouldn't lose that much, in fact. My pension won't kick in for another fifteen years, or even twenty, and even then it's meager. You know my salary, or you can guess. I'd lose living rent free in a shabby rectory. But think what I'd gain."

"Yes, half a million isn't to be sneezed at."

"I mean, Alex, my self-respect."

"Mab, you shock me. And in any case, you're wrong. That is precisely what you'd lose."

"I shock myself, in a way, but it's so. You see, it's something we used to talk about, Bing and I. Whether, given the way the Church has changed, it means the same thing to be a priest as it did when we were ordained."

"It's not the Church that's changed, Mab. In a way, that may be its problem—that it's in the nature of the Church that it *can't* change. What's changed is the world around us."

"Bullshit," said Father Mabbley.

"Mab, really," said Alexis, lowering his eyes reproachfully.

"All right, then, to be brutally honest, it's the hypocrisy. The sheer weight of it. And don't talk to me about shouldering the cross. Christ came down on hypocrisy more than on anything else. He hated hypocrites. And that's what we all are—those of us, anyhow, who wear the uniform of celibacy and don't practice it. Especially if we're gay, and you and I both know what percentage of us *are* gay."

"But how else are we to *change* the Church, Mab?" Alexis demanded. His tone of zestful debate had developed an edge of petulance. For if Father Mabbley was a hypocrite in these matters, Father Clareson had to be accounted one equally, and while he was perfectly ready to acknowledge any number of other sins with equanimity, Father Clareson prided himself on his intellectual honesty—at least when he was among friends.

"Has anyone been trying to change the Church?" Father Mabbley replied. "I hadn't noticed. Everyone I know is just looking out for his ass. Isn't any homosexual act still a mortal sin? Don't teenagers still attempt suicide when they realize they're gay and they can't help it? *You* did, Alex. You told me so."

"That's not fair, Mab. I told you that in strictest confidence."

"But you must see my point. It's *cruel* to make people go through that kind of suffering. Some don't survive, as we did, and *we* were warped by it. Not as badly as some are warped, I'll give you that. I hate to think of what it must be like for a poor bastard like Bryce. He probably can't help himself with the pedophilia. All he can do is try to deny his urges. But surely you can see that it's the *system*, the Church, that has shaped those urges. You don't think it's an accident, do you, that every diocese in the country is having a scandal with pedophile priests? We *attract* them. We are the culture in which they breed, like excited bacteria. Just because of the hypocrisy. People whose sexual desires have been declared criminal *have to be* hypocrites, they have no choice. And we extend them the same protection we've extended ourselves. We say, 'It's only human to be gay. So, maybe it's a sin. But I'll confess it. And sin again.' "

"It *is* only human, Mab. Come on! Did you miss the Renaissance or something? The Church can celebrate life as well as deny it. How about the wedding feast at Cana?"

"As I understand it, Alex, gays weren't invited to that party."

"Christ got it off with publicans and sinners."

"And as a result, we're all alkies. It's the one vice permitted us. And gambling, I forgot gambling."

"And hasn't gambling been your special ministry, Mab? Are you going to want to give that up? You've done inestimable good in helping gamblers recover. Don't deny it. I've even heard it said that you are to Nevada what Mother Teresa is to India."

"True enough. I'll miss that the most. But I'll tell you something, Alex—the twelve-step programs work better in that area than the Church. My entire ministry to gamblers is based on AA and GA, not on Church doctrine. The Church isn't *against* gambling; it *uses* it! That's been one of the hardest parts of working with gamblers who are Catholic. They swear off blackjack and turn to bingo. Bing used to tell me stories that would curl your hair, if you had any left. He was a bingo caller in Vegas, and he got to know the real addicts. And almost all of them were Catholics."

"So," said Alexis, in a tone of theatrical melancholy, "are there to be no more cakes and ale?"

"Of course there will. But I don't have to preach against cakes and ale when I know perfectly well that for most people they constitute one of the simple, accepted pleasures of life. Some people can't handle the ale; they're alcoholics, and they have to swear off it. Some can't handle gambling. And some can't handle sex. But in that category I don't include gays."

"Well, that's very generous of you, Mab. Considering the number of times I've sucked your cock."

"And I was grateful every time, Alex, believe me. Parting is such sweet sorrow, and all that."

"So why not just declare a policy of live and let live? Why become the Robespierre of the sexual revolution?"

"Robespierre? That seems a bit excessive. I'm not proposing to remove anyone's head. Only my own collar."

"And what of Bryce, Father? You're not hunting for *his* head?"

Father? he thought. He let it pass, but he was aware that by that form of address Alexis had moved to a different ground.

"Bryce is the particular subject, Alex, that I understood you didn't wish to be informed about. If it can be avoided."

"Indeed. I stand corrected. And"—Alexis brightened, and retreated to a tone of formal cordiality—"I have been inconsiderate in badgering you about what must be, except in its financial aspect, a painful dilemma. What, if I may ask, is to happen to the money if for some reason you *don't* remove your collar? Would it all go to this Greg Romano?"

"I was wondering when you'd think to ask that one. What would happen would be, from the Church's viewpoint, the worst possibility of all, and the lawyer tells me that that proviso is ironclad and incontestable. It would go to creating a memorial, in iron and concrete, to the victims of priestly pedophilia."

"Jesus Christ," said Alexis.

"That was my own first reaction."

"A memorial where?"

"In the front yard of his home in St. Paul."

"There are zoning laws!"

"I'm afraid not. There was a case recently about crossburning by the Klan that Wiley says—and he should know—establishes a clear precedent."

"And the *form* of this *memorial?* Is it to be a plaque, or—?"

"Bing had an artistic imagination. It is to take the form of the Christ Child, at something like the age of eleven, crowned with thorns, and crucified. He's to be shown life-size, but the cross is to be twelve feet high. He's commissioned a sketch of what's intended from the sculptor Donald Granger. Wiley showed it to me. It's impressive."

"Might I add: indecent?"

"Not ostensibly. There are no genitalia or wounds. It's all very aboveboard and symbolic. But the symbolism is powerful—I think you'd agree."

"Massey will shit his episcopal breeches."

"Which was another reason, it occurred to me, why it might be better, all around, for me to take the money and run."

"Oh, you sly fox," said Alex, smiling in a way that was once again friendly. "You *arranged* this with him!"

"I swear to God," Father Mabbley declared, crossing himself. "Never!"

"Well, it changes everything, doesn't it? You will leave the priesthood for the *sake* of the priesthood."

"I doubt that Bing looked at it that way."

"Ah, but he must have thought how *you* would look at it, so it amounts to the same thing."

"So, between my priestly vows and the prospect of scandal . . ."

"Mab, it's my *job* to avoid scandal."

"Well, we'll avoid that scandal, at least. With Bryce I can't offer any guarantees, just as I can't offer any information. But I do need a phone number, an address. Where is he?"

"Oh, you always know how to get what you want! Such a politician. But aren't we all. I'll tell Jeremiah to give you what you need to know. Over the phone. Unofficially. Mab, it's wonderful to see you. But I've got to say good night."

31

As many times as he had stood beneath the immense concrete ribs of the dome of the Shrine of Blessed Konrad of Paderborn, Gerhardt Ober never ceased to feel a chill of reverence. He had made pilgrimages to Rome, to Lourdes, to Oberammergau and Berchtesgaden. He had seen the great cathedrals of Chartres and Köln, and others whose names he'd forgotten, when he accompanied Monsignor O'Toole on his European speaking tour in 1951, but none of those edifices had inspired Gerhardt with the same sense of wonder. There had been in all of them something fussy and feminine, as though their architects had felt they must disguise the stark power of the masonry with filigrees of lace and bouquets of flowers. The architect of the Shrine had made no such concessions to mere prettiness. Here there were no frescoes of infant angels tumbling through gilded clouds, no stone carved to look like foliage—just the sheer muscling upward of the supporting pillars and the awful weight of the ferroconcrete dome they supported. To stand beneath this dome was to experience the Fear of God.

Gerhardt could see that he was not alone in that response. Father Bryce, though he had attended Étoile du Nord as a seminarian and later taught there, and must therefore have been familiar with the Shrine's somber majesty, was nevertheless goggling at the dome like any tourist entering this holy place for the first time.

"There was an article in *National Geographic* years back," Gerhardt declared proudly, "that called the Shrine one of the Seven Wonders of the Modern World. Right along with the Eiffel Tower and the Empire State Building."

"Truly," said Father Bryce, who had uttered scarcely a word on the long drive north, "it is a marvel. Such an immense dome, and there seems almost no visible support."

"Well, that's what they can do nowadays with ferroconcrete. From the time the foundation was dug—and the Shrine goes down as deep as it stands high—till the cross was put on top of the dome, this whole thing went up in less than five years."

"And we're here . . . alone," Father Bryce observed. "No other pilgrims have come to worship here."

"It's a shame, isn't it? When I was a young man, just out of high school, this place was filled with visitors on Sundays during the summer months. They'd drive here from all over the country. But now—" Gerhardt shook his head bitterly. "It's like the Church is ashamed of the place. There was a time when they were actually thinking of demolishing it. Only at that point it would have cost as much to raze as it had originally cost to put up. So they just try to pretend it doesn't exist. That's why they let us have it for Birth-Right. I think the Bishop would like to pretend we don't exist either. At least, that's what I've heard Father Cogling say."

"Ashamed of such magnificence," Father Bryce marveled.

"It's hard to believe, isn't it. And you want to know the reason, Father?" Gerhardt thrust out his bony jaw challengingly, and when Father Bryce nodded, he declared: "The Jews!"

"The Jews?" Father Bryce echoed, not in the tone of polite, cautioning skepticism that Gerhard was used to from all but a few priests of Father Bryce's generation, but in a tone, much more, of honest curiosity.

"First there was the stink, in the sixties, right before he was going to be canonized, about Blessed Konrad having been anti-Semitic. Because he preached against the Jews who defiled the Holy Eucharist! There were pickets right here outside the gates of the Shrine with signs that said BLESSED KONRAD—PATRON SAINT OF ANTI-SEMITES. You might have seen them on TV when you were a kid, though the media wasn't as biased then as it is now, and mostly the whole thing was kept off the TV news. But it was in the papers, all right, and you can bet those picketers were Jews. Or Commies. Or both, probably. And *then*, when they'd won that round, and the Vatican backed down and said Konrad wasn't even *Blessed* Konrad anymore and may never even have existed, that's when there was the fuss about the architect who built the shrine, Ernst Kurtzensohn. A Nazi, they said in the papers. Because he'd been an assistant for Albert Speer when he was a young man in Germany, and Speer was Hitler's favorite architect. Could the man help it he was born a German? Is that a crime? If it is, then *I'm* a criminal! But suddenly the papers are saying that the Shrine, because the lower levels are built to withstand a nuclear attack, is somehow the same as the bunkers where the Führer was killed. Kurtzensohn had been the structural engineer for the Berlin bunker, so that makes him some kind of war criminal! They even tried to deport him back to Germany to stand trial. A war criminal! When he was a member of Opus Dei!"

"It is hard to believe," Father Bryce murmured sympathetically.

"In the end, even Monsignor O'Toole turned against him."

"Did he?"

"Of course, the Monsignor was under pressure himself, and his first thought was always for the Shrine. He knew that the Jews would be after him next. And he was right."

Gerhardt fell silent, but for a moment the dome itself, with its marvelous acoustical sensitivity, resounded with its own, more abstract version of his fulminations, the meaning gone but the emotion intact.

"Amazing," Father Pat commented. "It sounds like an entire pack of hunting hounds."

A lot Father Pat would have known about the sound of hunting dogs, Gerhardt thought. But he did not venture to contradict the priest. Indeed, as the echoes died away, he had to admit the comparison was apt.

They had come to stand before the altar of the side chapel dedicated to the Monsignor's memory. Gerhardt pointed to the simple marble plaque that was the only memorial to O'Toole's accomplishments.

Father Bryce read the few words on the plaque and nodded respectfully. "I wonder if I might ask you, Gerhardt, for a few moments here alone by this altar. That I might pray?"

Gerhardt suspected that he was being manipulated in some way, but it was not a request he could reasonably refuse. "Certainly, Father. For as long as you like. But my sister is keeping your dinner warm, you know."

"God bless her," said Father Bryce, getting down on his knees on the lowest of three steps leading to the altar.

Gerhardt withdrew to a respectful distance and mulled over the situation. Things had been getting out of hand, and every time Gerhardt tried to come up with a solution, he seemed to make things worse. This was not the first time in his life he'd sinned for the sake of the Church, but it was the first time he had resisted the opportunity to go to confession as soon as it had presented itself. All during the long and mostly silent drive from the Twin Cities to the Shrine, Gerhardt had thought to ask Father Pat to hear his confession. Whatever opinion Gerhardt had of the man personally (and it was not high), he *was* a priest with the power of forgiveness that all priests inherit from Saint Peter, irrespective of their own grace or virtue. Father Pat might literally be reeking with sin and still administer the sacraments. But Gerhardt had gone to confession with Father Pat before, and he knew that it would not be enough to say "Forgive me, Father, I've sinned against the fifth commandment" and let it go at that. Father Pat would demand to know the exact nature of his sin against the fifth commandment, and there were compelling reasons why Father Pat should not be admitted into his confidence, even under the seal of the confessional.

There had been opportunities, even in the rush of events, to approach Father Cogling, but the priest had his own reasons for wanting to remain uninformed of what he surely suspected. President Reagan had often operated in the same way, and it showed good sense in both priest and president. As a man of God, Father Cogling should keep his hands clean. Even in the Middle Ages it wasn't the Church that had burned the heretics. All that side of things was handled by civil authorities—by laymen like Gerhardt Ober, who weren't afraid of dirtying themselves if that might help to preserve undefiled the Church's own immaculate garment. It was enough for Father Cogling to have expressed his concern to Gerhardt as to the fact of Father Pat's being blackmailed, which he'd learned from having chanced to monitor a phone conversation between Father Pat and the blackmailer. Father Cogling had naturally been concerned for the younger priest, but even more, as he'd explained to Gerhardt, he was alarmed at the possibility of a scandal that could involve the Church. Gerhardt had shared his alarm, and acted accordingly. Perhaps he'd been unwise.

And it had certainly been a mistake to have effected the disappearance of Father Pat's mother and twin brother, even though at the time they had seemed to pose an even greater threat of scandal—to the Church in general, and to Father Cogling in particular. Gerhardt was devoted to Father Cogling. No other priest in the entire archdiocese still honored the memory of Monsignor O'Toole and of the Shrine he had founded. Father Cogling was, in Gerhardt's estimation, a true saint. He may have sinned in his youth, but sin can be repented, especially the sins of the flesh, which are in their nature fleeting.

As it said somewhere in the Good Book, what's done can't be undone, and there was no use crying over spilled milk—or even, for that matter, blood. Repentance was not a matter of shedding tears, in any case, and that was a good thing for Gerhardt, since he'd never been one for crying. Repentance was something spiritual and sacramental; it took place between the sinner and the priest, and, as Father Cogling had explained it to him one time, it was one of the mysteries of the Faith. You had to put your soul into God's keeping and just let go. God would do the rest. So the fact that Gerhardt wasn't heartbroken over what he'd done was neither here nor there. God would be his judge.

Father Pat finally made a sign of the cross, got up off his knees, and turned to Gerhardt. "Well, now, shall we find out what your good sister has prepared for our dinner?"

"Right this way, Father," Gerhardt said, leading the way to the single elevator in the Shrine proper that was kept in operation. He rummaged among the many keys on the ring chained to his belt, inserted one in the lock, and then pressed the button that now could summon the elevator. Apparently Hedwig had not used the elevator since his departure that morning to chauffeur Father Pat to the Shrine, since the door opened at once.

"After you, Father. They're on the fourth level down."

Father Pat gave an odd look at the cage of the elevator. "There is no . . . stairway?"

"There is—that door over there—but it's only for emergencies. I doubt it's been used, though, since the Shrine was opened. If the local power fails, we've got an emergency generator that kicks in right away."

Father Pat seemed reluctant to enter the elevator.

"Elevators make you nervous, Father?"

"No. No, of course not. I was only . . . curious." He entered the elevator with obvious reluctance, and Gerhardt stepped in after him and pressed the button marked 4. The doors slid closed, and they descended.

The doors opened with a hiss, and Gerhardt stepped out. Father Pat followed him, stepping gingerly. He looked about at the gray concrete blocks of the corridor with almost as much amazement as when he'd entered the Shrine itself.

"We are in the crypt?" Father Pat asked.

"The crypt? I don't think I've heard anyone call it that since the Monsignor's day. Sometimes he'd say, 'Let's go down to the crypt, Gerhardt.' Other times he'd say these were his catacombs. Like in Rome. When we were in Rome, in 'fifty-one, he took me to a church called Santa Maria sopra Minerva, which he explained means 'Saint Mary on top of Minerva.' Minerva was one of the pagan goddesses, and they built the church on top of what used to be a temple to her, and there were catacombs under that. I served Mass for the Monsignor there."

"Gerhardt! Thank God you're here. I was going crazy."

While he was speaking, Gerhardt had advanced to the first turning of the corridor, and there was Hedwig ahead of him at the far end, outside the door to the main kitchen.

Gerhardt made a cautionary gesture. "Of course I'm here, Hedwig. And Father Pat is here with me."

"Oh," she said, in another voice entirely, as Father Pat followed Gerhardt around the turn of the corridor. "Oh, I see. Father Pat, how wonderful that you've been able to come here at last."

"God's will be done," said Father Pat with a benign smile. As he approached Hedwig, he extended his right hand, with the palm of it lowered and the fingers drooping, as though (Gerhardt thought) he expected Hedwig to kiss it.

Hedwig took it, somewhat disconcertedly, in her left hand, and that was odd, too.

"Hedwig," said Gerhardt, noticing how his sister held her right arm close to her body. "Have you hurt your arm?"

"It's nothing," said Hedwig, releasing Father Pat's hand and cupping her right hand, which was pressed against her stomach, with her left. "I had a small accident. It's of no importance."

"Did one of our young ladies—" He did not complete the question, not wanting to reveal his central anxiety about the operation of Birth-

Right to Father Pat, who would probably learn soon enough how rebellious his charges could be.

Hedwig smiled brightly. "No, no, nothing of that sort. It was my own foolishness." She gave her brother a warning grimace, then smiled more brightly still at Father Pat. "And it certainly didn't stop me from preparing . . . What do you think, Father?"

"I really can't imagine," said Father Pat.

"Sauerbraten! With spaetzle!"

"Is that so?" Father Pat replied, with a blank look.

"Father Pat loves sauerbraten," Gerhardt assured his sister.

"Oh yes," Father Pat agreed. "Very much. And the young ladies—will they be dining with us?"

Hedwig cast down her eyes. "No. Unfortunately. They've already had their dinner. It will just be the three of us. But I suppose you'd like to see your room now, and to freshen up. You'll be staying in the Monsignor's suite, with its own private chapel. And Gerhardt?"

"Yes, Hedwig?"

"Will you just make sure that everything is all right in the kitchen? I'll join you there as soon as I've seen Father Pat to his room."

Gerhardt went into the kitchen and stared sullenly at the pots on the gigantic electric range. The kitchen was of institutional proportions, having been designed for the eventuality of serving a small army of the faithful in the event of nuclear war. The metal countertops and shelves were festooned with huge stainless steel pots and pans and cooking utensils, all dully gleaming like armor. Hedwig had tried, here and there, to add a homier touch, but all the various houseplants, in their pots and baskets, tended to become sickly with no other source of light than the fluorescent bulbs, and the ceramic kittens and other knickknacks didn't produce the same effect of cozy good cheer that they had in Hedwig's own kitchen in Willowville. They seemed, much like the girls domiciled on the floor below, forlorn and resentful, and they awakened an answering resentment in Gerhardt. For a moment he felt tempted to take up the nearest figurine—an infant angel sitting, beelike, atop a daisy—and smash it to bits. But Gerhardt was not one to yield to such irrational impulses.

However, when Hedwig returned, he was snappish. "How in hell did you manage to break your arm?"

She didn't answer at once but stood in the doorway, glowering.

"Well?" he insisted.

"How do you *think?* By trying to move the corpse in the freezer!"

"Oh, shit," said Gerhardt.

"Please watch your tongue. I have to put up with enough filthy language from that Peck girl. I don't have to hear it from my own brother. And I think I'm owed some kind of explanation."

Gerhardt bit his lip. He had not wanted Hedwig—or anyone else—to know about Peter Bryce. If he had not been called back to the Twin Cities to bring Father Pat to the Shrine, this would not have happened. He had managed to dispose of the old woman without great difficulty, for there was, in fact, a literal catacomb in the sixth and lowest subbasement of the Shrine. The architect, Ernst Kurtzensohn, had foreseen the need to provide for the rapid interment of those who had been injured in the initial blast or later developed radiation illness and died after they'd been admitted to the shelter. So the Monsignor's reference to his "catacombs" had not been entirely a jest. Gerhardt was certain that no one any longer knew of the existence of this special facility, and so it seemed to have been made on purpose for the disposal of Mrs. Bryce's and her son's corpses.

The only difficulty had been with Peter. Because of the man's obesity, Gerhardt had been unable to raise him to the level of even the lowest of the burial chambers, which stood at a height of four feet above the floor. Even the old woman had taxed his strength. Indeed, he'd almost been unable to move Peter's body out of the back of the limousine and into the wheelbarrow beside it. So, when Father Cogling had called to insist that Gerhardt return to the city, he had trundled the body back into the elevator and up to the fourth subbasement and deposited him in the walk-in freezer until such time as he could deal with the matter in a less hasty fashion. He had intended either to rig up some kind of hoist or else to dismember the corpse into more liftable pieces, which might be done without unsightly gore if the body were given time to freeze solid.

What Gerhardt had not foreseen was that Hedwig would decide to enter the freezer herself to get one of the precooked sauerbratens stored there. She'd even said, before he'd driven off, that she meant to make sauerbraten to welcome Father Pat to the Shrine, but Gerhardt hadn't put two and two together.

"Hedwig," Gerhardt said in a tone of stern authority, "this is not a matter that I'm free to discuss with you."

"No?"

"No. I must ask you just to forget what happened today."

"And every time I go to the freezer to get some food, I must *overlook* the fact that there is the corpse of a fat man in a wheelbarrow there?"

"He will not remain there long. The corpse will be interred in the sixth subbasement, where provision has been made for exactly that."

Hedwig looked aghast. "You've been on six? Gerhardt, there are *bats* down there!"

"There *were* bats down there, Hedwig, but that was some long while ago. And I think the problem was taken care of when I sealed up the broken screen on the ventilator. In any case, I was down there yesterday and saw no sign of bats."

"A month ago you said you'd seen their . . . excrement."

"But not a great deal of it."

"I can see the bats outside at twilight. There are hundreds of them, Gerhardt. And that's where they must live. There's not anywhere else they could be. They've got some *cave* down there that they know how to get to. You promised me you wouldn't go down there again until we'd had professional exterminators check the entire floor."

"Exterminators are expensive, Hedwig. You know that."

"If you let bats get into other parts of the Shrine, Gerhardt, I won't remain here. There are limits to what you can ask of me. I will do what must be done for Birth-Right, even if it means I risk being put in prison. I will even forget that I have seen a corpse in the food locker. But I won't live here with bats."

"You're being irrational, Hedwig."

"Yes, about bats I will be as irrational as I like."

"We can't discuss this now, in any case. Father Pat will be expecting his dinner."

"I know that. But there's one more thing. You'll have to take me to the doctor in Leech Lake. I may have broken my wrist trying to move that wheelbarrow to get at the chest with the sauerbraten. The whole thing turned over on me, and for a while I thought I'd be trapped underneath it and freeze to death."

"I'll look at it myself once Father Pat is out of our hair."

"I've *looked* at it, Gerhardt. It's bruised dark purple. I need a doctor to look at it."

"Does it hurt?"

"Of course it hurts." But there was an affectionate note in her impatience. "But when has that ever stopped me?"

Gerhardt smiled his approbation. They might have their disagreements from time to time, but when it came right down to it, they were both Obers. He stood up and took her afflicted hand in his, and, as she winced, he lifted it to his lips and kissed it. "There. Now it will be all better."

"You're impossible," she told him, but he knew she'd been won round. Finally his sister always recognized his authority, and that was why he loved her so.

32

"Mary, my dear, are you awake? Mary?"

It was the voice of Hedwig Ober. Mary Tyler kept her eyes closed.

"I know she's not asleep, Father. Perhaps if *you* were to say something to her . . ."

"Mary?" It was a stranger's voice, not Gerhardt's. The way he spoke her name was almost a caress, and when he spoke again, he placed his hand on her shoulder with the same gentleness. "Mary, I'd like to talk with you."

The moment she opened her eyes, the tears welled up and began to roll down the sides of her face. The man whose touch had summoned the tears was standing at the side of the bed, and Mary found herself looking up into the familiar wrinkled face of Hedwig Ober, who was bent over her, attentive.

"You see, I knew it, she *is* awake," Hedwig said with a little squint of vindication. "And already she's begun to cry."

Mary tried to lift her hand to wipe away the tears, but she could raise it only a few inches from the bed before the canvas restraint prevented further movement.

"I should explain," said Hedwig, backing away from the bed. "It's not that Mary's ever shown any tendency to violence. Unlike the Peck girl, in Cell Four, who cannot be trusted at all. It's rather that she has developed an unfortunate nervous habit. She pulls out her hair. One after another, hair by hair. She understands that she mustn't do it, but she sometimes has no control over herself. The way some children can't be kept from biting their nails. Isn't that so, Mary?"

Mary could see the arm of the man touching her and, turning her head sideways, his shoulder and the front of his black suit, but unless she pushed her head back against the pillow she could not see his face. But she knew that he was a priest, for he had a white collar around his neck instead of a necktie. And there was a kind of comfort in having a priest beside her, touching her.

"Am I dying?" she asked the priest.

"Mary!" Hedwig scolded. "Such a question! As though one never saw a priest except on one's deathbed. For heaven's sake!"

The priest's fingers closed a little more tightly about the girl's shoulder. "We are all dying, Mary," he said in a gentle voice. "Each day that we live we are a little closer to our death, but we can never know when that day will be. The healthiest of us may die tomorrow, struck by the plague. Only God knows the hour that has been set. That is why we must always be prepared. Are you prepared?"

There was something strangely comforting in having her fears dealt with so directly instead of being told that she must buck up and smile and be more positive. It was like spinning the dial of the radio when you're very sad and finding a song as sad as you are. She closed her eyes and, without really knowing why, she said, "Thank you."

"I think," said the priest, letting loose her shoulder, "that Mary wants to go to confession."

"Naturally," said Hedwig. She moved farther away from the bed but showed no intention of leaving Mary's cell.

"So we must be alone," the priest insisted.

"Of course, Father. What am I thinking? When you're done, just press that buzzer there on the wall by the head of the bed, and I'll know you want me back."

"And if there is any way to extinguish the light . . . ?"

"You want to be in the dark?"

"Yes, since we can't use a proper confessional."

"Whatever you say, Father. It will take me a moment."

Hedwig left the cell without locking it behind her. Mary counted her footsteps, as she had so often before at bedtime. Twelve steps, and then a pause, and the light went out.

The priest wriggled his fingers under her head, pushing the pillow aside so that his hand bore the weight of her head. "Your name is Mary," he said.

"Yes," she agreed. "Mary Tyler."

"And you've been brought here, to this Shrine, because of your sins?"

If Hedwig or Gerhardt or almost anyone else had asked such a question of her, she would have become indignant, but here in the dark, with the priest whose face she'd never seen, she was able to accept that bitter truth.

"Yes, Father. I meant to get an abortion. I would have if my parents hadn't sent me here."

"That was an intended sin. But there must have been a sin committed first. A sin of the flesh."

Part of her still wanted to cry out that it had not been a sin—not, at least, on her part. The sin had been done *to* her. Instead, she surrendered to his authority and agreed. "Yes, Father. A sin of the flesh."

"You must tell me. What acts were performed? With whom? And how often?"

"It was only the once. And I don't even know his name. It was at a party, and things got out of control, I guess. I was drinking. I'm not used to alcohol. I don't remember many of the details."

"Were you tied down, my child, as you are now, or did you have the free use of your limbs?"

"No, I don't think I was tied down. It wasn't that kind of situation."

"That *kind* of situation?"

The tone of his voice seemed one of ordinary curiosity rather than scolding or disapproval. Suddenly she *wanted* to go to confession, though that had not been her intention at first. She wanted to stand naked before him and let her sins be washed away.

"I think there may have been more than one of them, Father," she whispered. She'd never told this to anyone before—not to the woman at the crisis center; not to her own confessor, when she'd finally gone to him; not even to the other girls here at Birth-Right. It had seemed too shameful to be spoken of.

The priest placed his other hand at the base of the great swelling that was to be her child. "How many, exactly?" he insisted.

"I don't know. Three. Possibly four."

"Where did they touch you, my child?" His voice seemed closer. She was certain she could feel his breath upon her face, and when she turned her head away, his lips brushed the lobe of her ear.

The fingers cradling her head tightened in her hair and forced her head back until, when he whispered again, she could feel his lips brushing hers. His other hand moved from her abdomen to her breast, at first in an exploratory way; then, when he had found the nipple, gripping it through the thin cotton of her nightgown between thumb and knuckle. "Here?" he insisted. "Did they touch you here? Were all their hands on you at once?"

When she opened her mouth to scream, he came down on her with his entire weight, his mouth on hers, so that the scream became a kiss. His free hand tugged her nightgown up to her waist and felt between her thighs to find her private parts.

She lacked the strength to struggle, and in any case all she could do was twist her pelvis from one side to the other. Even so, he could not penetrate her—not so much because she resisted him but because of the advanced state of her pregnancy. While his mouth was pressed against hers, her pregnant belly prevented her rape.

When he came to understand this, he spoke again, in the same tone of benign authority. "You must lie still, my child. You must be very quiet, and then you won't be hurt. Do you understand me?"

"But you're a *priest!*"

"And what are you? A whore! By your own admission, you cannot even name the father of your child. Now, if you want that child to live, lie still and be quiet."

She obeyed him. He still had some difficulty achieving penetration, because of the way her restraints positioned her on the bed, but once he was inside her, he spent himself quickly. At once he withdrew, and she waited, listening to his heavy breathing and her own, to know what he intended next.

In the darkness she could hear him fumbling with his clothing, then felt him drawing the damp cotton of her nightgown down to her knees. The pillow was plumped and placed beneath her head.

"You must say nothing of what has passed between us to the old woman when she returns. Do you understand that, Mary?"

"Yes, Father."

"And are you truly sorry for the sins you have committed?"

"Yes, Father."

"You should be, my child. Each time you sin you are driving a nail into the flesh of our Savior. Imagine what pain you must be causing Him. Yet His mercy is infinite, and He forgives you. *Ego te absolvo.*"

He pressed the buzzer, and a moment later the light went on.

He was looking down at her and smiling.

"You are a very beautiful girl, Mary. A very beautiful girl."

She was afraid to make any kind of reply, and when Hedwig returned to the cell, Mary was actually grateful for the old woman's presence.

"I think we should leave Mary alone now for a while," the priest told Hedwig.

"Whatever you say, Father." Hedwig glanced down at Mary with a questioning look, as she might have looked at a room in which someone had altered the ordained position of the furniture.

The priest, in leaving, pressed Mary's hand. "God be with you, my child."

She knew that he must be mad, but when she looked at him, he seemed like any other priest she'd ever known, anytime, anywhere. And that was the scariest thing about him.

XXXIII

He was huddled in the far corner of the cell in which Crispo had ordered him to be held, clutching the filthy woolen cloth that was the only garment allowed him, stupid with fear but too hungry to sleep, when the Legate, Durand du Fuaga, appeared, unannounced, and spoke his name. Only that. "Father Bryce," he said.

Then, after allowing some time for that to sink in, he continued, in English: "At last we can speak candidly."

There was just enough light in the corridor that Father Bryce could see the Legate's silhouette in the open doorway.

"Is he bound?" the Legate asked, and Crispo replied, "Fettered hand and foot, Your Holiness."

"Your Holiness?" Father Bryce repeated.

"You question my right to be addressed by that title, Father? Such punctilio, even in chains, is commendable. In fact, as Legate, I may be so addressed, not *in proprio persona* but as one who speaks with the Pope's voice. A borrowed authority, but then what authority is not?" He paused and continued in a more intimate tone: "Crispo says that you were present at the passion of our mutual friend, Mr. Boscage."

"His passion! Is that how Your Holiness speaks of murder?"

"Would not that diminish the significance of the man's suffering, Father Bryce? To be scourged and crowned with thorns and nailed to a cross; to die a lingering and inconceivably painful death: could there be a more perfect imitation of Christ's Passion than this?"

"It is sadism, nothing more."

"O ye of little faith," said Durand du Fuaga, stepping into the cell to become a part of the enveloping darkness. "Do you think, then, that the Roman soldiers who crucified Christ acted for nobler motives than Crispo? Christ died at the hands of men trained to be institutional sadists. What else are soldiers, Father? What have they ever been? And how else is power to be exercised except by the threat of terror? Cut off their heads or burn them at the stake or crucify them. One way or another, it's a job that has to be done."

Father Bryce fell silent, as an animal caught in a trap will sometimes leave off its struggling and give way to brute despair.

"Aren't you curious, Father, to know *why* this is being done? Have you no questions to ask me?"

"I'm sure you'll say it's all for the greater glory of the Church."

"How little you know me. What if I were to tell you it was for just the opposite reason? What if our object here—our very long-term object—were to destroy the Church? What if I told you that you are essential to that object, Father Bryce? That you are to be the evangel of a new Savior? One who suffered just as Christ did, but at the hands of the very Church His sufferings created?"

Despite himself, Father Bryce felt a stirring of hope. "Are you saying it is possible for me to . . . return?"

"Would you want to resume your old life, Father Bryce? Does the idea stir your blood? Is that how you've passed the time here in the darkness, imagining another Teddy Hamburg? Another Gabriel? How many were there altogether? Were you the sort to keep a record?"

Father Bryce made no reply. How could this man know these things? No one but Father Bryce himself knew the names of those boys.

"Let me read your mind, Father Bryce," the Inquisitor said. "You wonder how I can catalog your secret guilts so precisely. A little thought should solve the puzzle. Boscage and you and I all hail from a later time, but not the same later time. Boscage's transmentation, as he called it, took place in 1981. Yours more than a decade later. If you'd read the *Prolegomenon* when you had the opportunity, you would not be quite so mystified at what has been happening to you. I have the advantage of still wider hindsight, for I have been able, in my own time, to read all the news stories publishing your guilt, naming your victims, and execrating your crimes. You will be infamous, Father Bryce, a few centuries from now. More than all the other priestly pedophiles of your day and age, whose names are legion, you will come to signify the Church's deepest shame."

"I would rather die," said Father Bryce, "here in the dungeons of the Inquisition."

"And so you shall, Father. Crispo is already making the preparations. But as Paul remarks, 'Except a man die, he cannot be born again.' There is no other way to return to your own time and your own flesh. And I shall unfold a further secret, Father. It is your image that will be printed on the Shroud of Turin—not Boscage's, as the man supposed. He made rather a poor impression, if I may be forgiven a bad pun. We expect to do better with you. Your beard's grown out, while you've been our guest, to just the right length, and you've slimmed down, too. The likeness is quite uncanny."

"Cheap blasphemies," said Father Bryce with sincere scorn.

"There, that's what I like to see—a show of spirit! But really, Father, it's already been established that the cloth of the Shroud dates to the thirteenth century, at the earliest. And so it must have been a forgery. But it was not forgery within the skill of any painter of the time. It must have been created by another kind of artistry. And Crispo is that artist, with, of course, such latter-day technical advice as I've been able to provide concerning the best placement of the nails and the shape of the metal pellets attached to the scourge and all those other little details that have given the Shroud its peculiar, if limited, authenticity. Even now—that is to say, the 'now' you will soon return to—there are those who reverence the Shroud while knowing it cannot be authentic. Cardinal Ballestrero of Turin (who admittedly has a vested interest in the matter) is on record as saying that the Church 'reiterates her respect and her veneration for the Shroud.' "

"Forged relics are an old scandal. The Church has survived many such scandals. It will survive this one."

"If it were only the scandal, I agree. But what if the Shroud is proven to be not the image of Christ but of A. D. Boscage? Who was crucified, died, and resurrected centuries afterward—the Messiah of the Aquarian Age? That would put Receptivist Science on an entirely different footing than any other crackpot religion ever known."

"Messiah? Why not the Antichrist?"

"Why not, indeed, if that's your preference? He's been called that often enough."

Finally the question had to be asked, though Father Bryce knew better than to expect a truthful answer. "Who are you? And why are you doing this?"

"Whom do you suppose, Father?"

"You *look* like a younger version of an elderly parishioner from St. Bernardine's, Gerhardt Ober. But I can't suppose that's who you are."

"Resemblances—yes, they can be deceiving. Undoubtedly, when you look about you here, the people you see seem to be versions of people you knew in your own time. It was the same for Boscage, and for myself. In you I seem to recognize a priest I knew when I was a boy of fourteen. He tried to seduce me, and I tried to murder him. Now, at last, that karmic debt will be paid. What seems to be the case is that in our transmentated state we perceive spiritual resemblances as physical. In some way that I don't understand, I am the moral equivalent of this Gerhardt Ober, as you are the equivalent of my would-be seducer. Does that mean that this whole medieval mise-en-scène is a phantasmagoria? No, I think the truth is somewhere in between. We are here, in these borrowed bodies, like sleepwalkers, only half aware of the real world we stumble through. And for all you or I know, the same may be true of the lives we've left behind. But that is all philosophy. You have yet to answer my question."

"Who do I think you are? I think you may be the devil."

"I'm flattered, Father. Truly I am. The devil always cuts such a dashing figure. The ultimate scene-stealer. Of course, if I *were* the devil, I would have to deny it, wouldn't I? The Father of Lies, and all that. Allowing for that paradox, let me assure you I am not the devil. Would you like to try again?"

"This is madness."

"Now you flatter yourself, Father. Do you think your imagination so rich that I am just a figment of your fancy? Come to think of it, that is typical of pedophiles and rapists. They must believe that their victims solicited their attentions. Let someone only say hello, and you're unzipping your fly."

Father Bryce said nothing, and after a time the Legate interpreted his silence as his final tacit submission. He left the cell and Crispo entered, followed by a soldier bearing a torch.

Like a priest lifting up the Host for adoration, Crispo showed Father Bryce the crown of thorns that had been prepared for him.

34

"Gerhardt, I really must insist," Hedwig said. "I have to see a doctor. I am in intolerable pain. You can see how my whole lower arm is swollen up. If you can't drive me to Leech Lake, then I must call for a taxi."

"I'm sorry," said Gerhardt, "but I need you here now. I can't do everything that has to be done by myself. Not with *him* here. You said yourself he's been acting funny."

"Not funny. He's just obstinate sometimes. You're the same way; that doesn't make *you* funny."

"How was he obstinate? What did he want?"

She sighed. As soon as she'd let Father Bryce have his way, she'd regretted it, and had avoided telling Gerhardt about it. But perhaps it was best that he know. He would soon enough, in any case. "He wanted me to show him how to use the beeper. So that he could visit the girls without having me let him in and out of their cells. After all, he is officially in charge of the Shrine."

"You didn't give him the codes, did you?"

"How could I refuse?"

"For Christ's sake, Hedwig!" Gerhardt threw the scrub brush into the bucket, making the soapy water splash across the bib of his overalls. He was already exasperated at having to mop up the bloodstains on the floor of the walk-in freezer. Cleaning was not one of his responsibilities.

"I didn't give him the code for accessing the elevator, so he can't leave the dormitory floor. And what harm can he do if he's with the girls? You *surely* don't believe what that little Joyner girl said."

Gerhardt pursed his thin lips and shook his head. "No, I might have believed that about someone else, but not Father Bryce."

"Of course not him. The man's a priest, he's sworn to chastity. And I've always known that Janet was a little liar. She pretends to be this innocent, sweet child, but if she were, how did she come to be here in the first place? Pregnant at the age of twelve!"

"True, true. Did you tell *him* what she'd accused him of?"

"Perhaps I should have. But it just seemed too . . . ugly. Even now, thinking about it, I'd like to swat her again. That's why I have to see a doctor, Gerhardt. I did something to my wrist when I struck the girl. It hurts more than it did when I first broke it. And there are no painkillers left. We used up the last of them on Tara Seberg."

"You've just got to hang on, Hedwig," Gerhardt said, using the handle of the mop to help him rise to his feet. He'd been kneeling so long that the wet knees of his overalls had frozen to the metal floor of the freezer. "Have some brandy. That'll take off some of the edge. I've called Father Cogling and told him that we need his help. He said he'd come tomorrow, but I told him he had to come right away. And he said he would. That was a couple hours ago. Once he gets here, he can take you in to see a doctor. But there is one thing, Hedwig."

She sighed. "What is that?"

"It would be better not to tell Father Cogling about . . ." Gerhardt tilted his head to where the corpse of the fat man, now frozen quite solid, still lay in the wheelbarrow, waiting interment.

Hedwig had spread a linen tablecloth over the body as a kind of shroud. Gerhardt had yet to explain how the man's body had come to be here, and he probably never would. Nor did she want to know anything about it. Just as her brother resented being required to perform the woman's work of scrubbing a floor, so she resented being implicated in the masculine domain of violence. She understood that it was sometimes needful, in the interest of a higher cause, to perform illegal actions. Doctors who refused to stop performing abortions might, for instance, have to be dealt with in ways that the civil authorities would not sanction. But that was men's work, and women should not have to know about it. Whatever the motive that had impelled her brother to act as he had, Hedwig trusted that he'd done so in good conscience, but she did resent having been made a witness to it.

"Hedwig, I would appreciate it if you would go back down to the dormitory floor and look after things there. I don't like the idea of Father Pat being alone with those girls."

"Gerhardt—you don't believe that girl, do you?"

"No, nothing like that. But they might be telling him stories about the way things are run here. Which they wouldn't be doing if you were there."

"That can't be helped, Gerhardt. I can't be breathing down his neck every single moment."

"Even so, it's better you were with them."

Hedwig sighed with feigned reluctance. She would much prefer being with Father Pat and the girls than catching her death of cold while she watched her brother mopping up bloodstains.

"Do you have your own remote, or do I have to access the elevator for you?"

"No, I have mine. I gave Father Pat the spare."

The moment she was alone inside the cage of the elevator, Hedwig began to cry. She cried—silently, and without needing more than a pat or two of her hanky, but for someone so little given to weeping it amounted to a torrent. In part it was simply the pain of her broken wrist, but there was also a sense that Birth-Right was falling to pieces around them. Tara Seberg had died when her infant miscarried two weeks ago, and now Mary Tyler seemed to be going the same way. They should not have begun operating Birth-Right until they had been assured of being able to call on professional medical assistance for such emergencies. All the good work already done and the prospect of doing so much more seemed to be coming to nothing. Only a miracle could help the Shrine now to realize the rightful glory it had for so long been denied.

When the elevator doors opened, there was Father Bryce in the common room, with Mary Tyler and Alison Sanders sitting beside him on either side of the sofa. Hedwig was so taken aback that she did not step out into the corridor. Mary Tyler had not been out of her cell for the past two months. Sometimes she hadn't had the strength to cross the room to the toilet and Hedwig had had to resort to the unpleasantness of a bedpan. And here she was, in her bathrobe in the common room!

When they caught sight of Hedwig, all three of them sprang to their feet, smiling, and Alison called out, "Don't close those doors! Father Pat has had the most wonderful idea."

"My dear!" Hedwig remonstrated. "Really!" She jabbed at the button that would close the doors, but instead she hit—and with the wrong hand!—the one that held them open. The pain flashed up to her elbow and then down into her fingers.

And then there was Father Pat, with his hand on the door of the elevator, and both girls were inside of it, and Alison was saying, "I told him about the Shroud of Turin. How the Shrine has actual threads from the Shroud of Turin."

"To think of it," said Father Pat, advancing into the elevator so that Hedwig had to step back from the door. "The very cloth that wrapped His crucified body!"

"Surely you've known of that relic a long time, Father," said Hedwig as the doors of the elevator closed. "It was already here in your seminary days."

"Yes, of course," Alison continued in the same vein of overwrought reverence, "but it was Father Pat's idea to take the relic from where it's kept—"

"The reliquarium," said Hedwig. "But it's securely *locked.*"

"—and to let Mary *touch* it, or *kiss* it, or however you deal with a relic like that. Because she's been so sick. And it could make her well again, or anyhow a little better. Father Pat says relics can work miracles."

"Yes, of course, but—"

"If it *could* help me . . ." Mary ventured mildly.

Relics can work miracles. Hedwig accepted this as an article of faith. And she did know where to find the key to the reliquarium. And if Mary was to mend and have a successful delivery, something on the order of a miracle would be required. But more than all that, Birth-Right itself needed a miracle if it was to survive.

"Please," said Father Pat. "For their sake, and the sake of the children they are to bear."

Gerhardt would be furious. But really, what could be the risk? Even if they went up to the Shrine, its doors were secured. The girls could not get out of the building, even if they were foolish enough to try.

And relics *can* work miracles.

"Very well," said Hedwig. She took the remote from the pocket of her smock, aimed it at the control panel, and, with a flinch of pain, pressed 1.

35

The girl was an enchantress. She was like the most beautiful statue of the Virgin that ever craftsman fashioned—the belly rounded with child but not unbecomingly swollen; the face a perfect oval, except for a subtle sharpness to the chin; the arms, bare almost to her shoulders and the palest pink, an invitation to his embrace. She inspired a reverence of desire such as a harlot of Delilah's sort could never hope to arouse, though, like Delilah, this Alison had fingernails dyed red and carmined lips. Loveliest was the dark hair that streamed loosely about her face like the tresses of the Magdalene.

It did not matter to Silvanus that he could not possess her at once. Now he understood those voluptuaries who prided themselves on drawing out their dalliances with their paramours until love had left them weak and trembling rather than dealing with temptation in a brisk martial way. In any case, he had already satisfied his baser appetites only a little time before in the cell of the girl called Raven.

She had been no enchantress. When he had offered to hear her confession, she had spit out profanities that would have made a *routier* blush. When he had pressed himself upon her, she had resisted with a vigor that had prevented his carnal possession of her body until he'd wrung almost the last breath from her heaving lungs. Being bound hand and foot to the pallet in her cell, the minx had had no hope of effectively resisting him, and yet she would not yield. And so what mercy could there have been for her? None.

Now, too late, he regretted what he'd done, for he was certain that when one of the girls' elderly jailers discovered her lifeless body, there would be a price to pay. Even though it was they who'd brought the raucous "Raven" to this dungeon crypt and bound her to the pallet, the Ober woman seemed to expect that he would deal with the wanton, and with her fellow prisoners, only in his capacity as a priest. But in this antechamber of hell, this demesne of the Antichrist, how was Silvanus always to preserve a priestly demeanor? Confronting such temptations as had been placed in his path, what virile man could have done otherwise than he had done?

But this one, this Alison, this statue of the Holy Mother quickened into life, this was a new order of temptation. Her glance was like a woodland creature, a finch that would light upon his finger and at once go fluttering off. Her very piety served to entice, for when he'd asked her if she wished to confess her sins to him, first she'd agreed and then, when he'd sought to know in more intimate detail the nature of her transgressions (and chanced, at the same moment, to brush the soft underside of her arm with the back of his hand), oh, what a pretty panic there was. She had not been bound to her pallet, as Mary and later Raven had been, but enjoyed the liberty of her cell, as did the youngest of the four fair prisoners, Janet. Like Janet, too, she'd fled his first caress and looked at him with such a look! Just as flames of many colors may flicker at the wick of a lamp, so in her eyes he could see at one instant fear, at the next reproach, and then the fear would flare up more brightly, and you could see the very fear of death in her face as though in a flash of lightning. But then, at last, and most astonishing, he'd seen a yielding. Her lips had trembled and then tensed into a smile of sweetest acquiescence. But this was not a yielding dictated by fear; rather (he was certain), like the wise virgin of the parable, she acted at the promptings of reason and deliberation. She knew that ultimately she must please him, but she hoped, virginally, to delay that fated moment.

"Father," she'd told him, "I would like to go to confession. But not here. Can't we go up to the Shrine, where there's a proper confessional?"

"I wish it were possible, my child."

"Because you see, Father, there are things that I could tell you, if we were in the confessional, that somehow, here, like this . . ." She finished her sentence with a blush.

"The problem, my child, is the elevator. I am unable to summon it."

"But if you tell Hedwig you want to go up to the Shrine, she can't refuse you. She told us that you are in charge of the Shrine. You're her superior. And there's another reason, too."

"And what is that, my dear?"

She had told him then of the relic of the Holy Shroud that was kept in a reliquarium in one of the side chapels, and he had listened dumbfounded. To think that such a treasure could be so close by and no mention made of it till now! Why was not the Shrine teeming with pilgrims? Of course, there were spurious relics, but Alison had assured him that this was unassailably genuine. Many books had been written attesting to its authenticity. Alison had read one of them herself. She mentioned it now because it had been her hope, ever since she'd learned of the relic's presence at the Shrine, to be able to venerate it. She was certain that if she could press her lips to it, she and the child she carried could suffer no mischance when her time came. And beyond her concern for herself and her child, there was Mary Tyler, who was now very near her term and so sick that she almost required a miracle if she was not to miscarry.

Silvanus had let himself be persuaded to take Alison to Mary's cell, not without misgivings. He had not seen the girl since he had spent his seed upon her, and he was not certain if she would receive him in a spirit of humility or of grievance. She had seemed dazed at first, but then, as Alison had dwelt upon the benefits Mary might reap from being able to venerate the precious relic, she came to share her friend's fervor and insisted on having her restraints undone so that she might rise from her pallet and put on a loose robe over her bedclothes, in which habit she proposed to visit the Shrine.

All the while that Alison and Mary sang the praises of the Shroud and its miraculous powers, Silvanus began to formulate his own prayerful hope. For he, even more than these girls, stood in need of a miracle. They would pray to be delivered of healthy children, but he would pray for another kind of deliverance. Not knowing by what agency he'd been translated to this latter-day kingdom of the Antichrist, Silvanus had ceased to hope that he might be returned to his own era. "Lead us not into temptation," Christ had bade us pray, "but deliver us from evil." Never had those words rung with such urgency as now.

And yet, even as the hope stirred in his heart that the relic of the Shroud would enable him to return to the precincts of Notre Dame de

Gevaudon in his own kinder and more Christian era, the very temptation that he would escape from assailed him with more force than ever. He thought of being with Alison in the confessional, of pressing his ear against the black veil that separated priest and penitent until he could feel her breath upon his cheek. Her whispered sins would be a spice upon the air. Until (his fingers stroked the nape of his own neck in anticipation), of a sudden, his hand would rip through the veil and clasp her neck. He would draw her lips to his, let her protest as she might, let her writhe in that private darkness, nothing would avail against him, he would force her compliance, she would be his. As the dove is the falcon's, as the lamb is the wolf's, she would be his.

36

When the door of the elevator opened, Alison stepped out of the cage
with an unspoken but heartfelt *Thank you Jesus!* She knew that the gray
dome overhead represented only a larger prison cell than the one from
which she had just been released and to which she might have to return. But there was real summer sunlight streaming in through the
high, narrow windows, and a feeling of *space*. Not freedom. But at least
here freedom was visible.

Father Pat was right behind her, and in her delight and thankful-
ness she could almost have given him a hug. Mary Tyler had already
managed to warn her, by whispered hints, that the guy was some kind
of lech. Even without Mary's signals, Alison had got that message. A
year or two ago, she might have been shocked at the idea of a priest
wanting to do that kind of thing, but now it almost didn't register as
news. Maybe the only surprising thing was that he wasn't queer. For
the last couple of years the news on TV had been full of stories about
priests who'd been caught groping altar boys. She'd even heard Greg
tell a joke, the last time she'd seen him, about how do you get a nun
pregnant—by dressing her up as an altar boy. Not this priest. This one
was a plain, old-fashioned sleazeball. She could have wished he were
queer, except that in that case he probably wouldn't have been so eager
to follow up on her suggestion that they pay a visit to the Shrine to
look at the relic of the Shroud of Turin. Three threads did not seem
like a big deal, but Father Pat had reacted like it was a chance to kiss
Jesus in person. The same creep who two minutes earlier had been
trying to get into her pantyhose.

"It's so big," said Mary, looking across the great expanse of the nave. "I'd forgotten how big this place is."

"It is enormous," Father Pat agreed, slipping into his reverent tone of voice.

"It's like it was built for a city that isn't here. Instead, there's just us." Mary made a nervous sign of the cross.

"Where is the relic kept, Mrs. Ober?" Father Pat asked of Hedwig, who had remained inside the elevator.

"It's in the reliquarium, and the key to the reliquarium is in the sacristy, and I can't enter the sacristy without triggering the security system. Which means that nothing can be done until we're back down to Four, where I can turn off that part of the system."

"You surely don't need our help to do that," said Father Pat. "So while you take care of that, I can wait here with the girls."

"I'm not sure that's a good idea, Father," Hedwig said. "I'm not supposed to leave them on their own."

"They won't be on their own, will they? They'll be with me. Indeed, I'll be able to hear Alison's confession while you're away. Unless we need another key to open the confessional?"

"No, of course not. But, Mary, perhaps *you* should come with me."

Alison exchanged a glance with Mary.

"No," said Mary, in a tone of tentative self-assertion. "No, if I could, I'd like to say a prayer before the altar."

"A fine idea," Father Pat agreed.

Hedwig offered no further opposition beyond a reproachful lowering of her head.

When the elevator doors had closed, Alison almost skipped up the side aisle toward the nearest confessional, which was built on the same XXXL scale as the Shrine itself, though more old-fashioned in its style, with its dark wood carved into all kinds of twisty shapes and curlicues. She parted the heavy curtain and at once knelt down on the stone floor and felt under the kneeler for what she hoped would be there.

It wasn't, but there was still time (Father Pat had lingered beside Mary) to check out the compartment on the other side. And there it was, a smooth cylinder the size and weight of a flashlight. In the curtained darkness of the confessional it was too dark to examine the can of Mace to see if there were instructions on it explaining how it worked, but she assumed it was like any other aerosol, a deodorant or bug spray.

She heard the central half-door of the confessional opening, and a moment later, after some fumbling, Father Pat had pushed aside the panel separating confessor and penitent, and she could see, through the loose mesh of the screen, his bent head, in silhouette, black against the darkest of grays. "I'm here, my child," he whispered.

"Bless me, Father," she began, "for I have sinned. It's been—I don't know, a pretty long time—since my last confession. I haven't even been to Mass for a while. We haven't been able to, of course, until you came, but even before I was brought here—"

"Yes, yes, my child," said Father Pat impatiently, as though he knew that she was playing for time until Hedwig returned.

Which of course was what she was doing, but being inside the confessional she felt protected. He was a priest, after all, and had to play by the rules. Even so, it would probably make sense to offer him something more interesting than missing Mass or using profane language or even sins of disobedience. Confessing sins of that sort was a little like riding a bicycle with training wheels. It was what you confessed before your first communion, when you hadn't had a chance to find out what sin was all about. On the other hand, she didn't want to start with sex until she absolutely had to.

"Well, Father, one of the worst things . . ."

"Yes?"

"I did a lot of shoplifting." This was a lie. She'd done a little shoplifting. Mostly things like candy bars, or batteries for her Walkman, and, once or twice, clothes. But nothing expensive or risky. The last time, at Kmart, she'd almost been caught stealing pantyhose (the very ones she was wearing now and into which, under the waistband, she'd slipped the can of Mace), and that had cured her of shoplifting.

"Yes?" he said, but it was a different yes, not so much impatient as puzzled, as though shoplifting was a foreign concept.

So she began to invent details: shoes from Dayton's, CDs at Music Mart (even though she didn't have a CD player), and then, because she could tell his interest was flagging, she topped it off with, "And one time, at Walgreen's, I shoplifted some condoms. The thing is, I was just too embarrassed to take them to the cash register."

She was certain he'd want to know more about the condoms—especially whether they'd actually been used for their intended purpose—but evidently he was after bigger sins, because he didn't bother with the condoms but proceeded straight to the real sin that had brought her to Birth-Right.

"You're pregnant," he pointed out.

"Yes, Father. That was the time we didn't use condoms."

"Oh." And then another "Oh," as though he was just making the connection. In some ways Father Pat seemed awfully dim, even for a priest.

"You used these . . . condoms . . . to prevent the natural passage of the male essence?"

"Yes, Father." She might have fibbed and said she'd been worried about AIDS, but she knew that from a priest's point of view that probably didn't matter. She still remembered Father Cogling's little speech on the subject of contraception, how birth control was worse than incest.

"Oh, my dear child, that is a very grave offense!"

"I realize that, Father. That's why I felt such a strong need for confession."

"I can well understand."

"I know it's wrong, of course. A mortal sin. But my boyfriend insisted, and the truth of the matter is that if we had always used the condoms I wouldn't be here now."

"Your boyfriend"—he pronounced the word as though he were repeating an obscenity—"might insist that you follow him to hell. Would you do that? Would you like to spend eternity in flames that are never extinguished and that never consume but forever visit new pains upon your sinful flesh?"

Did he expect her to reply? He'd fallen silent and seemed to be waiting for her response, and for just a moment she imagined reaching into her pantyhose and taking out the Mace and squirting him with it right through the veil of cloth between them. That would have been stupid and definitely sinful. But how in the world do you answer such a question?

"I'm really very sorry," she said at last. "It was a terrible sin. I see that now."

"Tell me," he said in a gentler tone of voice, "how it is that you have come to be with child."

"Well, Greg and I—Greg is my boyfriend—I think the first time we went all the way—"

"You must be more specific, my child. How did you go 'all the way'?"

"When he— When we—" What did you call it when you were in the fucking confessional? "When we had intercourse."

"So." He sounded pleased. "When you had intercourse: Where were you? What led up to it? Were you cooperative, or did he force you?"

"No, he was kind of . . . insistent. But I wouldn't say I was forced. I mean, it wasn't the first time we were *together*. We both had— Oh, you know."

"Yes? Go on."

Maybe, Alison thought, he didn't know. Maybe he didn't have a clue. Maybe for all that he was certainly a lech, he hadn't had five minutes of practical experience, so the idea of her and Greg getting each other off was beyond his comprehension. She'd known kids like that in eighth and ninth grade, little wise guys who pretended they were sex fiends when in fact they'd never done anything but jerk off, if that. You had to feel sorry for them, in a way. But what could you feel for someone as old as Father Pat who was, sexually speaking, in eighth grade, and retarded at that?

Alison realized, to her complete astonishment, that in some very important ways—maybe in *the* most important way—she was more of a grown-up than the man on the other side of the confessional screen. Who was—she did the arithmetic in her head, not without difficulty— probably three times as old as she was.

It was just then that the alarm went off.

Alison was up off her knees and out of the confessional in a flash. But she came to a sudden stop as she felt the cylinder of Mace, as though by its own willpower, dislodge itself from the waistband of her pantyhose and fall to the floor of the Shrine. She scooped it up at once and glanced back at the confessional—while the *Whoop! Whoop! Whoop! Whoop!* of the alarm, magnified by the dome, filled the air of the Shrine—but Father Pat had not yet come out, and she was able to push the Mace back inside her pantyhose, this time shoving it down alongside her thigh, where it couldn't possibly escape.

The alarm went off, and at the same moment Father Pat emerged from his compartment of the confessional, looking thoroughly flustered and, unbelievably, fumbling with the zipper of his fly, just like the old men you hear about in porno movie houses with paper bags in their laps. At that moment she vowed she would *never* get inside a goddamned confessional again.

"Alison!" Mary Tyler called aloud into the sudden silence. "Are you all right?"

"I'm fine," Alison replied as Mary's question echoed through the Shrine. "Are you?"

"The alarm went off."

Alison sprinted down the main aisle till she stood beside Mary. "Yes, I heard." She glanced at Father Pat, standing before the confessional, frowning. People don't *run* in church.

"Whatever set the alarm off," Alison said with a smile, "it wasn't anything we did, Father Pat and me. I was worried about you. I thought you might have— I don't know what."

"Broken out of here through those metal doors? No, I didn't do that. I was praying, like I said I would. We *need* prayers."

"Well, maybe God heard them. Maybe that's why the alarm went off."

Father Pat had managed to deal with his zipper, and he came down the main aisle, looking stern and purposeful. But before he could act on his purpose, the elevator doors opened and a frazzled Hedwig appeared to explain the mystery of the alarm.

"It must have been my fault," she said. "Gerhardt has shown me how to work the control panel of the alarm system a dozen times, but there are so many different toggles, and I must have touched the wrong one, because when I entered the sacristy I set off the alarm. But I knew how to turn it off, so there's no harm done." She made an apologetic grimace. "I must have given you quite a start. Not to mention Gerhardt. I think this whole expedition has been ill advised, Father Pat, but if you really want to open the reliquarium, I have the key here."

"May I?" he asked, holding out his hand to receive a large key of tarnished brass, the kind you only see in movies, with a long stem like a pencil.

Hedwig, still grumbling misgivings, led them around behind the wall of statues inside niches that formed a semicircle around the main altar, and there, on the easternmost wall of the Shrine, in its own chapel, was the reliquarium. It had been built of great, rough-hewn slabs of dark marble that were supposed to look like the sepulcher in which Jesus had been buried when they'd taken him off the cross. The largest of the marble slabs served as the door of the sepulcher, and Alison couldn't imagine how they were ever going to get it open without construction equipment. But Hedwig explained that there was a system of weights and pulleys, like elevators used, that made it as easy to open and close as a car door.

And sure enough, when Father Pat put the key into the concealed keyhole and gave it a twist, the great artificial boulder swung forward to reveal a small empty room all of white marble, ceiling, walls, and floor. It looked like the bathroom of an expensive restaurant. At the far end was a little staircase of three steps that led to a second, much smaller door, and it was there, Hedwig explained, that the holy relic was kept.

"Who wishes to be first?" Father Pat asked, advancing into the little room of white marble to stand at the foot of the three steps.

"Can't you bring the monstrance out here?" Hedwig asked.

"I'm not sure that would be proper. Why else would the reliquarium have been built except to allow its special veneration here? Just here." He pointed to the lower step.

"I think," said Alison, "Hedwig should be first."

"Oh, that's very nice of you, my dear, but really—"

"She *should* be first," Mary insisted. "Not just because she's the oldest, but because she's looked after the Shrine so long."

"Well, if you both insist."

With a thin-lipped smile of disappointment, Father Pat gestured for Hedwig to enter the reliquarium and to kneel at the foot of the steps. Then he turned around and mounted the steps with due solemnity.

He made the sign of the cross, and genuflected, and placed his hand upon the small gold handle of the smaller door. Mary also made the sign of the cross and was about to kneel down when Alison pulled at her sleeve to make her move to the side of the outer door.

Father Pat opened the inner sanctum of the reliquarium and at once the bats, already disturbed in their sanctuary by the opening of the outer door, spilled out from the darkness into the light.

37

For generations, in the interstices of the Shrine, wherever no human might disturb their diurnal repose, the bats had multiplied like the tribes of Israel. Thanks to the anxious nature of its founder, Monsignor O'Toole, and to the experience of its architect, Ernst Kurtzensohn, in the building of the Berlin bunker, the Shrine had been supplied with a system of secret passages designed to allow the Monsignor to proceed from his own suite to the Shrine or to any of the other subbasements. It had been this system, whose existence the Monsignor had never confided to any of his aides, which the bats had been colonizing over the years, entering and exiting via the many defective ventilators by which the building drew in air. Only lately, as the Shrine's concrete had become brittle and begun to crumble, and as their own numbers had multiplied, had the bats spilled over from what could be said to be their own territory into that of the building's other residents, emerging first in the catacombs of the sixth subbasement and now, so much more spectacularly, into the Shrine proper. Bats have a natural urge to nest in the highest reaches of whatever space they lay claim to—in attics and belfries—and in the Shrine's system of colonized passages, the stairway that had led from the Monsignor's chambers to the reliquarium had offered the bats an equivalent to an attic. And so it was here that the bats swarmed in greatest abundance.

But once the door of the reliquarium was opened, there were new heights for the bats, all in a state of frenzied fear, to move to. Their little radar systems sensed, beyond the antechamber, a much wider and loftier space, almost a second sky—though when they quickly reached the limits of that second sky and could fly no higher, they began to circle the dome in ever increasing numbers.

Meanwhile, within the reliquarium there had been a grave mischance—almost, indeed, a fatality. For as the bats had poured out of the inner chamber of the reliquarium, Father Pat (or Silvanus, as we know him better) had backed away in panic—as who would not? Forgetting he stood on the third of three steps, he'd toppled backward, falling on the kneeling figure of Hedwig, who had not had time to realize that the worst fear of her life had just come true before she was knocked unconscious. Silvanus lay atop her, stunned, watching the multitudes of bats stream through the narrow white marble room.

Then, slowly, that room began to darken as Alison and Mary, with their arms covering their heads and faces to protect themselves from the bats (who, being bats, were in no danger of dashing themselves against anything their radar warned them of), put their shoulders against the simulated boulder that served as the sepulcher's door. As the boulder slipped into position, fewer and fewer bats were able to escape the inner chamber, and two of them had the misfortune of being crushed to death as the door, with a final joint effort by the two girls, slipped into its frame.

The little antechamber began to fill with the bats that had nested in the lower passageways, summoned by the cries of their fellows. Silvanus could no longer see them, for the sepulcher was once again perfectly dark, but he could hear their shrilling, and sometimes he could feel himself brushed by their wings.

He covered his face with his hands and, rolling away from Hedwig's body, pressed himself against the lowest of the three steps in an ecstasy of fear. He knew, at last, that he was in hell.

38

The dogs! Gerhardt thought, once he'd settled down again with his *Word-Search Magazine,* having assured himself that the alarm was in fact a false alarm. The security monitor had said SACRISTY and, under that, MISCHANCE, which meant that someone had accidentally triggered the sacristy alarm and then shut it off within the ten-second allotted period. It must have been Hedwig. There was nothing to worry about, except that the alarm would have released the dogs from their kennel, and they would be ranging about the property, which they considered theirs and were keen to defend against all comers. Ordinarily, Gerhardt would have let them enjoy their freedom for an hour or two, since the Shrine's twelve acres of scrub wood were enclosed by a ten-foot-high cyclone fence. But Father Cogling would be arriving any moment now, and he had his own key to the outer gate. The dogs had not been taught to recognize Father Cogling as a friend, so any encounter could be dangerous to the old priest. Gerhardt would have to go outside and fetch them back to the kennel.

He was getting to think that the dogs were more trouble than they were worth, what with the cost of feeding them and having to take them out twice a day to have their dump. They were beautiful animals, of course, and he'd seen them put through their paces after they'd completed their attack training, and it had been an impressive display. But so far there'd never been an occasion for them to translate their training into practice. They were beginning to look like a luxury.

Gerhardt went up to ground level on the freight elevator, exiting not through the Shrine proper but through the utility core. First he checked out the kennel, and sure enough the dogs were gone, leaving only a bad smell. He realized that he'd been remiss in the past two days with their feeding and exercise, what with his visits into the Twin Cities. They were probably in a mean temper. He took up the leashes from the hook by the door and went in search of them.

Even before he'd got around to the front of the Shrine, he could hear one of them barking up a storm. He could tell by her voice it was Sheba. And there she was, standing right in front of the main portal, behaving just as though she had cornered a trespasser and was holding him at bay. "Sheba!" he commanded. "Aus!" But "Aus!" didn't do the trick. Sheba turned her head, recognizing Gerhardt, and then went right on barking at the invisible intruder.

It wasn't possible that someone had got into the Shrine from out here, but something must have happened to have riled the dog, so Gerhardt went around to the side of the portal, where there was a lancet window of clear glass that would let him look inside if he boosted himself onto the ledge below it. But he didn't even have to get on the ledge to see what the problem was. The bats had gotten into the Shrine. He couldn't see much of the dome itself from where he stood, but even from the slice of the interior visible to him, he could see that there must have been a whole lot of bats in there.

He didn't know how it had happened, but he was certain that it was something Hedwig had done, perhaps when she'd gone into the sacristy. She was the only one besides himself who had access to the ground floor. Her—and now the bats.

"Damn!" he said, and then, this time with real conviction, "Aus!"

Sheba stopped growling, though she maintained attack posture.

Gerhardt took out his beeper and pressed the button that paged Hedwig. There was no response. He pressed it again, more firmly, and then a third time. Hedwig never went anywhere without her beeper in one of her pockets, and she had never failed to respond to his summons. Her silence was a greater cause for concern than having the dogs loose. He decided to enter the Shrine through the main portal and punched in the appropriate code on his security beeper. He waited a moment for the tumblers to respond and then tugged on one of the large brass handles. The right panel of the door yielded sluggishly at first; then, with the help of its own inertia, it was less of a strain. Even before the door had been folded into the recess designed for it, the first of the excited bats found its way outside.

Gerhardt went down the center aisle of the nave until he could see the whole of the dome. His heart sank. There were hundreds of bats, all caroming about like black popcorn inside a popcorn popper. How did you fumigate something the size of that dome? And if you didn't fumigate, how else could you get rid of them? And how in *hell* had such a swarm of bats got into the Shrine in the first place? If Hedwig had done this, he would brain her!

He tried his beeper one more time, and this time Hedwig answered. "Gerhardt? Damn this thing anyhow. Can you hear me?" She sounded simultaneously groggy and half-hysterical.

"I can hear you, Hedwig. And I would like an explanation. Where are you?"

"Gerhardt, I fell on my bad arm, I am in agony. And it's completely dark. How long have I been in here?"

"In where, Hedwig?"

"In the reliquarium. I was in here with Father Pat, and then he knocked me down, and after that . . . I don't know. I must have hit my head on the floor. I can feel blood on it, and . . . Gerhardt, something touched me!"

"Just keep calm, Hedwig. Tell me, how did you get *in* the reliquarium of all places?"

"Gerhardt, I can feel it on my *ankle!*"

Gerhardt realized that all the bats must have got into the Shrine when the reliquarium had been opened, but he couldn't understand why his sister would have remained there in that case. Bats sent her into conniptions. Somehow (he realized) she'd had an accident and wasn't aware of the bats.

Then she began to scream.

"Hedwig, just keep still. The bats won't hurt you. Just don't move about, or you'll excite them more. I'll be there in a moment."

He hurried down the aisle and then went around behind the main altar. Even before he could see the boulders of the simulated sepulcher in the chapel devoted to the reliquarium, he could hear Hedwig's muffled screams.

"I'm here, Hedwig! Now, quiet down! Do you hear me, Hedwig?" He was right beside the boulder that served as a door to the sepulcher. "I'm opening the door now, Hedwig!"

But the door wouldn't budge. It was locked, and the key was not in the lock. For a moment he thought his sister must have taken the key with her, but the door couldn't be locked from within, so if she did have the key, how had the door been locked?

"Gerhardt, are you there? Open the door, Gerhardt! Open it!"

"It's locked, Hedwig."

"Then use the key! I left it there in the lock."

"It's not there now, Hedwig. Was anyone else here with you, Hedwig?"

There was no response.

"Hedwig, answer me!"

He could hear her whimpering, and he feared she was beyond reach of his reasonable advice.

"Hedwig, I will have to go and get the other key that's in my safe. Just wait here, do you understand?" He realized, even as he said it, that there was something ridiculous in ordering her to do what she couldn't help doing in any case.

"I'll be right back." He tried to sound reassuring, but in fact he was thoroughly pissed off with her.

Someone—either Father Pat or one of the girls—must have closed the door on her, locked it, and taken away the key. Which meant that there was someone here in the Shrine besides the bats. He hadn't seen anyone, but then they might have hidden from him. They certainly couldn't have left the Shrine. Unless . . . He rushed back to the door he'd left open, but Sheba was still standing guard, barking at the occasional bat that had the wit or the luck to fly low enough to escape through the door.

There was also the possibility that the person who'd locked Hedwig in the reliquarium had stolen her security beeper and taken the elevator to one of the lower floors. Gerhardt recalled that she'd let Father Pat have a beeper of his own. It was him, then, the son of a bitch! Gerhardt didn't know what Father Pat thought he was up to, but if he'd figured out that he was a prisoner here as much as the girls and was trying to break out, he wasn't going to get very far. Sheba was guarding the main church door, and if he got past her, there was still Rambo and Trixie to contend with. If he'd gone to one of the floors below, Gerhardt would find him.

But all in good time. Gerhardt's first priority was to release his sister from the reliquarium. To a certain extent, she might have only herself to blame for the predicament she was in. She'd deferred too readily to Father Pat's authority, but then how could she have done otherwise?

Gerhardt took the elevator to 3 and went to his office. The safe where the spare key to the reliquarium was kept was an old-fashioned combination safe, and Gerhardt fumbled the combination twice.

Then, as he tried a third time, the alarm went off, and this time it didn't stop. Gerhardt hurried down the hall to the security office and checked the monitor. A message flashed on the screen: MAIN GATE—ATTEMPTED ENTRY. There was no video surveillance of the main gate, so Gerhardt had no way of knowing what was happening. The only other time there'd been a similar alarm had been last November, when Trixie had chased a young doe right into the fence at night. The deer had tried to scramble up the mesh of the fence and tangled itself in the chain that secured the gate to the post. Trixie had torn one haunch to shreds before Gerhardt could get there.

He had no hope that the reason for this alarm would be so harmless. When it rains, it pours. He would have to come to Hedwig's rescue later. There wasn't even time to get the key from the safe. Instead, he opened up the arms locker in the security office and helped himself to a 9mm Sig Sauer and a 12-gauge pump. He stuck the automatic inside the waistband of his trousers and, for good measure, pocketed another magazine.

XXXIX

The blade of the lance was poised, ready to pierce the right side of Father Bryce's breast. It was just such a blade, elliptical in shape, as the Roman legionnaires had used for the coup de grâce on such occasions. Amazingly, he was not yet dead. The torture of crucifixion had been developed to elicit maximum suffering for an extended period of time.

Father Bryce regarded Crispo and prayed for the mercy of death.

Their eyes met.

"It's time, isn't it, Father, to say *Consummatum est?*"

Father Bryce turned his head aside. The effort sent new signals of pain through his wracked flesh. He was no longer aware of any single pain. Pain had no locus; it was his whole existence.

"Or is it?" Crispo asked. "Perhaps, for all my efforts, your *mind* has not yet been obliterated. Perhaps there is still a part of you that wonders who I am and why I do this. And I would like to tell you, if I could, Father, but I am legion. I am Crispo, of course—dentist, surgeon, torturer, agent of the Holy Inquisition, and—would you believe?—paterfamilias. Oh, a very doting parent, a capable spouse, a solid citizen.

"But I have other names, different faces, a vast bibliography of crimes. A few, the most notorious, may ring a bell. I am Moloch first, a very god, if you believe such things. Herod, too, as myth blends into history, but still my pleasure is the slaughter of innocents, of innocence. What were your pleasures, Father? Weren't they much the same as mine?

"And after that? Nero, surely, but not only he, for the amphitheaters were packed to the upmost tiers for the spectacles I rejoiced in, and the whole audience shared my pleasure, you may be sure. Those extravaganzas were the first soul-warping traumas of your own pathetic creed, and your churches still honor the tradition—not just with the image you so vividly present to my private view at this moment, hanging there from the crossbar, my own delectable Grünewald, my do-it-yourself *Ecce homo*, but in myriad variations. There are churches in Rome, and indeed throughout all Christendom, that would put to shame Hollywood's sleaziest horrormongers. Decapitations, eyeballs served up on platters, you name it—in some chapel there is a vivid rendering. Fascinating works of art, and I am, I like to think, their most discerning connoisseur.

"And I have other names, not all in the realm of art history. Kings, generals, bishops, revolutionary firebrands, and ordinary civil servants. Anyone given enough power *must* succumb to such temptations. Why, even a little power can lead to infamies. Hasn't that been your experience? There's the old Jesuit saying, 'Give me a child for his first ten years, and I will give you a Catholic for life.' Give me a child, indeed—eh, Father? Then give me another. Can there ever be enough? It becomes an addiction. Oh, yes, it does.

"Who else am I? I am you, of course. I think that's been understood from the start. For there has to be a kind of reciprocity in these things. Doppelgängers, and all that. The devil in the flesh. The Other, who turns out, to our astonishment, to be none other than ourself.

"I didn't want you to die without *some* degree of enlightenment, Father Bryce. Or"—he thrust in the lance—"may I call you Pat?"

40

"Are you afraid of bats?" Mary asked Alison in a whisper as they huddled together inside the confessional. Alison was sitting on the chair the priest would have used, and Mary was on her lap with her right arm around Alison's shoulders.

"Well, I wouldn't want one to come in *here*," she said, "but right now I'd have to say I like bats. Seeing what they've done for us."

"I hadn't looked at it that way. That's funny." She was quiet for a while, and then she asked, "What do you think he's going to do, Alison? Don't you think he's going to come looking for us?"

"At some point he will."

"I wish we'd gone up that staircase. This will be the first place he looks."

"But I don't know where those stairs go. There's nothing *up* there, that I know of, but the dome. Shh! I think I can hear him."

Alison parted the curtain of the confessional, but all she could see was the nave and the main altar. The confessional was positioned so that she couldn't see the portal itself, only the sunlight streaming in across the marble floor. Which meant that the door had been left open. But she knew that the dog that had been barking just outside the portal was probably still there, even though it had stopped barking.

Then they heard, far off and muffled, Hedwig scream, and then Gerhardt shouting something at her. The dome magnified their voices but muddied them at the same time, so you couldn't tell what Gerhardt was saying.

Mary sighed. "She's still alive, anyhow. I was wondering what happened to the two of them, locked inside there. With all those bats, Jesus. What do you think Gerhardt will do?"

"I don't know."

"Do you know what I was thinking when we were pushing the door shut? I was thinking how it was just like in Hansel and Gretel, when the witch gets shoved into the oven."

Alison laughed. Not loudly, but with the same feeling of relief that comes from a good belly laugh. "That's just what Joyce said. It was all her idea, you know, getting them to go inside the reliquarium."

"It was Joyce's idea?" Mary asked.

"Well, she said it was Raven's idea originally. They'd planned it all out, back when they still were allowed to talk together by themselves."

"They never told me," said Mary, a little resentfully.

Alison shushed her. Gerhardt was shouting again, and Alison couldn't make any of it out, until the very last words—"I'll be right back." Alison leaned forward again and parted the curtain the least little bit. Mary's fingernails dug into her shoulder.

"There he is, I see him," Alison said. "He's off to the side from the altar, and he's just standing there, looking around."

"Don't hold the *curtain* open," Mary whispered urgently.

"Shh. There's no way he can see us. Now he's walking over to the elevator. Yes, he's getting *into* it! Oh, thank you, Jesus."

Alison tried to stand up, but Mary was sitting on her. "Get up, Mary. We've got to take care of that dog."

"No!" Mary tightly wrapped both arms around Alison.

"Mary, come on. We've already got this far. And I've got the Mace. It will work on dogs the same as on people. If you want to stay in the Shrine, that's okay, but let me get up."

Reluctantly, Mary stood up, and Alison found the little doorknob that opened the low half-door of the confessional. At the far end of the nave the portal was open. The dog that had been making such a racket saw Alison at the moment she saw the dog, and it started in again. But it didn't come rushing forward; it just stood right where it was, barking like mad.

Alison had had time, hiding in the confessional, to figure out what to do now. She went inside the compartment where she'd found the Mace and felt around along the top of the curtain. As she'd hoped, it was hung on a rod that lifted up easily from its supports. She took down the curtain and slid it off the rod, which was wooden and as thick as a broom handle, and offered the curtain rod to Mary.

Mary shook her head.

"Take it," Alison insisted. "It could be useful."

"I'm feeling sick."

"You'll feel sicker if we don't get out of here before fucking Gerhardt gets back."

Mary accepted the curtain rod. Sometimes a bit of obscenity is all it takes.

"Now, you hold up the top corner of the curtain, like this, so it's sideways, and I'll hold the bottom end. So. And now we walk toward that door. Slowly. But not too slowly—we want to get out of here. And if the dog rushes at us, just wait till it gets close and then try and get the curtain *over* it. It's pretty thick. It can't bite us through the curtain, can it?"

"Alison, those bats— Can't you *hear* them?"

"The bats aren't our problem, Mary. The dog is our problem."

"Right."

"So, what we'll do is—we'll walk to the center aisle first, and then up the aisle toward where the dog is. Okay?"

"Okay."

Alison held the left side of the curtain, so that she could use the can of Mace with her right hand. The Mace seemed like any other aerosol, with a little black button on the top that you pressed down to make it squirt. But there were no instructions as to how far away you had to be to use it.

When they got to the center aisle, the sound of the bats whirling around up in the dome suddenly became very loud. Very loud and very shrill. At the same time the dog in the doorway was still going at it, just as loud, not as shrill.

Mary giggled.

Alison shot her a questioning look.

"I was just thinking," Mary said. "It sounds like some kind of organ that's gone crazy. And the two of us are walking down the aisle. So it's kind of like the wedding we both never had. We're even wearing white."

"Very funny. Are you okay?"

"Uh-huh. I just wish you had a gun instead of a can of Mace, but I'm okay."

They'd gone half the distance toward the door, and the dog didn't seem to have any intention of coming into the Shrine after them. It just stood its ground and went on barking, which was probably good strategy from its point of view.

As they got closer, they automatically slowed down. When they were only about twenty feet away, the dog's behavior changed. It stopped barking and took a couple of steps backward and started to snarl. Its snarl was scarier.

"What do we do now?" Mary asked.

"Just keep going ahead, real slow."

When they were ten feet away, Alison could see the dog's body tensing, and she decided this would have to be the moment. She pressed the button on the can of Mace, and she could see the cone of vapor shoot out of the nozzle. But not, she could tell right away, far enough.

The dog didn't know about Mace, though. It only knew that some kind of action had been directed against it, and it lunged right into the cone of vapor, and the Mace did its work.

When the dog hit the center of the curtain, Mary dropped her end of it and ran for the portal. Alison closed her eyes and directed another solid squirt from the can in the general direction of the blinded dog, then followed Mary out into the open air, almost stumbling down the short flight of concrete steps.

At the bottom of the steps they both turned back to watch—to marvel, to applaud—the dog as it thrashed about, baffled, attacking the curtain for want of any better enemy.

Alison turned around. It was like looking down the road to heaven. There was a wide asphalt drive, lined on both sides with white birches. The asphalt was already speckled with the first yellow leaves off the birches. It had been a dry summer. The sky was blue, with white puffy clouds.

"Let's get out of here," she said, grabbing hold of Mary's wrist. Mary was still watching the dog as it spun around in circles, savaging the curtain. "Come on. Fast."

"I can't run," said Mary.

Alison realized immediately that she wasn't just playing for sympathy. She hadn't been out of her cell for a long time, and she was weak. And very near her term. "We don't have to run, Mary. But let's get going."

They headed down the drive as fast as Alison could propel Mary, tugging on her wrist. When they'd come to the first bend, Alison saw with dismay the asphalt drive stretching ahead of them with no sign of the highway that it must be taking them to. She had only a dim memory of arriving at the Shrine. There had been a gate, which Gerhardt had had to get out of the car to unlock. But between the gate and the Shrine? It couldn't have been that far. It couldn't.

"Alison," Mary said. "I *am* feeling sick. I have to stop a minute. Really."

"Sure. A little while. We're almost there."

"Here, take this." Mary handed Alison the curtain rod, then walked over to the side of the drive, holding her swollen abdomen, and vomited, politely, into high weeds. Then she stood still, waiting for the second spasm.

The silence was broken by the sound of another dog somewhere ahead of them. Shit, Alison thought, how many of them are there? Standing still, looking down the tree-lined drive, she felt exposed. If a dog came running at them along the drive, the Mace wouldn't be much of a defense.

When Mary felt she could walk again, Alison persuaded her that it would be better for them to make their way through the woods. It would slow them down, but it would also slow down a dog, and if a dog did come after them, they could get behind a tree trunk or a bush. Or even climb a tree, if need be.

"Alison, come on! I could no more climb a tree than I could . . . I don't know what. Jesus, I wish we hadn't got into this."

"Hey, we're almost *out* of it—that's the bright side. Try and make believe we're hikers. Looking at the beautiful scenery. The trees and . . . well, the trees are nice. I can't say I care much for the stuff close to the ground. Some of them have prickers."

"I know. I've already had one slice my ankle."

Mary started crying, but she cried a lot, and as long as it didn't slow her down, Alison decided she didn't have to go on with the pep talk. They were already making enough noise just walking through the woods, pushing aside dead branches and stepping on things that crackled. Bugs had started to find them, nasty little gnats, and once they did, there was no getting away from them. They tagged along like a private cloud.

The barking up ahead had become almost continuous—but that

could be a positive thing. Who would the dog be barking at that way? Not an animal. Unless the animal were up a tree. And if it were a person, if it were anyone but Gerhardt, they were almost home free. Alison tried to get Mary to move faster, but Mary was afraid of the dog ahead of them and slowed down to a snail's pace. At last she seized up altogether. She sat on a log and refused to budge. You could see there was no use arguing, so Alison told her to stay where she was. At least there were bushes all around, so she wouldn't be easy to see.

Alison went on by herself, directly toward where the barking seemed to be coming from. The trees were getting closer together, but there was less knee-level brush. She could move almost as fast as along the asphalt drive. And then ahead of her it got brighter and she could see, through the last trees, the glint of the metal fence.

She stopped at the edge of the woods. About twenty feet beyond the fence was a two-lane highway, but there was no traffic on it, and she wasn't sure someone in a car would see her this far away—or stop, if they did see her. The fence was about ten feet high, with barbed wire strung across the top. At the bottom was only a couple inches of leeway (she tried prying it with the curtain rod, which broke) and not enough give in the fence to be able to push her way out—not without taking the time to do some digging.

She had to choose. Either follow the curve of the fence in the direction the barking was coming from, or go the other way and hope that she could eventually flag down a car.

At that point she heard, behind the barking of the dog, a man's voice, not loud but urgent, and moments later a whistling sound, like a teakettle whistling on the stove when you're outside of the house. She realized, still undecided which way to go, that the whistling sound was the alarm inside the Shrine that had gone off before.

She chose—and began to jog alongside the fence toward the sound of the barking, keeping a firm grip on the can of Mace. As the fence curved, a large ornamental gateway came into sight, and parked beside it was a car that Alison recognized at a glance as Greg's red junker Olds.

She broke into a run and called out his name, and there he was, there outside the locked gate. He looked up and shouted "Alison!" but the dog had seen her at the same moment, another German shepherd like the one outside the Shrine, and it came bounding toward her.

Alison didn't think, she just kept running straight for the dog, and when they were almost ready to collide, she veered to one side and closed her eyes and pressed the nozzle on the Mace and didn't stop squirting until the dog had knocked her over and she'd rolled into the fence. The dog made a kind of howling noise she'd never heard before, so she was sure she'd got him in the eyes. But she'd got herself, too, a little. It felt like what happens if you rub your eyes after you've eaten something with Tabasco sauce.

She made herself blink tears and tried to see what the dog was doing. It was shaking its head from one side to the other, like it was trying to shake off water, but at the same time it was staggering toward her. It was blind, and probably unable to smell anything either, but it was angrier than ever, just the way the dog outside the Shrine had been when it was tearing the curtain to shreds.

"Alison." It was Greg. He was down on his knees right on the other side of the fence, near enough to touch.

"Greg," she said. "Oh, Jesus. I love you."

"Alison, you got to get away from the dog. Can you climb the fence? Try and climb high enough that the dog can't get to you."

It sounded like a dumb thing to do and probably impossible, but she would try. She grabbed hold of the mesh and pulled herself to her feet. Her eyes were on fire, and she really couldn't see anything now. She fitted her toe into the mesh of the fence. She'd climbed mesh fences before, when she was little, and her feet were still small enough so she could jam in her toe and get a purchase. She got a higher handhold and pulled herself up, and Greg, on the other side of the fence, was coaching her.

The dog lunged into the fence, off to the side from where she was, and she lost a toehold. Her leg was dangling down like bait.

Then there was a huge explosion, and the dog stopped barking. Someone had shot it, and her first thought was simply despair, because she couldn't think who would have had a gun except Gerhardt.

"Fucking hell," said Greg, but not to her. "You had a gun all this time and you didn't *use* it?"

"Against a dog that was doing only what it was supposed to do? Until this young lady appeared— Are you all right, Miss?"

"I'm fine," said Alison, who was back on terra firma. "But my eyes hurt. There's Mace in them, it's like pepper."

"I think," said the stranger with Greg, "that there is still some water left in the car. Let me go see."

"Are you all right?" Greg asked, trying to touch her through the mesh. They managed to twine their fingers together with the wire between.

"I'm fine. My eyes hurt. Oh, I'm so happy to *see* you." She laughed. "And I *can't* see you."

They managed to kiss, and then the other man was there with the water. He told her to make a cup of her hands and hold them close to the fence, and then he poured a little water into them. She doused her eyes, and for just a moment it was heaven, but the stinging started up again, almost as bad. He continued pouring and she continued washing her eyes until she became aware that the man pouring the water into her hands was wearing a Roman collar.

She let her hands drop, dismayed, blinking, still half-blind. "You're a priest," she said.

"Yes. But don't let that alarm you. I'm no part of this unholy operation. I'm here with your friend to help you get away. When you appeared, Greg had been trying to use the tire iron from the car to break the lock on the gate. I confess that I tried to dissuade him. Apparently, the situation here is worse than we could have imagined."

"A whole lot worse," said Alison. "There's another priest in there, and he's some kind of— Oh God, I can't explain, it's a mess. I thought that dog was going to kill me. Where's Greg?"

"He's back by the gate, trying to break the chain with the tire iron. But I don't hold out much hope of success. It's a very thick chain. And we have no way of cutting the wire at the top of the fence, so I don't see how we can get you to our side. What I mean to suggest to Greg, who, by the way, is very much in love with you, if I'm any judge at all—"

"You are," said Alison gratefully. "He's wonderful."

As they talked, they walked together, slowly, brushing against the fence that separated them, in the direction of the gate. "What I mean to suggest is that I leave you here with Greg, and with my gun—which I never in my *life* thought that I would use, I'm very much opposed to them, but living in the West, as I have for so long— But never mind all that. I think I'm a little upset myself. What I mean to suggest," he began again, "is that I take Greg's car and find the nearest phone and summon the police."

"I think that's a very good idea," said Alison.

When they had reached the gate, where Greg was trying to break the chain, the strange priest began to explain what he thought they should do. Greg didn't agree right away, and he wanted to hear from Alison what was happening in the Shrine, but before she could begin to explain, another car, big and black, pulled up alongside Greg's junker.

"May I ask," said the driver, stepping out of the black car, "what in the world is happening here?"

Oh, Jesus, Alison thought—this time, not thankfully. Because, even though everything was still mostly a blur, she recognized the man's voice.

It was Father Cogling.

41

Father Mabbley was shaken. He was not cut out for this sort of thing. Violence. And yet, providentially, he had had the gun on his person. A gun he'd always sworn he would never use. And yet he'd brought it with him, concealed under his suit coat, and he *had* used it, and it seemed quite certain now that if he hadn't, the poor girl they'd come to help would almost certainly have been savaged by the dog he'd killed. A justifiable use of violence—but still he felt this irrational guilt for having shot the dog, for having used the gun he'd sworn never to use.

His hands were trembling. More accurately, they were twitching in an odd way, and there was a feeling, around his rib cage, that was both elevating and vaguely distressing, like the one time he'd yielded to the temptation of cocaine. It was, in an asexual way, a little like being horny.

He wished he were anywhere else but here. He wished he'd never left Las Vegas. He wished he'd never grown up. But here he was, and now here was another priest (Father Cogling, he presumed, just by the sound of his voice), in high dudgeon, railing about the dead dog. Greg, God bless him, was railing right back, and so Father Mabbley didn't have to switch into rhetorical mode himself. He could try to lower his blood pressure (or whatever it was) and regain his sanity.

Think, he told himself. Think what to do.

But there wasn't time for that, because while Greg was still giving Father Cogling what for, a new player appeared on the other side of the cyclone fence, a scrawny old coot with a face as deathly as life allows, and carrying the kind of gun one hopes to see only in movies.

"Gerhardt!" said Father Cogling. "Thank heaven you're here. I just caught these two trying to break open the gate."

"I heard a gunshot," the skull croaked.

"And a good thing you did," said Greg. "My wife was almost killed by your damned dog."

"Son of a bitch," said Gerhardt, looking toward the dog's body, where it lay beside the fence. "Trixie? Goddamn."

"I saw it happen, Gerhardt," said Father Cogling, in, for him, a placatory tone. "And I will say they had little choice. The dog *was* attacking this girl." For the first time Cogling seemed to take notice of Alison and said, "Oh. It's you. I might have known." Then he turned to Father Mabbley and said, in another tone of voice that was *entre nous*, in a specifically priestly way, "No one has yet to explain what you are doing here, or why you were trying to break open the gate."

"Let's take care of explanations later, okay?" said Gerhardt, unlocking the gate and swinging it open. "You folks wanted to get in here. The gate's open. Get in."

"I think," said Father Mabbley, "that at this point we would prefer to take this young lady with us to somewhere she can receive suitable medical attention."

"Get in," Gerhardt repeated, lifting his lethal weapon. "She can get the attention she needs right here." He looked toward Father Cogling. "Which of them has a gun? Get it from him."

Father Cogling approached Father Mabbley. "I think it would be best if you gave me your weapon. We don't want a shooting match here, do we?"

Father Mabbley gave his gun to Father Cogling, who put it in the inside breast pocket of his suit. As he did so, Greg gave Father Mabbley a look of withering scorn. Father Mabbley could scarcely blame him. It must have looked like craven submission.

"And who's got the keys to the red car?" Gerhardt wanted to know. When there was no answer, he turned his weapon on Greg. "It's got to be yours. So put the keys on the ground in front of you, and go inside the gate, and you walk with the girl there along the drive. Slowly. I'll be right behind you in your car. Father Willy, you bring your friend along in your car, but lock up the gate behind you. Okay?"

Cogling nodded.

When these things had been duly accomplished, and they had begun the slow procession toward the Shrine, Father Mabbley said, "I should inform you now, Father Cogling, that the Chancery is aware of my coming here. I don't know what your *henchman* thinks he's doing in abducting us in this fashion, but he will have to answer for it. As will you, Father, if you allow him to continue to violate our rights."

"Violate *your* rights, is it? Your right to break and enter? I should inform *you*, Father, that the girls being cared for at this facility are here for their own protection, and for the protection of the unborn life within them."

"A strange way to protect them, if I may say so."

"I don't know what was happening with the dog. I do know the girl shouldn't have been loose on the grounds. The dogs are there for the protection of the Shrine. From those"—he gave Father Mabbley a sideways look—"who might try to break in."

Father Mabbley felt he'd achieved no more than a stalemate. Cogling's righteous indignation seemed equal to his own. So he changed course.

"Actually, my original purpose in coming here did not have to do with securing the release of Miss Sanders."

"Oh," said Father Cogling sarcastically. "She's a Miss now, is she? A moment ago your friend had claimed her for his wife."

"My original purpose," Father Mabbley persisted, "was to speak with the purported director of Birth-Right, Patrick Bryce."

"Well, in that case, you'll be disappointed in both your purposes. *Miss* Sanders is not about to be released, and Father Bryce is not receiving visitors."

"Shouldn't Father Bryce be able to decide that for himself?"

Cogling made no reply, and Father Mabbley might well not have taken it in if he had, for he was wonderstruck. There ahead of them stood one of the Seven Wonders of the Totalitarian World, the Shrine of the infamous Blessed Konrad of Paderborn, the patron saint of anti-Semites and one of the holy places of the Cold War. He'd seen photographs of the Shrine before, but photographs can never convey the nature of an atrocity. The Shrine was the perfect combination of a cathedral and a bunker, with a lead-gray dome of cast concrete that seemed to be sinking into the earth rather than soaring from it. Every detail was expressive of the whole, though detail, as such, had not been the architect's forte. It was, quite arrogantly, One Big Idea, and that idea was Authority. Authority that had no use for the landscape around it, or for the people who might enter it, but only for its own swollen and ill-conceived *terribilità*. It was, as the poets say, a sermon in stone (or ferroconcrete) and *such* an indictment of the institution that had erected it that Father Mabbley, for the first time since he had come to the decision that he would leave the priesthood, felt a sense of, if not exactly jubilation, joyful relief. What bliss it would be no longer to be implicated in what that building represented! To be a priest no more and a human being again.

Cogling brought his car to a stop and got out. Greg and Alison were standing at the foot of the steps leading to the entrance of the monstrosity, and Gerhardt was urging them to enter with motions of his lethal weapon. There was *another* dead dog lying on the steps, and—the topper—there were *bats* flittering out of the lowering Romanesque doorway. In its own gothic way, it was almost beautiful.

Father Mabbley got out of the car. He wondered, as he did from time to time, if he was about to die. He hoped not, but it was always possible, and if he were to die, there was at least this consolation: that he couldn't have done it in higher style. This place was the very entrance to the city of Dis. Dante would have felt right at home.

He followed Cogling into the Shrine without demur, simply marveling. The dome, which was more oppressive from within than from without, was *filled* with bats, circling about in anticlockwise gyres, like the souls of the lustful caught up in the cyclones of the second circle of the Inferno. Father Mabbley customarily felt a normative dread of bats, but these bats were so *à propos* that he could not but rejoice in them. And the *noise* they made as they whirled about—it was Bach and Richard Strauss and Philip Glass, all sent to hell in the same handbasket.

While Father Mabbley marveled, Cogling and his henchman were conferring, and the result of their conference was Cogling's demanding to know of Alison Sanders what had become of a key that she had taken from the Shrine. Miss Sanders, after some equivocation, produced the key demanded of her, and Gerhardt, after closing and locking the central portal of the Shrine, led the way (Father Mabbley followed out of sheer fascination) toward the altar, and then around it, to stand before an object of art as wonderful in its way as the Shrine itself.

It was a parody of the sepulcher—squat and lumpy and obviously *faux*, with an effete angel posing off to one side like a gargoyle that had lost its way from Mussolini's Rome.

Gerhardt opened the sepulcher with the key that Alison had given him, and then there was sheer pandemonium. The tomb virtually exploded. Bats streamed out of it like, what else, bats out of hell. Millions of bats! Billions of bats! Father Cogling threw himself to the floor, and even his skull-faced henchman took cover behind the half-open door of the tomb as the bats streamed out and up and all about and filled the air around them.

Father Mabbley looked on, as at the burning bush of Moses. It didn't occur to him to hit the deck, and the torrent of bats flew by without touching a thread of his clothes or a hair on his head.

Gradually they diminished, and Father Mabbley, as the only person still in possession of his faculties, approached the door of the sepulcher and pulled it open wider. The last and timidest bats departed the space within, and there, prostrate on the floor of the room within, with a few dead bats speckling the white marble floor about them, were the bodies of a man and a woman.

At first, entering, he supposed they were both dead, that seeming the most suitable fate for bodies found within a sepulcher. And the woman assuredly was. One could tell it without stooping to feel if there was a pulse (though he did, in common courtesy, do that). Astonishingly (if astonishment still was possible), she had the same face, in death, that Cogling's henchman had in life, and it made Father Mabbley think, uncharitably, that perhaps her death had been deserved. But one should never judge by appearances.

The man was alive. His right hand was scrabbling, with weak convulsivity, at the marble floor. Father Mabbley got down on his knees and rolled him over on his back, intending mouth-to-mouth resuscitation, if that seemed suitable. He realized, looking down at the face and the Roman collar, that this must be the very man he'd been looking for, Father Patrick Bryce. In the innocence of its unconsciousness, you could see what, years ago, Bing must have seen in that face. The simple need that could never be satisfied and that would call to those who were fated never to satisfy the needs of others. The poor doomed fool.

Father Bryce's eyes opened. Eyes that had been transfigured by terror. "I'm alive," he said.

"Yes," said Father Mabbley. "We both are. Let us thank God for that."

"You're a priest."

Father Mabbley neither affirmed nor denied the assertion. He was, after all, wearing the collar.

"Will you hear my confession?"

"It can't wait?"

"No. If you will. Please."

Father Mabbley made the sign of the cross and waited for Bryce to begin.

"I have been . . . how can I say this . . . the slave of Satan."

"We have all sinned, Father."

"No. That isn't what I mean. I'll show you." He began to pull off his collar and then to undo the snaps of his black tunic. He didn't stop until he'd bared his chest.

"Why did you do that?" Father Mabbley demanded, disconcerted and even a little embarrassed.

"So that you could see the tattoo."

Father Mabbley looked down at the man's chest. "I don't see any tattoo," said Father Mabbley. "There's no tattoo there."

The man looked up at him with such a look. Once Father Mabbley had had to tell a woman that her only child had died. It was a look like that.

Then Father Bryce's face began to grow dark. Father Mabbley looked up. Someone was closing the door of the sepulcher upon them. Well, he thought, let them.

"Go on," he said to Father Bryce, "with your confession. How did you become the slave of Satan? Begin at the beginning."

42

Father Cogling was in a state of barely suppressed fury. Gerhardt had let things at the Shrine get utterly out of hand. Just how much out of hand he didn't realize until Gerhardt had pushed shut the door of the reliquarium, locking the two priests inside. Then he revealed that the situation was even worse than Father Cogling could have supposed. Two of the girls in the Birth-Right program were dead—three, if one added the death of Tara Seberg, of which he'd already been apprised. The Seberg girl had died after a miscarriage, so her death, however regrettable, had been the sort of mischance that the program would probably have had to face eventually. The Obers could not reasonably be held to account for it.

The two other deaths were another matter. The Tyler girl had been attacked by one of the guard dogs when she had tried to escape with Alison Sanders from the Shrine. Gerhardt had discovered her body in the woods only a few minutes earlier. In a sense, even that death could be accounted accidental. The dog had not been directly incited to kill her.

It was the death of Raven Peck that was confounding, for Gerhardt had found her in her own cell, in restraints, the apparent victim of strangulation. She could not conceivably have committed suicide, but who would have done such a thing? Gerhardt had said with a perfectly straight face that he believed Father Pat was responsible. The only grounds for this suggestion was that another of the girls, the youngest, had told Hedwig that Father Pat had attempted to molest her, but the

Obers had not believed the girl, who was an accomplished liar, and neither did Father Cogling.

Father Cogling was more inclined to believe that one of the Obers had killed Raven Peck than that Father Pat had done so. Father Pat's sexual drive did not tend in the direction of teenage girls, and Father Cogling doubted whether that was the sort of thing that changed overnight. So the girl's murder had to be accounted, at this point, a mystery—and one that there was not time, now, to investigate in the spirit of an amateur detective. For Gerhardt was determined to find where the Sanders girl and her meddling boyfriend had gone off to.

"We can't just stand around gassing," Gerhardt insisted, without any of his usual deference to Father Cogling's authority. "If they manage to get away now, this whole thing could blow up."

"It seems to have blown up already," said Father Cogling acerbically.

"What I mean to say, Father, is that we could all of us end up in jail. You and me and Father Pat, and even my poor sister, who has been another Mother Teresa toward these girls."

"So what do you propose to do, Gerhardt? Hunt down the boy and girl like a pair of animals?"

Gerhardt's reply was a steely silence. Father Cogling realized that that was exactly what Gerhardt intended.

"What about the priest who's locked in the reliquarium?"

"Isn't he the one you said was pestering you on the phone about his friend, the faggot who started this whole mess? You think he isn't going to the police after what's happened?"

This time it was Father Cogling who had no reply.

"We deal with him like we dealt with his friend," said Gerhardt. "We deal with *all* of them that way. I honestly don't see any alternative, Father. We've discussed before what we'd do if one of the girls died. We'd tell her parents that she ran away from Birth-Right and we don't know where she went. None of the parents know each other. All they know is that their kid is a runaway. It happens all the time."

"And the priest, Mabbley? And the girl's boyfriend? Mabbley says the Chancery knows that he was coming here. The *Chancery*, Gerhardt!"

"We say they never got here. Or maybe *they* helped the Sanders girl break out of here and ran off with her. By the time someone starts looking for them, we'll have had a chance to get things back in order here."

"And what about Father Pat?"

"What about him? You don't think he's going to go to the police, do you? Fat chance of that happening. Father, this is not the time to be talking things over. We got to find those two kids. Am I right?"

Father Cogling nodded, and then added, prudentially, "But you're not to hurt them."

"Right, right. Now, here's what I suggest. You stay here in front of the altar, where you can see most of the church, and I'll check out all the nooks and crannies where they might be. Fortunately, the way the Shrine is built, there's not that many possibilities for them. But if they try to scoot out of one while I'm checking into another, you'll be able to see them."

"I understand," said Father Cogling.

It took Gerhardt no more than fifteen minutes to check out all the side chapels, starting with those behind the main altar, and the confessionals.

"No sign of them?" asked Father Cogling when Gerhardt returned to him.

"No, but that means I know where they've got to be. It's the only place left. And it's just where I want them. They're up there." He pointed with his shotgun at the bats circling in the dome.

Father Cogling snorted derisively. "And how did they get there? Did they fly?"

"There's a stairway that goes up there. There's no door on it. It goes all the way up to the base of the dome. See that railing that goes all around the bottom part of the dome, like a little fence?"

"The balustrade?"

"Mm-hm. Well, there's a little walkway behind it, just wide enough for one person to go along it. Apparently, the idea was for tourists to be able to go up there and have a view of the whole Shrine."

"Yes, it's a common feature of churches that have impressive domes."

"That's where they must have gone. And that's where we're going after them."

"No, Gerhardt, please leave me out of it."

"Sorry, Father, but there has to be two of us. 'Cause the pathway goes all around the dome. And there's just the one way to enter or to leave. By the stairway that goes up there. So if I went up there by myself, and they were on the opposite side of the dome, I couldn't flush them out. 'Cause if I go to the side where they are, then they can just keep opposite me and get back to the door. Unless there's somebody *by* the door. You see the logic, don't you?"

Father Cogling hated having to keep taking his cues from Gerhardt, but he did see the logic.

"You're certain that's where they are?"

Gerhardt smiled and nodded. "In fact, Father, if you look up there right now, you can see the girl. Or a bit of her white dress. They're crouched down behind the balustrade, looking at us and wondering if they fooled us."

Father Cogling sighed. "I'm afraid your eyes are better than mine, Gerhardt."

Gerhardt nodded. "They're there. And they can probably see us looking at them. And where they are they'll be able to see us heading to the stairwell. So they'll know we're coming up there. Which means, since I've got a twelve-gauge pump, I should be ahead of you on the stairs."

Father Cogling readily agreed.

It was a long climb. Gerhardt, despite his years, seemed indefatigable, and Father Cogling had to beg more than once for a respite. In his youth, on visits to various cathedrals in Europe, Father Cogling had been obliged, as a responsible tourist and a devout Catholic, to undertake similar ascents into domes and bell towers. Even then he'd considered it a form of pious madness.

But the long climb did give him an opportunity to think. Gerhardt had performed many services for him that Father Cogling did not like to think about. If the police began to examine him (as now seemed inevitable), Father Cogling doubted that the man, for all his proven loyalty, would have the courage to shoulder all the responsibility for everything that had happened. Indeed, so much had happened that it would probably not be possible for Gerhardt, if he began to be asked questions, to avoid implicating Father Cogling—and (this was surely the most important consideration) compromising the Church.

The more Father Cogling pondered these matters, the clearer it seemed that the best service Gerhardt could perform would be to sacrifice himself *before* he was interrogated.

When they reached the top of the staircase and emerged into the bat-infested madness of the dome, Father Cogling had also reached his decision. And, thanks to the gun that he had appropriated from Father Mabbley, he was in a position to carry it out.

As Gerhardt had foreseen, the guilty couple had crawled along the walkway to the side of the dome opposite the doorway. Father Cogling was able to discern, once Gerhardt had pointed it out, the telltale white of the girl's dress and the blue of the boy's jeans through the massive balusters supporting the railing.

"You stay here by the door," Gerhardt told him. "I'll walk around this way and flush them out. And don't let yourself be spooked by the bats."

Father Cogling nodded. He did not have time to hesitate, but he wasn't familiar with the operation of the handgun. He knew there was supposed to be some kind of mechanism called a safety that had to be released. Like cocking back the thingamajig on a cap pistol. He couldn't discover any such device, however, and he decided that the gun was ready to be fired. But Gerhardt had already progressed too far along the walkway, and Father Cogling wanted to be sure of his aim. He followed after him as quickly as he could.

Gerhardt turned around. "I thought I told you—" he began.

Father Cogling took aim and pulled the trigger. There was only a muted click.

"Well, you goddamned son of a bitch," said Gerhardt. He lifted the 12-gauge pump and aimed it at the priest.

Father Cogling pulled the trigger again. The gun had been used to kill the dog: There could not have been just a single bullet in it. But in fact (for Father Mabbley had had peculiar scruples in the matter of guns), such was the case. There was only a click.

Gerhardt fired. The charge tore off the cap of Father Cogling's left shoulder and, striking the concrete, ricocheted all about the dome. A few bats died and dropped to the floor of the Shrine, but Father Cogling was still alive. He ran toward the door of the stairway.

Gerhardt fired again. Father Cogling's body smashed into the concrete base of the dome and, rebounding, toppled over the balustrade to plunge to the floor of the Shrine.

Gerhardt leaned over the balustrade, amazed at what he'd done.

It was the moment Greg had waited for. During the time that Gerhardt's attention had been focused on the priest who had betrayed him, Greg had run forward in a crouch, as near as he thought he would have to get for his aim to be true. Then he hurled the brass candlestick he'd taken from the main altar, and the candlestick connected. Gerhardt fell, dazed, onto the railing of the balustrade.

Greg didn't hesitate. He was there beside him at once. The old man still had enough of his wits about him to sense what Greg intended. He was able to lift his hand and to say, "Don't."

Greg caught hold of Gerhardt by the calf of his scrawny leg and tipped him into the Shrine's central void.

Gerhardt's body landed atop that of the man he'd just killed. Together their corpses formed a kind of sign of the cross.

43

The following is excerpted from Appendix B of A Prolegomenon to Receptivist Science, *Revised Edition, by A. D. Boscage (Exegete Press, 1993):*

In the interval since the appearance of the first edition of this investigation, I have been harshly dealt with by many so-called critics, who have pointed out real and pretended inconsistencies in my text. Many have done so in a spirit of open derision that has been a cause of real distress to myself and to the many others who have had experiences similar to my own and have had the courage to speak of them. What kind of "critic" is it who points the finger of laughter at those whose only fault is to have exhibited the psychic scars—or the still bleeding stigmata!—of sufferings such as I have recounted in these pages? Perhaps these wounds were inflicted by weapons unknown to the limited perspective of "scientific" investigation. I have never professed to be able to offer a complete scientific explanation for all that I have been a witness to. I leave that to those who will come after me. I have only been able to offer suggestions, hypotheses, *hints,* that may pierce the dark veil surrounding events that often do seem inexplicable.

Perhaps the cruelest of all these critiques was that offered by someone I had supposed to be a friend. "Tripping with the UFO Messiah" appeared in a monthly magazine of limited circulation but high reputation (a reputation that has been irreparably tarnished by the publication of such a mean-spirited "hatchet job"), and it bore the byline of Héloïse Vendelle. As a rule, I refuse to read the screeds of those who have no other purpose than ridicule and vilification, but I knew Héloïse Vendelle! She it was with whom I journeyed in 1981 to the ruined abbey church at Montpellier-le-Vieux. With her I had marveled at the picturesque remains of that abandoned city. She it was who had discovered me as I emerged dazed and confused from the crypt of Notre Dame de Gevaudon, after my experience of transmentation, and it was she who was my companion in the blisses of love for the three weeks that followed.

What a very different account of that experience Héloïse Vendelle related in the pages of that magazine which I forbear to name. According to her, there is no such city as Montpellier-le-Vieux! According to her, there has never been such a city! The blocks of stone that once formed the pillars of Notre Dame de Gevaudon are nothing, according to her, but geological formations of a peculiar character, the work not of medieval stonemasons but of eroding winds and rains! She quoted passages from reference books and even supplied her own poor-quality snapshots of what *she* claimed was Montpellier-le-Vieux. I looked at them and could not believe my eyes, for these were *not* the ruins we had visited!

Héloïse claimed, further, that at the time of this visit I was under the influence of illicit substances—both amphetamines and hallucinogens. I have already written that Lorraine had purchased amphetamines when we were in Rodez, but they were entirely for her own use. I *did* prepare myself with a megadose of Vitamin C, and was in a state of heightened receptivity to my external environment. But I categorically deny using any hallucinogens, a kind of drug whose use I have forsworn since 1976. Perhaps *Héloïse Vendelle* was dropping acid unbeknownst to me, but *I* was not!

Unless (it suddenly occurs to me) she gave me acid without my knowing she did so! Oh, perfidy, if so! But why would she have done such a thing—she, whom for a little while I had loved and who had returned that love? Unless (which I shudder to suppose) she had been acting all along as an agent of the Alphanes! Unless she had been intending *from the first* to throw my credibility into question by muddying the waters with this disinformation about "natural, geological formations"!

With the advantage of hindsight, no other explanation seems possible.

But what, then, of my experiences as Bonamico? Were they all mere hallucinations? Could they be false memories induced by mnemocytes? I cannot believe it; they are too vivid, too circumstantial. Bonamico lived, and, for a while, his life was mine—if not in the Middle Ages recorded by historians, then at some other, deeper level of reality.

I have never been certain whether our Alphane visitors have come to us from the vasty reaches of outer space or from the no less vasty reaches of Inner Space. Extraterrestrial or supernatural? We cannot answer that question until they choose to make us privy to their secrets. Similarly, it may be that my transmentation to the Dark Ages took me not to an earlier century but to another realm altogether, a higher reality, such as philosophy has always posited, in which the irregularities and inconsistencies of our mundane existence have been effaced and one dwells among those figures Jung calls archetypes.

There can be no final answer. Surely, the crude, material skepticism of those who would use the testimony of Héloïse Vendelle to invalidate the whole of Receptivist Science offers no kind of answer at all. *I know what happened to me.* I felt it in my flesh. The wounds are visible on my soul. Those who have eyes can see them.

44

"It's such a lovely *rug*," Janet said, sitting down on it and petting it as though it were the fur of some gigantic pet. "But a *white* rug? How can you keep it clean?"

"I don't have to worry about that," Alison said, sitting down beside Janet in front of the fireplace, which was all set up with logs in it so they could light a fire after dinner. "I've got a woman who comes in, and she does all the cleaning."

"That's on top of the baby-sitter who looks after Cindi?"

"Mm-hm. Except she's not really a baby-sitter. She's an au pair."

"O-pear?"

"That's what the French call their baby-sitters when they live in your house full-time. At least, according to Father Mab."

"And he lives here, too, along with the baby-sitter? The O-pear, I mean?"

"Almost. You see, the house really belongs to him. We just have the use of it for five years, while Greg gets his degree. Greg doesn't have any idea why the Anker guy wrote him into his will, except that he didn't have any closer relatives. But he's not complaining. The nice thing is, the house belongs to Greg—for the next five years anyhow—plus, he gets money that pays for his tuition and a whole lot besides. He wanted to get a Harley, but I told him I wouldn't ride on it. So he got a Cherokee LTD instead."

"I saw it in the driveway. Leather seats!"

"It's got everything. Anyhow, with the house and the money he's got, Greg doesn't have to feel like he's living off of me. Not that I'd mind, I've got so much, but I think he might."

"How much did you get, if you don't mind my asking?"

"You won't believe. Five million dollars."

"No shit? Jesus, that's *twice* what I got. I guess I went to the wrong lawyer."

"Well, you might have got more if you hadn't given up your kid for adoption. Half of the five million is in a trust fund for Cindi, and we can't touch that. Except that the au pair gets paid out of that money, and Cindi's tuition when she goes to college. Mr. Kennedy, that's our lawyer, said the Church didn't even put up that much of a fight. They knew they'd lose their shirts if it went to a court case, that's what Mr. Kennedy said."

"Yeah, that's what I was told, too. I wonder where they'll get that kind of money. Besides us, they've had to buy off Raven Peck's family, and Mary's, and Tara Seberg's. What'll they do, sell their cathedral?"

"Well, according to Father Mab, who's got a friend who's in charge of the Chancery, which is like the business office, they're going to have to sell the Shrine."

"And tear it down, I hope. Who'd buy an old monstrosity like that?"

"Apparently, there's this religious group down in Texas that they're trying to strike a deal with. Reverend Somebody-or-other. You can see him on cable TV."

"Isn't it *great* having cable! So anyhow, you started out explaining about Father Mab and how he 'almost' lives here. What's that all about?"

"Well, he's practically made himself part of the family. He's back in the kitchen right now with Greg, fixing dinner. He loves to cook, and he's pretty good, except that he makes fish more often than I care for."

"Not tonight, I hope. I hate fish. Mrs. Findley—that's my new mom—is always making fish. *Steamed* fish. And brown rice with everything. She's some kind of health nut, I think."

"Do you like her?"

"Better than the first couple I got sent to live with. They were real creeps. I knew right from the start they just thought of me as a meal ticket. 'Cause they knew I'd be getting a lot of money when the legal business was settled. At least the Findleys aren't adopting me for my money. Mr. Findley is some kind of millionaire himself. He's the Findley with the dry-cleaning stores all over town. And you should see their house. It's right on Lake Calhoun, and all brick, with a third floor that isn't an attic. I mean, it's a mansion."

"Are there other kids?"

"Four of them, but two are already married and the other two are in college. I've got my own room, plus there's a room they call the rec room in the basement, with a pool table, and I'm the only one who ever uses it. And I can have friends over anytime. It's a nice situation, except for the fish."

"Well, don't worry. Father Mab isn't making fish. *Or* brown rice. He likes to eat pretty much the same things we do. He doesn't cook *all* the time. We have a lot of takeout—pizzas, Chinese, barbecued ribs. *He's* certainly no health nut."

"Do you think he'd mind if I had a cigarette?"

"*I'd* mind, Janet. When did you start smoking? You're only twelve years old."

Janet sighed resignedly. "I started smoking when I was ten, for Christ's sake. And I'm not twelve, I'm thirteen and a half, almost. Mrs. Findley is just like you, she won't let me smoke anywhere in the house."

"Well, you shouldn't, it's bad for you. And it's especially bad for babies. I made Greg stop. For Cindi's sake."

"Boy, you've really got him jumping through the hoop. No Harley, no smoking. Does he have to be in bed by eleven? *I* do."

"He doesn't have to be. But we usually are. It's like we're still on our honeymoon."

"Oh, don't talk about sex. Not with me. I go to this therapist in Edina three times a week, and she's always wanting to talk about sex. I would just like to *forget* all that, and she says that's just what I *should* do. But then she wants me to talk about how I feel about my parents, my real ones, who are in jail, which is just where they belong. But how can I talk about my dad and forget all that shit at the same time? I like the therapist in a lot of ways, she's got a sense of humor, and I think she actually likes me, too. Only how can you tell if someone really likes you when she's getting paid a hundred bucks an hour?"

"I know what you mean. I go to my therapist twice a week now, but for a while it was four times a week. What my therapist said was to look at it as a job. If I didn't have a lot of mental anguish, I wouldn't be getting such a huge settlement."

"Yeah, that makes sense."

There was a light rap on the door. It was Thérèse, the au pair. She'd brought in Cindi for her good-night kiss. She was already half-asleep, so Alison didn't make a big fuss, and she knew that Janet didn't have much use for babies at this point, even a baby as sweet as Cindi.

When Thérèse had taken Cindi back to her nursery, Janet said, "She's older than you are."

"Yeah, it feels a little weird sometimes. I mean, she goes to college at night, and she's always studying stuff whenever Cindi's napping, and I'm still taking makeup courses to get a high school diploma. It feels funny telling *her* what to do. But it's great having the free time."

"I don't know. It must be different if you're married. I wouldn't know what to do with myself if I weren't back at school."

"You like school? You don't get hassled?"

"There wasn't all the publicity in the papers for me that there was for you. I don't think the other kids know. And it turns out I'm really good at science. I get A's without half trying."

"You're bright, that's why."

"Yeah, I guess I am. It's nice. And it's a really fancy school. You should see the gym. It's got *two* trampolines. I love bouncing on those things. I think I'll be on the gymnastics team next year. Maybe I'll be the next Olga Korbut, that's what my gym teacher says."

"Who's Olga Korbut?" Alison asked.

Janet shrugged. "I don't know, but I'll be the next one."

Greg came in from the dining room, wearing his brand-new Giorgio Armani suit with a midnight blue silk shirt under it and two gold chains peeking out from behind the open collar. "Dinner is served," he announced.

He led the way into the dining room, where the table was set with the genuine sterling silver flatware and the china that had cost $240 for each of the place settings (and that had been on sale) and little bouquets of flowers in front of each plate in addition to the big bouquet in the center of the table she'd gotten already made up by the florist for $75. Alison had never done anything like this in her life, but Father Mabbley had helped her with the details, and the final result really did look like a picture in a book. You almost didn't want to sit down and eat off the plates. But Father Mabbley had said that now that they were nouveaux riches (which was another French word for when you suddenly came into a pile of money), this sort of thing was expected of you.

If you didn't show off, people would think you weren't grateful for God's blessings.

"My gosh," said Janet. "That is really something."

"Isn't it," Alison agreed.

"Should we sit down now?" Greg asked. "Or should we wait for Father Mab?"

"Sit down," Father Mabbley called out from behind the louvered door that led to the kitchen. "I'll be with you in no time at all."

Greg pulled out a chair for Janet, who sat down and very carefully unfolded the linen napkin that was on her plate. Alison and Greg sat down on either side of her, but then Greg got to his feet again. "The candles! I forgot to light the candles."

There were seven red candles mounted on a big silver candle-holder, and Greg didn't get the last of them lit until Father Mabbley entered the dining room, pushing a wheeled table with the dinner he'd prepared. There was a Caesar salad, and a big chicken potpie, and hot rolls sprinkled with sesame seeds, and yams baked with honey and walnuts, and little peas cooked in cream with bits of Italian ham. Janet *oo*-ed and *ah*-ed over her first taste of everything but the rolls, but it was the peas she went on about.

"These are just incredible, Father," she gushed. "I never thought I'd ask for a second helping of *peas*. Jesus, they're delicious!"

"I'm glad you like them," said Father Mabbley modestly.

"This is better than any holiday dinner I ever had."

"Mm," said Greg, nodding his head and swallowing. "I could say the same. Even if I did do half the cooking."

"You did?" Janet marveled, helping herself to more of the peas. "That's amazing."

Aside from the compliments to the chefs, there was not a lot of conversation at the table. They all had second helpings of everything, and there were still leftovers, except for the peas, which Janet polished off after Father Mabbley insisted.

Then they all went into the living room, leaving the unwashed dishes on the table. Greg lit a fire in the fireplace, and they settled down on different sections of the maroon leather sectional, with Father Mabbley sitting in the middle, where it curved.

"I can't tell you," Father Mabbley began, "how happy I am to be allowed to meet you at last, Janet. After all these months."

"My lawyer explained to me," said Janet, "that until everything was settled with the Church's lawyers, I shouldn't see anything of Alison. I guess their idea was that the Church's lawyers would say we were making things up if we had a chance to be with each other. As though we *needed* to make things up!"

"That's over now, thank heaven," Father Mabbley said, "and it's all turned out for the best. At least for the four of us. I felt a similar frustration all this long while, because I was unable to talk about all the things I learned from Father Bryce and from the police—not even with Alison and Greg. In part, that's because his first confidences were told to me under the seal of the confessional."

"But you're not a priest anymore," Greg pointed out.

"That doesn't relieve me of an obligation to my vows. It only means that I don't draw my salary from the Church anymore. In any case, Father Bryce eliminated that scruple by insisting that he would tell the police what they wanted to know only if I acted as his interrogator. He was quite obstinate, and the police indulged him in his whim. And so I learned the whole of the story again, in extraordinary detail. And almost all of it turned out to be pure fantasy."

"But I thought he'd confessed to everything," said Janet. "That's why there wasn't any trial."

"Indeed, he pleaded guilty. But most of the crimes he confessed to me, often in great detail, weren't the crimes he committed. And vice versa. In fact, it's hard to be perfectly sure what crimes he did commit. For instance, I don't think it was Father Bryce who killed my friend and Greg's cousin, Bing Anker."

"That's news to me," said Alison. "I mean, that was one of the few cases where there was a witness. The woman who saw him in back of Bing's house, getting into his car. That much was in the newspaper."

"Yes, but then the police ballistics test showed that the gun that killed Bing belonged to Gerhardt Ober. And we're quite certain that Gerhardt also killed Father Bryce's mother and twin brother at about the same time."

"Why would he do that?" Greg asked.

"The police had no idea at first. Unless he'd been told to by Father Cogling. They *think* that's why he killed Bing Anker."

"Father Cogling ordered a hit?" Greg marveled. "Jesus, these Catholics."

"Not *all* Catholics do such things, Greg," Father Mabbley chided. "Only a few."

"So Father Cogling had his henchman kill your buddy so that Father Bryce wouldn't be blackmailed?"

"More likely, he acted to spare the Church further scandal. The Church abhors scandal, as you have learned. Didn't you sign papers as part of your settlement agreeing never to talk about any of this to the press?"

"We had to," said Alison.

"We *all* had to," said Janet impatiently. "But what I don't understand is, how did Father Cogling *know* there was a scandal in the works? Were they *both* sleeping with the altar boys?"

"No, there's never been a breath of scandal about Father Cogling in *that* regard. The police *think* that Father Cogling was in the habit of listening to Father Bryce's phone conversations, and that while I was eavesdropping on Father Bryce and Bing, when Bing was being such a rash fool (may he rest in peace), Father Cogling was doing the same thing on his end of the line without Father Bryce's knowledge. It's all very complicated."

"You bet," said Greg.

"Really," said Father Mabbley, "I should begin at the beginning. But if I might impose on your hospitality, Alison, I *would* like a bit of brandy at this point. I know that I was the one who insisted that we have only Diet Coke with our dinner, but I am beginning, a little, to fade."

"Surely, Father Mab. Greg, would you get him something? We *could* have had wine with dinner."

"Ah, but you see, we didn't have the *right* wine. And the wrong wine is worse than none at all."

Greg returned with two brandy snifters and a bottle of Rémy Martin. He poured brandy in both snifters, gave one to Father Mabbley, and took the other himself.

"You don't offer any to your guests?" Janet said reproachfully.

"Janet," Alison scolded, "you're thirteen."

Janet settled back in the sectional. "Well, at least you got *that* right this time. At *home* Mr. Findley lets me have wine. Except I have to put water in it, so I almost can't taste it. It doesn't matter. I just hate being treated like a child."

"You are a child," said Alison, smiling.

"Am not!"

"Are so!"

"She only *seems* to be a child," said Father Mabbley, having had a judicious sip of his brandy. "In fact, she may be the most adult person here."

"Thank you, Father," said Janet.

"It wasn't necessarily a compliment, my dear. Now, where were we? Oh yes, I was beginning at the beginning. Have you all seen *Psycho*?"

"Oh, come on," said Janet. "I've seen it maybe a dozen times. It's always on TV. Did Father Pat think he was his own *mother*? He really *was* crazy."

"I've never seen *Psycho*," said Greg, "so I guess you should explain."

"Well, then, this is what happened, as nearly as we can tell. By 'we' I mean myself and the two psychiatrists who were working for the prosecution. Father Bryce had multiple personalities. He also had a drinking problem, which is one reason, Miss Joyner—"

"I'm Miss Findley now."

"Very well, Miss Findley. One reason not to drink. Rum *is* a demon. Likewise bourbon, which was Father Bryce's undoing, by his own account. He had blackouts. Which is to say, times when he did things he didn't remember afterward. Most alcoholics do have black-outs. It's a convenient way to avoid a consciousness of sin. At some point on his road to perdition, probably after he'd had dealings with a young man who committed suicide, Father Bryce began to receive phone calls from another young man, who called himself Clay. Whether there ever was a real Clay, or whether he was, from the first, a fantasy in the poor man's mind, there's no way to know. But it seems certain that when he began receiving phone calls from Clay, the voice that Father Bryce heard was purely internal. The voice, one might say, of conscience. Conscience can be a cruel taskmaster, and Clay was no exception. Clay was Father Bryce's first taskmaster, and, not unlike my friend Bing, he imposed a task that wasn't simply a cash payment. He told Father Bryce to go to a tattoo parlor in Little Canada and have himself tattooed in an obscene manner. If you had heard Father Bryce's confession, you'd have been entirely taken in by his story, until he insisted on showing you the tattoo that he supposed to be on his chest. There *was* no tattoo."

"Jesus," said Mary and Alison in unison.

"That was my own reaction."

"When was this?" Greg asked.

"The first time was at the Shrine, when I heard his confession. He insisted on taking off his shirt to show me the tattoo that wasn't there. And I thought, this man is crazy. But he was also dangerous, so I looked at the tattoo that wasn't there respectfully and asked him to go on with his story. Later on I heard the story repeated, in greater detail, and I've no doubt at all that he believed every word of what he told me. Oh, my goodness, I see that this is becoming a very long story."

"Go on," said Alison. "Don't be a tease."

"You've had fair warning. Because the imaginary tattoo was just the beginning. I suppose that, psychologically speaking, the tattoo was a kind of self-imposed punishment for the death of the young man by the name of Kramer. The police suppose that Father Bryce learned of the boy's suicide in the newspaper and that that triggered the fantasy of being tattooed. It was after that that Bing called him to deliver his own threat of blackmail, and *that* is when Father Bryce totally freaked. That is when he became Silvanus de Roquefort, the Bishop of Rodez and Montpellier-le-Vieux."

"How's that again?" said Greg, pouring more brandy into his own and Father Mabbley's snifters.

"No more for me," said Father Mabbley, once Greg had put down the bottle. "And it is a mouthful, isn't it? So let us just call him Silvanus. A Catholic bishop in the south of France during the Middle Ages, when they were burning heretics at the stake. A period of history that the Church would rather forget. Apparently, Father Bryce had read about it, for his account was very circumstantial. Even though I was perfectly sure he was bonkers, because I'd seen that his supposed tattoo didn't exist, I had a hard time *dis*-believing in the story he told me about all the things that he said had happened to him when he became Silvanus."

"He *became* him?" Alison asked.

"He became him, and at the same time, Silvanus became Father Bryce. *That* was the problem. Father Bryce may be the first case of interactive multiple personalities. Because while Father Bryce was adventuring back in the Middle Ages, Silvanus took over the body, mind, and soul of Father Bryce. When you dealt with the man at the Shrine, it wasn't Father Bryce you dealt with. Not at all. It was Silvanus."

"You mean," said Janet, "the way that when Janet Leigh gets stabbed in the shower it isn't really Tony Perkins, it's his mother?"

"Just so," said Father Mabbley. "But, at the same time, somehow,

Father Bryce was enjoying the life of the imaginary Silvanus de Roque-fort. With—and here's *another* complication—input from a book he must have read at some point, by a whacked-out sci-fi writer, A. D. Boscage."

"The *Prolegomenon?*" Greg asked, perking up. "I've read that. It's wild."

"I have to agree," said Father Mabbley. "Also, as the revised edition suggests, it was a complete fabrication. Though, in charity, it seems possible that Boscage was just as crazy as Father Bryce and believed everything he wrote. Though I doubt that. I think the man was just a canny charlatan. In any case, Father Bryce picked up on his medieval phantasmagoria, which turns out to be just that, for the site of his fantasy, Montpellier-le-Vieux, is nothing but a remarkable rock formation in the south of France; it never was the city Boscage describes in such fetching detail. The man is a novelist."

"You're sure of that?" Greg asked, setting down his snifter on the white carpet. "I drank it in."

"You were meant to. Boscage was a professional, in his own weird way. I suppose Father Bryce drank it in as well, while he imbibed. He *swears* he never read the book after the first chapter. But it *fueled* his imagination, and when he snapped, he became a character in Boscage's book. He became Silvanus. He fantasized an entire and complete day-by-day existence in the approximate era of the Albigensian Crusade. We think his Silvanus fantasies began even before his first phone call from Clay, during his blackout periods. He would check into a motel with a quart of booze and sail away into a hypnagogic haze."

"Hypna-who?" Janet demanded.

"Gogic. It's a strange, more intense kind of dreaming that happens on the borderline between sleep and waking. People who swear they've been abducted by aliens in UFOs have probably had hypnagogic hallu-cinations, the ones who aren't simply lying. And there's often a vision-ary component to hypnagogic dreams, the way there is to the dream journeys of shamans and Indian medicine men. They're not only more intense, they *signify*. When Father Bryce traveled back in time to become Silvanus, he was becoming a more perfect priest, almost an archetypal priest."

"I know what 'archetypal' means," said Janet smugly. "It's like in myths and fairy tales."

"He was a bishop at a time when the Church's power was at its height—for good and for ill. Instead of being what he was here and now—a parish priest in an institution that is falling to pieces. He was also, when he was Silvanus, a heterosexual—or, at least, a nightmare version of a heterosexual as filtered through the mind of someone who conceives of the sexual act as essentially obscene and violent. The Catholic Church's view of sex has never been that friendly toward women."

"We found that out," said Alison, "at the Shrine."

"I suppose, in a way, his attraction to altar boys may have been a kind of psychological barrier erected to prevent the woman-hating Silvanus from expressing himself. But Silvanus, once he'd begun to stir in the murk of Father Bryce's blackouts, wanted out. So, unfortunately for you young ladies, when Father Bryce became Silvanus, Silvanus became Father Bryce."

"Wait," said Alison. "I thought he was Clay."

"No, no." Janet spelled it out: "It's like *The Three Faces of Eve* with What's-her-name."

"Joanne Woodward," Father Mabbley filled in.

"Right! Sometimes he was Clay, and sometimes he was—what was the other name?"

"Silvanus."

"So," Greg asked, "when he thought he was this Silvanus, that's when he started killing everyone?"

"Yes, that's what he *thought*. But the first murder he committed, which he described in dreadful detail, probably never happened. Delilah, her name was. Isn't that classic? But she was only his fantasy, along with the tattoo parlor where he claims to have met her. The police went there, and it had been a tattoo parlor once, some four years ago. It was near a motel that Father Bryce often visited for his bouts of solitary drinking, so he must have taken it in, and it became a permanent fixture of his unconscious, along with the contents of the Boscage book. Then he did his best bit of interactive insanity, according to the prosecution's psychiatrists: He appeared, as Clay, at the scene of the imaginary crime (which was an actual trailer court near Little Canada) and chauffeured himself back, as Silvanus, to his rectory in Willowville. From that point it was Silvanus who was in charge of Father Bryce's mortal flesh, while Father Bryce was relegated to a medieval existence that became increasingly more horrific."

"But if Father Bryce thought he was back living in the Middle Ages, how could he have told you about what was happening when he was Silvanus?"

Father Mabbley beamed at Janet. "*That,*" he said, "is the sixty-four-thousand-dollar question. When he first confessed to me, at the Shrine, he claimed to have no recollection of his doings in the days just gone by, when he was with you there. But then the clouds began to part. He remembered attacking Raven Peck when he'd entered her cell alone and found her in restraints. By this time the police already knew that he had violated her, because they'd tested the . . . fluids he'd left."

"Let's not talk about all that stuff, huh?" said Janet. "It gives me the creeps."

"Same here," said Alison. "Sometimes, when I think how close I came to the same thing happening to me . . ."

"Father Bryce felt much the same way about it. Horror and disgust over Silvanus's behavior. Which was expressed, in Father Bryce's imaginary medieval existence, in the most drastic possible way. He had himself crucified by one of the torturers working for the Inquisition. A priest, after all, is supposed to be reenacting Christ's sacrifice on the cross each time he says Mass. And the details of the Crucifixion are impressed on a priest's imagination by the need to deliver sermons on that subject at least once a year. You might say that he died for Silvanus's sins."

"I've heard those sermons," said Janet. "They used to scare the shit out of me."

"Did the Church actually *crucify* heretics back then?" Greg asked. "I thought they burned them at the stake."

"Quite so. The rationale for Father Bryce's crucifixion was another borrowing from the Boscage book, and Boscage in turn had taken his idea from a British writer, Joseph Cornwell, who proposed that the Shroud of Turin was the work of forgers of relics (a major industry in the Middle Ages), who created the uncanny image of the crucified Christ by duplicating the original process."

"Gross," commented Janet. "Do *you* think that's what really happened?"

"It's not for me to speculate. We know the Shroud is a forgery; that's embarrassing enough from the Church's viewpoint. If it was made in such a way, I can't believe that any clergyman would have been directly involved. It seems the ultimate sacrilege, and that is probably why Father Bryce incorporated it into his vision of the Middle Ages. So. At the suggestion of our hostess, Silvanus entered the reliquarium that had been built to hold the threads from the Shroud, praying that it would be a doorway back to his own era, and when he opened the inner door, his prayers were answered. He returned whence he came, and it was Father Bryce who awoke in the darkness of the tomb, with the bats about him, beside the dead body of Hedwig Ober. He told me that he supposed he'd gone to hell."

"Yeah," said Janet. "It's too bad he didn't. He deserved it more than she did, though I can't say I feel *that* sorry for her. Not after all that happened."

"It was an awful way to die," said Alison. "But my therapist says I shouldn't blame myself for it. I didn't know about the bats. Nobody did."

"I think it can be fairly said," said Father Mabbley, "that she had only herself to blame." He turned to Greg. "Do you know, I think I wouldn't mind just another drop of brandy."

"Do you think there's any chance that Silvanus will decide to come back?" Janet asked. "If he did, he'd sure give a scare to some of the other prisoners in that prison."

"No, I don't think there's any chance of that. I think Silvanus died at the hands of the Inquisition. That's what Father Bryce believes, anyhow, and he's the expert."

"Well, *that's* a relief," said Alison. "I don't expect he'll ever escape from prison, but if he did—"

"I don't think you have to worry about either Father Bryce *or* Silvanus getting out of prison. Silvanus is dead (or gone to hell), and Father Bryce seems resigned to life without parole. I wouldn't say he's repented his sins. Pedophiles rarely do, because they don't believe they've sinned. And while he deplores the crimes that Silvanus committed, he doesn't feel that he's responsible for them."

"That's bullshit," said Greg. "No one else killed Raven Peck. No one else raped Mary Tyler. He did."

"Yeah, I know," said Alison, "and I'm glad he's locked away and is never going to be paroled. But there's a part of me that feels sorry for him, in a way."

"It must be the same part that likes snakes," said Janet.

"But that's just it, he wasn't a snake. Even when he thought he was

Silvanus, and when he was hearing my confession that first time in my cell and started to come on about how pretty I was, and said I looked like the Virgin Mary—"

"The Virgin Mary?" said Greg. "You never mentioned that before."

"I'd actually forgot about it. But even then, when I was most scared of him, he made me think of Jimmy Norton, who was this kid back in the eighth grade who tried to put the make on me. Only he was so afraid of *touching* me that it was almost comical. And sad, at the same time. I mean, yes, in one way he was just a creep, but in another way you knew that he'd always be like that, even if he got married someday. He would always be afraid of sex and think it was dirty but at the same time that it was something that he had to do."

"Yes," said Father Mabbley, looking down into his brandy glass with a sad smile, "I think that's just who he was. There are a lot of Jimmy Nortons in our seminaries. I've known a few of them very well. And you're quite right about what becomes of them. They may grow older, but they don't grow up."

He finished off his brandy and set down the glass decisively. "Well, there it is, the whole, uncensored story. Now let's try to forget it, shall we?"

"There is nothing," said Janet, "I'd rather forget."

"Good, then let me vanish into the kitchen for no more than five minutes to whip the cream. I hope you all like strawberry shortcake?"

"I *love* strawberry shortcake," said Janet.

When Father Mabbley had gone into the kitchen and Greg was clearing the dishes from the dining room table, Janet looked into the flames licking up from the logs for a while, and then, with a sigh of contentment, turned to Alison and said, "Is he making real whipped cream, not the stuff out of a plastic tub?"

"He always does."

"Boy, isn't this the life, Alison? Isn't it great to be rich?"

45

Clay woke up with the mother of all headaches. The kind of headache where you could wish you didn't exist, where all you wanted was to return to the nothingness of dreamless sleep. But there was no returning, he was awake.

He reached to the side of the bed, where he always kept a pack of Marlboros. But there was no pack there, there wasn't even a table, and the bed almost wasn't a bed, just some kind of cot, with another cot above it, bunk-bed-style. He couldn't even sit up to take in where it was; he had to ease out of it sideways.

That's when he saw the bars.

Shit! he thought.

How in hell? He couldn't have got so drunk that he'd forgotten everything between doing whatever had landed him here and this present, very unpleasant moment. But his mind was a fucking blank. Like a big eraser had rubbed out a few months of his existence. Like he'd been dipped in Liquid Paper.

Something was wrong. Something more than the fact that he'd woken up in a fucking prison cell without knowing how he'd got here. Something internal. His hand reached down to his prick, and at least that was okay.

Except for one thing. It was cut. He had no foreskin.

Something was very wrong indeed.

He stood up, dropped the prison-issue shorts he'd been sleeping in, and looked down at his dick.

It wasn't his. His *hands* weren't his. There was something wrong with his whole body. It wasn't the feeling you get from being massively hungover.

He looked around for a mirror, but he was looking around a prison cell (and a pretty ratty cell at that), and a mirror was not one of the amenities provided. There was the bunk bed, with its sagging mattresses (and no one in the upper bunk), a bench bolted to the opposite wall, a toilet with no lid in one corner, and in the other a kind of school desk with a few books on top of it and a plastic chair beside it. Clay had thought this kind of minimum-comfort prison cell had been made illegal sometime back in the seventies.

Three concrete-block walls, one of which featured a fucking crucifix, and a fourth wall of steel bars.

All he wanted to do was to look at his own face, but in prison you can't always get what you want.

The toilet bowl, he thought. There'll be water in the toilet, it'll work like a mirror.

But when he knelt down beside the toilet to peer into its porcelain bowl, he couldn't make out anything but his shadow. The cell was too dark, and of course, being a cell, there was no light switch.

Then, like a wish, the lights came on, and there was a guard outside the bars looking down at him, grinning. The guard was black.

"Hey, Father Rat," the guard said, "I got a joke for you."

"Fuck off." Clay reacted with knee-jerk automatism.

"Hey, what kind of language is that? Anyhow, I want to tell you the joke. How do you get a nun pregnant?"

"Go fuck yourself."

"You dress her up as an altar boy."

Clay, who'd got up on his feet again, had no more ready invective. He just scowled.

"I guess you heard that one before, huh? Anyhow, I got good news for you, Father Rat. All your commotion about how it's cruel and unusual for you to be locked up all on your lonesome has made a dent. You are to have a roommate, and you won't be so lonely anymore. Congratulations."

"Have you got a cigarette?" Clay asked. "I need a cigarette."

"Since when did you start smoking?"

"You want me to say please, I'll say please. I need a fucking cigarette. I don't feel good."

"Sure thing," said the guard. He took a pack of Kools from his pocket, lighted one, and handed it through the bars.

Clay inhaled gratefully. For one brief shining moment he felt okay. Then he felt sick again.

"You know, Father Rat, this shouldn't be for me to say, but you aren't looking very well. I don't think you're taking care of yourself. Maybe you need more exercise. Maybe it's your diet. But you don't look well."

Clay tried to concentrate on the cigarette and ignore the guard.

Another guard appeared, also black, with a prisoner in handcuffs and manacles. While the guard who'd been harassing Clay unlocked the cell door, the other guard took off the new prisoner's cuffs and manacles and pushed him into the cell.

"Enjoy yourselves, boys," said the first guard, and then they both went off, before Clay could think to bum another cigarette.

The new prisoner plopped down on the lower of the two bunks with a sigh. He was a big dude, about Clay's age, with a dago mustache and a build that looked like he'd already served a few years and spent all his time in the weight room. He looked up at Clay, and their eyes locked. It was like arm wrestling, and Clay lost the first match.

"I read about you," the guy said.

"Yeah? What'd you read?"

"What I read made me think we got a few things in common. That may be why they put us together. Birds of a feather?"

"You got a cigarette, buddy?"

"You got one in your mouth. Cocksucker."

Clay went onto red alert. "Hey, you watch *your* mouth."

The guy just smiled, almost in a lazy way. "No offense intended. I guess you like to be addressed . . . how? As Father? That's okay with me."

There was a silence. Clay smoked. The guy went on looking.

When Clay threw the butt of the cigarette into the toilet bowl, the guy held out his hand and said, "Let me introduce myself." There was a pentagram tattooed across the back of his hand. "Crispo. Donald Crispo. Does it ring a bell?"

Clay didn't offer his own hand. "Should it?"

"Well, I'd like to think so. I'm not going to have any more opportunities anytime soon to reach the attention of the media. And neither will you, right? Life without parole is one of the things we got in common."

It hit him like a sledgehammer. "Life without parole?"

"So I guess we'll have to learn to be friends. But I figure we can."

Another long silence. Then Crispo said, "I'll tell you something funny, Father."

"What's that?"

"I got psychic powers. No—really. Like, when I was going after the next one? I could tell. I could tell if he really wanted it. 'Cause some of them do, you know. Even the kids. Some of them have such shitty lives they really deep-down would rather be dead. And those ones I just left alone. 'Cause what would be the satisfaction? It's like eating an animal that died of natural causes. But with you, the minute I saw you, I knew: This guy is ready. This guy needs me. You know how I knew?"

"No. I don't know anything anymore. I don't know my own fucking name."

"I knew," Crispo went on, " 'cause I could see the tattoo."

"The tattoo?"

"On your chest. The mark of Satan. I can see it."

Only now did it dawn on Clay what had happened. He'd been switched. Boscage had set him up! All the training he'd undergone in the transmentation process had been a scam. Boscage had taken over Clay's younger, abler body and shunted Clay's psyche into the sinking, stinking vessel that he'd intended to receive it all along.

Clay didn't have to look into a mirror now. He knew now who he was. Who the guards and Crispo and all the rest of the world would *think* he was.

"I could see it," Crispo went on, "right through your fucking T-shirt. It said in the papers how you thought you had this tattoo that wasn't there. But it is there. It's Satan's face, escaped from hell. And I can see it. And you know why I can do that, Father? 'Cause it's on me, too."

Crispo fell silent for a spell, and a sad look came over his face. "You never read about me? Or seen anything on TV?"

Clay shook his head.

Crispo sighed. "Well, that's fame for you. Fifteen fucking minutes."

"What did you do?" Clay asked.

"You honestly never heard?"
Clay shook his head.
"I was Crispo, the Mad Dentist."
Clay made no response.
Crispo smiled. "But I also tattoo."

A NOTE ON THE TYPE

This book was set in Janson, a typeface long thought to have been made by the Dutchman Anton Janson, who was a practicing typefounder in Leipzig during the years 1668 to 1687. However, it has been conclusively demonstrated that these types are actually the work of Nicholas Kis (1650–1702), a Hungarian, who most probably learned his trade from the master Dutch typefounder Dirk Voskens. The type is an excellent example of the influential and sturdy Dutch types that prevailed in England up to the time William Caslon (1692–1766) developed his own incomparable designs from them.

Composed by ComCom, an R. R. Donnelley & Sons Company,
Allentown, Pennsylvania
Printed and bound by Quebecor Printing,
Fairfield, Pennsylvania
Designed by Virginia Tan